The Kailyard Authors

The Little Minister

James Matthew Barrie was born in Kirriemuir in Forfarshire on 9 May 1860. Educated at Glasgow Academy, Forfar Academy and Dumfries Academy, he matriculated in Edinburgh University in 1878. While an undergraduate he wrote articles for the *Edinburgh Courant* and in 1883 moved south to work as a leader writer on the *Nottingham Journal*. He returned to Kirriemuir in 1884 and after contributing to many other papers arrived in London on 28 March 1885 determined to make his living from literature. He contributed to the cost of production of his first book, *Better Dead* (1887), and in 1888 published a novel, *When a Man's Single*. In the same year, he issued a collection of sketches entitled *Auld Licht Idylls*. Based on his mother's memories of her childhood in Kirriemuir, the book was compiled from previously published articles in the *St James's Gazette* and *Home Chimes* and told of life in 'Thrums', Barrie's fictional name for his native town. Its success prompted Barrie to issue a second volume, *A Window in Thrums*, the following year, and in 1891 the novel *The Little Minister* was published to critical and commercial success. Two longer and more ambitious novels followed, *Sentimental Tommy* (1896) and *Tommy and Grizel* (1900). Barrie also published a memoir of his mother, *Margaret Ogilvy* (1896).

In 1894 Barrie married the actress Mary Ansell but the marriage was not a success and the couple were divorced in 1909. Around 1897 Barrie met and befriended the family of Sylvia and Arthur Llewelyn Davies, taking an active part in the lives of their young sons. *The Little White Bird* (1902) is a fictionalised account of this relationship which provided the raw material for the play *Peter Pan*, first staged in 1904. Barrie had turned his attention to the theatre in the late 1890s, scoring an immense box-office success with a dramatised version of *The Little Minister* (1897). Many other highly successful plays followed, including *Quality Street* (1902), *The Admirable Crichton* (1902), *What Every Woman Knows* (1908), *Dear Brutus* (1917) and *Mary Rose* (1920). In 1931 he returned to the theme of his early fiction with the novella *Farewell Miss Julie Logan*. His final play, *The Boy David*, appeared in 1936.

Barrie became one of the most successful and best-known writers of his day. He died on 19 June 1937, aged 77. He was buried in the family grave in Kirriemuir.

Series editor:
Andrew Nash,
University of Reading.

The Little Minister

by J. M. Barrie

with an introduction by
Melodee R. Mattson

Kennedy & Boyd
an imprint of
Zeticula
57 St Vincent Crescent
Glasgow
G3 8NQ
Scotland

http://www.kennedyandboyd.co.uk
admin@kennedyandboyd.co.uk

First published in 1891

ISBN-13 978 1 904999 62 1
ISBN-10 1 904999 62 X

Introduction

> It is of another minister I am to tell, but only to those who can sympathise. Others will find these pages as colourless as our little square would have been that day for the weaver, had the love-light never shone in his own eyes, lit at the only fire where it may be lit, a woman's heart. By this light alone should a love-story be read (ch. 1, p. 5).

The appearance of J.M. Barrie's novels was at one time considered a literary event equal to the publication of Thomas Hardy's: 'At the present moment,' wrote an 1892 reviewer, '"everybody" is reading either *The Little Minister* or *Tess of the D'Urbervilles*.'[1] The review went on to criticize both novels, and it is interesting to ponder why Hardy's reputation survived censure while Barrie's, in large measure, did not. With respect to *The Little Minister*, we can attribute much of the latter's fall from grace to mistaken expectations and a misunderstanding of his artistic aims.

Barrie had gained a following with his early collections of stories, *Auld Licht Idylls* and *A Window in Thrums,* both of which had tremendous appeal for a Victorian market craving regionalism. Like Hardy's Wessex, Barrie's Thrums was clearly modelled on a real place (his hometown of Kirriemuir), and his use of local color and Scottish dialect strengthened his links to the type of regional fiction popular at the time. As these authors fictionalized real places, however, many readers interpreted the fiction as fact. The regional trappings of *Auld Licht Idylls* and *A Window in Thrums* led the majority of reviewers to categorise Barrie as a 'realist' author. That the word 'improbable' is frequent in reviews of *The Little Minister* indicates that his subsequent fiction was judged by how well it measured up to the realist standards initially applied to his work. The reception of the novel was cautiously positive, but puzzled. Reviewers focused their praise on the scenes most reminiscent of *A Window in Thrums,* but seemed quite uncomfortable with the appearance of a strange Egyptian woman in the predictable setting of Thrums; there was no room for Babbie in their pre-determined critical parameters.

We have an advantage over the contemporary critics, however; access to Barrie's later work enables us to see *The Little Minister* as a transitional work in his *oeuvre.* As his first attempt at a full-length novel, it certainly has its technical faults, yet at the same time it represents a significant advance in his ability to write a sustained story and to develop three-dimensional characters. Here, for the first time, Thrums is a fully realized place. Characters that were mere names and shadows in *Auld Licht Idylls* and *A Window in Thrums* are crafted with more personality and substance.

With greater intensity of character, Barrie seeks to raise a higher level of emotion in his audience. While twenty-first-century readers may feel such a strategy falls into sentimentality, Victorian authors and readers alike applauded a text that elicited emotion because it enlarged sympathy for fellow man and shed understanding on the human heart. Such emotion-inducing literature often found expression in the genre of the Victorian idyll, as described by Shelagh Hunter: 'The Victorian idylls are, above all, explorations of basic human emotions; the springs of feeling are sought in simple surroundings and an isolable network of family and community relationships.'[2] Barrie's early works fit this genre, and *The Little Minister* borrows from it as well. In Barrie's case the 'springs of feeling' are those of humor and pathos, flowing from sympathy, which, in an essay on Kipling, he calls 'the blood of the novel.'[3] He elaborates on this point in a further essay on Sabine Baring-Gould written for the *Contemporary Review:*

> Sympathy is the ink in which all fiction should be written; indeed, we shall find, on examination, that the humour, which some say is the novelist's greatest gift, and the power of character-drawing by which others hold, are streams from this same source. [...] Give humour and pathos a chance, and they run into one like two drops of water; keep them apart, and they die for want of each other.'[4]

Humor and pathos certainly go hand in hand in *The Little Minister.* The narrator's sad personal history runs like a dark undercurrent throughout the novel, adding depth and seriousness to the romantic comedy enacted by the young couple. Gavin Dishart is a humorous figure, with his boyish foolishness and narrow self-righteousness, but for the moment when 'in the hour of trial he proved himself a man' (*TLM* ch.45, p. 325); Babbie's light and witty exterior hides a wounded and neglected heart. The community of Thrums is full of similar examples. While the villagers are sometimes caricatured for comic effect, Barrie offers glimpses of their inner life and struggles, their gratitude and pain: Nanny Webster, with her terror of the poor house; Tammas Whamond, whose strict and loveless exterior slips just once to show the emotion suppressed within; and Rob Dow, the relapsed drunkard on whom the final happiness of Gavin and Babbie depends. In his exploration of character and continual blending of humor and pathos, Barrie continues the idyllic goals of his earlier work in *The Little Minister*. Surely it is his concern, as well as his narrator's, that we will 'neither laugh nor cry with Gavin and Babbie' (*TLM* ch.1, p. 7).

While continuing in an idyllic vein, however, Barrie moves further from a 'realist' label by manipulating realist conventions and blending them with romance. Despite the inclusion of scenes that comfortably sit under the banner of social realism (including references to a real-life 1839 Chartist riot), Barrie clearly intimates from the beginning that *The Little Minister* is not about reality, but about illusion:

> A ghost show used to come yearly to Thrums at the merry Muckle Friday, in which the illusion was effected with a glass hung between the audience and the stage. [...] We discovered afterwards that T'nowhead had been sitting at the end of a form where he saw round the glass, and consequently saw no ghost. I fear lest my audience may be in the same predicament. I see the little minister as he was at one-and-twenty; but can I provide the glass for them? (*TLM* ch.1 p.7)

The narrator likens himself to the creator of an illusion, and the analogy emphasizes the stylized nature of the novel. By highlighting the narrator's self-doubt about his ability to provide the 'glass,' Barrie invites his audience to read the novel on two levels: they should read the story through the glass, or framework, the narrator provides, but they should also peer around the glass like T'nowhead and study the narrator himself.

The glass of *The Little Minister* is not a straightforward 'window in Thrums.' This time Thrums is not the object of semi-journalistic observation as in *Auld Licht Idylls*, nor is it the only location of the novel: Barrie presents an intersection between the 'real,' identifiable, Kirriemuir-like Thrums, and the more ambiguous Caddam Wood, a land associated with fairy tale. Gavin finds himself in this Wood at midnight; for a moment he forgets that he is a minister, and loses himself in the legend of Caddam, with its lost maiden singing on fine nights and weeping on stormy ones:

> Gavin was in the Caddam of past days, where the beautiful maiden wanders ever, waiting for him who is

> so pure that he may find her. [...] Then he remembered who and where he was, and stopped to pick up his staff. But he did not pick it up, for as his fingers were closing on it the lady began to sing (*TLM* ch. 4, p. 39).

The lady is Babbie, entering Gavin's life in the guise of the mythical spirit of Caddam. She upsets his conventional outlook and forces him to face something 'other'—a woman, a gypsy, a fairy tale. Babbie represents a world antithetical to Gavin's: he views life from the comfort of an Auld Licht manse, while her more carefree vantage point is the top of a tree (or so she claims). The novel is not just about their love story; it is about different perspectives of reality, the clash of worldviews. In this framework, the world of fantasy or fairy tale does not represent an escape from 'real life' but rather a challenge to one's preconceptions about life. Babbie challenges Gavin's narrow, prejudiced outlook about women and outsiders; Gavin's response in turn challenges Babbie's cynical, irresponsible attitude toward men and relationships.

If the novel is about perspective, perhaps none is more important than that of the dominie, Gavin Ogilvy, who narrates the story. The dominie's presentation of Gavin and Babbie's story is his own perception of reality posing as an objective, even 'realist,' account. He claims to be a knowledgeable biographer, setting down Gavin's story as it really happened. He has 'only to write over with ink what [Gavin] has written in pencil' (*TLM* ch. 1 p. 9). Some critics, by accepting the dominie's own claims, complain that in using a 'trustworthy' narrator Barrie demands a passive audience that uncritically submits itself entirely into his hands.[5] This overlooks the implicit question Barrie poses to his readers in the text: should we trust the dominie's perceptions, or should we challenge them? Is he as objective as he thinks he is? In the first chapter Barrie hints that while the narrator of the novel may desire a passive audience, the *author* of the novel calls for an active one that looks 'around the glass,' critically weighing the dominie's claims.

Several techniques alert us to the subjective nature of the narration. First is the obvious fact that the dominie is far from an omniscient narrator; he is only occasionally an eyewitness, and most of his information is filtered through the gossip of Gavin's parishioners, whose zeal for observing their minister is matched only by their creativity in interpreting his behavior. The omnipresence of gossip in the narrative emphasizes the fact that the dominie's interpretation of events is one among many.

A second, and related, technique is found only in the version of the novel serialized in *Good Words* in 1891 (subsequently used as the text for several early American editions), where Barrie uses the device of a fictional editor who, in a series of footnotes, undermines the authority of the dominie's interpretations. The editor is not objective any more than the dominie is—she is the 'little maid' for whom he is writing the book, 'Margaret the Second'—but by challenging his opinions, she encourages the reader to consider the possibility that he is often wrong.[6] This fictional editor illustrates that the dominie is less interested in producing a true, 'factual' account than in producing a work of art. In fact, contrary to his initial claim that he is merely a biographer, he has artistic ambitions beyond that of a chronicler: 'Up here in the glen school-house after my pupils have straggled home, there comes to me at times, and so sudden that it may be while I am infusing my tea, a hot desire to write great books' (*TLM* ch. 24 p.188). It is as an artist that he collects the bits and pieces of gossip, memory, and impression; he sifts them with an eye to his story and makes his own subjective choices as to what to include and what to discard. As Andrew Nash suggests, this presentation of the dominie as a conscious artist signals a transition in Barrie's fiction 'away from the relatively neutral presentation of an idealised past found in the Auld Licht stories toward what would become in later novels a sophisticated, complex interest in the relationship between art and life.'[7]

Barrie's most important clue as to the subjectivity of the narration is the dominie's role as a *character* in the story. His own personal involvement precludes any objectivity in his view of things. His life has been dominated by a single, tragic event, the circumstances of which are not fully revealed until near the end of the novel. Despite his initial assurances that 'this is to be Gavin's story, not mine,' his own story is the recurring reference-point for his narrative (*TLM* ch. 1, p.10). Indeed, it frames the entire novel: the opening paragraph sets the stage for a happy ending of his own, yet the final words of his story are devoted, not to Gavin and Babbie, but to his own dashed expectations and tortured sense of failure. Barrie has skillfully created a narrator who tells the audience one thing but unwittingly communicates another; there is a frequent discordance between his professions and his actions. His perspective of life and reality is tragically skewed by his need to relive his worst experience, and this colours his narrative. Gavin's success is an overwhelming reminder of his failure, and thus he catches himself at times infusing the young couple's love story with his own bitterness and envy.

Barrie's fascinating use of the dominie as a narrator is nevertheless an uneven affair. At times the narrator moves so far into the background as to nearly disappear, reporting conversations and events with such an 'omniscient' flair that it stretches belief that, as a character, he could have gleaned this information second-hand. This inconsistency in presentation is a sign that Barrie was still an inexperienced novelist at the time of *The Little Minister.* In its overall effect, however, the presentation of the dominie as both an artist and as a character with personal involvement in the story showcases the difficulties an artist has in reporting 'reality.'

An important theme that emerges from Barrie's portrait of the dominie is the conflict between one's adopted mask, or role, and one's true identity. This theme, introduced for the first time in *The Little Minister,* is explored extensively in Barrie's later novels, *Sentimental Tommy, Tommy & Grizel,* and *The Little White Bird,* culminating in the play, *Peter Pan.* These later works emphasize the importance of discarding role-playing in favor of authenticity in human relationships by showing its negative and destructive consequences, but *The Little Minister* presents a much more positive picture.

Gavin begins as a 'little' man play-acting the minister. The adjective 'little' is multi-faceted: it refers to his height, of course, but it also indicates a littleness of mind, demonstrated by his initial pompous, prejudiced, and narrow outlook. Gavin has admirable qualities—love for his mother, zeal for his work, fervent sincerity in prayer—but at the beginning of the novel he is young and dominated by his insecurities. From an early age, when he mimicked the gestures of the preacher from his pew, Gavin adopted the role of 'minister' as a compensation for his weaknesses. As a minister he has an important position of authority; he is a 'big man' in the community despite his short stature. His real power is negligible, but he is seduced by the appearance of power, and is quick to condemn Babbie as a 'sinful woman' when she undermines his authority. Gavin's ministry is not of the heart: it is a façade he adopts that hides his true warm-heartedness. He escapes it in unguarded moments, only to revert immediately to his play-acting of 'proper' ministerial behavior:

The transformation begins when Gavin forgets his own position in concern for another person, when he looks at Babbie and sees 'that this fragile girl might have a history far sadder and more turbulent than his' (*TLM* ch. 15. p.127). At this moment he abandons the role of the self-righteous, cardboard 'minister' who condemningly addresses her as

'Woman,' and instead calls her compassionately by name. In doing so he symbolically moves toward a more relationship with God and his congregation as well as with Babbie; in the end he becomes a minister in heart, not merely in name, prompting a parishioner to exclaim, 'That man has a religion to last him all through' (*TLM* ch. 44. p. 321).

As Gavin begins to love honestly and sacrificially, Babbie is forced to drop her own façade. Her role is that of a carefree gypsy, and she plays it with relish. With her quick wit and playful demeanor, she takes pleasure in making fools of those in authority, whether it is Captain Halliwell or Gavin Dishart. She is a creature of impulse, 'a dozen women in the hour,' ever-changing and ever-confusing (*TLM* ch. 23 p. 185). Critics who judge her based on first impressions invariably criticize Barrie for writing such a strange heroine: 'What a mere circus caricature is the central personage, that inhuman 'Egyptian woman!'[8] Such readings fail to see that Babbie's flightiness is an act, a protective mask worn to shield herself from men. As her story unfolds, it becomes clear that things are not always as they seem: there is unhappiness behind the gaiety, bondage behind the freedom, and a broken woman behind the mischievous gypsy. Interestingly, the misconceptions about Babbie's character might in fact have been fuelled by Barrie's own very popular stage adaptation of the novel. In the adaptation, the plot is modified such that Babbie's complexities are almost entirely absent. According to his secretary, Cynthia Asquith, Barrie was unhappy with the play and did not want it included in future editions of his works.[9]

Some have accused *The Little Minister* of 'bowing to fantasy' or 'playing to the gallery.'[10] Such charges might appropriately be applied to the stage version, but the novel is clearly a more ambitious project than a mere pot-boiler popular romance. Here Barrie experiments with narrative techniques that highlight the conflict between perspective and reality, he encourages the reader to approach the novel on two levels, and he explores the difficulty of unmasking one's true identity. His premise seems clear: happiness and fulfillment are only possible when people *reject* the 'fantasy' of playing roles that mask their genuine selves. Despite falling, at times, into melodrama, the novel is a successful first attempt at more complex subject-matter.

Critics of the Kailyard authors have long charged them with failing to produce an accurate depiction of Scotland as it was at the end of the nineteenth century, but the fact remains that Thrums is not Scotland, nor does it claim to be. It is, rather, the backdrop that highlights Barrie's literary development: from idyll to romance to an exposé of the dangers of fantasy. He wrote his early works in an established literary genre—the Victorian idyll—based upon established theories of the need for literature to enlarge the reader's sympathies. *The Little Minister* was a transition away from these comfortable methods, as he began to experiment with elements of fantasy and romance to address more complex themes through his characters. This important hinge in his *oeuvre* has long been neglected, but it is to be hoped that this new edition will facilitate a renewed interest in both the novel and in the rest of J.M. Barrie's diverse work.

[1] Francis Adams, 'Some Recent Novels,' *Fortnightly Review,* LII (1892) 17.

[2] Shelagh Hunter, *Victorian Idyllic Fiction: Pastoral Strategies* (London and Basingstoke: Macmillan, 1984), p. 222.

[3] J.M. Barrie, 'Mr. Kipling's Stories,' *Contemporary Review* (March 1891) 371.

[4] J.M. Barrie, 'Mr. Baring-Gould's Novels,' *Contemporary Review* (February 1890) 206.

[5] See, for example, Lynette Hunter's discussion of the dominie in 'J.M. Barrie: The Rejection of Fantasy,' *Scottish Literary Journal,* 5:1 (May 1978) 39-52.

[6] For example, at one point the 'editor,' taking offence at a description

of Babbie, indignantly writes, 'I wanted him to let me strike out this passage, as conveying a false impression of Babbie's character, but he would not (*The Little Minister*, serial version, *Good Words* (1891), 563).

[7] Andrew Nash, 'From Realism to Romance: Gender and Narrative Technique in J.M. Barrie's *The Little Minister,' Scottish Literary Journal,* 26:1 (June 1999) 83.

[8] Adams, 19.

[9] Cynthia Asquith, *Portrait of Barrie* (London: Robert Cunningham & Sons, 1954), p. 21.

[10] Lynette Hunter, 41; J.H. Millar, *A Literary History of Scotland* (London: T. Fisher Unwin, 1903), p. 656.

Further Reading

The most recent biography is by Lisa Chaney, *Hide-and-Seek with Angels* (2005). The first authorized biography, *The Story of J.M.B.*, (1941) by Denis Mackail, is idiosyncratic but essential in its detail. Another important study is Andrew Birkin's *J.M. Barrie & the Lost Boys* (1979, repr. 2003). *J.M. Barrie: An Annotated Secondary Bibliography* (1989), by Carl Markgraf, provides a wealth of references for *The Little Minister* and Barrie's work in general.

Critical studies of the Kailyard with discussions of the novel include Thomas Knowles, *Ideology, Art and Commerce* (1983) and Andrew Nash, *Kailyard and Scottish Literature* (2007). Leonee Ormond's *J.M. Barrie* (1987) is a compact introduction.

In addition to the articles by Nash and Hunter cited in the Notes, the reader should also consult Christopher Harvie, "The Barrie who Never Grew Up: An Apologia for *The Little Minister*" in Horst W. Drescher and Joachim Schwend (eds) *Studies in Scottish Fiction: Nineteenth Century* (1985), pp. 321–35.

Preface to the American Collected Edition of 1896

THE editor of *Good Words*, in which "The Little Minister" appeared, was dissatisfied with the size of the heroine's mouth and implored me to make it larger. Otherwise the book would always disturb him. So with charming good-nature I enlarged Babbie's mouth, and he was again the most genial man in Glasgow.

But no one could persuade me to add half an inch to the stature of the little minister. In real life small men have their affairs of the heart equally with their big brothers, they even bring them to a successful issue (wait at the church door and you will presently see a little bridegroom emerge with a tall bride); but in fiction these things are not so; you know when the short man is introduced that he is to be a mere foil to a six-footer, that he must love in vain, that at the most the lady will offer to be a sister to him. Gavin is not only among the shortest heroes in fiction: so far as my researches go, he is one of the very few who are not six-footers; were all the heroes of the novels to meet on some vast plain you could pick him out at once, not because he was preaching to the others (though that is what he would be doing), but solely because of his lack of inches. "Who is the little man?" you would ask inquisitively, and if Mr. Dishart heard you, perhaps he would not wince, but I cannot guarantee this.

I am afraid I have already mentioned his only claim to distinction. He begins pretty well, I think, but there comes a time — I see it now, though I did not see it then — when Rob Dow might with advantage have left Babbie alone and turned his attention to the author.

Contents

Chapter I

The Love Light

Long ago in the days when our caged blackbirds never saw a king's soldier without whistling impudently, "Come ower the water to Charlie," a minister of Thrums was to be married, but something happened, and he remained a bachelor. Then, when he was old, he passed in our square the lady who was to have been his wife, and her hair was white, but she, too, was still unmarried. The meeting had only one witness, a weaver, and he said solemnly afterwards, "They didna speak, but they just gave one another a look, and I saw the love light in their een." No more is remembered of these two, no being now living ever saw them, but the poetry that was in the soul of a battered weaver makes them human to us for ever.

It is of another minister I am to tell, but only to those who know that light when they see it. I am not bidding good-bye to many readers, for though it is true that some men, of whom Lord Rintoul was one, live to an old age without knowing love, few of us can have met them, and of women so incomplete I never heard.

Gavin Dishart was barely twenty-one when he and his mother came to Thrums, light-hearted like the traveller who knows not what awaits him at the bend of the road. It was the time of year when the ground is carpeted beneath the firs with brown needles, when splitnuts patter all day from the beech, and children lay yellow corn on the dominie's desk to remind him that now they are needed in the fields. The day was so silent that carts could be heard rumbling a mile away. All Thrums was out in its wynds and closes — a few of the weavers still in knee-breeches — to look at the new Auld Licht minister. I was there too, the dominie of Glen Quharity, which is four miles from Thrums; and heavy was my heart as I stood afar off so that Gavin's mother might not have the pain of seeing me. I was the only one in the crowd who looked at her more than at her son.

Eighteen years had passed since we parted. Already her hair had lost the brightness of its youth, and she seemed to me smaller and more fragile; and the face that I loved when I was a hobbledehoy, and loved when I looked once more upon it in Thrums, and always shall love till I die, was soft and worn. Margaret was an old woman, and she was only forty-three: and I am the man who made her old. As Gavin put his eager boyish face out at the carriage window, many saw that he was holding her hand, but none could be glad at the sight as the dominie was glad, looking on at a happiness in which he dared not mingle. Margaret was crying because she was so proud of her boy. Women do that. Poor sons to be proud of, good mothers, but I would not have you dry those tears.

When the little minister looked out at the carriage window, many of the people drew back humbly, but a little boy in a red frock with black spots pressed forward and offered him a sticky parly, which Gavin accepted, though not without a tremor, for children were more terrible to him then than bearded men. The boy's mother, trying not to look elated, bore him away, but her face said that he was made for life. With this little incident Gavin's career in Thrums began. I remembered it suddenly the other day when wading across the wynd where it took place. Many scenes in the little minister's life come back to me in this way. The first time I ever thought of writing his love story as an old man's gift to a little maid since grown tall, was one night while I sat alone in the school-house; on my knees a fiddle that has been my only living companion since I sold my hens. My mind had drifted back to the first time I saw Gavin and the Egyptian together, and what set it wandering to that midnight meeting was my garden gate shaking in the wind. At a gate on the hill I had first encountered these two. It rattled in his hand, and I looked up and saw them, and neither knew why I had such cause to start at the sight. Then the gate swung to. It had just such a click as mine.

These two figures on the hill are more real to me than things that happened yesterday, but I do not know that I can make them live to others. A ghostshow used to come yearly to Thrums on the merry Muckle Friday, in which the illusion was contrived by hanging a glass between the onlookers and the stage. I cannot deny that the comings and goings of the ghost were highly diverting, yet the farmer of T'nowhead only laughed because he had paid his money at the hole in the door like the rest of us. T'nowhead sat at the end of a form where he saw round the glass and so saw no ghost. I fear my public may be in the same predicament. I see the little minister as he was at one-and-twenty, and the little girl to whom this story is to belong sees him, though the things I have to tell happened before she came into the world. But there are reasons why she should see; and I do not know that I can provide the glass for others. If they see round it, they will neither laugh nor cry with Gavin and Babbie.

When Gavin came to Thrums he was as I am now, for the pages lay before him on which he was to write his life. Yet he was not quite as I am. The life of every man is a diary in which he means to write one story, and writes another; and his humblest hour is when he compares the volume as it is with what he vowed to make it. But the biographer sees the last chapter while he is still at the first, and I have only to write over with ink what Gavin has written in pencil.

How often is it a phantom woman who draws the man from the way he meant to go? So was man created, to hunger for the ideal that is above himself, until one day there is magic in the air, and the eyes of a girl rest upon him. He does not know that it is he himself who crowned her, and if the girl is as pure as he, their love is the one form of idolatry that is not quite ignoble. It is the joining of two souls on their way to God. But if the woman be bad, the test of the man is when he wakens from his dream. The nobler his ideal, the further will he have been hurried down the wrong way, for those who only run after little things will not go far. His love may now sink into passion, perhaps only to stain its wings and rise again, perhaps to drown.

Babbie, what shall I say of you who make me write these things? I am not your judge. Shall we not laugh at the student who chafes when between him and his book comes the song of the thrushes, with whom, on the mad night you danced into Gavin's life, you had more in common than with Auld Licht ministers? The gladness of living was in your step, your voice was melody, and he was wondering what love might be. You were the daughter of a summer night, born where all the birds are free, and the moon christened you with her soft light to dazzle the eyes of man. Not our little minister alone was stricken by you into his second childhood.

To look upon you was to rejoice that so fair a thing could be; to think of you is still to be young. Even those who called you a little devil, of whom I have been one, admitted that in the end you had a soul, though not that you had been born with one. They said you stole it, and so made a woman of yourself. But again I say I am not your judge, and when I picture you as Gavin saw you first, a bare-legged witch dancing up Windyghoul, rowan berries in your black hair, and on your finger a jewel the little minister could not have bought with five years of toil, the shadows on my pages lift, and I cannot wonder that Gavin loved you.

Often I say to myself that this is to be Gavin's story, not mine. Yet must it be mine too, in a manner, and of myself I shall sometimes have to speak; not willingly, for it is time my little tragedy had died of old age. I have kept it to myself so long that now I would stand at its grave alone. It is true that when I heard who was to be the new minister I hoped for a day that the life broken in Harvie might be mended in Thrums, but two minutes' talk with Gavin showed me that Margaret had kept from him the secret which was hers and mine, and so knocked the bottom out of my vain hopes. I did not blame her then, nor do I blame her now, nor shall anyone who blames her ever be called friend by me; but it was bitter to look at the white manse among the trees and know that I must never enter it. For Margaret's sake I had to keep aloof, yet this new trial came upon me like our parting at Harvie. I thought that in those eighteen years my passions had burned like a ship till they sank, but I suffered again as on that awful night when Adam Dishart came back, nearly killing Margaret and tearing up all my ambitions by the root in a single hour. I waited in Thrums until I had looked again on Margaret, who thought me dead, and Gavin who had never heard of me, and then I trudged back to the school-house. Something I heard of them from time to time during the winter — for in the gossip of Thrums I was well posted — but much of what is to be told here I only learned afterwards from those who knew it best. Gavin heard of me at times as the dominie in the glen who had ceased to attend the Auld Licht kirk, and Margaret did not even hear of me. It was all I could do for them.

Chapter II

Runs Alongside The Making Of A Minister

ON the east coast of Scotland, hidden, as if in a quarry, at the foot of cliffs that may one day fall forward, is a village called Harvie. So has it shrunk since the day when I skulked from it that I hear of a traveller's asking lately at one of its doors how far he was from a village; yet Harvie throve once and was celebrated even in distant Thrums for its fish. Most of our weavers would have thought it as unnatural not to buy harvies in the square on the Muckle Friday, as to let Saturday night pass without laying in a sufficient stock of halfpennies to go round the family twice.

Gavin was born in Harvie, but left it at such an early age that he could only recall thatched houses with nets drying on the roofs, and a sandy shore in which coarse grass grew. In the picture he could not pick out the house of his birth, though he might have been able to go to it had he ever returned to the village. Soon he learned that his mother did not care to speak of Harvie, and perhaps he thought that she had forgotten it too, all save one scene to which his memory still guided him. When his mind wandered to Harvie, Gavin saw the door of his home open and a fisherman enter, who scratched his head and then said, "Your man's drowned, missis." Gavin seemed to see many women crying, and his mother staring at them with a face suddenly painted white, and next to hear a voice that was his own saying, "Never mind, mother; I'll be a man to you now, and I'll need breeks for the burial." But Adam required no funeral, for his body lay deep in the sea.

Gavin thought that this was the tragedy of his mother's life,and the most memorable event of his own childhood. But it was neither. When Margaret, even after she came to Thrums, thought of Harvie, it was not at Adam's death she shuddered, but at the recollection of me.

It would ill become me to take a late revenge on Adam Dishart now by saying what is not true of him. Though he died a fisherman he was a sailor for a great part of his life, and doubtless his recklessness was washed into him on the high seas, where in his time men made a crony of death, and drank merrily over dodging it for another night. To me his roars of laughter without cause were as repellent as a boy's drum; yet many faces that were long in my company brightened at his coming, and women, with whom, despite my learning, I was in no wise a favourite, ran to their doors to listen to him as readily as to the bell-man. Children scurried from him if his mood was savage, but to him at all other times, while me they merely disregarded. There was always a smell of the sea about him. He had a rolling gait, unless he was drunk, when he walked very straight, and before both sexes he boasted that any woman would take him for his beard alone. Of this beard he took prodigious care, though otherwise thinking little of his appearance, and I now see that he understood women better than I did, who had nevertheless reflected much about them. It cannot be said that he was vain, for though he thought he attracted women strangely, that, I maintain, is a weakness common to all men, and so no more to be marvelled at than a stake in a fence. Foreign oaths were the nails with which he held his talk together, yet I doubt not they were a curiosity gathered at sea, like his chains of shells, more for his own pleasure than for others' pain. His friends gave them no weight, and when he wanted to talk emphatically he kept them back, though they were then as troublesome to him as eggs to the bird-nesting boy who has to speak with his spoil in his mouth.

Adam was drowned on Gavin's fourth birthday, a year after I had to leave Harvie. He was blown off his smack in a storm, and could not reach the rope his partner flung him. "It's no go, lad," he shouted; "so long, Jim," and sank. A month afterwards Margaret sold her share in the smack, which was all Adam left her, and the furniture of the house was rouped. She took Gavin to Glasgow, where her only brother needed a housekeeper, and there mother and son remained until Gavin got his call to Thrums. During those seventeen years I lost knowledge of them as completely as Margaret had lost knowledge of me. On hearing of Adam's death I went back to Harvie to try to trace her, but she had feared this, and so told no one where she was going.

According to Margaret, Gavin's genius showed itself while he was still a child. He was born with a brow whose nobility impressed her from the first. It was a minister's brow, and though Margaret herself was no scholar, being as slow to read as she was quick at turning bannocks on the girdle, she decided, when his age was still counted by months, that the ministry had need of him. In those days the first question asked of a child was not "Tell me your name," but "What are you to be?" and one child in every family replied "A minister." He was set apart for the Church as doggedly as the shilling a week for the rent, and the rule held good though the family consisted of only one boy. From his earliest days Gavin thought he had been fashioned for the ministry as certainly as a spade for digging, and Margaret rejoiced and marvelled thereat, though she had made her own puzzle. An enthusiastic mother may bend her son's mind as she chooses if she begins at once; nay, she may do stranger things. I know a mother in Thrums who loves "features," and had a child born with no chin to speak of. The neighbours expected this to bring her to the dust, but it only showed what a mother can do. In a few months that child had a chin with the best of them.

Margaret's brother died, but she remained in his single room, and, ever with a picture of her son in a pulpit to repay her, contrived to keep Gavin at school. Everything a woman's fingers can do Margaret's did better than most, and among the wealthy people who employed her — would that I could have the teaching of the sons of such as were good to her in those hard days! — her gentle manner was spoken of. For though Margaret had no schooling, she was a lady at heart, moving and almost speaking as one even in Harvie, where they did not perhaps like her the better for it.

At six Gavin hit another boy hard for belonging to the Established Church, and at seven he could not lose himself in the Shorter Catechism. His mother expounded the Scriptures to him till he was eight, when he began to expound them to her. By this time he was studying the practical work of the pulpit as enthusiastically as ever medical student cut off a leg. From a front pew in the gallery Gavin watched the minister's every movement, noting that the first thing to do on ascending the pulpit is to cover your face with your hands, as if the exalted position affected you like a strong light, and the second to move the big Bible slightly, to show that the kirk officer, not having had a university education, could not be expected to know the very spot on which it ought to lie. Gavin saw that the minister joined in the singing more like one countenancing a seemly thing than because he needed it himself, and that he only sang a mouthful now and again after the congregation was in full pursuit of the precentor. It was noteworthy that the first prayer lasted longer than all the others, and that to read the intimations about the Bible-class and the collection elsewhere than immediately before the last Psalm would have been as sacrilegious as to insert the dedication to King James at the end of Revelation. Sitting under a minister justly honoured in his day, the boy was often some words in advance of him, not vainglorious of his memory, but fervent, eager, and regarding the preacher as hardly less sacred than the Book. Gavin was encouraged by his frightened yet admiring mother to saw the air from their pew as the minister sawed it in the pulpit, and two benedictions were pronounced twice a Sabbath in that church, in the same words, the same manner, and simultaneously.

There was a black year when the things of this world, especially its pastimes, took such a grip of Gavin that he said to Margaret he would rather be good at the high jump than the author of "The Pilgrim's Progress." That year passed, and Gavin came to his right mind. One afternoon Margaret was at home making a glengarry for him out of a piece of carpet, and giving it a tartan edging, when the boy bounded in from school, crying, "Come quick, mother, and you'll see him." Margaret reached the door in time to see a street musician flying from Gavin and his friends. "Did you take stock of him, mother?" the boy asked when he reappeared with the mark of a muddy stick on his back. "He's a Papist! — a sore sight, mother, a sore sight. We stoned him for persecuting the noble Martyrs."

When Gavin was twelve he went to the university, and also got a place in a shop as errand boy. He used to run through the streets between his work and his classes. Potatoes and salt fish, which could then be got at twopence the pound if bought by the halfhundredweight, were his food. There was not always a good meal for two, yet when Gavin reached home at night there was generally something ready for him, and Margaret had supped "hours ago." Gavin's hunger urged him to fall to, but his love for his mother made him watchful.

"What did you have yourself, mother?" he would demand suspiciously.

"Oh, I had a fine supper, I assure you."

"What had you?"

"I had potatoes, for one thing."

"And dripping?"

"You may be sure."

"Mother, you're cheating me. The dripping hasn't been touched since yesterday."

"I dinna — don't — care for dripping — no much."

Then would Gavin stride the room fiercely, a queer little figure.

"Do you think I'll stand this, mother? Will I let myself be pampered with dripping and every delicacy while you starve?"

"Gavin, I really dinna care for dripping."

"Then I'll give up my classes, and we can have butter."

"I assure you I'm no hungry. It's different wi' a growing laddie."

"I'm not a growing laddie," Gavin would say, bitterly; "but, mother, I warn you that not another bite passes my throat till I see you eating too."

So Margaret had to take her seat at the table, and when she said "I can eat no more," Gavin retorted sternly, "Nor will I, for fine I see through you."

These two were as one far more than most married people, and, just as Gavin in his childhood reflected his mother, she now reflected him. The people for whom she sewed thought it was contact with them that had rubbed the broad Scotch from her tongue, but she was only keeping pace with Gavin. When she was excited the Harvie words came back to her, as they come back to me. I have taught the English language all my life, and I try to write it, but everything I say in this book I first think to myself in the Doric. This, too, I notice, that in talking to myself I am broader than when gossiping with the farmers of the glen, who send their children to me to learn English, and then jeer at them if they say "old lights" instead of "auld lichts."

To Margaret it was happiness to sit through the long evenings sewing, and look over her work at Gavin as he read or wrote or recited to himself the learning of the schools. But she coughed every time the weather changed, and then Gavin would start.

"You must go to your bed, mother," he would say, tearing himself from his books; or he would sit beside her and talk of the dream that was common to both — a dream of a manse where Margaret was mistress and Gavin was called the minister. Every night Gavin was at his mother's bedside to wind her shawl round her feet, and while he did it Margaret smiled.

"Mother, this is the chaff pillow you've taken out of my bed, and given me your feather one."

"Gavin, you needna change them. I winna have the feather pillow."

"Do you dare to think I'll let you sleep on chaff? Put up your head. Now, is that soft?"

"It's fine. I dinna deny but what I sleep better on feathers. Do you mind, Gavin, you bought this pillow for me the moment you got your bursary money?"

The reserve that is a wall between many of the Scottish poor had been broken down by these two. When he saw his mother sleeping happily, Gavin went back to his work. To save the expense of a lamp, he would put his book almost beneath the dying fire, and, taking the place of the fender, read till he was shivering with cold.

"Gavin, it is near morning, and you not in your bed yet! What are you thinking about so hard?"

"Oh, mother, I was wondering if the time would ever come when I would be a minister, and you would have an egg for your breakfast every morning."

So the years passed, and soon Gavin would be a minister. He had now sermons to prepare, and every one of them was first preached to Margaret. How solemn was his voice, how his eyes flashed, how stern were his admonitions.

"Gavin, such a sermon I never heard. The spirit of God is on you. I'm ashamed you should have me for a mother."

"God grant, mother," Gavin said, little thinking what was soon to happen, or he would have made this prayer on his knees, "that you may never be ashamed to have me for a son."

"Ah, mother," he would say wistfully, "it is not a great sermon, but do you think I'm preaching Christ? That is what I try, but I'm carried away and forget to watch myself."

"The Lord has you by the hand, Gavin; and mind, I dinna say that because you're my laddie."

"Yes you do, mother, and well I know it, and yet it does me good to hear you."

That it did him good, I who would fain have shared those days with them, am very sure. The praise that comes of love does not make us vain, but humble rather. Knowing what we are, the pride that shines in our mother's eyes as she looks at us, is about the most pathetic thing a man has to face, but he would be a devil altogether if it did not burn some of the sin out of him.

Not long before Gavin preached for our kirk and got his call, a great event took place in the little room at Glasgow. The student appeared for the first time before his mother in his ministerial clothes. He wore the black silk hat, that was destined to become a terror to evil-doers in Thrums, and I dare say he was rather puffed up about himself that day. You would probably have smiled at him.

"It's a pity I'm so little, mother," he said with a sigh.

"You're no what I would call a particularly long man," Margaret said, "but you're just the height I like."

Then Gavin went out in his grandeur, and Margaret cried for an hour. She was thinking of me as well as of Gavin, and as it happens, I know that I was thinking at the same time of her. Gavin kept a diary in those days, which I have seen, and by comparing it with mine, I discovered that while he was showing himself to his mother in his black clothes, I was on my way back from Tilliedrum, where I had gone to buy a sand-glass for the school. The one I bought was so like another Margaret had used at Harvie that it set me thinking of her again all the way home. This is a matter hardly worth mentioning, and yet it interests me.

Busy days followed the call to Thrums, and Gavin had difficulty in forcing himself to his sermons when there was always something more to tell his mother about the weaving town they were going to, or about the manse or the furniture that had been transferred to him by the retiring minister. The little room which had become so familiar that it seemed one of a family party of three had to be stripped, and many of its contents were sold. Among what were brought to Thrums was a little exercise book, in which Margaret had tried, unknown to Gavin, to teach herself writing and grammar, that she might be less unfit for a manse. He found it accidentally one day. It was full of "I am, thou art, he is," and the like, written many times in a shaking hand. Gavin put his arms round his mother when he saw what she had been doing. The exercise book is in my desk now, and will be my little maid's when I die.

"Gavin, Gavin," Margaret said many times in those last days at Glasgow, "to think it has all come true!"

"Let the last word you say in the house be a prayer of thankfulness," she whispered to him when they were taking a final glance at the old home.

In the bare room they called the house, the little minister and his mother went on their knees, but, as it chanced, their last word there was not addressed to God.

"Gavin," Margaret whispered as he took her arm. "do you think this bonnet sets me?"

Chapter III

The Night-Watchers

WHAT first struck Margaret in Thrums was the smell of the caddis. The town smells of caddis no longer, but whiffs of it may be got even now as one passes the houses of the old, where the lay still swings at little windows like a great ghost pendulum. To me it is a homely smell, which I draw in with a great breath, but it was as strange to Margaret as the weavers themselves, who, in their coloured nightcaps and corduroys streaked with threads, gazed at her and Gavin. The little minister was trying to look severe and old, but twenty-one was in his eye.

"Look, mother, at that white house with the green roof. That is the manse."

The manse stands high, with a sharp eye on all the town. Every back window in the Tenements has a glint of it, and so the back of the Tenements is always better behaved than the front. It was in the front that Jamie Don, a pitiful bachelor all his life because he thought the women proposed, kept his ferrets, and here, too, Beattie hanged himself, going straight to the clothes-posts for another rope when the first one broke, such was his determination. In the front Sanders Gilruth openly boasted (on Don's potato-pit) that by having a seat in two churches he could lie in bed on Sabbath and get the credit of being at one or other. (Gavin made short work of him.) To the right-minded the Auld Licht manse was as a family Bible, ever lying open before them, but Beattie spoke for more than himself when he said, "Dagone that manse! I never gie a swear but there it is glowering at me."

The manse looks down on the town from the north-east, and is reached from the road that leaves Thrums behind it in another moment by a wide, straight path, so rough that to carry a fraught of water to the manse without spilling was to be superlatively good at one thing. Packages in a cart it set leaping like trout in a fishing-creel. Opposite the opening in the garden wall of the manse, where for many years there had been an intention of putting up a gate, were two big stones a yard apart, standing ready for the winter, when the path was often a rush of yellow water, and this the only bridge to the glebe dyke, down which the minister walked to church.

When Margaret entered the manse on Gavin's arm, it was a whitewashed house of five rooms, with a garret in which the minister could sleep if he had guests, as during the Fast week. It stood with its garden within high walls, and the roof facing southward was carpeted with moss that shone in the sun in a dozen shades of green and yellow. Three firs guarded the house from west winds, but blasts from the north often tore down the steep fields and skirled through the manse, banging all its doors at once. A beech, growing on the east side, leant over the roof as if to gossip with the well in the courtyard. The garden was to the south, and was over full of gooseberry and currant bushes. It contained a summer seat, where strange things were soon to happen.

Margaret would not even take off her bonnet until she had seen through the manse and opened all the presses. The parlour and kitchen were downstairs, and of the three rooms above, the study was so small that Gavin's predecessor could touch each of its walls without shifting his position. Every room save Margaret's had long-lidded beds, which close as if with shutters, but hers was coff-fronted, or comparatively open, with carving on the wood like the ornamentation of coffins. Where there were children in the house they liked to slope the boards of the closed-in bed against the dresser, and play at sliding down mountains on them.

But for many years there had been no children in the manse. He in whose ways Gavin was to attempt the heavy task of walking had been a widower three months after his marriage, a man narrow when he came to Thrums, but so large-hearted when he left it that I, who know there is good in all the world because of the lovable souls I have met in this corner of it, yet cannot hope that many are as near to God as he. The most gladsome thing in the world is that few of us fall very low; the saddest that, with such capabilities, we seldom rise high. Of those who stand perceptibly above their fellows I have known very few; only Mr. Carfrae and two or three women.

Gavin only saw a very frail old minister who shook as he walked, as if his feet were striking against stones. He was to depart on the morrow to the place of his birth, but he came to the manse to wish his successor God-speed. Strangers were so formidable to Margaret that she only saw him from her window.

"May you never lose sight of God, Mr. Dishart," the old man said in the parlour. Then he added, as if he had asked too much, "May you never turn from Him as I often did when I was a lad like you."

As this aged minister, with the beautiful face that God gives to all who love Him and follow His commandments, spoke of his youth, he looked wistfully around the faded parlour.

"It is like a dream," he said. "The first time I entered this room the thought passed through me that I would cut down that cherry-tree, because it kept out the light, but, you see, it outlives me. I grew old while looking for the axe. Only yesterday I was the young minister, Mr. Dishart, and to-morrow you will be the old one, bidding good-bye to your successor."

His eyes came back to Gavin's eager face.

"You are very young, Mr. Dishart?"

"Nearly twenty-one."

"Twenty-one! Ah, my dear sir, you do not know how pathetic that sounds to me. Twenty-one! We are children for the second time at twenty-one, and again when we are grey and put all our burden on the Lord. The young talk generously of relieving the old of their burdens, but the anxious heart is to the old when they see a load on the back of the young. Let me tell you, Mr. Dishart, that I would condone many things in one-and-twenty now that I dealt hardly with at middle age. God Himself, I think, is very willing to give one-and-twenty a second chance."

"I am afraid," Gavin said anxiously, "that I look even younger."

"I think," Mr. Carfrae answered smiling, "that your heart is as fresh as your face; and that is well. The useless men are those who never change with the years. Many views that I held to in my youth and long afterwards are a pain to me now, and I am carrying away from Thrums memories of errors into which I fell at every stage of my ministry. When you are older you will know that life is a long lesson in humility."

He paused.

"I hope," he said nervously, "that you don't sing the Paraphrases?"

Mr. Carfrae had not grown out of all his prejudices, you see; indeed, if Gavin had been less bigoted than he on this question they might have parted stiffly. The old minister would rather have remained to die in his pulpit than to surrender it to one who read his sermons. Others may blame him for this, but I must say here plainly that I never hear a minister reading without wishing to send him back to college.

"I cannot deny," Mr. Carfrae said, "that I broke down more than once to-day. This forenoon I was in Tillyloss, for the last time, and it so happens that there is scarcely a house in it in which I have not had a marriage or prayed over a coffin. Ah, sir, these are the scenes that make the minister more than all his sermons. You must join the family, Mr. Dishart, or you are only a minister once a week. And remember this, if your call is from above it is a call to stay. Many such partings in a lifetime as I have had to-day would be too heartrending."

"And yet," Gavin said, hesitatingly, "they told me in Glasgow that I had received a call from the mouth of hell."

"Those were cruel words, but they only mean that people who are seldom more than a day's work in advance of want sometimes rise in arms for food. Our weavers are passionately religious, and so independent that they dare any one to help them, but if their wages were lessened they could not live. And so at talk of reduction they catch fire. Change of any kind alarms them, and though they call themselves Whigs, they rose a few years ago over the paving of the streets and stoned the workmen, who were strangers, out of the town.

"And though you may have thought the place quiet to-day, Mr. Dishart, there was an ugly outbreak only two months ago, when the weavers turned on the manufacturers for reducing the price of the web, made a bonfire of some of their doors, and terrified one of them into leaving Thrums. Under the command of some Chartists, the people next paraded the streets to the music of fife and drum, and six policemen who drove up from Tilliedrum in a light cart were sent back tied to the seats."

"No one has been punished?"

"Not yet, but nearly two years ago there was a similar riot, and the sheriff took no action for months. Then one night the square suddenly filled with soldiers, and the ringleaders were seized in their beds. Mr. Dishart, the people are determined not to be caught in that way again, and ever since the rising a watch has been kept by night on every road that leads to Thrums. The signal that the soldiers are coming is to be the blowing of a horn. If you ever hear that horn, I implore you to hasten to the square.'

"The weavers would not fight?

"You do not know how the Chartists have fired this part of the country. One misty day,a week ago,I was on the hill; I thought I had it to myself, when suddenly I heard a voice cry sharply, 'Shoulder arms.' I could see no one, and after a moment I put it down to a freak of die wind. Then all at once the mist before me blackened, and a body of men seemed to grow out of it. They were not shadows; they were Thrums weavers drilling, with pikes in their hands.

'They broke up," Mr. Carfrae continued, after a pause, "at my entreaty, but they have met again since then."

"And there were Auld Lichts among them?" Gavin asked. "I should have thought they would be frightened at our precentor, Lang Tammas, who seems to watch for backsliding in the congregation as if he had pleasure in discovering it."

Gavin spoke with feeling, for the precentor had already put him through his catechism, and it was a stiff ordeal.

'The precentor!" said Mr. Carfrae. "Why, he was one of them."

The old minister, once so brave a figure, tottered as he rose to go, and reeled in a dizziness until he had walked a few paces. Gavin went with him to the foot of the manse road; without his hat, as all Thrums knew before bedtime.

"I begin," Gavin said, as they were parting, "where you leave off, and my prayer is that I may walk in your ways."

"Ah, Mr. Dishart," the white-haired minister said, with a sigh, "the world does not progress so quickly as a man grows old. You only begin where I began."

He left Gavin, and then, as if the little minister's last words had hurt him, turned and solemnly pointed his staff upward. Such men are the strong nails that keep the world together.

The twenty-one-years-old minister returned to the manse somewhat sadly, but when he saw his mother at the window of her bed-room, his heart leapt at the thought that she was with him and he had eighty pounds a year. Gaily he waved both his hands to her, and she answered with a smile, and then, in his boyishness, he jumped over a gooseberry bush. Immediately afterwards he reddened and tried to look venerable, for while in the air he had caught sight of two women and a man watching him from the dyke. He walked severely to the door, and, again forgetting himself, was bounding upstairs to Margaret, when Jean, the servant, stood scandalized in his way.

"I don't think she caught me," was Gavin's reflection, and "The Lord preserve's!" was Jean's.

Gavin found his mother wondering how one should set about getting a cup of tea in a house that had a servant in it. He boldly rang the bell, and the willing Jean answered it so promptly (in a rush and jump) that Margaret was as much startled as Aladdin the first time he rubbed his lamp.

Manse servants of the most admired kind move softly, as if constant contact with a minister were goloshes to them; but Jean was new and raw, only having got her place because her father might be an elder any day. She had already conceived a romantic affection for her master; but to say "sir" to him as she thirsted to do would have been as difficult to her as to swallow oysters. So anxious was she to please that when Gavin rang she fired herself at the bed-room, but bells were novelties to her as well as to Margaret, and she cried, excitedly, "What is't?" thinking the house must be on fire.

"There's a curran folk at the back door," Jean announced later, "and their respects to you, and would you gie them some water out o' the well? It has been a drouth this aucht days, and the pumps is locked. Na," she said, as Gavin made a too liberal offer, "that would toom the well, and there's jimply enough for oursels. I should tell you, too, that three o' them is no Auld Lichts."

"Let that make no difference," Gavin said grandly, but Jean changed his message to: "A bowlful apiece to Auld Lichts; all other denominations one cupful."

"Ay,ay," said Snecky Hobart, letting down the bucket, "and we'll include atheists among other denominations." The conversation came to Gavin and Margaret through the kitchen doorway.

"Dinna class Jo Cruickshanks wi' me," said Sam'l Langlands the U.P.

"Na, na," said Cruickshanks the atheist, "I'm ower independent to be religious. I dinna gang to the kirk to cry, 'Oh, Lord, gie, gie, gie.'

"Take tent o' yoursel', my man," said Lang Tammas sternly, "or you'll soon be whaur you would neifer the warld for a cup o' that cauld water."

"Maybe you've ower keen an interest in the devil, Tammas," retorted the atheist, "but, ony way,if it's heaven for climate, it's hell for company."

"Lads," said Snecky, sitting down on the bucket, "we'll send Mr. Dishart to Jo. He'll make another Rob Dow o' him."

"Speak mair reverently o' your minister," said the precentor. "He has the gift."

"I hinna naturally your solemn rasping word, Tammas, but in the heart I speak in all reverence. Lads, the minister has a word! I tell you he prays near like one giving orders."

"At first," Snecky continued, "I thocht yon lang candidate was the earnestest o' them a', and I dinna deny but when I saw him wi' his head bowed-like in prayer during the singing I says to mysel', 'Thou art the man.' Ay, but Betsy wraxed up her head, and he wasna praying. He was combing his hair wi' his fingers on the sly."

"You ken fine, Sneck," said Cruickshanks, "that you said, 'Thou art the man' to ilka ane o' them, and just voted for Mr. Dishart because he preached hinmost."

"I didna say it to Mr. Urquhart, the ane that preached second," Sneck said: "That was the lad that gaed through ither."

"Ay," said Susy Tibbits, nicknamed by Haggart "the Timidest Woman" because she once said she was too young to marry, "but I was fell sorry for him, him just being over anxious. He began bonny, flinging himself, like ane inspired, at the pulpit door, but after Hendry Munn pointed at it and cried out, 'Be cautious, the sneck's loose,' he a' gaed to bits. What a coolness Hendry has, though I suppose it was his duty, him being kirk-officer."

"We didna want a man," Lang Tammas said, "that could be put out by sic a sma' thing as that. Mr. Urquhart was in sic a ravel after it that when he gies out the first line o' the hunder and nineteenth psalm for singing, say he, 'And so on to the end.' Ay, that finished his chance."

"The noblest o' them to look at," said Tibbie Birse, "was that ane frae Aberdeen, him that had sic a saft side to Jacob."

"Ay," said Snecky, "and I speired at Dr. McQueen if I should vote for him. 'Looks like a genius, does he?' says the Doctor. 'Weel, then,' says he, 'dinna vote for him, for my experience is that there's no folk sic idiots as them that looks like geniuses.'"

"Sal," Susy said, "it's a guid thing we've settled, for I enjoyed sitting like a judge upon them so muckle that I sair doubt it was a kind o' sport to me."

"It was no sport to them, Susy, I'se uphaud, but it is a blessing we've settled, and ondoubtedly we've got the pick o' them. The only thing Mr. Dishart did that made me oneasy was his saying the word Caesar as if it began wi' a *k*."

"He'll startle you mair afore you're done wi' him," the atheist said maliciously. "I ken the ways o' thae ministers preaching for kirks. Oh, they're cunning. You was a' pleased that Mr. Dishart spoke about looms and webs, but, lathies, it was a trick. Ilka ane o' thae young ministers has a sermon about looms for weaving congregations, and a second about beating swords into ploughshares for country places, and another on the great catch of fishes for fishing villages. That's their stock-in-trade; and just you wait and see if you dinna get the ploughshares and the fishes afore the month's out. A minister preaching for a kirk is one thing, but a minister placed in't may be a very different berry."

"Joseph Cruickshanks," cried the precentor, passionately, "none o' your d—d blasphemy!"

They all looked at Whamond, and he dug his teeth into his lips in shame.

"Wha's swearing now?" said the atheist.

But Whamond was quick.

"Matthew, twelve and thirty-one," he said.

"Dagont, Tammas," exclaimed the baffled Cruickshanks, "you're aye quoting Scripture. How do you no quote Feargus O'Connor?"

"Lads," said Snecky, "Jo hasna heard Mr. Dishart's sermons. Ay, we get it scalding when he comes to the sermon. I canna thole a minister that preaches as if heaven was round the corner."

"If you're hitting at our minister, Snecky," said James Cochrane, "let me tell you he's a better man than yours."

"A better curler, I dare say."

"A better prayer."

"Ay, he can pray for a black frost as if it was ane o' the Royal Family. I ken his prayers, 'O Lord, let it haud for anither day, and keep the snaw awa'.' Will you pretend, Jeames, that Mr. Duthie could make ony thing o' Rob Dow?"

"I admit that Rob's awakening was an extraordinary thing, and sufficient to gie Mr. Dishart a name. But Mr. Carfrae was baffled wi' Rob, too."

"Jeames, if you had been in our kirk that day Mr. Dishart preached for't you would be wearying the now for Sabbath, to be back in't again. As you ken, that wicked man there, Jo Cruickshanks, got Rob Dow, drucken, cursing, poaching Rob Dow, to come to the kirk to annoy the minister. Ay, he hadna been at that work for ten minutes when Mr. Dishart stopped in his first prayer and ga'e Rob a look. I couldna see the look, being in the precentor's box, but as sure as death I felt it boring through me. Rob is hard wood, though, and soon he was at his tricks again. Weel, the minister stopped a second time in the sermon, and so awful was the silence that a heap o' the congregation couldna keep their seats. I heard Rob breathing quick and strong. Mr. Dishart had his arm pointed at him a' this time, and at last he says sternly, 'Come forward.' Listen, Joseph Cruickshanks, and tremble. Rob gripped the board to keep himsel' frae obeying, and again Mr. Dishart says, 'Come forward,' and syne Rob rose shaking, and tottered to the pulpit stair like a man suddenly shot into the Day of Judgment. 'You hulking man of sin,' cries Mr. Dishart, not a tick fleid, though Rob's as big as three o' him, 'sit down on the stair and attend to me, or I'll step doun frae the pulpit and run you out of the house of God.'

"And since that day," said Hobart, "Rob has worshipped Mr. Dishart as a man that has stepped out o' the Bible. When the carriage passed this day we was discussing the minister, and Sam'l Dickie wasna sure but what Mr. Dishart wore his hat rather far back on his head. You should hae seen Rob. 'My certie,' he roars, 'there's the shine frae Heaven on that little minister's face, and them as says there's no has me to fecht.'"

"Ay, weel," said the U.P., rising, "we'll see how Rob wears — and how your minister wears too. I wouldna like to sit in a kirk whaur they daurna sing a paraphrase."

"The Psalms of David," retorted Whamond, "mount straight to heaven, but your paraphrases sticks to the ceiling o' the kirk."

"You're a bigoted set, Tammas Whamond, but I tell you this, and it's my last words to you the nicht, the day'll come when you'll hae Mr. Duthie, ay, and even the U.P. minister, preaching in the Auld Licht kirk."

"And let this be my last words to you," replied the precentor, furiously; "that rather than see a U.P. preaching in the Auld Licht kirk I would burn in hell fire for ever!"

This gossip increased Gavin's knowledge of the grim men with whom he had now to deal. But as he sat beside Margaret after she had gone to bed, their talk was pleasant.

"You remember, mother," Gavin said, "how I almost prayed for the manse that was to give you an egg every morning. I have been telling Jean never to forget the egg."

"Ah, Gavin, things have come about so much as we wanted that I'm a kind o' troubled. It's hardly natural, and I hope nothing terrible is to happen now."

Gavin arranged her pillows as she liked them, and when he next stole into the room in his stocking soles to look at her, he thought she was asleep. But she was not. I dare say she saw at that moment Gavin in his first frock, and Gavin in knickerbockers, and Gavin as he used to walk into the Glasgow room from college, all still as real to her as the Gavin who had a kirk.

The little minister took away the lamp to his own room, shaking his fist at himself for allowing his mother's door to creak. He pulled up his blind. The town lay as still as salt. But a steady light showed in the south, and on pressing his face against the window he saw another in the west. Mr. Carfrae's words about the night-watch came back to him. Perhaps it had been on such a silent night as this that the soldiers marched into Thrums. Would they come again?

Chapter IV

First Coming Of The Egyptian Woman

A learned man says in a book, otherwise beautiful with truth, that villages are family groups. To him Thrums would only be a village, though town is the word we have ever used, and this is not true of it. Doubtless we have interests in common, from which a place so near (but the road is heavy) as Tilliedrum is shut out, and we have an individuality of our own too, as if, like our red houses, we came from a quarry that supplies no other place. But we are not one family. In the old days, those of us who were of the Tenements seldom wandered to the Croft head, and if we did go there we saw men to whom we could not always give a name. To flit from the Tanage brae to Haggart's roady was to change one's friends. A kirk-wynd weaver might kill his swine and Tillyloss not know of it until boys ran westward hitting each other with the bladders. Only the voice of the dulsemen could be heard all over Thrums at once. Thus even in a small place but a few outstanding persons are known to everybody.

In eight days Gavin's figure was more familiar in Thrums than many that had grown bent in it. He had already been twice to the cemetery, for a minister only reaches his new charge in time to attend a funeral. Though short of stature he cast a great shadow. He was so full of his duties, Jean said, that though he pulled to the door as he left the manse, he had passed the currant bushes before it snecked. He darted through courts, and invented ways into awkward houses. If you did not look up quickly he was round the corner. His visiting exhausted him only less than his zeal in the pulpit, from which, according to report, he staggered damp with perspiration to the vestry, where Hendry Munn wrung him like a wet clout. A deaf lady, celebrated for giving out her washing, compelled him to hold her trumpet until she had peered into all his crannies, with the Shorter Catechism for a lantern. Janet Dundas told him, in answer to his knock, that she could not abide him, but she changed her mind when he said her garden was quite a show. The wives who expected a visit scrubbed their floors for him, cleaned out their presses for him, put diamond socks on their bairns for him, rubbed their hearthstones blue for him, even tidied up the garret for him, and triumphed over the neighbours whose houses he passed by. For Gavin blundered occasionally by inadvertence, as when he gave dear old Betty Davie occasion to say bitterly:—

"Ou ay, you can sail by my door and gang to Easie's, but I'm thinking you would stop at mine too if I had a brass handle on't."

So passed the first four weeks, and then came the fateful night of the seventeenth of October, and with it the strange woman. Family worship at the manse was over, and Gavin was talking to his mother, who never crossed the threshold save to go to church (though her activity at home was among the marvels Jean sometimes slipped down to the Tenements to announce), when Weary world the policeman came to the door "with Rob Dow's compliments, and if you're no wi' me by ten o'clock I'm to break out again." Gavin knew what this meant, and at once set oft for Rob's.

"You'll let me gang a bit wi' you," the policeman entreated, "for till Rob sent me on this errand not a soul has spoken to me the day; ay, mony a ane hae I spoken to, but not a man, woman, nor bairn would fling me a word."

"I often meant to ask you," Gavin said as they went along the Tenements, which smelled at that hour of roasted potatoes, "why you are so unpopular."

"It's because I'm police. I'm the first ane that has ever been in Thrums, and the very folk that appointed me at a crown a week looks upon me as a disgraced man for accepting. It's Gospel that my ain wife is short wi' me when I've on my uniform, though weel she kens that I would rather hae stuck to the loom if I hadna ha'en sic a queer richt leg. Nobody feels the shame o' my position as I do mysel', but this is a town without pity."

"It should be a consolation to you that you are discharging useful duties."

"But I'm no. I'm doing harm. There's Charles Dickson says that the very sicht o' my uniform rouses his dander so muckle that it makes him break windows, though a peaceably-disposed man till I was appointed. And what's the use o' their haeing a policeman when they winna come to the lock-up after I lay hands on them?"

"Do they say they won't come?"

"Say! Catch them saying onything! They just gie me a wap into the gutters. If they would speak I wouldna complain, for I'm nat'rally the sociablest man in Thrums."

"Rob, however, had spoken to you."

"Because he had need o' me. That was ay Rob's way, converted or no converted. When he was blind drunk he would order me to see him safe hame, but would he crack wi' me? Na, na."

Weary world, who was so called because of his forlorn way of muttering, "It's a weary warld, and nobody bides in't" as he went his melancholy rounds, sighed like one about to cry, and Gavin changed the subject.

"Is the watch for the soldiers still kept up?" he asked.

"It is, but the watchers winna let me in aside them. I'll let you see that for yoursel' at the head o' the Roods, for they watch there in the auld windmill."

Most of the Thrums lights were already out, and that in the windmill disappeared as footsteps were heard.

"You're desperate characters," the policeman cried, but got no answer. He changed his tactics.

"A fine nicht for the time o' year," he cried. No answer.

"But I wouldna wonder," he shouted, "though we had rain afore morning." No answer.

"Surely you could gie me a word frae ahint the door. You're doing an onlawful thing, but I dinna ken wha you are."

"You'll swear to that?" some one asked gruffly.

"I swear to it, Peter?"

Wearyworld tried another six remarks in vain.

"Ay," he said to the minister, "that's what it is to be an onpopular man. And now I'll hae to turn back, for the very anes that winna let me join them would be the first to complain if I gaed out o' bounds."

Gavin found Dow at New Zealand, a hamlet of mud houses, whose tenants could be seen on any Sabbath morning washing themselves in the burn that trickled hard by. Rob's son, Micah, was asleep at the door, but he brightened when he saw who was shaking him.

"My father put me out," he explained, "because he's daft for the drink, and was fleid he would curse me. He hasna cursed me," Micah added, proudly, "for an aucht days come Sabbath. Hearken to him at his loom. He daurna take his feet oft the treadles for fear o' running straucht to the drink."

Gavin went in. The loom, and two stools, the one four-footed and the other a buffet, were Rob's most conspicuous furniture. A shaving-strap hung on the wall. The fire was out, but the trunk of a tree, charred at one end, showed how he heated his house. He made a fire of peat, and on it placed one end of a tree trunk that might be six feet long. As the tree burned away it was pushed further into the fireplace, and a roaring fire could always be got by kicking pieces of the smouldering wood and blowing them into flame with the bellows. When Rob saw the minister he groaned relief and left his loom. He had been weaving, his teeth clenched, his eyes on fire, for seven hours.

"I wasna fleid," little Micah said to the neighbours afterwards, "to gang in wi' the minister. He's a fine man that. He didna ca' my father names. Na, he said, 'You're a brave fellow, Rob,' and he took my father's hand, he did. My father was shaking after his fecht wi' the drink, and, says he, 'Mr. Dishart, he says, 'if you'll let me break out nows and nans, I could bide straucht atween times, but I canna keep sober if I hinna a drink to look forrit to.' Ay, my father prigged sair to git one fou day in a month, and he said, 'Syne if I die sudden, there's thirty chances to one that I gang to heaven, so it's worth risking.' But Mr. Dishart wouldna hear o't, and he cries, 'No, by God,' he cries, 'we'll wrestle wi' the devil till we throttle him,' and down him and my father gaed on their knees.

"The minister prayed a lang time till my father said his hunger for the drink was gone, 'but,' he says, 'it swells up in me o' a sudden aye, and it may be back afore you're name.' 'Then come to me at once,' says Mr. Dishart; but my father says, 'Na, for it would haul me into the public-house as if it had me at the end o' a rope, but I'll send the laddie.'

"You saw my father crying the minister back? It was to gie him twa pound, and, says my father, 'God helping me,' he says, 'I'll droon mysel in the dam rather than let the drink master me, but in case it should get haud o' me and I should die drunk, it would be a michty gratification to me to ken that you had the siller to bury me respectable without ony help frae the poor's rates.' The minister wasna for taking it at first, but he took it when he saw how earnest my father was. Ay, he's a noble man. After he gaed awa my father made me learn the names o' the apostles frae Luke sixth, and he says to me, 'Miss out Bartholomew,' he says, 'for he did little, and put Gavin Dishart in his place.'

Feeling as old as he sometimes tried to look, Gavin turned homeward. Margaret was already listening for him. You may be sure she knew his step. I think our steps vary as much as the human face. My bookshelves were made by a blind man who could identify by their steps nearly all who passed his window. Yet he has admitted to me that he could not tell wherein my steps differed from others; and this I believe, though rejecting his boast that he could distinguish a minister's step from a doctor's, and even tell to which denomination the minister belonged.

I have sometimes asked myself what would have been Gavin's future had he gone straight home that night from Dow's. He would doubtless have seen the Egyptian before morning broke, but she would not have come upon him like a witch. There are, I dare say, many lovers who would never have been drawn to each other had they met for the first time, as, say, they met the second time. But such dreaming is to no purpose. Gavin met Sanders Webster, the mole-catcher, and was persuaded by him to go home by Caddam Wood.

Gavin took the path to Caddam, because Sanders told him the Wild Lindsays were there, a gypsy family that threatened the farmers by day and danced devilishly, it was said, at night. The little minister knew them by repute as a race of giants, and that not many persons would have cared to face them alone at midnight, but he was feeling as one wound up to heavy duties, and meant to admonish them severely.

Sanders, an old man who lived with his sister Nanny on the edge of the wood, went with him, and for a time both were silent. But Sanders had something to say.

"Was you ever at the Spittal, Mr. Dishart?" he asked.

"Lord Rintoul's house at the top of Glen Quharity? No."

"Hae you ever looked on a lord?"

"No."

"Or on an auld lord's young leddyship? I have."

"What is she?"

"You surely ken that Rintoul's auld, and is to be married on a young leddyship. She's no a leddyship yet, but they're to be married soon, so I may say I've seen a leddyship. Ay, an impressive sicht. It was yestreen.".

"Is there a great difference in their ages?"

"As muckle as atween auld Peter Spens and his wife, wha was saxteen when he was saxty, and she was playing at dumps in the street when her man was waiting for her to make his porridge. Ay, sic a differ doesna suit wi' common folk, but of course earls can please themsels. Rintoul's so fond of the leddyship 'at is to be, that when she was at the school in Edinbury he wrote to her ilka day. Kaytherine Crummie telled me that, and she says aince you're used to it, writing letters is as easy as skinning moles. I dinna ken what they can write sic a heap about, but I daur say he gies her his views on the Chartist agitation and the potato disease, and she'll write back about the romantic sichts o' Edinbury and the sermons o' the grand preachers she hears. Sal, though, thae grand folk has no religion to speak o', for they're a' English kirk. You're no' speiring what her leddyship said to me?"

"What did she say?"

"Weel, you see, there was a dancing ball on, and Kaytherine Crummie took me to a window whaur I could stand on a flowerpot and watch the critturs whirling round in the ball like teetotums. What's mair, she pointed out the leddyship that's to be to me,and I just glowered at her, for thinks I, 'Take your fill, Sanders, and whaur there's lords and leddyships, dinna waste a minute on colonels and honourable misses and sic like dirt.' Ay, but what wi' my een blinking at the blaze o' candles, I lost sicht o' her till all at aince somebody says at my lug, 'Well, my man, and who is the prettiest lady in the room?' Mr. Dishart, it was her leddyship. She looked like a star."

"And what did you do?'

"The first thing I did was to fall aff the flower-pot, but syne I came to, and says I, wi' a polite smirk, I'm thinking your leddyship,' says I, 'as you're the bonniest yoursel'."

"I see you are a cute man, Sanders."

"Ay, but that's no' a'. She lauched in a pleased way and tapped me wi' her fan, and says she, 'Why do you think me the prettiest?' I dinna deny but what that staggered me, but I thocht a minute, and took a look at the other dancers again, and syne I says, michty sly like, 'The other leddies,' I says, 'has sic sma' feet.'

Sanders stopped here and looked doubtingly at Gavin.

"I canna make up my mind," he said, "whether she liked that, for she rapped my knuckles wi' her fan fell sair, and aff she gaed. Ay, I consulted Tammas Haggart about it, and he says, 'The flirty crittur,' he says. What would you say, Mr. Dishart?"

Gavin managed to escape without giving an answer, for here their roads separated. He did not find the Wild Lindsays, however. Children of whim, of prodigious strength while in the open, but destined to wither quickly in the hot air of towns, they had gone from Caddam, leaving nothing of themselves behind but a black mark burned by their fires into the ground. Thus they branded the earth through many counties until some hour when the spirit of wandering again fell on them, and they forsook their hearths with as little compunction as the bird leaves its nest.

Gavin had walked quickly, and he now stood silently in the wood, his hat in his hand. In the moonlight the grass seemed tipped with hoar frost. Most of the beeches were already bare, but the shoots, clustering round them, like children at their mothers' skirts, still retained their leaves red and brown. Among the pines these leaves were as incongruous as a wedding-dress at a funeral. Gavin was standing on grass, but there were patches of heather within sight, and broom, and the leaf of the blaeberry. Where the beeches had drawn up the earth with them as they grew, the roots ran this way and that, slippery to the feet and looking like disinterred bones. A squirrel appeared suddenly on the charred ground, looked doubtfully at Gavin to see if he was growing there, and then glided up a tree, where it sat eyeing him, and forgetting to conceal its shadow. Caddam was very still. At long intervals came from far away the whack of an axe on wood. Gavin was in a world by himself, and this might be someone breaking into it.

The mystery of woods by moonlight thrilled the little minister. His eyes rested on the shining roots, and he remembered what had been told him of the legend of Caddam, how once on a time it was a mighty wood, and a maiden most beautiful stood on its confines, panting and afraid, for a wicked man pursued her; how he drew near, and she ran a little way into the wood, and he followed her, and she still ran, and still he followed, until both were for ever lost, and die bones of her pursuer lie beneath a beech, but the lady may still be heard singing in the woods, if the night be fine, for then she is a glad spirit, but weeping when there is wild wind, for then she is but a mortal seeking a way out of the wood.

The squirrel slid down the fir and was gone. The axe's blows ceased. Nothing that moved was in sight. The wind that has its nest in trees was circling around with many voices, that never rose above a whisper, and were often but the echo of a sigh.

Gavin was in the Caddam of past days, where the beautiful maiden wanders ever, waiting for him who is so pure that he may find her. He will wander over the tree-tops looking for her, with the moon for his lamp, and some night he will hear her singing. The little minister drew a deep breath, and his foot snapped a brittle twig. Then he remembered who and where he was, and stooped to pick up his staff. But he did not pick it up, for as his fingers were closing on it the lady began to sing.

For perhaps a minute Gavin stood stock still, like an intruder. Then he ran towards the singing, which seemed to come from Windyghoul, a straight road through Caddam that farmers use in summer, but leave in the back end of the year to leaves and pools. In Windyghoul there is either no wind or so much that it rushes down the sieve like an army, entering with a shriek of terror, and escaping with a derisive howl. The moon was crossing the avenue. But Gavin only saw the singer.

She was still fifty yards away, sometimes singing gleefully, and again letting her body sway lightly as she came dancing up Windyghoul. Soon she was within a few feet of the little minister, to whom singing, except when out of tune, was a suspicious thing, and dancing a device of the devil. His arm went out wrathfully, and his intention was to pronounce sentence on this woman.

But she passed, unconscious of his presence, and he had not moved nor spoken. Though really of the average height, she was a little thing to the eyes of Gavin, who always felt tall and stout except when he looked down. The grace of her swaying figure was a new thing in the world to him. Only while she passed did he see her as a gleam of colour, a gypsy elf poorly clad, her bare feet flashing beneath a short green skirt, a twig of rowan berries stuck carelessly into her black hair. Her face was pale. She had an angel's loveliness. Gavin shook.

Still she danced onwards, but she was very human, for when she came to muddy water she let her feet linger in it, and flung up her arms, dancing more wantonly than before. A diamond on her finger shot a thread of fire over the pool. Undoubtedly she was the devil.

Gavin leaped into the avenue, and she heard him and looked behind. He tried to cry; "Woman!" sternly, but lost the word, for now she saw him, and laughed with her shoulders, and beckoned to him, so that he shook his fist at her. She tripped on, but often turning her head beckoned and mocked him, and he forgot his dignity and his pulpit and all other things, and ran after her. Up Windyghoul did he pursue her, and it was well that the precentor was not there to see. She reached the mouth of the avenue, and kissing her hand to Gavin, so that the ring gleamed again, was gone.

The minister's one thought was to find her, but he searched in vain. She might be crossing the hill on her way to Thrums, or perhaps she was still laughing at him from behind a tree. After a longer time than he was aware of, Gavin realised that his boots were chirping and his trousers streaked with mud. Then he abandoned the search and hastened homewards in a rage.

From the hill to the manse the nearest way is down two fields, and the little minister descended them rapidly. Thrums, which is red in daylight, was grey and still as the cemetery. He had glimpses of several of its deserted streets. To the south the watchlight showed brightly, but no other was visible. So it seemed to Gavin, and then — suddenly — he lost the power to move. He had heard the horn. Thrice it sounded, and thrice it struck him to the heart.

He looked again and saw a shadow stealing along the Tenements, then another, then half-a-dozen. He remembered Mr. Carfrae's words, "If you ever hear that horn, I implore you to hasten to the square," and in another minute he had reached the Tenements.

Now again he saw the gypsy. She ran past him, half-a-score of men, armed with staves and pikes, at her heels. At first he thought they were chasing her, but they were following her as a leader. Her eyes sparkled as she waved them to the square with her arms.

"The soldiers, the soldiers!" was the universal cry.

"Who is that woman?" demanded Gavin, catching hold of a frightened old man.

"Curse the Egyptian limmer," the man answered, "she's egging my laddie on to fecht."

"Bless her rather," the son cried, "for warning us that the sojers is coming. Put your ear to the ground, Mr. Dishart, and you'll hear the dirl o' their feet."

The young man rushed away to the square, flinging his father from him. Gavin followed. As he turned into the school wynd, the town drum began to beat, windows were thrown open, and sullen men ran out of closes where women were screaming and trying to hold them back. At the foot of the wynd Gavin passed Sanders Webster.

"Mr. Dishart," the mole-catcher cried, "hae you seen that Egyptian? May I be struck dead if it's no' her little leddyship."

But Gavin did not hear him.

Chapter V

A Warlike Chapter, Culminating In The Flouting Of The Minister By The Woman

"MR. DISHART!" Jean had clutched at Gavin in Bank Street. Her hair was streaming, and her wrapper but half buttoned.

"Oh, Mr. Dishart, look at the mistress! I couldna keep her in the manse."

Gavin saw his mother beside him, bare-headed, trembling.

"How could I sit still, Gavin, and the town full o' the skirls of women and bairns? Oh, Gavin, what can I do for them? They will suffer most this night."

As Gavin took her hand he knew that Margaret felt for the people more than he.

"But you must go home, mother," he said, "and leave me to do my duty. I will take you myself if you will not go with Jean. Be careful of her, Jean."

"Ay, will I," Jean answered, then burst into tears. "Mr. Dishart," she cried, "if they take my father they'd best take my mither too."

The two women went back to the manse, where Jean re-lit the fire, having nothing else to do, and boiled the kettle, while Margaret wandered in anguish from room to room.

Men nearly naked ran past Gavin, seeking to escape from Thrums by the fields he had descended. When he shouted to them they only ran faster. A Tillyloss weaver whom he tried to stop struck him savagely and sped past to the square. In Bank Street, which was full of people at one moment and empty the next, the minister stumbled over old Charles Yuill.

"Take me and welcome," Yuill cried, mistaking Gavin for the enemy. He had only one arm through the sleeve of his jacket, and his feet were bare.

"I am Mr. Dishart. Are the soldiers already in the square, Yuill?"

"They'll be there in a minute."

The man was so weak that Gavin had to hold him.

"Be a man, Charles. You have nothing to fear. It is not such as you the soldiers have come for. If need be, I can swear that you had not the strength even if you had the will, to join in the weavers' riot."

"For Godsake, Mr. Dishart," Yuill cried, his hands chattering on Gavin's coat, "dinna swear that. My laddie was in the thick o' the riot; and if he's ta'en there's the poor's-house gaping for Kitty and me, for I couldna weave half a web a week. If there's a warrant agin onybody o' the name o' Yuill, swear it's me; swear I'm a desperate character, swear I'm michty strong for all I look palsied; and if when they take me, my courage breaks down, swear the mair, swear I confessed my guilt to you on the Book."

As Yuill spoke the quick rub-a-dub of a drum was heard.

"The soldiers!" Gavin let go his hold of the old man, who hastened away to give himself up.

"That's no the sojers," said a woman; "it's the folk gathering in the square. This'll be a watery Sabbath in Thrums."

"Rob Dow," shouted Gavin, as Dow flung past with a scythe in his hand, "lay down that scythe."

"To hell wi' religion!" Rob retorted, fiercely; "it spoils a' thing."

"Lay down that scythe; I command you."

Rob stopped undecidedly, then cast the scythe from him, but its rattle on the stones was more than he could bear.

"I winna," he cried, and, picking it up, ran to the square.

An upper window in Bank Street opened, and Dr. McQueen put out his head. He was smoking as usual.

"Mr. Dishart," he said, "you will return home at once if you are a wise man; or, better still, come in here. You can do nothing with these people tonight."

"I can stop their fighting."

"You will only make black blood between them and you."

"Dinna heed him, Mr. Dishart," cried some women.

"You had better heed him," cried a man.

"I will not desert my people," Gavin said.

"Listen, then, to my prescription," the doctor replied. "Drive that gypsy lassie out of the town before the soldiers reach it. She is firing the men to a red-heat through sheer devilry."

"She brocht the news, or we would have been nipped in our beds," some people cried.

"Does any one know who she is?" Gavin demanded, but all shook their heads. The Egyptian, as they called her, had never been seen in these parts before.

"Has any other person seen the soldiers?" he asked. "Perhaps this is a false alarm."

"Several have seen them within the last few minutes," the doctor answered: 'They came from Tilliedrum, and were advancing on us from the south, but when they heard that we had got the alarm they stopped at the top of the brae, near T'nowhead's farm. Man, you would take these things more coolly if you smoked."

"Show me this woman," Gavin said sternly to those who had been listening. Then a stream of people carried him into the square.

The square has altered little, even in these days of enterprise, when Tillyloss has become Newton Bank, and the Craft Head Croft Terrace, with enamelled labels on them for the guidance of slow people, who forget their address and have to run to the end of the street and look up every time they write a letter. The stones on which the butter-wives sat have disappeared, and with them the clay walls and the outside stairs. Gone, too, is the stair of the town-house, from the top of which the drummer roared the gossip of the week on Sabbaths to country folk, to the scandal of all who knew that the proper thing on that day is to keep your blinds down; but the town-house itself, round and red, still makes exit to the south troublesome. Wherever streets meet the square there is a house in the centre of them, and thus the heart of Thrums is a box, in which the stranger finds himself suddenly, wondering at first how he is to get out, and presently how he got in.

To Gavin, who never before had seen a score of people in the square at once, here was a sight strange and terrible. Andrew Struthers, an old soldier, stood on the outside stair of the town-house, shouting words of command to some fifty weavers, many of them scantily clad, but all armed with pikes and poles. Most were known to the little minister, but they wore faces that were new to him. New-comers joined the body every moment. If the drill was clumsy the men were fierce. Hundreds of people gathered around, some screaming, some shaking their fists at the old soldier, many trying to pluck their relatives out of danger. Gavin could not see the Egyptian. Women and old men, fighting for the possession of his ear, implored him to disperse the armed band. He ran up the town-house stair, and in a moment it had become a pulpit.

"Dinna dare to interfere, Mr. Dishart," Struthers said savagely.

"Andrew Struthers," said Gavin solemnly, "in the name of God I order you to leave me alone. If you don't," he added ferociously, "I'll fling you over the stair."

"Dinna heed him, Andrew," some one shouted; and another cried, "He canna understand our sufferings; he has dinner ilka day."

Struthers faltered, however, and Gavin cast his eye over the armed men.

"Rob Dow," he said, "William Carmichael, Thomas Whamond, William Munn, Alexander Hobart, Henders Haggart, step forward."

These were Auld Lichts, and when they found that the minister would not take his eyes off them, they obeyed, all save Rob Dow.

"Never mind him, Rob," said the atheist, Cruickshanks, "it's better playing cards in hell than singing psalms in heaven."

"Joseph Cruickshanks," responded Gavin grimly, "you will find no cards down there."

Then Rob also came to the foot of the stair. There was some angry muttering from the crowd, and young Charles Yuill exclaimed, "Curse you, would you lord it ower us on week-days as weel as on Sabbaths?"

"Lay down your weapons," Gavin said to the six men.

They looked at each other. Hobart slipped his pike behind his back.

"I hae no weapon," he said slily.

"Let me hae my fling this nicht," Dow entreated, "and I'll promise to bide sober for a twelvemonth."

"Oh, Rob, Rob!" the minister said bitterly, "are you the man I prayed with a few hours ago?"

The scythe fell from Rob's hands.

"Down wi' your pikes," he roared to his companions, "or I'll brain you wi' them."

"Ay, lay them down," the precentor whispered, "but keep your feet on them."

Then the minister, who was shaking with excitement, though he did not know it, stretched forth his arms for silence, and it came so suddenly as to frighten the people in the neighbouring streets.

"If he prays we're done for," cried young Charles Yuill, but even in that hour many of the people unbonneted.

"Oh, Thou who art the Lord of hosts," Gavin prayed, "we are in Thy hands this night. These are Thy people, and they have sinned, but Thou art a merciful God, and they were sore tried, and knew not what they did. To Thee, our God, we turn for deliverance, for without Thee we are lost."

The little minister's prayer was heard all round the square, and many weapons were dropped as an Amen to it.

"If you fight," cried Gavin, brightening as he heard the clatter of the iron on the stones, "your wives and children may be shot in the streets. These soldiers have come for a dozen of you; will you be benefited if they take away a hundred?"

"Oh, hearken to him," cried many women.

"I winna," answered a man, "for I'm ane o' the dozen. Whaur's the Egyptian?"

"Here."

Gavin saw the crowd open, and the woman of Windyghoul come out of it, and, while he should have denounced her, he only blinked, for once more her loveliness struck him full in the eyes. She was beside him on the stair before he became a minister again.

"How dare you, woman?" he cried; but she flung a rowan berry at him.

"If I were a man," she exclaimed, addressing the people, "I wouldna let mysel be catched like a mouse in a trap."

"We winna," some answered.

"What kind o' women are you," cried the Egyptian, her face gleaming as she turned to her own sex, "that bid your men folk gang to gaol when a bold front would lead them to safety? Do you want to be husbandless and nameless?"

"Disperse, I command you!" cried Gavin. "This abandoned woman is inciting you to riot."

"Dinna heed this little man," the Egyptian retorted.

It is curious to know that even at that anxious moment Gavin winced because she called him little.

"She has the face of a mischief-maker," he shouted, "and her words are evil."

"You men and women o' Thrums," she responded, "ken that I wish you weel by the service I hae done you this nicht. Wha telled you the sojers was coming?"

"It was you; it was you!"

"Ay, and mony a mile I ran to bring the news. Listen, and I'll tell you mair."

"She has a false tongue," Gavin cried; "listen not to the brazen woman."

"What I have to tell," she said, "is as true as what I've telled already, and how true that is you a' ken. You're wondering how the sojers has come to a stop at the tap o' the brae instead o' marching on the town. Here's the reason. They agreed to march straucht to the square if the alarm wasna given, but if it was they were to break into small bodies and surround the town so that you couldna get out. That's what they're doing now."

At this the screams were redoubled, and many men lifted the weapons they had dropped.

"Believe her not," cried Gavin. "How could a wandering gypsy know all this?"

"Ay, how can you ken?" some demanded.

"It's enough that I do ken," the Egyptian answered. "And this mair I ken, that the captain of the soldiers is confident he'll nab every one o' you that's wanted unless you do one thing."

"What is't?"

"If you a' run different ways you're lost, but if you keep thegither you'll be able to force a road into the country, whaur you can scatter. That's what he's fleid you'll do."

"Then it's what we will do."

"It is what you will not do," Gavin said passionately. "The truth is not in this wicked woman."

But scarcely had he spoken when he knew that startling news had reached the square. A murmur arose on the skirts of the mob, and swept with the roar of the sea towards the town-house. A detachment of the soldiers were marching down the Roods from the north.

"There's some coming frae the east-town end," was the next intelligence, "and they've gripped Sanders Webster, and auld Charles Yuill has gien himsel' up."

"You see, you see," the gypsy said, flashing triumph at Gavin."

"Lay down your weapons," Gavin cried, but his power over the people had gone.

"The Egyptian spoke true," they shouted; "dinna heed the minister."

Gavin tried to seize the gypsy by the shoulders, but she slipped past him down the stair, and crying "Follow me!" ran round the town-house and down the brae.

"Woman!" he shouted after her, but she only waved her arms scornfully. The people followed her, many of the men still grasping their weapons, but all in disorder. Within a minute after Gavin saw the gleam of the ring on her finger, as she waved her hands, he and Dow were alone in the square.

"She's an awfu' woman that," Rob said. "I saw her lauching."

Gavin ground his teeth.

"Rob Dow," he said, slowly, "if I had not found Christ I would have throttled that woman. You saw how she flouted me?"

Chapter VI

In Which The Soldiers Meet The Amazons Of Thrums

Dow looked shamefacedly at the minister, and then set off up the square. "Where are you going, Rob?"

"To gie myself up. I maun do something to let you see there's one man in Thrums that has mair faith in you than in a fliskmahoy."

"And only one, Rob. But I don't know that they want to arrest you."

"Ay, I had a hand in tying the polissman to the—"

"I want to hear nothing about that," Gavin said, quickly.

"Will I hide, then?"

"I dare not advise you to do that. It would be wrong."

Half a score of fugitives tore past the town-house, and were out of sight without a cry. There was a tread of heavier feet, and a dozen soldiers, with several policemen and two prisoners, appeared suddenly on the north side of the square.

"Rob," cried the minister in desperation, "run!"

When the soldiers reached the town-house, where they locked up their prisoners, Dow was skulking eastward, and Gavin running down the brae.

"They're fechting," he was told, "they're fechting on the brae, the sojers is firing, a man's killed!"

But this was an exaggeration.

The brae, though short, is very steep. There is a hedge on one side of it, from which the land falls away, and on the other side a hillock. Gavin reached the scene to see the soldiers marching down the brae, guarding a small body of policemen. The armed weavers were retreating before them. A hundred women or more were on the hillock, shrieking and gesticulating. Gavin joined them, calling on them not to fling the stones they had begun to gather.

The armed men broke into a rabble, flung down their weapons, and fled back towards the town-house. Here they almost ran against the soldiers in the square, who again forced them into the brae. Finding themselves about to be wedged between the two forces, some crawled through the hedge, where they were instantly seized by policemen. Others sought to climb up the hillock and then escape into the country. The policemen clambered after them. The men were too frightened to fight, but a woman seized a policeman by the waist and flung him head foremost among the soldiers. One of these shouted "Fire!" but the captain cried "No." Then came showers of missiles from the women. They stood their ground and defended the retreat of the scared men.

Who flung the first stone is not known, but it is believed to have been the Egyptian. The policemen were recalled, and the whole body ordered to advance down the brae. Thus the weavers who had not escaped at once were driven before them, and soon hemmed in between the two bodies of soldiers, when they were easily captured. But for two minutes there was a thick shower of stones and clods of earth.

It was ever afterwards painful to Gavin to recall this scene, but less on account of the shower of stones than because of the flight of one divit in it. He had been watching the handsome young captain, Halliwell, riding with his men; admiring him, too, for his coolness. This coolness exasperated the gypsy, who twice flung at Halliwell and missed him. He rode on smiling contemptuously.

"Oh, if I could only fling straight!" die Egyptian moaned.

Then she saw the minister by her side, and in the tick of a clock something happened that can never be explained. For the moment Gavin was so lost in misery over the probable effect of the night's rioting that he had forgotten where he was. Suddenly the Egyptian's beautiful face was close to his, and she pressed a divit into his hand, at the same time pointing at the officer, and whispering "Hit him."

Gavin flung the clod of earth, and hit Halliwell on the head.

I say I cannot explain this. I tell what happened, and add with thankfulness that only the Egyptian witnessed the deed. Gavin, I suppose, had flung the divit before he could stay his hand. Then he shrank in horror.

"Woman!" he cried again.

"You are a dear," she said, and vanished.

By the time Gavin was breathing freely again, the lock-up was crammed with prisoners, and the Riot Act had been read from the town-house stair. It is still remembered that the baron-bailie, to whom this duty fell, had got no further than, "Victoria, by the Grace of God," when the paper was struck out of his hands.

When a stirring event occurs up here we smack our lips over it for months, and so I could still write a history of that memorable night in Thrums. I could tell how the doctor, a man whose shoulders often looked as if they had been caught in a shower of tobacco ash, brought me the news to the schoolhouse, and how, when I crossed the fields to dumfounder Waster Lunny with it, I found Birse, the post, reeling off the story to him as fast as a fisher could let out line. I know who was the first woman on the Marywell brae to hear the horn, and how she woke her husband, and who heard it first at the Denhead and the Tenements, with what they immediately said and did. I had from Dite Deuchar's own lips the curious story of his sleeping placidly throughout the whole disturbance, and on wakening in the morning yoking to his loom as usual; and also his statement that such ill-luck was enough to shake a man's faith in religion. The police had knowledge that enabled them to go straight to the houses of the weavers wanted, but they sometimes brought away the wrong man, for such of the people as did not escape from the town had swopped houses for the night — a trick that served them better than all their drilling on the hill. Old Yuill's son escaped by burying himself in a peat-rick, and Snecky Hobart by pretending that he was a sack of potatoes. Less fortunate was Sanders Webster, the mole-catcher already mentioned. Sanders was really an innocent man. He had not even been in Thrums on the night of the rising against the manufacturers, but thinking that the outbreak was to be left unpunished, he wanted his share in the glory of it. So he had boasted of being a ringleader until many believed him, including the authorities. His braggadocio undid him. He was run to earth in a pig-sty, and got nine months. With the other arrests I need not concern myself, for they have no part in the story of the little minister.

While Gavin was with the families whose breadwinners were now in the lock-up, a cell that was usually crammed on fair nights and empty for the rest of the year, the sheriff and Halliwell were in the round-room of the town-house, not in a good temper. They spoke loudly, and some of their words sank into the cell below.

"The whole thing has been a fiasco," the sheriff was heard saying, "owing to our failing to take them by surprise. Why, three-fourths of those taken will have to be liberated, and we have let the worst offenders slip through our hands."

"Well," answered Halliwell, who was wearing a heavy cloak, "I have brought your policemen into the place, and that is all I undertook to do."

"You brought them, but at the expense of alarming the country-side. I wish we had come without you."

"Nonsense! My men advanced like ghosts. Could your police have come down that brae alone to-night?"

"Yes, because it would have been deserted. Your soldiers, I tell you, have done the mischief. This woman, who, so many of our prisoners admit, brought the news of our coming, must either have got it from one of your men or have seen them on the march."

"The men did not know their destination. True, she might have seen us despite our precautions, but you forget that she told them how we were to act in the event of our being seen. That is what perplexes me."

"Yes, and me too, for it was a close secret between you and me and Lord Rintoul and not half-a-dozen others."

"Well, find the woman, and we shall get the explanation. If she is still in the town she cannot escape, for my men are everywhere."

"She was seen ten minutes ago."

"Then she is ours. I say, Riach, if I were you I would set all my prisoners free and take away a cartload of their wives instead. I have only seen the backs of the men of Thrums, but, on my word, I very nearly ran away from the women. Hallo! I believe one of your police has caught our virago single-handed."

So Halliwell exclaimed, hearing some one shout, "This is the rascal!" But it was not the Egyptian who was then thrust into the round-room. It was John Dunwoodie, looking very sly. Probably there was not, even in Thrums, a cannier man than Dunwoodie. His religious views were those of Cruickshanks, but he went regularly to church "on the offchance of there being a God after all; so I'm safe, whatever side may be wrong."

"This is the man," exclaimed a policeman, "who brought the alarm. He admits himself having been in Tilliedrum just before we started."

"Your name, my man?" the sheriff demanded.

"It micht be John Dunwoodie," the tinsmith answered cautiously.

"But is it?"

"I dinna say it's no."

"You were in Tilliedrum this evening?"

"I micht hae been."

"Were you?"

"I'll swear to nothing."

"Why not?"

"Because I'm a canny man."

"Into the cell with him," Halliwell cried, losing patience.

"Leave him to me," said the sheriff. "I understand the sort of man. Now, Dunwoodie, what were you doing in Tilliedrum?"

"I was taking my laddie down to be prenticed to a writer there," answered Dunwoodie, falling into the sheriff's net.

"What are you yourself?"

"I micht be a tinsmith to trade."

"And you, a mere tinsmith, dare to tell me that a lawyer was willing to take your son into his office? Be cautious, Dunwoodie."

"Weel, then, the laddie's highly edicated and I hae siller, and that's how the writer was to take him and make a gentleman o' him."

"I learn from the neighbours," the policeman explained, "that this is partly true, but what makes us suspect him is this. He left the laddie at Tilliedrum, and yet when he came home the first person he sees at the fireside is the laddie himself. The laddie had run home, and the reason plainly was that he had heard of our preparations and wanted to alarm the town."

"There seems something in this, Dunwoodie," the sheriff said, "and if you cannot explain it I must keep you in custody."

"I'll make a clean breast o't," Dunwoodie replied, seeing that in this matter truth was best. "The laddie was terrible against being made a gentleman, and when he saw the kind o' life he would hae to lead — clean hands, clean dickies, and no gutters on his breeks — his heart took mair scunner at genteelity than ever, and he ran hame. Ay, I was mad when I saw him at the fireside, but he says to me, 'How would you like to be a gentleman yoursel', father?' he says, and that so affected me 'at I'm to gie him his ain way."

Another prisoner, Dave Langlands, was confronted with Dunwoodie.

"John Dunwoodie's as innocent as I am mysel," Dave said, "and I'm most michty innocent. It wasna John but the Egyptian that gave the alarm. I tell you what, sheriff, if it'll make me innocenter-like I'll picture the Egyptian to you just as I saw her, and syne you'll be able to catch her easier."

"You are an honest fellow," said the sheriff.

"I only wish I had the whipping of him," growled Halliwell, who was of a generous nature.

"For what business had she," continued Dave righteously, "to meddle in other folks' business? She's no a Thrums lassie, and so I say, 'Let the law take its course on her.'"

"Will you listen to such a cur, Riach?" asked Halliwell.

"Certainly. Speak out, Langlands."

"Weel, then, I was in the windmill the nicht."

"You were a watcher?"

"I happened to be in the windmill wi' another man," Dave went on, avoiding the officer's question.

"What was his name?" demanded Halliwell.

"It was the Egyptian I was to tell you about," Dave said, looking to the sheriff.

"Ah, yes, you only tell tales about women," said Halliwell.

"Strange women," corrected Dave. "Weel, we was there, and it would maybe be twal o'clock, and we was speaking (but about lawful things) when we heard some ane running yont the road. I keeked through a hole in the door, and I saw it was an Egyptian lassie 'at I had never clapped een on afore. She saw the licht in the window, and she cried, 'Hie, you billies in the windmill, the sojers is coming!' I fell in a fricht, but the other man opened the door, and again she cries, 'The sojers is coming; quick, or you'll be ta'en.'

At that the other man up wi' his bonnet and ran, but I didna make off so smart."

"You had to pick yourself up first," suggested the officer.

"Sal, it was the lassie picked me up; ay, and she picked up a horn at the same time.

" 'Blaw on that,' she cried, 'and alarm the town.' But, sheriff, I didna do't. Na, I had ower muckle respect for the law."

"In other words," said Halliwell, "you also bolted, and left the gypsy to blow the horn herself."

"I dinna deny but what I made my feet my friend, but it wasna her that blew the horn. I ken that for I looked back and saw her trying to do't, but she couldna, she didna ken the way."

"Then who did blow it?"

'The first man she met, I suppose. We a' kent that the horn was to be the signal except Wearywarld. He's police, so we kept it frae him."

"That is all you saw of the woman?"

"Ay, for I ran straucht to my garret, and there your men took me. Can I gae hame now, sheriff?"

"No, you cannot. Describe the woman's appearance."

"She had a heap o' rowan berries stuck in her hair, and, I think, she had on a green wrapper and a red shawl. She had a most extraordinar face. I canna exact describe it, for she would be lauchin' one second and syne solemn the next. I tell you her face changed as quick as you could turn the pages o' a book. Ay, here comes Weary warld to speak up for me."

Wearyworld entered cheerfully.

"This is the local policeman," a Tilliedrum officer said; "we have been searching for him everywhere, and only found him now."

"Where have you been?" asked the sheriff, wrathfully.

"Whaur maist honest men is at this hour," replied Wearyworld; "in my bed."

"How dared you ignore your duty at such a time?"

"It's a long story," the policeman answered, pleasantly, in anticipation of a talk at last.

"Answer me in a word."

"In a word!" cried the policeman, quite crestfallen. "It canna be done. You'll need to cross-examine me, too. It's my lawful richt."

"I'll take you to the Tilliedrum gaol for your share in this night's work if you do not speak to the purpose. Why did you not hasten to our assistance?"

"As sure as death I never kent you was here. I was up the Roods on my rounds when I heard an awfu' din down in the square, and thinks I, there's rough characters about, and the place for honest folk is their bed. So to my bed I gaed, and I was in't when your men gripped me."

"We must see into this before we leave. In the meantime you will act as a guide to my searchers. Stop! Do you know anything of this Egyptian?"

"What Egyptian? Is't a lassie wi' rowans in her hair?"

"The same. Have you seen her?"

"That I have. There's nothing agin her, is there? Whatever it is, I'll uphaud she didna do't, for a simpler, franker-spoken critter couldna be."

"Never mind what I want her for. When did you see her?"

"It would be about twal o'clock," began Wearyworld unctuously, "when I was in the Roods, ay, no lang afore I heard the disturbance in the square. I was standing in the middle o' the road, wondering how the door o' the windmill was swinging open, when she came up to me.

" 'A fine nicht for the time o' year,' I says to her, for nobody but the minister had spoken to me a' day.

" 'A very fine nicht,' says she, very frank, though she was breathing quick like as if she had been running. 'You'll be police?' says she.

" 'I am,' says I, 'and wha be you?'

" 'I'm just a puir gypsy lassie,' she says.

" 'And what's that in your hand?' says I.

" 'It's a horn I found in the wood,' says she, 'but it's rusty and winna blaw.'

"I laughed at her ignorance, and says I, 'I warrant I could blaw it.'

" 'I dinna believe you,' says she.

" 'Gie me haud o't,' says I, and she gae it to me, and I blew some bonny blasts on't. Ay, you see she didna ken the way o't. 'Thank you, kindly,' says she, and she ran awa without even minding to take the horn back again."

"You incredible idiot!" cried the sheriff. "Then it was you who gave the alarm?"

'What hae I done to madden you?" honest Wearyworld asked in perplexity.

"Get out of my sight, sir!" roared the sheriff.

But the captain laughed.

"I like your doughty policeman, Riach," he said. "Hie, obliging friend, let us hear how this gypsy struck you. How was she dressed?"

"She was snod, but no unca snod," replied Wearyworld, stiffly.

"I don't understand you."

"I mean she was couthie, but no sair in order."

"What on earth is that?"

"Weel, a tasty stocky, but gey orra put on."

"What language are you speaking, you enigma?"

"I'm saying she was naturally a bonny bit kimmer rather than happit up to the nines."

"Oh, go away," cried Halliwell; whereupon Wearyworld descended the stair haughtily, declaring that the sheriff was an unreasonable man, and that he was a queer captain who did not understand the English language.

"Can I gae hame now, sheriff?" asked Langlands, hopefully.

"Take this fellow back to his cell," Riach directed, shortly, "and whatever else you do, see that you capture this woman. Halliwell, I am going out to look for her myself. Confound it, what are you laughing at?"

"At the way this vixen has slipped through your fingers."

"Not quite that, sir, not quite that. She is in Thrums still, and I swear I'll have her before day breaks. See to it, Halliwell, that if she is brought here in my absence she does not slip through your fingers."

"If she is brought here," said Halliwell, mocking him, "you must return and protect me. It would be cruelty to leave a poor soldier in the hands of a woman of Thrums."

"She is not a Thrums woman. You have been told so a dozen times."

"Then I am not afraid."

In the round-room (which is oblong) there is a throne on which the bailie sits when he dispenses justice. It is swathed in red cloths that give it the appearance of a pulpit. Left to himself, Halliwell flung off his cloak and taking a chair near this dais rested his legs on the bare wooden table, one on each side of the lamp. He was still in this position when the door opened, and two policemen thrust the Egyptian into the room.

Chapter VII

Has The Folly Of Looking Into Women's Eyes By Way Of Text

"THIS is the woman, captain," one of the policemen said in triumph, "and, begging your pardon, will you keep a grip of her till the sheriff comes back?"

Halliwell did not turn his head.

"You can leave her here," he said carelessly.

"Three of us are not needed to guard a woman."

"But she's a slippery customer."

"You can go," said Halliwell; and the policemen withdrew slowly, eyeing their prisoner doubtfully until the door closed. Then the officer wheeled round languidly, expecting to find the Egyptian gaunt and muscular.

"Now, then," he drawled, "why — By Jove!"

The gallant soldier was as much taken aback as if he had turned to find a pistol at his ear. He took his feet off the table. Yet he only saw the gypsy's girlish figure in its red and green, for she had covered her face with her hands. She was looking at him intently between her fingers, but he did not know this. All he did want to know just then was what was behind the hands.

Before he spoke again she had perhaps made up her mind about him, for she began to sob bitterly. At the same time she slipped a finger over her ring.

"Why don't you look at me?" asked Halliwell, selfishly.

"I daurna."

"Am I so fearsome?"

"You're a sojer, and you would shoot me like a craw."

Halliwell laughed, and taking her wrists in his hands, uncovered her face.

"Oh, by Jove!" he said again, but this time to himself.

As for the Egyptian, she slid the ring into her pocket and fell back before the officer's magnificence.

"Oh," she cried, "is all sojers like you?"

There was such admiration in her eyes that it would have been self-contempt to doubt her. Yet having smiled complacently, Halliwell became uneasy.

"Who on earth are you?" he asked, finding it wise not to look her in the face. "Why do you not answer me more quickly?"

"Dinna be angry at that, captain," the Egyptian implored. "I promised my mither aye to count twenty afore I spoke, because she thocht I was ower glib. Captain, how is't that you're so fleid to look at me?"

Thus put on his mettle, Halliwell again faced her, with the result that his question changed to "Where did you get those eyes?" Then was he indignant with himself.

"What I want to know," he explained severely, "is how you were able to acquaint the Thrums people with our movements? That you must tell me at once, for the sheriff blames my soldiers. Come now, no counting twenty!"

He was pacing the room now, and she had her face to herself. It said several things, among them that the officer evidently did not like this charge against his men.

"Does the shirra blame the sojers?" exclaimed this quick-witted Egyptian.! "Weel, that cows, for he has nane to blame but himsel'."

"What!" cried Halliwell, delighted. "It was the sheriff who told tales? Answer me. You are counting a hundred this time."

Perhaps the gypsy had two reasons for withholding her answer. If so, one of them was that as the sheriff had told nothing, she had a story to make up. The other was that she wanted to strike a bargain with the officer.

"If I tell you," she said eagerly, "will you set me free?"

"I may ask the sheriff to do so."

"But he mauna see me," the Egyptian said in distress. "There's reasons, captain."

"Why, surely you have not been before him on other occasions," said Halliwell, surprised.

"No in the way you mean," muttered the gypsy, and for the moment her eyes twinkled. But the light in them went out when she remembered that the sheriff was near, and she looked desperately at the window as if ready to fling herself from it. She had very good reasons for not wishing to be seen by Riach, though fear that he would put her in gaol was not one of them.

Halliwell thought it was the one cause of her woe, and great was his desire to turn the tables on the sheriff.

"Tell me the truth," he said, "and I promise to befriend you."

"Weel, then," the gypsy said, hoping still to soften his heart, and making up her story as she told it, "yestreen I met the shirra, and he telled me a' I hae telled the Thrums folk this nicht."

"You can scarcely expect me to believe that. Where did you meet him?"

"In Glen Quharity. He was riding on a horse."

"Well, I allow he was there yesterday, and on horseback. He was on his way back to Tilliedrum from Lord Rintoul's place. But don't tell me that he took a gypsy girl into his confidence."

"Ay, he did, without kenning. He was gieing his horse a drink when I met him, and he let me tell him his fortune. He said he would gaol me for an impostor if I didna tell him true, so I gaed about it cautiously, and after a minute or twa I telled him he was coming to Thrums the nicht to nab the rioters."

"You are trifling with me," interposed the indignant soldier. "You promised to tell me not what you said to the sheriff, but how he disclosed our movements to you."

"And that's just what I am telling you, only you hinna the rummelgumption to see it. How do you think fortunes is telled? First we get out o' the man, without his seeing what we're after, a' about himsel', and syne we repeat it to him. That's what I did wi' the shirra."

"You drew the whole thing out of him without his knowing?"

" 'Deed I did, and he rode awa' saying I was a witch."

The soldier heard with the delight of a school-boy.

"Now if the sheriff does not liberate you at my request," he said, "I will never let him hear the end of this story. He was right; you are a witch. You deceived the sheriff: yes, undoubtedly you are a witch."

He looked at her with fun in his face, but the fun disappeared, and a wondering admiration took its place.

"By Jove!" he said, "I don't wonder you bewitched the sheriff. I must take care or you will bewitch the captain, too."

At this notion he smiled, but he also ceased looking at her.

Suddenly the Egyptian again began to cry.

"You're angry wi' me," she sobbed. "I wish I had never set een on you."

"Why do you wish that?" Halliwell asked.

"Fine you ken," she answered, and again covered her face with her hands.

He looked at her undecidedly.

"I am not angry with you," he said, gently. "You are an extraordinary girl."

Had he really made a conquest of this beautiful creature? Her words said so, but had he? The captain could not make up his mind. He gnawed his moustache in doubt.

There was silence, save for the Egyptian's sobs. Halliwell's heart was touched, and he drew nearer her.

"My poor girl—"

He stopped. Was she crying? Was she not laughing at him rather? He became red.

The gypsy peeped at him between her fingers, and saw that he was of two minds. She let her hands fall from her face, and undoubtedly there were tears on her cheeks.

"If you're no angry wi' me," she said, sadly, "how will you no look at me?"

"I am looking at you now."

He was very close to her, and staring into her wonderful eyes. I am older than the captain, and those eyes have dazzled me.

"Captain dear."

She put her hand in his. His chest rose. He knew she was seeking to beguile him, but he could not take his eyes off hers. He was in a worse plight than a woman listening to the first whisper of love.

Now she was further from him, but the spell held. She reached the door, without taking her eyes from his face. For several seconds he had been as a man mesmerised.

Just in time he came to. It was when she turned from him to find the handle of the door. She was turning it when his hand fell on hers so suddenly that she screamed. He twisted her round.

"Sit down there," he said hoarsely, pointing to the chair upon which he had flung his cloak. She dared not disobey. Then he leant against the door, his back to her, for just then he wanted no one to see his face. The gypsy sat very still and a little frightened.

Halliwell opened the door presently, and called to the soldier on duty below.

"Davidson, see if you can find the sheriff. I want him. And Davidson—"

The captain paused.

"Yes," he muttered, and the old soldier marvelled at his words, "it is better. Davidson, lock this door on the outside."

Davidson did as he was ordered, and again the Egyptian was left alone with Halliwell.

"Afraid of a woman!" she said, contemptuously, though her heart sank when she heard the key turn in the lock.

"I admit it," he answered, calmly.

He walked up and down the room, and she sat silently watching him.

"That story of yours about the sheriff was not true," he said at last.

"I suspect it wasna," answered the Egyptian coolly. "Hae you been thinking about it a' this time? Captain, I could tell you what you're thinking now. You're wishing it had been true, so that the ane o' you couldna lauch at the other."

"Silence!" said the captain, and not another word would he speak until he heard the sheriff coming up the stair. The Egyptian trembled at his step, and rose in desperation.

"Why is the door locked?" cried the sheriff, shaking it.

"All right," answered Halliwell; "the key is on your side."

At that moment the Egyptian knocked the lamp off the table, and the room was at once in darkness. The officer sprang at her,and catching her by the skirt, held on.

"Why are you in darkness?" asked the sheriff, as he entered.

"Shut the door," cried Halliwell. "Put your back to it."

"Don't tell me the woman has escaped?"

"I have her, I have her! She capsized the lamp, the little jade. Shut the door."

Still keeping firm hold of her, as he thought, the captain relit the lamp with his other hand. It showed an extraordinary scene. The door was shut, and the sheriff was guarding it. Halliwell was clutching the cloth of the bailie's seat. There was no Egyptian.

A moment passed before either man found his tongue.

"Open the door. After her!" cried Halliwell.

But the door would not open. The Egyptian had fled and locked it behind her.

What the two men said to each other, it would not be fitting to tell. When Davidson, who had been gossiping at the corner of the town-house, released his captain and the sheriff, the gypsy had been gone for some minutes.

"But she shan't escape us," Riach cried, and hastened out to assist in the pursuit.

Halliwell was in such a furious temper that he called up Davidson and admonished him for neglect of duty.

Chapter VIII

3 A.M. — Monstrous Audacity of the Woman

NOT till the stroke of three did Gavin turn homeward, with the legs of a ploughman, and eyes rebelling against over-work. Seeking to comfort his dejected people, whose courage lay spilt on the brae, he had been in as many houses as the policemen. The soldiers marching through the wynds came frequently upon him, and found it hard to believe that he was always the same one. They told afterwards that Thrums was remarkable for the ferocity of its women, and the number of its little ministers.

The morning was nipping cold, and the streets were deserted, for the people had been ordered within doors. As he crossed the Roods, Gavin saw a gleam of red-coats. In the back wynd he heard a bugle blown. A stir in the Banker's close spoke of another seizure. At the top of the school wynd two policemen, of whom one was Wearyworld, stopped the minister with the flash of a lantern.

"We dauredna let you pass, sir," the Tilliedrum man said, "without a good look at you. That's the orders."

"I hereby swear," said Wearyworld, authoritatively, "that this is no the Egyptian. Signed, Peter Spens, policeman, called by the vulgar, Wearyworld. Mr. Dishart, you can pass, unless you'll bide a wee and gie us your crack."

"You have not found the gypsy, then?" Gavin asked.

"No," the other policeman said, "but we ken she's within cry o' this very spot, and escape she canna."

"What mortal man can do," Wearyworld said, "we're doing: ay, and mair, but she's auld wecht, and may find bilbie in queer places. Mr. Dishart, my official opinion is that this Egyptian is fearsomely like my snuff-spoon. I've kent me drap that spoon on the fender, and be beat to find it in an hour. And yet, a' the time I was sure it was there. This is a gey mysterious world, and women's the uncanniest things in't. It's hardly mous to think how uncanny they are."

"This one deserves to be punished," Gavin said, firmly; "she incited the people to riot."

"She did," agreed Wearyworld, who was supping ravenously on sociability; "ay, she even tried her tricks on me, so that them that kens no better thinks she fooled me. But she's cracky. To gie her her due, she's cracky, and as for her being a cuttie, you've said yoursel', Mr. Dishart, that we're all desperately wicked. But we're sair tried. Has it ever struck you that the trouts bites best on the Sabbath? God's critters tempting decent men."

"Come alang," cried the Tilliedrum man, impatiently.

"I'm coming, but I maun give Mr. Dishart permission to pass first. Hae you heard, Mr. Dishart," Wearyworld whispered, "that the Egyptian diddled baith the captain and the shirra? It's my official opinion that she's no better than a roasted onion, the which, if you grip it firm, jumps out o' sicht, leaving its coat in your fingers. Mr. Dishart, you can pass."

The policemen turned down the school wynd, and Gavin, who had already heard exaggerated accounts of the strange woman's escape from the town-house, proceeded along the Tenements. He walked in the black shadows of the houses, though across the way there was the morning light.

In talking of the gypsy, the little minister had, as it were, put on the black cap; but now, even though he shook his head angrily with every thought of her, the scene in Windyghoul glimmered before his eyes. Sometimes when he meant to frown he only sighed, and then having sighed he shook himself. He was unpleasantly conscious of his right hand, which had flung the divit. Ah, she was shameless, and it would be a bright day for Thrums that saw the last of her. He hoped the policemen would succeed in—. It was the gladsomeness of innocence that he had seen dancing in the moonlight. A mere woman could not be like that. How soft — And she had derided him; he, the Auld Licht minister of Thrums, had been flouted before his people by a hussy. She was without reverence, she knew no difference between an Auld Licht minister, whose duty it was to speak and hers to listen, and herself. This woman deserved to be — And the look she cast behind her as she danced and sang! It was sweet, so wistful; the presence of purity had silenced him. Purity! Who had made him fling that divit? He would think no more of her. Let it suffice that he knew what she was. He would put her from his thoughts. Was it a ring on her finger?

Fifty yards in front of him Gavin saw the road end in a wall of soldiers. They were between him and the manse, and he was still in darkness. No sound reached him, save the echo of his own feet. But was it an echo? He stopped, and turned round sharply. Now he heard nothing, he saw nothing. Yet was not that a human figure standing motionless in the shadow behind?

He walked on, and again heard the sound. Again he looked behind, but this time without stopping. The figure was following him. He stopped. So did it. He turned back, but it did not move. It was the Egyptian!

Gavin knew her, despite the lane of darkness, despite the long cloak that now concealed even her feet, despite the hood over her head. She was looking quite respectable, but he knew her.

He neither advanced to her nor retreated. Could the unhappy girl not see that she was walking into the arms of the soldiers? But doubtless she had been driven from all her hiding-places. For a moment Gavin had it in his heart to warn her. But it was only for a moment. The next a sudden horror shot through him. She was stealing toward him, so softly that he had not seen her start. The woman had designs on him! Gavin turned from her. He walked so quickly that judges would have said he ran.

The soldiers, I have said, stood in the dim light. Gavin had almost reached them, when a little hand touched his arm.

"Stop," cried the sergeant, hearing some one approaching, and then Gavin stepped out of the darkness with the gypsy on his arm.

"It is you, Mr. Dishart," said the sergeant, "and your lady?"

"I—," said Gavin.

His lady pinched his arm.

"Yes," she answered, in an elegant English voice that made Gavin stare at her, "but, indeed, I am sorry I ventured into the streets tonight. I thought I might be able to comfort some of these unhappy people, captain, but I could do little, sadly little."

"It is no scene for a lady, ma'am, but your husband has — Did you speak, Mr. Dishart?"

"Yes, I must inf—"

"My dear," said the Egyptian, "I quite agree with you, so we need not detain the captain."

"I'm only a sergeant, ma'am."

"Indeed!" said the Egyptian, raising her pretty eyebrows, "and how long are you to remain in Thrums, sergeant?"

"Only for a few hours, Mrs. Dishart. If this gypsy lassie had not given us so much trouble, we might have been gone by now."

"Ah, yes, I hope you will catch her, sergeant."

"Sergeant," said Gavin, firmly, "I must—"

"You must, indeed, dear," said the Egyptian, "for you are sadly tired. Good-night, sergeant."

"Your servant, Mrs. Dishart. Your servant, sir."

"But—," cried Gavin.

"Come, love," said the Egyptian, and she walked the distracted minister through the soldiers and up the manse road.

The soldiers left behind, Gavin flung her arm from him, and, standing still, shook his fist in her face.

"You—you—woman!" he said.

This, I think, was the last time he called her a woman.

But she was clapping her hands merrily.

"It was beautiful!" she exclaimed.

"It was iniquitous!" he answered. "And I a minister!"

"You can't help that," said the Egyptian, who pitied all ministers heartily.

"No," Gavin said, misunderstanding her, "I could not help it. No blame attaches to me."

"I meant that you could not help being a minister. You could have helped saving me, and I thank you so much."

"Do not dare to thank me. I forbid you to say that I saved you. I did my best to hand you over to the authorities."

"Then why did you not hand me over?"

Gavin groaned.

"All you had to say," continued the merciless Egyptian, "was, 'This is the person you are in search of.' I did not have my hand over your mouth. Why did you not say it?"

"Forbear!" said Gavin, woefully.

"It must have been," the gypsy said, "because you really wanted to help me."

"Then it was against my better judgment," said Gavin.

"I am glad of that," said the gypsy. "Mr. Dishart, I do believe you like me all the time."

"Can a man like a woman against his will?" Gavin blurted out.

"Of course he can," said the Egyptian, speaking as one who knew. "That is the very nicest way to be liked."

Seeing how agitated Gavin was, remorse filled her, and she said in a wheedling voice—

"It is all over, and no one will know."

Passion sat on the minister's brow, but he said nothing, for the gypsy's face had changed with her voice, and the audacious woman was become a child.

"I am very sorry," she said, as if he had caught her stealing jam. The hood had fallen back, and she looked pleadingly at him. She had the appearance of one who was entirely in his hands.

There was a torrent of words in Gavin, but only these trickled forth—

"I don't understand you."

"You are not angry any more?" pleaded the Egyptian.

"Angry!" he cried, with the righteous rage of one who when his leg is being sawn off is asked gently if it hurts him.

"I know you are," she sighed, and the sigh meant that men are strange.

"Have you no respect for law and order?" demanded Gavin.

"Not much," she answered, honestly.

He looked down the road to where the red-coats were still visible, and his face became hard. She read his thoughts.

"No," she said, becoming a woman again, "it is not yet too late. Why don't you shout to them?"

She was holding herself like a queen, but there was no stiffness in her. They might have been a pair of lovers, and she the wronged one. Again she looked timidly at him, and became beautiful in a new way. Her eyes said that he was very cruel, and she was only keeping back her tears till he had gone. More dangerous than her face was her manner, which gave Gavin the privilege of making her unhappy; it permitted him to argue with her; it never implied that though he raged at her he must stand afar off; it called him a bully, but did not end the conversation.

Now (but perhaps I should not tell this) unless she is his wife a man is shot with a thrill of exultation every time a pretty woman allows him to upbraid her.

"I do not understand you," Gavin repeated weakly, and the gypsy bent her head under this terrible charge.

"Only a few hours ago," he continued, "you were a gypsy girl in a fantastic dress, bare-footed—"

The Egyptian's bare foot at once peeped out mischievously from beneath the cloak, then again retired into hiding.

"You spoke as broadly," complained the minister, somewhat taken aback by this apparition, "as any woman in Thrums, and now you fling a cloak over your shoulders, and immediately become a fine lady. Who are you?"

"Perhaps," answered the Egyptian, "it is the cloak that has bewitched me." She slipped out of it. "Ay, ay, ou losh!" she said, as if surprised, "it was just the cloak that did it, for now I'm a puir ignorant bit lassie again. My, certie, but claithes does make a differ to a woman!"

This was sheer levity, and Gavin walked scornfully away from it.

"Yet, if you will not tell me who you are," he said, looking over his shoulder, "tell me where you got the cloak."

"Na faags," replied the gypsy out of the cloak. "Really, Mr. Dishart, you had better not ask," she added, replacing it over her.

She followed him, meaning to gain the open by the fields to the north of the manse.

"Good-bye," she said, holding out her hand, "if you are not to give me up."

"I am not a policeman," replied Gavin, but he would not take her hand.

"Surely, we part friends, then?" said the Egyptian, sweetly.

"No," Gavin answered. "I hope never to see your face again."

"I cannot help," the Egyptian said, with dignity, "your not liking my face." Then, with less dignity, she added, "There is a splotch of mud on your own, little minister; it came off the divit you flung at the captain."

With this parting shot she tripped past him, and Gavin would not let his eyes follow her. It was not the mud on his face that distressed him, nor even the hand that had flung the divit. It was the word "little." Though even Margaret was not aware of it, Gavin's shortness had grieved him all his life. There had been times when he tried to keep the secret from himself. In his boyhood he had sought a remedy by getting his larger comrades to stretch him. In the company of tall men he was always self-conscious. In the pulpit he looked darkly at his congregation when he asked them who, by taking thought, could add a cubit to his stature. When standing on a hearthrug his heels were frequently on the fender. In his bedroom he has stood on a footstool and surveyed himself in the mirror. Once he fastened high heels to his boots, being ashamed to ask Hendry Munn to do it for him; but this dishonesty shamed him, and he tore them off. So the Egyptian had put a needle into his pride, and he walked to the manse gloomily.

Margaret was at her window, looking for him, and he saw her though she did not see him. He was stepping into the middle of the road to wave his hand to her, when some sudden weakness made him look towards the fields instead. The Egyptian saw him and nodded thanks for his interest in her, but he scowled and pretended to be studying the sky. Next moment he saw her running back to him.

"There are soldiers at the top of the field," she cried. "I cannot escape that way."

"There is no other way," Gavin answered.

"Will you not help me again?" she entreated.

She should not have said "again." Gavin shook his head, but pulled her closer to the manse dyke, for his mother was still in sight.

"Why do you do that?" the girl asked, quickly, looking round to see if she were pursued. "Oh, I see," she said, as her eyes fell on the figure at the window.

"It is my mother," Gavin said, though he need not have explained, unless he wanted the gypsy to know that he was a bachelor.

"Only your mother?"

"Only! Let me tell you she may suffer more than you for your behaviour to-night!"

"How can she!"

"If you are caught, will it not be discovered that I helped you to escape?"

"But you said you did not."

"Yes, I helped you," Gavin admitted. "My God! what would my congregation say if they knew I had let you pass yourself off as — as my wife?"

He struck his brow, and the Egyptian had the propriety to blush.

"It is not the punishment from men I am afraid of," Gavin said, bitterly, "but from my conscience. No, that is not true. I do fear exposure, but for my mother's sake. Look at her; she is happy, because she thinks me good and true; she has had such trials as you cannot know of, and now, when at last I seemed able to do something for her, you destroy her happiness. You have her life in your hands."

The Egyptian turned her back upon him, and one of her feet tapped angrily on the dry ground. Then, child of impulse as she always was, she flashed an indignant glance at him, and walked quickly down the road.

"Where are you going?" he cried.

"To give myself up. You need not be alarmed; I will clear you."

There was not a shake in her voice, and she spoke without looking back.

"Stop!" Gavin called, but she would not, until his hand touched her shoulder.

"What do you want?" she asked.

"Why—" whispered Gavin, giddily, "why — why do you not hide in the manse garden? — No one will look for you there."

There were genuine tears in the gypsy's eyes now.

"You are a good man," she said; "I like you."

"Don't say that," Gavin cried in horror. "There is a summer-seat in the garden."

Then he hurried from her, and without looking to see if she took his advice, hastened to the manse. Once inside, he snibbed the door.

Chapter IX

The Woman Considered in Absence - Adventures of a Military Cloak

ABOUT six o'clock Margaret sat up suddenly in bed, with the conviction that she had slept in. To her this was to ravel the day: a dire thing. The last time it happened Gavin, softened by her distress, had condensed morning worship into a sentence that she might make up on the clock.

Her part on waking was merely to ring her bell, and so rouse Jean, for Margaret had given Gavin a promise to breakfast in bed, and remain there till her fire was lit. Accustomed all her life, however, to early rising, her feet were usually on the floor before she remembered her vow, and then it was but a step to the window to survey the morning. To Margaret, who seldom went out, the weather was not of great moment, while it mattered much to Gavin, yet she always thought of it the first thing, and he not at all until he had to decide whether his companion should be an umbrella or a staff.

On this morning Margaret only noticed that there had been rain since Gavin came in. Forgetting that the water obscuring the outlook was on the other side of the panes she tried to brush it away with her fist. It was of the soldiers she was thinking. They might have been awaiting her appearance at the window as their signal to depart, for hardly had she raised the blind when they began their march out of Thrums. From the manse she could not see them, but she heard them, and she saw some people at the Tenements run to their houses at sound of the drum. Other persons, less timid, followed the enemy with execrations halfway to Tilliedrum. Margaret, the only person, as it happened, then awake in the manse, stood listening for some time. In the summer-seat of the garden, however, there was another listener protected from her sight by thin spars.

Despite the lateness of the hour Margaret was too soft-hearted to rouse Jean, who had lain down in her clothes, trembling for her father. She went instead into Gavin's room to look admiringly at him as he slept. Often Gavin woke to find that his mother had slipped in to save him the enormous trouble of opening a drawer for a clean collar, or of pouring the water into the basin with his own hand. Sometimes he caught her in the act of putting thick socks in the place of thin ones, and it must be admitted that her passion for keeping his belongings in boxes, and the boxes in secret places, and the secret places at the back of drawers, occasionally led to their being lost when wanted. "They are safe, at any rate, for I put them away some gait," was then Margaret's comfort, but less soothing to Gavin. Yet if he upbraided her in his hurry, it was to repent bitterly his temper the next, and to feel its effects more than she, temper being a weapon that we hold by the blade. When he awoke and saw her in his room he would pretend, unless he felt called upon to rage at her for self-neglect, to be still asleep, and then be filled with tenderness for her. A great writer has spoken sadly of the shock it would be to a mother to know her boy as he really is, but I think she often knows him better than he is known to cynical friends. We should be slower to think that the man at his worst is the real man, and certain that the better we are ourselves the less likely is he to be at his worst in our company. Every time he talks away his own character before us he is signifying contempt for ours.

On this morning Margaret only opened Gavin's door to stand and look, for she was fearful of awakening him after his heavy night. Even before she saw that he still slept she noticed with surprise that, for the first time since he came to Thrums, he had put on his shutters. She concluded that he had done this lest the light should rouse him. He was not sleeping pleasantly, for now he put his open hand before his face, as if to guard himself, and again he frowned and seemed to draw back from something. He pointed his finger sternly to the north, ordering the weavers, his mother thought, to return to their homes, and then he muttered to himself so that she heard the words, "And if thy right hand offend thee cut it off, and cast it from thee, for it is profitable for thee that one of thy members should perish, and not that thy whole body should be cast into hell." Then suddenly he bent forward, his eyes open and fixed on the window. Thus he sat, for the space of half a minute, like one listening with painful intentness. When he lay back Margaret slipped away. She knew he was living the night over again, but not of the divit his right hand had cast, nor of the woman in the garden.

Gavin was roused presently by the sound of voices from Margaret's room, where Jean, who had now gathered much news, was giving it to her mistress. Jean's cheerfulness would have told him that her father was safe had he not wakened to thoughts of the Egyptian. I suppose he was at the window in an instant, unsnibbing the shutters and looking out as cautiously as a burglar might have looked in. The Egyptian was gone from the summer-seat. He drew a great breath.

But his troubles were not over. He had just lifted his ewer of water when these words from the kitchen capsized it:

"Ay, an Egyptian. That's what the auld folk call a gypsy. Weel, Mrs. Dishart, she led the police and sojers sic a dance through Thrums as would baffle description, though I kent the fits and fors o't as I dinna. Ay, but they gripped her in the end, and the queer thing is—"

Gavin listened to no more. He suddenly sat down. The queer thing, of course, was that she had been caught in his garden. Yes, and doubtless queerer things about this hussy and her "husband" were being bawled from door to door. To the girl's probable sufferings he gave no heed. What kind of man had he been a few hours ago to yield to the machinations of a woman who was so obviously the devil? Now he saw his folly in the face.

The tray in Jean's hands clattered against the dresser, and Gavin sprang from his chair. He thought it was his elders at the front door.

In the parlour he found Margaret sorrowing for those whose mates had been torn from them, and Jean with a face flushed by talk. On ordinary occasions the majesty of the minister still cowed Jean, so that she could only gaze at him without shaking when in church, and then because she wore a veil. In the manse he was for taking a glance at sideways and then going away comforted, as a respectable woman may once or twice in a day look at her brooch in the pasteboard box as a means of helping her with her work. But with such a to-do in Thrums, and she the possessor of exclusive information, Jean's reverence for Gavin only took her to-day as far as the door, where she lingered half in the parlour and half in the lobby, her eyes turned politely from the minister, but her ears his entirely.

"I thought I heard Jean telling you about the capture of the — of an Egyptian woman," Gavin said to his mother, nervously.

"Did you cry to me?" Jean asked, turning round longingly. "But maybe the mistress will tell you about the Egyptian herself."

"Has she been taken to Tilliedrum?" Gavin asked in a hollow voice.

"Sup up your porridge, Gavin," Margaret said. "I'll have no speaking about this terrible night till you've eaten something."

"I have no appetite," the minister replied, pushing his plate from him. "Jean, answer me."

'Deed, then," said Jean willingly, "they hinna ta'en her to Tilliedrum."

"For what reason?" asked Gavin, his dread increasing.

"For the reason that they couldna catch her," Jean answered. "She spirited herself awa', the magerful crittur."

"What! But I heard you say—"

"Ay, they had her aince, but they couldna keep her. It's like a witch story. They had her safe in the town-house, and baith shirra and captain guarding her, and syne in a clink she wasna there. A' nicht they looked for her, but she hadna left so muckle as a footprint ahint her, and in the tail of the day they had to up wi' their tap in their lap and march awa without her."

Gavin's appetite returned.

"Has she been seen since the soldiers went away?" he asked, laying down his spoon with a new fear. "Where is she now?"

"No human eye has seen her," Jean answered impressively. "Whaur is she now? Whaur does the flies vanish to in winter? We ken they're some gait, but whaur?"

"But what are the people saying about her?"

"Daft things," said Jean. "Old Charles Yuill gangs the length o' hinting that she's dead and buried."

"She could not have buried herself, Jean," Margaret said, mildly.

"I dinna ken. Charles says she's even capable o' that."

Then Jean retired reluctantly (but leaving the door ajar), and Gavin fell to on his porridge. He was no so cheerful that Margaret wondered.

"If half the stories about this gypsy be true," she said, "she must be more than a mere woman."

"Less, you mean, mother," Gavin said, with conviction. "She is a woman, and a sinful one."

"Did you see her, Gavin?"

"I saw her. Mother, she flouted me!"

"The daring tawpie!" exclaimed Margaret.

"She is all that," said the minister.

"Was she dressed just like an ordinary gypsy body? "But you don't notice clothes much, Gavin."

"I noticed hers," Gavin said, slowly, "she was in green and red, I think, and barefooted."

"Ay," shouted Jean from the kitchen, startling both of them, "but she had a lang grey-like cloak too. She was seen jouking up closes in't."

Gavin rose, considerably annoyed, and shut the parlour door.

"Was she as bonny as folks say?" asked Margaret. "Jean says they speak of her beauty as unearthly."

"Beauty of her kind," Gavin explained learnedly, "is neither earthly nor heavenly." He was seeing things as they are very clearly now. "What," he said, "is mere physical beauty? Pooh!"

"And yet," said Margaret, "the soul surely does speak through the face to some extent."

"Do you really think so, mother?" Gavin asked, a little uneasily.

"I have always noticed it," Margaret said, and then her son sighed.

"But I would let no face influence me a jot," he said, recovering.

"Ah, Gavin, I'm thinking I'm the reason you pay so little regard to women's faces. It's no natural."

"You've spoilt me, you see, mother, for ever caring for another woman. I would compare her to you, and then where would she be?"

"Sometime," Margaret said, "you'll think differently."

"Never," answered Gavin, with a violence that ended the conversation.

Soon afterwards he set off for the town, and in passing down the garden walk cast a guilty glance at the summer-seat. Something black was lying in one corner of it. He stopped irresolutely, for his mother was nodding to him from her window. Then he disappeared into the little arbour. What had caught his eye was a Bible. On the previous day, as he now remembered, he had been called away while studying in the garden, and had left his Bible on the summer-seat, a pencil between its pages. Not often probably had the Egyptian passed a night in such company.

But what was this? Gavin had not to ask himself the question. The gypsy's cloak was lying neatly folded at the other end of the seat. Why had the woman not taken it with her? Hardly had he put this question when another stood in front of it. What was to be done with the cloak? He dared not leave it there for Jean to discover. He could not take it into the manse in daylight. Beneath the seat was a tool-chest without a lid, and into this he crammed the cloak. Then, having turned the box face downwards he went about his duties. But many a time during the day he shivered to the marrow, reflecting suddenly that at this very moment Jean might be carrying the accursed thing (at arms' length, like a dog in disgrace) to his mother.

Now let those who think that Gavin has not yet paid toll for taking the road with the Egyptian, follow the adventures of the cloak. Shortly after gloaming fell that night Jean encountered her master in the lobby of the manse. He was carrying something, and when he saw her he slipped it behind his back. Had he passed her openly she would have suspected nothing, but this made her look at him.

"Why do you stare so, Jean?" Gavin asked, conscience-stricken, and he stood with his back to the wall until she had retired in bewilderment.

"I have noticed her watching me sharply all day," he said to himself, though it was only he who had been watching her.

Gavin carried the cloak to his bed-room, thinking to lock it away in his chest, but it looked so wicked lying there that he seemed to see it after the lid was shut.

The garret was the best place for it. He took it out of the chest and was opening his door gently, when there was Jean again. She had been employed very innocently in his mother's room, but he said tartly—

"Jean, I really cannot have this," which sent Jean to the kitchen with her apron at her eyes.

Gavin stowed the cloak beneath the garret bed, and an hour afterwards was engaged on his sermon, when he distinctly heard some one in the garret. He ran up the ladder with a terrible brow for Jean, but it was not Jean; it was Margaret.

"Mother," he said in alarm, "what are you doing here?"

"I am only tidying up the garret, Gavin."

"Yes, but — it is too cold for you. Did Jean — did Jean ask you to come up here?"

"Jean? She knows her place better."

Gavin took Margaret down to the parlour, but his confidence in the garret had gone. He stole up the ladder again, dragged the cloak from its lurking place, and took it into the garden. He very nearly met Jean in the lobby again, but hearing him coming she fled precipitately, which he thought very suspicious.

In the garden he dug a hole, and there buried the cloak, but even now he was not done with it. He was wakened early by a noise of scraping in the garden, and his first thought was "Jean!" But peering from the window, he saw that the resurrectionist was a dog, which already had its teeth in the cloak.

That forenoon Gavin left the manse unostentatiously, carrying a brown-paper parcel. He proceeded to the hill, and having dropped the parcel there, retired hurriedly. On his way home, nevertheless, he was overtaken by D. Fittis, who had been cutting down whins. Fittis had seen the parcel fall, and running after Gavin, returned it to him. Gavin thanked D. Fittis, and then sat down gloomily on the cemetery dyke. Half an hour afterwards he flung the parcel into a Tillyloss garden.

In the evening Margaret had news for him, got from Jean.

"Do you remember, Gavin, that the Egyptian every one is still speaking of, wore a long cloak? Well, would you believe it, the cloak was Captain Halliwell's, and she took it from the town-house when she escaped. She is supposed to have worn it inside out. He did not discover that it was gone until he was leaving Thrums."

"Mother, is this possible?" Gavin said.

"The policeman, Wearyworld, has told it. He was ordered, it seems, to look for the cloak quietly, and to take any one into custody in whose possession it was found."

"Has it been found?"

"No."

The minister walked out of the parlour, for he could not trust his face. What was to be done now? The cloak was lying in mason Baxter's garden, and Baxter was therefore, in all probability, within four-and-twenty hours of the Tilliedrum gaol.

"Does Mr. Dishart ever wear a cap at nichts?" Femie Wilkie asked Sam'l Fairweather three hours later.

"Na, na, he has ower muckle respect for his lum hat," answered Sam'l; "and richtly, for it's the crowning stone o' the edifice."

"Then it couldna hae been him I met at the back o'Tillyloss the now," said Femie, "though like him it was. He joukit back when he saw me."

While Femie was telling her story in the Tenements, mason Baxter, standing at the window which looked into his garden, was shouting, "Wha's that in my yard?" There was no answer, and Baxter closed his window, under the impression that he had been speaking to a cat. The man in the cap then emerged from the corner where he had been crouching, and stealthily felt for something among the cabbages and pea sticks. It was no longer there, however, and by-and-by he retired empty-handed.

"The Egyptian's cloak has been found," Margaret was able to tell Gavin next day. "Mason Baxter found it yesterday afternoon."

"In his garden?" Gavin asked hurriedly.

"No; in the quarry, he says, but according to Jean he is known not to have been at the quarry to-day. Some seem to think that the gypsy gave him the cloak for helping her to escape, and that he has delivered it up lest he should get into difficulties."

"Whom has he given it to, mother?" Gavin asked.

"To the policeman."

"And has Wearyworld sent it back to Halliwell?"

"Yes. He told Jean he sent it off at once, with the information that the masons had found it in the quarry."

The next day was Sabbath, when a new trial, now to be told, awaited Gavin in the pulpit; but it had nothing to do with the cloak, of which I may here record the end. Wearyworld had not forwarded it to its owner; Meggy, his wife, took care of that. It made its reappearance in Thrums, several months after the riot, as two pairs of Sabbath breeks for her sons, James and Andrew.

Chapter X

First Sermon Against Women

ON the afternoon of the following Sabbath, as I have said, something strange happened in the Auld Licht pulpit. The congregation, despite their troubles, turned it over and peered at it for days, but had they seen into the inside of it they would have weaved few webs until the session had sat on the minister. The affair baffled me at the time, and for the Egyptian's sake I would avoid mentioning it now, were it not one of Gavin's milestones. It includes the first of his memorable sermons against Woman.

I was not in the Auld Licht church that day, but I heard of the sermon before night, and this, I think, is as good an opportunity as another for showing how the gossip about Gavin reached me up here in the Glen school-house. Since Margaret and her son came to the manse I had kept the vow made to myself and avoided Thrums. Only once had I ventured to the kirk, and then, instead of taking my old seat, the fourth from the pulpit, I sat down near the plate, where I could look at Margaret without her seeing me. To spare her that agony I even stole away as the last word of the benediction was pronounced, and my haste scandalised many, for with Auld Lichts it is not customary to retire quickly from church after the manner of the godless U.P.'s (and the Free Kirk is little better), who have their hats in their hand when they rise for the benediction, so that they may at once pour out like a burst dam. We resume our seats, look straight before us, clear our throats and stretch out our hands for our womenfolk to put our hats into them. In time we do get out, but I am never sure how.

One may gossip in a glen on Sabbaths, though not in a town, without losing his character, and I used to await the return of my neighbour, the farmer of Waster Lunny, and of Silva Birse, the Glen Quharity post, at the end of the school-house path. Waster Lunny was a man whose care in his leisure hours was to keep from his wife his great pride in her. His horse, Catlaw, on the other hand, he told outright what he thought of it, praising it to its face and blackguarding it as it deserved, and I have seen him, when completely baffled by the brute, sit down before it on a stone and thus harangue: "You think you're clever, Catlaw, my lass, but you're mista'en. You're a thrawn limmer, that's what you are. You think you have blood in you. You hae blood! Gae away, and dinna blether. I tell you what, Catlaw, I met a man yestreen that kent your mither,and he says she was a feikie fushionless besom. What do you say to that?"

As for the post, I will say no more of him than that his bitter topic was the unreasonableness of humanity, which treated him graciously when he had a letter for it, but scowled at him when he had none, "aye implying that I hae a letter, but keep it back."

On the Sabbath evening after the riot, I stood at the usual place awaiting my friends, and saw before they reached me that they had something untoward to tell. The farmer, his wife and three children, holding each other's hands, stretched across the road. Birse was a little behind, but a conversation was being kept up by shouting. All were walking the Sabbath pace, and the family having started half a minute in advance, the post had not yet made up on them.

"It's sitting to snaw," Waster Lunny said, drawing near, and just as I was to reply, "It is so," Silva slipped in the words before me.

"You wasna at the kirk," was Elspeth's salutation. I had been at the Glen church, but did not contradict her, for it is the Established, and so neither here nor there. I was anxious, too, to know what their long faces meant, and so asked at once—

"Was Mr. Dishart on the riot?"

"Forenoon, ay; afternoon, no," replied Waster Lunny, walking round his wife to get nearer me. "Dominie, a queery thing happened in the kirk this day, sic as—"

"Waster Lunny," interrupted Elspeth sharply; "have you on your Sabbath shoon or have you no on your Sabbath shoon?"

"Guid care you took I should hae the dagont oncanny things on," retorted the farmer.

"Keep out o' the gutter, then," said Elspeth, "on the Lord's day."

"Him," said her man, "that is forced by a foolish woman to wear genteel 'lastic-sided boots canna forget them till he takes them aff. Whaur's the extra reverence in wearing shoon twa sizes ower sma?"

"It mayna be mair reverent," suggested Birse,to whom Elspeth's kitchen was a pleasant place, "but it's grand, and you canna expect to be baith grand and comfortable."

I reminded them that they were speaking of Mr. Dishart.

"We was saying," began the post briskly, "that—"

"It was me that was saying it," said Waster Lunny. "So, Dominie—"

"Haud your gabs, baith o' you," interrupted Elspeth. "You've been roaring the story to ane another till you're hoarse."

"In the forenoon," Waster Lunny went on determinedly, "Mr. Dishart preached on the riot, and fine he was. Oh, dominie, you should hae heard him ladling it on to Lang Tammas, no by name but in sic a way that there no mistaking wha he was preaching at. Sal! oh losh! Tammas got it strong."

"But he's dull in the uptake," broke in the post, "by what I expected. I spoke to him after the sermon, and I says, just to see if he was properly humbled, 'Ay, Tammas,' I says, 'them that discourse was preached against, winna think themselves seven feet men for a while again.' 'Ay, Birse,' he answers, 'and glad I am to hear you admit it, for he had you in his eye.' I was fair scunnered at Tammas the day."

"Mr. Dishart was preaching at the whole clanjamfray o' you," said Elspeth.

"Maybe he was," said her husband, leering; "but you needna cast it at us, for, my certie, if the men got it frae him in the forenoon, the women got it in the afternoon."

"He redd them up most michty," said the post. "Thae was his very words or something like them. 'Adam,' says he, 'was an erring man, but aside Eve he was respectable.'"

"Ay, but it wasna a' women he meant," Elspeth explained, "for when he said that, he pointed his ringer direct at T'nowhead's lassie, and I hope it'll do her good."

"But I wonder," I said, "that Mr. Dishart chose such a subject to-day. I thought he would be on the riot at both services."

"You'll wonder mair," said Elspeth, "when you hear what happened afore he began the afternoon sermon. But I canna get in a word wi' that man o' mine.

"We've been speaking about it," said Birse, "ever since we left the kirk door. Tod, we've been sawing it like seed a' alang the glen."

"And we meant to tell you about it at once," said Waster Lunny; "but there's aye so muckle to say about a minister. Dagont, to hae ane keeps a body out o' langour. Ay, but this breaks the drum. Dominie, either Mr. Dishart wasna weel, or he was in the devil's grip."

This startled me, for the farmer was looking serious.

"He was weel eneuch," said Birse, "for a heap o' fowk speired at Jean if he had ta'en his porridge as usual, and she admitted he had. But the lassie was skeered hersel', and said it was a mercy Mrs. Dishart wasna in the kirk."

"Why was she not there?" I asked anxiously.

"Oh, he winna let her out in sic weather."

"I wish you would tell me what happened," I said to Elspeth.

"So I will," she answered, "if Waster Lunny would haud his wheesht for a minute. You see the afternoon diet began in the ordinary way, and a' was richt until we came to the sermon. 'You will find my text,' he says, in his piercing voice, 'in the eighth chapter of Ezra.'"

"And at thae words," said Waster Lunny, "my heart gae a loup, for Ezra is an unca ill book to find; ay, and so is Ruth."

"I kent the books o' the Bible by heart," said Elspeth, scornfully, "when I was a sax year auld."

"So did I," said Waster Lunny, "and I ken them yet, except when I'm hurried. When Mr. Dishart gave out Ezra he a sort o' keeked round the kirk to find out if he had puzzled onybody, and so there was a kind o' a competition among the congregation wha would lay hand on it first. That was what doited me. Ay, there was Ruth when she wasna wanted, but Ezra, dagont, it looked as if Ezra had jumped clean out o' the Bible."

"You wasna the only distressed crittur," said his wife. "I was ashamed to see Eppie McLaren looking up the order o' the books at the beginning o' the Bible."

"Tibbie Birse was even mair brazen," said the post, "for the sly cuttie opened at Kings and pretended it was Ezra."

"None o' thae things would I do," said Waster Lunny, "and sal, I dauredna, for Davit Lunan was glowering over my shuther. Ay, you may scowl at me, Elspeth Proctor, but as far back as I can mind,

Ezra has done me. Mony a time afore I start for the kirk I take my Bible to a quiet place and look Ezra up. In the very pew I says canny to mysel', 'Ezra, Nehemiah, Esther, Job,' the which should be a help, but the moment the minister gi'es out that awfu' book, away goes Ezra like the Egyptian."

"And you after her," said Elspeth, "like the weavers that wouldna fecht. You make a windmill of your Bible."

"Oh, I winna admit I'm beat. Never mind, there's queer things in the world forby Ezra. How is cripples aye so puffed up mair than other folk? How does flour-bread aye fall on the buttered side?"

"I will mind," Elspeth said, "for I was terrified the minister would admonish you frae the pulpit."

"He couldna hae done that, for was he no baffled to find Ezra himsel'?"

"Him no find Ezra!" cried Elspeth. "I hae telled you a dozen times he found it as easy as you could yoke a horse."

"The thing can be explained in no other way," said her husband, doggedly, "if he was weel and in sound mind."

"Maybe the dominie can clear it up," suggested the post, "him being a scholar."

"Then tell me what happened," I asked.

"Godsake, hae we no telled you?" Birse said. "I thocht we had."

"It was a terrible scene," said Elspeth, giving her husband a shove. "As I said, Mr. Dishart gave out Ezra eighth. Weel, I turned it up in a jifify, and syne look cautiously to see how Eppie McLaren was getting on. Just at that minute I heard a groan frae the pulpit. It didna stop short o' a groan. Ay, you may be sure I looked quick at the minister, and there I saw a sicht that would hae made the grandest gape. His face was as white as a baker's, and he had a sort of fallen against the back o' the pulpit, staring demented-like at his open Bible."

"And I saw him," said Birse, "put up his hand atween him and the Book, as if he thocht it was to jump at him."

"Twice," said Elspeth, "he tried to speak, and twice he let the words fall."

"That," said Waster Lunny, "the whole congregation admits, but I didna see it mysel', for a' this time you may picture me hunting savage-like for Ezra. I thocht the minister was waiting till I found it."

"Hendry Munn," said Birse, "stood upon one leg, wondering whether he should run to the session-house for a glass of water."

"But by that time," said Elspeth, "the fit had left Mr. Dishart, or rather it had ta'en a new turn. He grew red, and it's gospel that he stamped his foot."

"He had the face of one using bad words," said the post. "He didna swear, of course, but that was the face he had on."

"I missed it," said Waster Lunny, "for I was in full cry after Ezra, with the sweat running down my face."

"But the most astounding thing has yet to be telled," went on Elspeth. "The minister shook himsel' like one wakening frae a nasty dream, and he cries in a voice of thunder, just as if he was shaking his fist at somebody—"

"He cries," Birse interposed, cleverly, "he cries, 'You will find the text in Genesis, chapter three, verse six.'"

"Yes," said Elspeth, "first he gave out one text, and then he gave out another, being the most amazing thing to my mind that ever happened in the town of Thrums. What will our children's children think o't? I wouldna hae missed it for a pound note."

"Nor me," said Waster Lunny, "though I only got the tail o't. Dominie, no sooner had he said Genesis third and sixth, than I laid my finger on Ezra. Was it no provoking? Onybody can turn up Genesis, but it needs an able-bodied man to find Ezra."

"He preached on the Fall," Elspeth said, "for an hour and twenty-five minutes, but powerful though he was I would rather he had telled us what made him gie the go-by to Ezra."

"All I can say," said Waster Lunny, "is that I never heard him mair awe-inspiring. Whaur has he got sic a knowledge of women? He riddled them, he fair riddled them, till I was ashamed o' being married."

"It's easy kent whaur he got his knowledge of women," Birse explained, "it's a' in the original Hebrew. You can howk ony mortal thing out o' the original Hebrew, the which all ministers hae at their finger ends. What else makes them ken to jump a verse now and then when giving out a psalm?"

"It wasna women like me he denounced," Elspeth insisted, "but young lassies that leads men astray wi' their abominable wheedling ways."

"Tod," said her husband, "if they try their hands on Mr. Dishart they'll meet their match."

"They will," chuckled the post. "The Hebrew's a grand thing, though teuch, I'm telled, mighty teuch."

"His sublimest burst," Waster Lunny came back to tell me, "was about the beauty o' the soul being everything and the beauty o' the face no worth a snuff. What a scorn he has for bonny faces and toom souls! I dinna deny but what a bonny face fell takes me, but Mr. Dishart wouldna gie a blade o' grass for't. Ay, and I used to think that in their foolishness about women there was dagont little differ atween the unlearned and the highly edicated."

The gossip about Gavin brought hitherto to the school-house had been as bread to me, but this I did not like. For a minister to behave thus was as unsettling to us as a change of Government to Londoners, and I decided to give my scholars a holiday on the morrow and tramp into the town for fuller news. But all through the night it snowed, and next day, and then intermittently for many days, and every fall took the school miles farther away from Thrums.

Birse and the crows had now the glen road to themselves, and even Birse had twice or thrice to bed with me. At these times had he not been so interested in describing his progress through the snow, maintaining that the crying want of our glen road was palings for postmen to kick their feet against, he must have wondered why I always turned the talk to the Auld Licht minister.

"Ony explanation o' his sudden change o' texts?" Birse said, repeating my question. "Tod, and there is and to spare, for I hear tell there's saxteen explanations in the Tenements alone. As Tammas Haggart says, that's a blessing, for if there had just been twa explanations the kirk micht hae split on them."

"Ay," he said at another time, "twa or three even dared to question the minister, but I'm thinking they made nothing o't. The majority agrees that he was just inspired to change his text. But Lang Tammas is dour. Tammas telled the session a queer thing. He says that after the diet o' worship on that eventful afternoon Mr. Dishart carried the Bible out o' the pulpit instead o' leaving that duty as usual to the kirk-officer. Weel, Tammas, being precentor, has a richt, as you ken, to leave the kirk by the session-house door, just like the minister himsel'. He did so that afternoon, and what, think you, did he see? He saw Mr. Dishart tearing a page out o' the Bible, and flinging it savagely into the session-house fire. You dinna credit it? Weel, it's staggering, but there's Hendry Munn's evidence too. Hendry took his first chance o' looking up Ezra in the minister's Bible, and, behold, the page wi' the eighth chapter was gone. Them that thinks Tammas wasna blind wi' excitement hauds it had been Ezra eighth that gaed into the fire. Onyway, there's no doubt about the page's being missing, for whatever excitement Tammas was in, Hendry was as cool as ever."

A week later Birse told me that the congregation had decided to regard the incident as adding lustre to their kirk. This was largely, I fear, because it could then be used to belittle the Established minister. That fervent Auld Licht, Snecky Hobart, feeling that Gavin's action was unsound, had gone on the following Sabbath to the parish kirk and sat under Mr. Duthie. But Mr. Duthie was a close reader, so that Snecky flung himself about in his pew in misery. The minister concluded his sermon with these words: "But on this subject I will say no more at present." "Because you canna," Snecky roared, and strutted out of the church. Comparing the two scenes, it is obvious that the Auld Lichts had won a victory. After preaching impromptu for an hour and twenty-five minutes, it could never be said of Gavin that he needed to read. He became more popular than ever. Yet the change of texts was not forgotten. If in the future any other indictments were brought against him, it would certainly be pinned to them.

I marvelled long over Gavin's jump from Ezra to Genesis, and at this his first philippic against Woman, but I have known the cause for many a year. The Bible was the one that had lain on the summer-seat while the Egyptian hid there. It was the great pulpit Bible which remains in the church as a rule, but Gavin had taken it home the previous day to make some of its loose pages secure with paste. He had studied from it on the day preceding the riot, but had used a small Bible during the rest of the week. When he turned in the pulpit to Ezra, where he had left the large Bible open in the summer-seat, he found this scrawled across chapter eight:—

"I will never tell who flung the clod at Captain Halliwell. But why did you fling it? I will never tell that you allowed me to be called Mrs. Dishart before witnesses. But is not this a Scotch marriage? Signed, Babbie the Egyptian."

Chapter XI

Tells in a Whisper of Man's Fall During the Curling Season

No snow could be seen in Thrums by the beginning of the year, though clods of it lay in Waster Lunny's fields, where his hens wandered all day as if looking for something they had dropped. A black frost had set in, and one walking on the glen road could imagine that through the cracks in it he saw a loch glistening. From my door I could hear the roar of curling stones at Rashie-bog, which is almost four miles nearer Thrums. On the day I am recalling, I see that I only made one entry in my diary, "At last bought Waster Lunny's bantams." Well do I remember the transaction, and no wonder, for I had all but bought the bantams every day for a six months.

About noon the doctor's dog-cart was observed by all the Tenements standing at the Auld Licht manse. The various surmises were wrong. Margaret had not been suddenly taken ill; Jean had not swallowed a darning-needle; the minister had not walked out at his study window in a moment of sublime thought. Gavin stepped into the dog-cart, which at once drove off in the direction of Rashiebog, but equally in error were those who said that the doctor was making a curler of him.

There was, however, ground for gossip; for Thrums folk seldom called in a doctor until it was too late to cure them, and McQueen was not the man to pay social visits. Of his skill we knew fearsome stories, as that, by looking at Archie Allardyce, who had come to broken bones on a ladder, he discovered which rung Archie fell from. When he entered a stuffy room he would poke his staff through the window to let in fresh air, and then fling down a shilling to pay for the breakage. He was deaf in the right ear, and therefore usually took the left side of prosy people, thus, as he explained, making a blessing of an affliction. "A pity I don't hear better?" I have heard him say. "Not at all. If my misfortune, as you call it, were to be removed, you can't conceive how I should miss my deaf ear." He was a fine fellow, though brusque, and I never saw him without his pipe until two days before we buried him, which was five-and-twenty years ago come Martinmas.

"We're all quite weel," Jean said apprehensively as she answered his knock on the manse door, and she tried to be pleasant, too, for well she knew that, if a doctor willed it, she could have fever in five minutes.

"Ay, Jean, I'll soon alter that," he replied ferociously. "Is the master in?"

"He's at his sermon," Jean said with importance.

To interrupt the minister at such a moment seemed sacrilege to her, for her up-bringing had been good. Her mother had once fainted in the church, but though the family's distress was great, they neither bore her out, nor signed to the kirk-officer to bring water. They propped her up in the pew in a respectful attitude, joining in the singing meanwhile, and she recovered in time to look up 2nd Chronicles, 21st and 7th.

"Tell him I want to speak to him at the door," said the doctor fiercely, "or I'll bleed you this minute."

McQueen would not enter, because his horse might have seized the opportunity to return stablewards. At the houses where it was accustomed to stop, it drew up of its own accord, knowing where the Doctor's "cases" were as well as himself, but it resented new patients.

"You like misery, I think, Mr. Dishart," McQueen said when Gavin came to him, "at least I am always finding you in the thick of it, and that is why I am here now. I have a rare job for you if you will jump into the machine. You know Nanny Webster, who lives on the edge of Windyghoul? No, you don't, for she belongs to the other kirk. Well, at all events, you knew her brother, Sanders, the mole-catcher?"

"I remember him. You mean the man who boasted so much about seeing a ball at Lord Rintoul's place?"

"The same, and, as you may know, his boasting about maltreating policemen whom he never saw led to his being sentenced to nine months in gaol lately."

"That is the man," said Gavin. "I never liked him."

"No, but his sister did," McQueen answered, drily, "and with reason, for he was her bread-winner, and now she is starving."

"Anything I can give her—"

"Would be too little, sir."

"But the neighbours—"

"She has few near her, and though the Thrums poor help each other bravely, they are at present nigh as needy as herself. Nanny is coming to the poorhouse, Mr. Dishart."

"God help her!" exclaimed Gavin.

"Nonsense," said the doctor, trying to make himself a hard man. "She will be properly looked after there, and — and in time she will like it."

"Don't let my mother hear you speaking of taking an old woman to that place," Gavin said, looking anxiously up the stair. I cannot pretend that Margaret never listened.

"You all speak as if the poorhouse was a gaol," the doctor said testily. "But so far as Nanny is concerned, everything is arranged. I promised to drive her to the poorhouse to-day, and she is waiting for me now. Don't look at me as if I was a brute. She is to take some of her things with her to the poorhouse, and the rest is to be left until Sanders's return, when she may rejoin him. At least we said that to her to comfort her."

"You want me to go with you?"

"Yes, though I warn you it may be a distressing scene; indeed, the truth is that I am loth to face Nanny alone to-day. Mr. Duthie should have accompanied me, for the Websters are Established Kirk; ay, and so he would if Rashiebog had not been bearing. A terrible snare this curling, Mr. Dishart" — here the doctor sighed — "I have known Mr. Duthie wait until midnight struck on Sabbath, and then be off to Rashie-bog with a torch."

"I will go with you," Gavin said, putting on his coat.

"Jump in then. You won't smoke? I never see a respectable man not smoking, sir, but I feel indignant with him for such sheer waste of time."

Gavin smiled at this, and Snecky Hobart, who happened to be keeking over the manse dyke, bore the news to the Tenements. "I'll no sleep the nicht," Snecky said, "for wondering what made the minister lauch. Ay, it would be no trifle."

A minister, it is certain, who wore a smile on his face would never have been called to the Auld Licht kirk, for life is a wrestle with the devil, and only the frivolous think to throw him without taking off their coats. Yet, though Gavin's zeal was what the congregation reverenced, many loved him privately for his boyishness. He could unbend at marriages, of which he had six on the last day of the year, and at every one of them he joked (the same joke) like a layman. Some did not approve of his playing at the teetotum for ten minutes with Kitty Dundas's invalid son, but the way Kitty boasted about it would have disgusted anybody. At the present day there are probably a score of Gavins in Thrums, all called after the little minister, and there is one Gavinia, whom he hesitated to christen. He made humorous remarks (the same remark) about all these children, and his smile as he patted their heads was for thinking over when one's work was done for the day.

The doctor's horse clattered up the back wynd noisily, as if a minister behind made no difference to it. Instead of climbing the Roods, however, the nearest way to Nanny's, it went westward, which Gavin, in a reverie, did not notice. The truth must be told. The Egyptian was again in his head.

"Have I fallen deaf in the left ear, too?" said the doctor. "I see your lips moving, but I don't catch a syllable."

Gavin started, coloured, and flung the gypsy out of the trap.

"Why are we not going up the Roods?" he asked.

"Well," said the doctor, slowly, "at the top of the Roods there is a stance for circuses, and this old beast of mine won't pass it. You know, unless you are behind in the clashes and clavers of Thrums, that I bought her from the manager of a travelling show. She was the horse ('Lightning' they called her), that galloped round the ring at a mile an hour, and so at the top of the Roods she is still unmanageable. She once dragged me to the scene of her former triumphs, and went revolving round it, dragging the machine after her."

"If you had not explained that," said Gavin, "I might have thought that you wanted to pass by Rashie-bog."

The doctor, indeed, was already standing up to catch a first glimpse of the curlers.

"Well," he admitted, "I might have managed to pass the circus ring, though what I have told you is true. However, I have not come this way merely to see how the match is going. I want to shame Mr. Duthie for neglecting his duty. It will help me to do mine, for the Lord knows I am finding it hard, with the music of these stones in my ears."

"I never saw it played before," Gavin said, standing up in his turn. "What a din they make! McQueen, I believe they are fighting!"

"No, no," said the excited doctor, "they are just a bit daft. That's the proper spirit for the game. Look, that's the baron-bailie near standing on his head, and there's Mr. Duthie off his head a' thegither. Yon's twa weavers and a mason cursing the laird, and the man wi' the besom is the Master of Crumnathie."

"A democracy, at all events," said Gavin.

"By no means," said the doctor, "it's an aristocracy of intellect. Gee up, Lightning, or the frost will be gone before we are there."

"It is my opinion, doctor," said Gavin, "that you will have bones to set before that game is finished. I can see nothing but legs now."

"Don't say a word against curling, sir, to me," said McQueen, whom the sight of a game in which he must not play had turned crusty. "Dangerous! It is the best medicine I know of. Look at that man coming across the field. It is Jo Strachan. Well, sir, curling saved Jo's life after I had given him up. You don't believe me? Hie, Jo, Jo Strachan, come here and tell the minister how curling put you on your legs again."

Strachan came forward, a tough, little, wizened man, with red flannel round his ears to keep out the cold.

"It's gospel what the doctor says, Mr. Dishart," he declared. "Me and my brither Sandy was baith ill, and in the same bed, and the doctor had hopes o' Sandy, but nane o' me. Ay, weel, when I heard that, I thocht I micht as weel die on the ice as in my bed, so I up and on wi' my claethes. Sandy was mad at me, for he was no curler,and he says, 'Jo Strachan, if you gang to Rashie-bog you'll assuredly be brocht hame a corp.' I didna heed him, though, and off I gaed."

"And I see you did not die," said Gavin.

"Not me," answered the fish cadger, with a grin. "Na, but the joke o't is, it was Sandy that died."

"Not the joke, Jo," corrected the doctor, "the moral."

"Ay, the moral; I'm aye forgetting the word."

McQueen, enjoying Gavin's discomfiture, turned Lightning down the Rashie-bog road, which would be impassable as soon as the thaw came. In summer Rashie-bog is several fields in which a cart does not sink unless it stands still, but in winter it is a loch with here and there a spring where dead men are said to lie. There are no rushes at its east end, and here the dog-cart drew up near the curlers, a crowd of men dancing, screaming, shaking their fists and sweeping, while half a hundred onlookers got in their way, gesticulating and advising.

"Hold me tight," the doctor whispered to Gavin, "or I'll be leaving you to drive Nanny to the poorhouse by yourself."

He had no sooner said this than he tried to jump out of the trap.

"You donnert fule, John Robbie," he shouted to a player, "soop her up, man, soop her up; no, no, dinna, dinna; leave her alane. Bailie, leave her alane, you blazing idiot. Mr. Dishart, let me go; what do you mean, sir, by hanging on to my coat tails? Dang it all, Duthie's winning. He has it, he has it!"

"You're to play, Doctor?" some cried, running to the dog-cart. "We hae missed you sair."

"Jeames, I — I — . No, I daurna."

"Then we get our licks. I never saw the minister in sic form. We can do nothing against him."

"Then," cried McQueen, "I'll play. Come what will, I'll play. Let go my tails, Mr. Dishart, or I'll cut them off. Duty? Fiddlesticks!"

"Shame on you, sir," said Gavin; "yes, and on you others who would entice him from his duty."

"Shame!" the doctor cried. "Look at Mr. Duthie. Is he ashamed? And yet that man has been reproving me for a twelvemonths because I've refused to become one of his elders. Duthie," he shouted, "think shame of yourself for curling this day."

Mr. Duthie had carefully turned his back to the trap, for Gavin's presence in it annoyed him. We seldom care to be reminded of our duty by seeing another do it. Now, however, he advanced to the dog-cart, taking the far side of Gavin.

"Put on your coat, Mr. Duthie," said the doctor, "and come with me to Nanny Webster's. You promised."

Mr. Duthie looked quizzically at Gavin, and then at the sky.

"The thaw may come at any moment," he said.

"I think the frost is to hold," said Gavin.

"It may hold over to-morrow," Mr. Duthie admitted; "but to-morrow's the Sabbath, and so a lost day."

"A what?" exclaimed Gavin, horrified.

"I only mean," Mr. Duthie answered, colouring, "that we can't curl on the Lord's day. As for what it may be like on Monday, no one can say. No, doctor, I won't risk it. We're in the middle of a game, man."

Gavin looked very grave.

"I see what you are thinking, Mr. Dishart," the old minister said doggedly; "but then, you don't curl. You are very wise. I have forbidden my sons to curl."

"Then you openly snap your fingers at your duty, Mr. Duthie?" said the doctor, loftily. ("You can let go my tails now, Mr. Dishart, for the madness has passed.")

"None of your virtuous airs, McQueen," said Mr. Duthie, hotly. "What was the name of the doctor that warned women never to have bairns while it was hauding?"

"And what," retorted McQueen, "was the name of the minister that told his session he would neither preach nor pray while the black frost lasted?"

"Hoots, doctor," said Duthie, "don't lose your temper because I'm in such form."

"Don't lose yours, Duthie, because I aye beat you."

"You beat me, McQueen! Go home, sir, and don't talk havers. Who beat you at—"

"Who made you sing small at—"

"Who won—"

"Who—"

"Who—"

"I'll play you on Monday for whatever you like!" shrieked the doctor

"If it holds," cried the minister, "I'll be here the whole day. Name the stakes yourself. A stone?"

"No," the doctor said, "but I'll tell you what we'll play for. You've been dinging me doited about that eldership, and we'll play for't. If you win I accept office."

"Done," said the minister, recklessly.

The dog-cart was now turned toward Windyghoul, its driver once more good-humoured, but Gavin silent.

"You would have been the better of my deaf ear just now, Mr. Dishart," McQueen said after the loch had been left behind. "Aye, and I'm thinking my pipe would soothe you. But don't take it so much to heart, man. I'll lick him easily. He's a decent man, the minister, but vain of his play, ridiculously vain. However, I think the sight of you, in the place that should have been his, has broken his nerve for this day, and our side may win yet."

"I believe," Gavin said, with sudden enlightenment, "that you brought me here for that purpose."

"Maybe," chuckled the doctor; "maybe." Then he changed the subject suddenly. "Mr. Dishart," he asked, "were you ever in love?"

"Never!" answered Gavin violently.

"Well, well," said the doctor, "don't terrify the horse. I have been in love myself. It's bad, but it's nothing to curling."

Chapter XII

Tragedy of a Mud House

THE dog-cart bumped between the trees of Caddam, flinging Gavin and the doctor at each other as a wheel rose on some beech-root or sank for a moment in a pool. I suppose the wood was a pretty sight that day, the pines only white where they had met the snow, as if the numbed painter had left his work unfinished, the brittle twigs snapping overhead, the water as black as tar. But it matters little what the wood was like. Within a squirrel's leap of it an old woman was standing at the door of a mud house, listening for the approach of the trap that was to take her to the poorhouse. Can you think of the beauty of the day now?

Nanny was not crying. She had redd up her house for the last time and put on her black merino. Her mouth was wide open while she listened. If you had addressed her you would have thought her polite and stupid. Look at her. A flabby-faced woman she is now, with a swollen body, and no one has heeded her much these thirty years. I can tell you something; it is almost droll. Nanny Webster was once a gay flirt, and in Airlie Square there is a weaver with an unsteady head who thought all the earth of her. His loom has taken a foot from his stature, and gone are Nanny's raven locks on which he used to place his adoring hand. Down in Airlie Square he is weaving for his life, and here is Nanny, ripe for the poorhouse, and between them is the hill where they were lovers. That is all the story save that when Nanny heard the dog-cart she screamed.

No neighbour was with her. If you think this hard, it is because you do not understand. Perhaps Nanny had never been very lovable except to one man, and him, it is said, she lost through her own vanity; but there was much in her to like. The neighbours, of whom there were two not a hundred yards away, would have been with her now but they feared to hurt her feelings. No heart opens to sympathy without letting in delicacy, and these poor people knew that Nanny would not like them to see her being taken away. For a week they had been aware of what was coming, and they had been most kind to her, but that hideous word, the poorhouse, they had not uttered. Poorhouse is not to be spoken in Thrums, though it is nothing to tell a man that you see death in his face. Did Nanny think they knew where she was going? was a question they whispered to each other, and her suffering eyes cut scars on their hearts. So now that the hour had come they called their children into their houses and pulled down their blinds.

"If you would like to see her by yourself," the doctor said eagerly to Gavin, as the horse drew up at Nanny's gate, "I'll wait with the horse. Not," he added, hastily, "that I feel sorry for her. We are doing her a kindness."

They dismounted together, however, and Nanny, who had run from the trap into the house, watched them from her window.

McQueen saw her and said glumly, "I should have come alone, for if you pray she is sure to break down. Mr. Dishart, could you not pray cheerfully?"

"You don't look very cheerful yourself," Gavin said sadly.

"Nonsense," answered the doctor. "I have no patience with this false sentiment. Stand still, Lightning, and be thankful you are not your master today."

The door stood open, and Nanny was crouching against the opposite wall of the room — such a poor, dull kitchen, that you would have thought the furniture had still to be brought into it. The blanket and the piece of old carpet that was Nanny's coverlet were already packed in her box. The plate rack was empty. Only the round table and the two chairs, and the stools and some pans were being left behind.

"Well, Nanny," the doctor said, trying to bluster, "I have come, and you see Mr. Dishart is with me."

Nanny rose bravely. She knew the doctor was good to her, and she wanted to thank him. I have not seen a great deal of the world myself, but often the sweet politeness of the aged poor has struck me as beautiful. Nanny dropped a curtsey, an ungainly one maybe, but it was an old woman giving the best she had.

"Thank you kindly, sirs," she said; and then two pairs of eyes dropped before hers.

"Please to take a chair," she added timidly. It is strange to know that at that awful moment, for let none tell me it was less than awful, the old woman was the one who could speak.

Both men sat down, for they would have hurt Nanny by remaining standing. Some ministers would have known the right thing to say to her, but Gavin dared not let himself speak. I have again to remind you that he was only one-and-twenty.

"I'm drouthy, Nanny," the doctor said, to give her something to do, "and I would be obliged for a drink of water."

Nanny hastened to the pan that stood behind her door, but stopped before she reached it.

"It's toom," she said, "I — I didna think I needed to fill it this morning." She caught the doctor's eye, and could only half restrain a sob. "I couldna help that," she said, apologetically. "I'm richt angry at myself for being so ungrateful like."

The doctor thought it best that they should depart at once. He rose.

"Oh, no, doctor," cried Nanny in alarm.

"But you are ready?"

"Ay," she said, "I have been ready this twa hours, but you micht wait a minute. Hendry Munn and Andrew Allardyce is coming yont the road, and they would see me."

"Wait, doctor," Gavin said.

"Thank you kindly, sir," answered Nanny.

"But Nanny," the doctor said, "you must remember what I told you about the poo— , about the place you are going to. It is a fine house, and you will be very happy in it."

"Ay, I'll be happy in't," Nanny faltered, "but, doctor, if I could just hae bidden on here though I wasna happy!"

"Think of the food you will get; broth nearly every day."

"It — it'll be terrible enjoyable," Nanny said.

"And there will be pleasant company for you always," continued the doctor, "and a nice room to sit in. Why, after you have been there a week, you won't be the same woman."

"That's it!" cried Nanny with sudden passion. "Na, na; I'll be a woman on the poor's rates. Oh, mither, mither, you little thocht when you bore me that I would come to this!"

"Nanny," the doctor said, rising again, "I am ashamed of you."

"I humbly speir your forgiveness, sir," she said, "and you micht bide just a wee yet. I've been ready to gang these twa hours, but now that the machine is at the gate, I dinna ken how it is, but I'm terrible sweer to come awa'. Oh, Mr. Dishart, it's richt true what the doctor says about the — the place, but I canna just take it in. I'm — I'm gey auld."

"You will often get out to see your friends," was all Gavin could say.

"Na, na, na," she cried, "dinna say that; I'll gang, but you mauna bid me ever come out, except in a hearse. Dinna let onybody in Thrums look on my face again."

"We must go," said the doctor firmly. "Put on your mutch, Nanny."

"I dinna need to put on a mutch," she answered, with a faint flush of pride. "I have a bonnet."

She took the bonnet from her bed, and put it on slowly.

"Are you sure there's naebody looking?" she asked.

The doctor glanced at the minister, and Gavin rose.

"Let us pray," he said, and the three went down on their knees.

It was not the custom of Auld Licht ministers to leave any house without offering up a prayer in it, and to us it always seemed that when Gavin prayed, he was at the knees of God. The little minister pouring himself out in prayer in a humble room, with awed people around him who knew much more of the world than he, his voice at times thick and again a squeal, and his hands clasped not gracefully, may have been only a comic figure, but we were old-fashioned, and he seemed to make us better men. If I only knew the way, I would draw him as he was, and not fear to make him too mean a man for you to read about. He had not been long in Thrums before he knew that we talked much of his prayers, and that doubtless puffed him up a little. Sometimes, I daresay, he rose from his knees feeling that he had prayed well to-day, which is a dreadful charge to bring against anyone. But it was not always so, nor was it so now.

I am not speaking harshly of this man, whom I have loved beyond all others, when I say that Nanny came between him and his prayer. Had he been of God's own image, unstained, he would have forgotten all else in his Maker's presence, but Nanny was speaking too, and her words choked his. At first she only whispered, but soon what was eating her heart burst out painfully, and she did not know that the minister had stopped. They were such moans as these that brought him back to earth:—

"I'll hae to gang . . . I'm a base woman no' to be mair thankfu' to them that is so good to me ... I dinna like to prig wi' them to take a roundabout road, and I'm sair fleid a' the Roods will see me ... If it could just be said to poor Sanders when he comes back that I died hurriedly, syne he would be able to haud up his head . . . Oh, mither! . . . I wish terrible they had come and ta'en me at nicht . . . It's a dog-cart, and I was praying it micht be a cart, so that they could cover me wi' straw."

"This is more than I can stand," the doctor cried.

Nanny rose frightened.

"I've tried you, sair," she said, "but, oh, I'm grateful, and I'm ready now."

They all advanced toward the door without another word, and Nanny even tried to smile. But in the middle of the floor something came over her, and she stood there. Gavin took her hand, and it was cold. She looked from one to the other, her mouth opening and shutting.

"I canna help it," she said.

"It's cruel hard," muttered the doctor. "I knew this woman when she was a lassie."

The little minister stretched out his hands.

"Have pity on her, O God!" he prayed, with the presumptuousness of youth.

Nanny heard the words.

"Oh, God," she cried, "you micht!"

God needs no minister to tell Him what to do, but it was His will that the poorhouse should not have this woman. He made use of a strange instrument, no other than the Egyptian, who now opened the mud house door.

Chapter XIII

Second Coming of the Egyptian Woman

The gypsy had been passing the house, perhaps on her way to Thrums for gossip, and it was only curiosity, born suddenly of Gavin's cry, that made her enter. On finding herself in unexpected company she retained her hold of the door, and to the amazed minister she seemed for a moment to have stepped into the mud house from his garden. Her eyes danced, however, as they recognized him, and then he hardened. "This is no place for you," he was saying fiercely, when Nanny, too distraught to think, fell crying at the Egyptian's feet. "They are taking me to the poorhouse," she sobbed; "dinna let them, dinna let them."

The Egyptian's arms clasped her, and the Egyptian kissed a sallow cheek that had once been as fair as yours, madam, who may read this story. No one had caressed Nanny for many years, but do you think she was too poor and old to care for those young arms around her neck? There are those who say that women cannot love each other, but it is not true. Woman is not undeveloped man, but something better, and Gavin and the doctor knew it as they saw Nanny clinging to her protector. When the gypsy turned with flashing eyes to the two men she might have been a mother guarding her child.

"How dare you!" she cried, stamping her foot; and they quaked like malefactors.

"You don't see—" Gavin began, but her indignation stopped him.

"You coward!" she said.

Even the doctor had been impressed, so that he now addressed the gypsy respectfully.

"This is all very well," he said, "but a woman's sympathy—"

"A woman! — ah, if I could be a man for only five minutes!"

She clenched her little fists, and again turned to Nanny.

"You poor dear," she said tenderly, "I won't let them take you away."

She looked triumphantly at both minister and doctor, as one who had foiled them in their cruel designs.

"Go!" she said, pointing grandly to the door.

"Is this the Egyptian of the riots," the doctor said in a low voice to Gavin, "or is she a queen? Hoots, man, don't look so shamefaced. We are not criminals. Say something."

Then to the Egyptian Gavin said firmly—

"You mean well, but you are doing this poor woman a cruelty in holding out hopes to her that cannot be realised. Sympathy is not meal and bedclothes, and these are what she needs."

"And you who live in luxury," retorted the girl, "would send her to the poorhouse for them. I thought better of you!"

"Tuts!" said the doctor, losing patience, "Mr. Dishart gives more than any other man in Thrums to the poor, and he is not to be preached to by a gypsy. We are waiting for you, Nanny."

"Ay, I'm coming," said Nanny, leaving the Egyptian. "I'll hae to gang, lassie. Dinna greet for me."

But the Egyptian said, "No, you are not going. It is these men who are going. Go, sirs, and leave us."

'And you will provide for Nanny?" asked the doctor, contemptuously.

"Yes."

"And where is the siller to come from?"

"That is my affair, and Nanny's. Begone, both of you. She shall never want again. See how the very mention of your going brings back life to her face."

"I won't begone," the doctor said roughly, "till I see the colour of your siller."

"Oh, the money," said the Egyptian scornfully. She put her hand into her pocket confidently, as if used to well-filled purses, but could only draw out two silver pieces.

"I had forgotten," she said aloud, though speaking to herself.

"I thought so," said the cynical doctor. "Come, Nanny."

"You presume to doubt me!" the Egyptian said, blocking his way to the door.

"How could I presume to believe you?" he answered. "You are a beggar by profession, and yet talk as if — pooh, nonsense."

"I would live on terrible little," Nanny whispered, "and Sanders will be out again in August month."

"Seven shillings a week," rapped out the doctor.

"Is that all?" the Egyptian asked. "She shall have it."

"When?"

"At once. No, it is not possible to-night, but tomorrow I will bring five pounds; no, I will send it; no, you must come for it."

"And where, O daughter of Dives, do you reside?" the doctor asked.

No doubt the Egyptian could have found a ready answer had her pity for Nanny been less sincere; as it was, she hesitated, wanting to propitiate the doctor, while holding her secret fast.

"I only asked," McQueen said, eyeing her curiously, "because when I make an appointment I like to know where it is to be held. But I suppose you are suddenly to rise out of the ground as you have done to-day, and did six weeks ago."

"Whether I rise out of the ground or not," the gypsy said, keeping her temper with an effort, "there will be a five-pound note in my hand. You will meet me to-morrow about this hour at — say the Kaims of Cushie?"

"No," said the doctor after a moment's pause; "I won't. Even if I went to the Kaims I should not find you there. Why can you not come to me?"

"Why do you carry a woman's hair," replied the Egyptian, "in that locket on your chain?"

Whether she was speaking of what she knew, or this was only a chance shot, I cannot tell, but the doctor stepped back from her hastily, and could not help looking down at the locket.

"Yes," said the Egyptian calmly, "it is still shut; but why do you sometimes open it at nights?"

"Lassie," the old doctor cried, "are you a witch?"

"Perhaps," she said; "but I ask for no answer to my questions. If you have your secrets, why may I not have mine? Now will you meet me at the Kaims?"

"No; I distrust you more than ever. Even if you came, it would be to play with me as you have done already. How can a vagrant have five pounds in her pocket when she does not have five shillings on her back?"

"You are a cruel, hard man," the Egyptian said, beginning to lose hope. "But, see," she cried, brightening, "look at this ring. Do you know its value?"

She held up her finger, but the stone would not live in the dull light.

"I see it is gold," the doctor said cautiously, and she smiled at the ignorance that made him look only at the frame.

"Certainly it is gold," said Gavin, equally stupid.

"Mercy on us!" Nanny cried; "I believe it's what they call a diamond."

"How did you come by it?" the doctor asked suspiciously.

"I thought we had agreed not to ask each other questions," the Egyptian answered drily. "But, see, I will give it you to hold in hostage. If I am not at the Kaims to get it back you can keep it."

The doctor took the ring in his hand and examined it curiously.

"There is a quirk in this," he said at last, "that I don't like. Take back your ring, lassie. Mr. Dishart, give Nanny your arm, and I'll carry her box to the machine."

Now all this time Gavin had been in the dire distress of a man possessed of two minds, of which one said, "This is a true woman," and the other, "Remember the seventeenth of October." They were at war within him, and he knew that he must take aside, yet no sooner had he cast one out than he invited it back. He did not answer the doctor.

"Unless," McQueen said, nettled by his hesitation, "you trust this woman's word."

Gavin tried honestly to weigh those two minds against each other, but could not prevent impulse from jumping into one of the scales.

"You do trust me," the Egyptian said, with wet eyes; and now that he looked on her again—

"Yes," he said firmly, "I trust you," and the words that had been so difficult to say were the right words. He had no more doubt of it.

"Just think a moment first," the doctor warned him. "I decline to have anything to do with this matter. You will go to the Kaims for the siller?"

"If it is necessary," said Gavin.

"It is necessary," the Egyptian said.

"Then I will go."

Nanny took his hand timidly and would have kissed it had he been less than a minister.

"You dare not, man," the doctor said gruffly, "make an appointment with this gypsy. Think of what will be said in Thrums."

I honour Gavin for the way in which he took this warning. For him, who was watched from the rising of his congregation to their lying down, whose every movement was expected to be a text to Thrums, it was no small thing that he had promised. This he knew, but he only reddened because the doctor had implied an offensive thing in a woman's presence.

"You forget yourself, doctor," he said sharply.

"Send some one in your place," advised the doctor, who liked the little minister.

"He must come himself and alone," said the Egyptian. "You must both give me your promise not to mention who is Nanny's friend, and she must promise too."

"Well," said the doctor, buttoning up his coat, "I cannot keep my horse freezing any longer. Remember, Mr. Dishart, you take the sole responsibility of this."

"I do," said Gavin, "and with the utmost confidence."

"Give him the ring then, lassie," said McQueen.

She handed the minister the ring, but he would not take it.

"I have your word," he said; "that is sufficient."

Then the Egyptian gave him the first look that he could think of afterwards without misgivings.

"So be it," said the doctor. "Get the money, and I will say nothing about it, unless I have reason to think that it has been dishonestly come by. Don't look so frightened at me, Nanny. I hope for your sake that her stocking-foot is full of gold."

"Surely it's worth risking," Nanny said, not very brightly, "when the minister's on her side."

"Ay, but on whose side, Nanny?" asked the doctor. "Lassie, I bear you no grudge; will you not tell me who you are?"

"Only a puir gypsy, your honour," said the girl, becoming

mischievous now that she had gained her point; "only a wandering hallen-shaker, and will I tell you your fortune, my pretty gentleman?"

"No, you shan't," replied the doctor, plunging his hands so hastily into his pockets that Gavin laughed.

"I don't need to look at your hand," said the gypsy, "I can read your fortune in your face."

She looked at him fixedly, so that he fidgeted.

"I see you," said the Egyptian in a sepulchral voice, and speaking slowly, "become very frail. Your eyesight has almost gone. You are sitting alone in a cauld room, cooking your ain dinner ower a feeble fire. The soot is falling down the lum. Your bearish manners towards women have driven the servant lassie frae your house, and your wife beats you."

"Ay. you spoil your prophecy there," the doctor said, considerably relieved, "for I'm not married; my pipe's the only wife I ever had."

"You will be married by that time," continued the Egyptian, frowning at this interruption, "for I see your wife. She is a shrew. She marries you in your dotage. She lauchs at you in company. She doesna allow you to smoke."

"Away with you, you jade," cried the doctor in a fury,and feeling nervously for his pipe. "Mr. Dishart, you had better stay and arrange this matter as you choose., but I want a word with you outside."

"And you're no angry wi' me, doctor, are you?" asked Nanny wistfully. "You've been richt good to me, but I canna thole the thocht o' that place. And, oh, doctor, you winna tell naebody that I was so near taen to it?"

In the garden McQueen said to Gavin—

"You may be right, Mr. Dishart, in this matter, for there is this in our favour, that the woman can gain nothing by tricking us. She did seem to feel for Nanny. But who can she be? You saw she could put on and off the Scotch tongue as easily as if it were a cap."

"She is as much a mystery to me as to you," Gavin answered, "but she will give me the money, and that is all I ask of her."

"Ay, that remains to be seen. But take care of yourself; a man's second childhood begins when a woman gets hold of him."

"Don't alarm yourself about me, doctor. I daresay she is only one of those gypsies from the South. They are said to be wealthy, many of them, and even, when they like, to have a grand manner. The Thrums people had no doubt but that she was what she seemed to be."

"Ay, but what does she seem to be? Even that puzzles me. And then there is this mystery about her which she admits herself, though perhaps only to play with us."

"Perhaps," said Gavin, "she is only taking precautions against her discovery by the police. You must remember her part in the riots."

"Yes, but we never learned how she was able to play that part. Besides, there is no fear in her, or she would not have ventured back to Thrums. However, good luck attend you. But be wary. You saw how she kept her feet among her shalls and wills? Never trust a Scotch man or woman who does not come to grief among them."

The doctor took his seat in the dog-cart.

"And, Mr. Dishart," he called out, "that was all nonsense about the locket."

Chapter XIV

The Minister Dances to the Woman's Piping

GAVIN let the doctor's warnings fall in the grass. In his joy over Nanny's deliverance he jumped the garden gate, whose hinges were of yarn, and cleverly caught his hat as it was leaving his head in protest. He then re-entered the mud house staidly. Pleasant was the change. Nanny's home was as a clock that had been run out, and is set going again. Already the old woman was unpacking her box, to increase the distance between herself and the poorhouse. But Gavin only saw her in the background, for the Egyptian, singing at her work, had become the heart of the house. She had flung her shawl over Nanny's shoulders, and was at the fireplace breaking peats with the leg of a stool. She turned merrily to the minister to ask him to chop up his staff for firewood, and he would have answered wittily but could not. Then, as often, the beauty of the Egyptian surprised him into silence. I could never get used to her face myself in the afterdays. It has always held me wondering, like my own Glen Quharity on a summer day, when the sun is lingering and the clouds are on the march, and the glen is never the same for two minutes, but always so beautiful as to make me sad. Never will I attempt to picture the Egyptian as she seemed to Gavin while she bent over Nanny's fire, never will I describe my glen. Yet a hundred times have I hankered after trying to picture both.

An older minister, believing that Nanny's anguish was ended, might have gone on his knees and finished the interrupted prayer, but now Gavin was only doing this girl's bidding.

"Nanny and I are to have a dish of tea, as soon as we have set things to rights," she told him. "Do you think we should invite the minister, Nanny?"

"We couldna dare," Nanny answered quickly. "You'll excuse her, Mr. Dishart, for the presumption?"

"Presumption!" said the Egyptian, making a face.

"Lassie," Nanny said, fearful to offend her new friend, yet horrified at this affront to the minister, "I ken you mean weel, but Mr. Dishart'll think you're putting yourself on an equality wi' him."

She added in a whisper, "Dinna be so free, he's the Auld Licht minister."

The gypsy bowed with mock awe, but Gavin let it pass. He had, indeed, forgotten that he was anybody in particular, and was anxious to stay to tea.

"But there is no water," he remembered, "and is there any tea?"

"I am going out for them and for some other things," the Egyptian explained. "But no," she continued, reflectively, "if I go for the tea, you must go for the water."

"Lassie," cried Nanny, "mind wha you're speaking to. To send a minister to the well!"

"I will go," said Gavin, recklessly lifting the pitcher: "The well is in the wood, I think?"

"Gie me the pitcher, Mr. Dishart," said Nanny, in distress. "What a town there would be if you was seen wi't!"

"Then he must remain here and keep the house till we come back," said the Egyptian, and thereupon departed, with a friendly wave of her hand to the minister.

"She's an awfu' lassie," Nanny said, apologetically, "but it'll just be the way she has been brought up."

"She has been very good to you, Nanny."

"She has; leastwise, she promises to be. Mr. Dishart, she's awa'; what if she doesna come back?"

Nanny spoke nervously, and Gavin drew a long face.

"I think she will," he said faintly. "I am confident of it," he added in the same voice.

"And has she the siller?"

"I believe in her," said Gavin, so doggedly that his own words reassured him. "She has an excellent heart."

"Ay," said Nanny, to whom the minister's faith was more than the Egyptian's promise, "and that's hardly natural in a gaen-aboot body. Yet a gypsy she maun be, for naebody would pretend to be ane that wasna. Tod, she proved she was an Egyptian by dauring to send you to the well."

This conclusive argument brought her prospective dower so close to Nanny's eyes that it hid the poorhouse.

"I suppose she'll gie you the money," she said, "and syne you'll gie me the seven shillings a week?"

"That seems the best plan," Gavin answered.

"And what will you gie it me in?" Nanny asked, with something on her mind. "I would be terrible obliged if you gae it to me in saxpences."

"Do the smaller coins go farther?" Gavin asked, curiously.

"Na, it's no that. But I've heard tell o' folk giving away half-crowns by mistake for twa-shilling bits; ay, and there's something dizzying in ha'en fower-and-twenty pennies in one piece; it has sic terrible little bulk. Sanders had aince a gold sovereign, and he looked at it so often that it seemed to grow smaller and smaller in his hand till he was feared it micht just be a half after all."

Her mind relieved on this matter, the old woman set off for the well. A minute afterwards Gavin went to the door to look for the gypsy, and, behold, Nanny was no farther than the gate. Have you who read ever been sick near to death, and then so far recovered that you could once again stand at your window? If so, you have not forgotten how the beauty of the world struck you afresh, so that you looked long and said many times, "How fair a world it is!" like one who had made a discovery. It was such a look that Nanny gave to the hill and Caddam while she stood at her garden gate.

Gavin returned to the fire and watched a girl in it in an officer's cloak playing at hide and seek with soldiers. After a time he sighed, then looked round sharply to see who had sighed, then, absent-mindedly, lifted the empty kettle and placed it on the glowing peats. He was standing glaring at the kettle, his arms folded, when Nanny returned from the well.

"I've been thinking," she said, "of something that proves the lassie to be just an Egyptian. Ay, I noticed she wasna nane awed when I said you was the Auld Licht minister. Weel, I'se uphaud that came frae her living ower muckle in the open air. Is there no smell o' burning in the house?"

"I have noticed it," Gavin answered, sniffing, "since you came in. I was busy until then, putting on the kettle. The smell is becoming worse."

Nanny had seen the empty kettle on the fire as he began to speak, and so solved the mystery. Her first thought was to snatch the kettle out of the blaze, but remembering who had put it there, she dared not. She sidled toward the hearth instead, and saying craftily, "Ay, here it is; it's a clout among the peats," softly laid the kettle on the earthen floor. It was still red with sparks, however, when the gypsy reappeared.

"Who's burned the kettle?" she asked, ignoring Nanny's signs.

"Lassie," Nanny said, "it was me;" but Gavin, flushing, confessed his guilt.

"Oh, you stupid!" exclaimed the Egyptian, shaking her two ounces of tea (which then cost six shillings the pound) in his face.

At this Nanny wrung her hands, crying, "That's waur than swearing."

"If men," said the gypsy, severely, "would keep their hands in their pockets all day, the world's affairs would be more easily managed."

"Wheesht!" cried Nanny, "if Mr. Dishart cared to set his mind to it, he could make the kettle boil quicker than you or me. But his thochts is on higher things."

"No higher than this," retorted the gypsy, holding her hand level with her brow. "Confess, Mr. Dishart, that this is the exact height of what you were thinking about. See, Nanny, he is blushing as if I meant that he had been thinking about me. He cannot answer, Nanny: we have found him out."

"And kindly of him it is no to answer," said Nanny, who had been examining the gypsy's various purchases; "for what could he answer, except that he would need to be sure o' living a thousand years afore he could spare five minutes on you or me? Of course it would be different if we sat under him."

"And yet," said the Egyptian, with great solemnity, "he is to drink tea at that very table. I hope you are sensible of the honour, Nanny."

"Am I no?" said Nanny, whose education had not included sarcasm. "I'm trying to keep frae thinking o't till he's gone, in case I should let the teapot fall."

"You have nothing to thank me for, Nanny," said Gavin, "but much for which to thank this —this —"

"This haggarty-taggarty Egyptian," suggested the girl. Then, looking at Gavin curiously, she said, "But my name is Babbie."

"That's short for Barbara," said Nanny; "but Babbie what?";

"Yes, Babbie Watt," replied the gypsy, as if one name was as good as another.

"Weel, then, lift the lid off the kettle, Babbie," said Nanny, "for it's boiling ower."

Gavin looked at Nanny with admiration and envy, for she had said Babbie as coolly as if it was the name of a pepper-box.

Babbie tucked up her sleeves to wash Nanny's cups and saucers, which even in the most prosperous days of the mud house had only been in use once a week, and Gavin was so eager to help that he bumped his head on the plate-rack.

"Sit there," said Babbie, authoritatively, pointing, with a cup in her hand, to a stool, "and don't rise till I give you permission."

To Nanny's amazement, he did as he was bid.

"I got the things in the little shop you told me of," the Egyptian continued, addressing the mistress of the house, "but the horrid man would not give them to me until he had seen my money."

"Enoch would be suspicious o' you," Nanny explained, "you being an Egyptian."

"Ah," said Babbie, with a side-glance at the minister, "I am only an Egyptian. Is that why you dislike me, Mr. Dishart?"

Gavin hesitated foolishly over his answer, and the Egyptian, with a towel round her waist, made a pretty gesture of despair.

"He neither likes you nor dislikes you," Nanny explained; "you forget he's a minister."

"That is what I cannot endure," said Babbie, putting the towel to her eyes, "to be neither liked nor disliked. Please hate me, Mr. Dishart, if you cannot lo—ove me."

Her face was behind the towel, and Gavin could not decide whether it was the face or the towel that shook with agitation. He gave Nanny a look that asked, "Is she really crying?" and Nanny telegraphed back, "I question it."

"Come, come," said the minister, gallantly, "I did not say that I disliked you."

Even this desperate compliment had not the desired effect, for the gypsy continued to sob behind her screen.

"I can honestly say," went on Gavin, as solemnly as if he were making a statement in a court of justice, "that I like you."

Then the Egyptian let drop her towel, and replied with equal solemnity:

"Oh, tank oo! Nanny, the minister says me is a dood 'ittle dirl."

"He didna gang that length," said Nanny sharply, to cover Gavin's confusion. "Set the things, Babbie, and I'll make the tea."

The Egyptian obeyed demurely, pretending to wipe her eyes every time Gavin looked at her. He frowned at this, and then she affected to be too overcome to go on with her work.

"Tell me, Nanny," she asked presently, "what sort of man this Enoch is, from whom I bought the things?"

"He is not very regular, I fear," answered Gavin, who felt that he had sat silent and self-conscious on his stool too long.

"Do you mean that he drinks?" asked Babbie.

"No, I mean regular in his attendance."

The Egyptian's face showed no enlightenment.

"His attendance at church," Gavin explained.

"He's far frae it," said Nanny, "and as a body kens, Joe Cruickshanks, the atheist, has the wite o' that. The scoundrel telled Enoch that the great ministers in Edinbury and London believed in no hell except sic as your ain conscience made for you, and ever since syne Enoch has been careless about the future state."

"Ah," said Babbie, waving the Church aside, "what I want to know is whether he is a single man."

"He is not," Gavin replied; "but why do you want to know that?"

"Because single men are such gossips. I am sorry he is not single, as I want him to repeat to everybody what I told him."

"Trust him to tell Susy," said Nanny, "and Susy to tell the town."

"His wife is a gossip?"

"Ay, she's aye tonguing, especially about her teeth. They're folk wi' siller, and she has a set o' false teeth. It's fair scumfishing to hear her blawing about thae teeth, she's so fleid we dinna ken that they're false."

Nanny had spoken jealously, but suddenly she trembled with apprehension.

"Babbie," she cried, "you didna speak about the poorhouse to Enoch?"

The Egyptian shook her head, though of the poorhouse she had been forced to speak, for Enoch, having seen the doctor going home alone, insisted on knowing why.

"But I knew," the gypsy said, "that the Thrums people would be very unhappy until they discovered where you get the money I am to give you, and as that is a secret I hinted to Enoch that your benefactor is Mr. Dishart."

" You should not have said that," interposed Gavin. "I cannot foster such a deception."

"They will foster it without your help," the Egyptian said. "Besides, if you choose, you can say you get the money from a friend."

"Ay, you can say that," Nanny entreated with such eagerness that Babbie remarked a little bitterly:

"There is no fear of Nanny's telling any one that the friend is a gypsy girl."

"Na, na," agreed Nanny, again losing Babbie's sarcasm. "I winna let on. It's so queer to be befriended by an Egyptian."

"It is scarcely respectable," Babbie said.

"It's no," answered simple Nanny.

I suppose Nanny's unintentional cruelty did hurt Babbie as much as Gavin thought. She winced, and her face had two expressions, the one cynical, the other pained. Her mouth curled as if to tell the minister that gratitude was nothing to her, but her eyes had to struggle to keep back a tear. Gavin was touched, and she saw it, and for a moment they were two people who understood each other.

"I, at least," Gavin said in a low voice, "will know who is the benefactress, and think none the worse of her because she is a gypsy."

At this Babbie smiled gratefully to him, and then both laughed, for they had heard Nanny remarking to the kettle, "But I wouldna hae been nane angry if she had telled Enoch that the minister was to take his tea here. Susy'll no believe't though I tell her, as tell her I will."

To Nanny the table now presented a rich appearance, for besides the teapot there were butter and loaf-bread and cheesies: a biscuit of which only Thrums knows the secret.

"Draw in your chair, Mr. Dishart," she said, in suppressed excitement.

"Yes," said Babbie, "you take this chair, Mr. Dishart, and Nanny will have that one, and I can sit humbly on the stool."

But Nanny held up her hands in horror.

"Keep us a'!" she exclaimed; "the lassie thinks her and me is to sit down wi' the minister! We're no to gang that length, Babbie; we're just to stand and serve him, and syne we'll sit down when he has risen.'

'Delightful!" said Babbie, clapping her hands.

"Nanny, you kneel on that side of him, and I will kneel on this. You will hold the butter and I the biscuits.'

But Gavin, as this girl was always forgetting, was a lord of creation.

"Sit down both of you at once!" he thundered, "I command you."

Then the two women fell into their seats; Nanny in terror, Babbie affecting it.

Chapter XV

The Minister Bewitched - Second Sermon Against Women

To Nanny it was a dizzying experience to sit at the head of her own table, and, with assumed calmness, invite the minister not to spare the loaf-bread. Babbie's prattle, and even Gavin's answers, were but an indistinct noise to her, to be as little regarded, in the excitement of watching whether Mr. Dishart noticed that there was a knife for the butter, as the music of the river by a man who is catching trout. Every time Gavin's cup went to his lips Nanny calculated (correctly) how much he had drunk, and yet, when the right moment arrived, she asked in the English voice that is fashionable at ceremonies, "if his cup was toom."

Perhaps it was well that Nanny had these matters to engross her, for though Gavin spoke freely, he was saying nothing of lasting value, and some of his remarks to the Egyptian, if preserved for the calmer contemplation of the morrow, might have seemed frivolous to himself. Usually his observations were scrambled for, like ha'pence at a wedding, but to-day they were only for one person. Infected by the Egyptian's high spirits, Gavin had laid aside the minister with his hat, and what was left was only a young man. He who had stamped his feet at thought of a soldier's cloak now wanted to be reminded of it. The little minister, who used to address himself in terms of scorn every time he wasted an hour, was at present dallying with a teaspoon. He even laughed boisterously, flinging back his head, and little knew that behind Nanny's smiling face was a terrible dread, because his chair had once given way before.

Even though our thoughts are not with our company, the mention of our name is a bell to which we usually answer. Hearing hers Nanny started.

"You can tell me, Nanny," the Egyptian had said, with an arch look at the minister. "Oh, Nanny, for shame! How can you expect to follow our conversation when you only listen to Mr. Dishart?"

"She is saying, Nanny," Gavin broke in, almost gaily for a minister, "that she saw me recently wearing a cloak. You know I have no such thing."

"Na," Nanny answered artlessly, "you have just the thin brown coat wi' the braid round it, forby the ane you have on the now."

"You see," Gavin said to Babbie, "I could not have a new neckcloth, not to speak of a cloak, without everybody in Thrums knowing about it. I dare say Nanny knows all about the braid, and even what it cost."

"Three bawbees the yard at Kyowowy's shop," replied Nanny, promptly, "and your mother sewed it on. Sam'l Fair weather has the marrows o't on his top coat. No that it has the same look on him."

"Nevertheless," Babbie persisted, "I am sure the minister has a cloak; but perhaps he is ashamed of it. No doubt it is hidden away in the garret."

"Na, we would hae kent o't if it was there," said Nanny.

"But it may be in a chest, and the chest may be locked," the Egyptian suggested.

"Ay, but the kist in the garret isna locked," Nanny answered.

"How do you get to know all these things, Nanny?" asked Gavin, sighing.

"Your congregation tells me. Naebody would lay by news about a minister."

"But how do they know?"

"I dinna ken. They just find out, because they're so fond o' you."

"I hope they will never become so fond of me as that," said Babbie. "Still, Nanny, the minister's cloak is hidden somewhere."

"Losh, what would make him hod it?" demanded the old woman. "Folk that has cloaks doesna bury them in boxes."

At the word "bury" Gavin's hand fell on the table,and he turned to Nanny apprehensively.

"That would depend on how the cloak was got," said the cruel Egyptian. "If it was not his own—"

"Lassie," cried Nanny, "behave yoursel'."

"Or if he found it in his possession against his will?" suggested Gavin, slyly. "He might have got it from some one who picked it up cheap."

"From his wife, for instance," said Babbie, whereupon Gavin suddenly became interested in the floor.

"Ay, ay, the minister was hitting at you there, Babbie," Nanny explained, "for the way you made off wi' the captain's cloak. The Thrums folk wondered less at your taking it than at your no keeping it. It's said to be michty grand."

"It was rather like the one the minister's wife gave him," said Babbie.

"The minister has neither a wife nor a cloak," retorted Nanny.

"He isn't married?" asked Babbie, the picture of incredulity.

Nanny gathered from the minister's face that he deputed to her the task of enlightening this ignorant girl, so she replied with emphasis, "Na, they hinna got him yet, and I'm cheated if it doesna tak them all their time."

Thus do the best of women sell their sex for nothing.

"I did wonder," said the Egyptian, gravely, "at any mere woman's daring to marry such a minister."

"Ay," replied Nanny, spiritedly, "but there's dauring limmers wherever there's a single man."

"So I have often suspected," said Babbie, duly shocked. "But, Nanny, I was told the minister had a wife, by one who said he saw her."

"He lied, then," answered Nanny, turning to Gavin for further instructions.

"But, see, the minister does not deny the horrid charge himself."

"No, and for the reason he didna deny the cloak: because it's no worth his while. I'll tell you wha your friend had seen. It would be somebody that would like to be Mrs. Dishart. There's a hantle o' that kind. Ay, lassie, but wishing winna land a woman in a manse."

"It was one of the soldiers," Babbie said, "who told me about her. He said Mr. Dishart introduced her to him."

"Sojers!" cried Nanny. "I could never thole the name o' them. Sanders in his young days hankered after joining them, and so he would, if it hadna been for the fechting. Ay, and now they've ta'en him awa to the gaol, and sworn lies about him. Dinna put any faith in sojers, lassie."

"I was told," Babbie went on, "that the minister's wife was rather like me."

"Heaven forbid!" ejaculated Nanny, so fervently that all three suddenly sat back from the table.

"I'm no meaning," Nanny continued hurriedly, fearing to offend her benefactress, "but what you're the bonniest tid I ever saw out o' an almanack. But you would ken Mr. Dishart's contempt for bonny faces if you had heard his sermon against them. I didna hear it mysel', for I'm no Auld Licht, but it did the work o' the town for an audit days."

If Nanny had not taken her eyes oft Gavin for the moment she would have known that he was now anxious to change the topic. Babbie saw it, and became suspicious.

"When did he preach against the wiles of women, Nanny?"

"It was long ago," said Gavin, hastily.

"No so very lang syne," corrected Nanny. "It was the Sabbath after the sojers was in Thrums; the day you changed your text so hurriedly. Some thocht you wasna weel, but Lang Tammas—"

"Thomas Whamond is too officious," Gavin said with dignity. "I forbid you, Nanny, to repeat his story."

"But what made you change your text?" asked Babbie.

"You see he winna tell," Nanny said, wistfully. "Ay, I dinna deny but what I would like richt to ken. But the session's as puzzled as yoursel', Babbie."

"Perhaps more puzzled," answered the Egyptian, with a smile that challenged Gavin's frowns to combat and overthrew them. "What surprises me, Mr. Dishart, is that such a great man can stoop to see whether women are pretty or not. It was very good of you to remember me to-day. I suppose you recognised me by my frock?"

"By your face," he replied, boldly; "by your eyes."

"Nanny," exclaimed the Egyptian, "did you hear what the minister said?"

"Woe is me," answered Nanny, "I missed it."

"He says he would know me anywhere by my eyes."

"So would I mysel', said Nanny.

"Then what colour are they, Mr. Dishart?" demanded Babbie. "Don't speak, Nanny, for I want to expose him."

She closed her eyes tightly. Gavin was in a quandary. I suppose he had looked at her eyes too long to know much about them.

"Blue," he guessed at last.

"Na, they're black," said Nanny, who had doubtless known this for an hour. I am always marvelling over the cleverness of women, as every one must see who reads this story.

"No but what they micht be blue in some lichts," Nanny added, out of respect to the minister.

"Oh, don't defend him, Nanny," said Babbie, looking reproachfully at Gavin. "I don't see that any minister has a right to denounce women when he is so ignorant of his subject. I will say it, Nanny, and you need not kick me beneath the table."

Was not all this intoxicating to the little minister, who had never till now met a girl on equal terms? At twenty-one a man is a musical instrument given to the other sex, but it is not as instruments learned at school, for when She sits down to it she cannot tell what tune she is about to play. That is because she has no notion of what the instrument is capable. Babbie's kind-heartedness, her gaiety, her coquetry, her moments of sadness, had been a witch's fingers, and Gavin was still trembling under their touch. Even in being taken to task by her there was a charm, for every pout of her mouth, every shake of her head, said, "You like me, and therefore you have given me the right to tease you." Men sign these agreements without reading them. But, indeed, man is a stupid animal at the best, and thinks all his life that he did not propose until he blurted out, "I love you."

It was later than it should have been when the minister left the mud house, and even then he only put on his hat because Babbie said that she must go.

"But not your way," she added. "I go into the wood and vanish. You know, Nanny, I live up a tree."

"Dinna say that," said Nanny, anxiously, "or I'll be fleid about the siller."

"Don't fear about it. Mr. Dishart will get some of it to-morrow at the Kaims. I would bring it here, but I cannot come so far to-morrow."

"Then I'll hae peace to the end o' my days," said the old woman, "and, Babbie, I wish the same to you wi' all my heart."

"Ah," Babbie replied, mournfully, "I have read my fortune, Nanny, and there is not much happiness in it."

"I hope that is not true," Gavin said, simply.

They were standing at the door, and she was looking toward the hill, perhaps without seeing it. All at once it came to Gavin that this fragile girl might have a history far sadder and more turbulent than his.

"Do you really care?" she asked, without looking at him.

"Yes," he said, stoutly, "I care."

"Because you do not know me," she said.

"Because I do know you," he answered.

Now she did look at him.

"I believe," she said, making a discovery, "that you misunderstand me less than those who have known me longer."

This was a perilous confidence, for it at once made Gavin say "Babbie."

"Ah," she answered, frankly, "I am glad to hear that. I thought you did not really like me, because you never called me by my name."

Gavin drew a great breath.

"That was not the reason," he said.

The reason was now unmistakable.

"I was wrong," said the Egyptian, a little alarmed; you do not understand me at all."

She returned to Nanny, and Gavin set off, holding his head high, his brain in a whirl. Five minutes afterwards, when Nanny was at the fire, the diamond ring on her little finger, he came back, looking like one who had just seen sudden death.

"I had forgotten," he said, with a fierceness aimed at himself, "that to-morrow is the Sabbath."

"Need that make any difference?" asked the gypsy.

"At this hour on Monday," said Gavin, hoarsely, "I will be at the Kaims."

He went away without another word, and Babbie watched him from the window. Nanny had not looked up from the ring.

What a pity he is a minister!" the girl said, reflectively. "Nanny, you are not listening."

The old woman was making the ring flash by the light of the fire.

"Nanny, do you hear me? Did you see Mr. Dishart come back?"

"I heard the door open," Nanny answered, without taking her greedy eyes off the ring. "Was it him? Whaur did you get this, lassie?"

"Give it me back, Nanny, I am going now."

But Nanny did not give it back; she put her other hand over it to guard it, and there she crouched, warming herself not at the fire, but at the ring.

"Give it me, Nanny."

"It winna come off my finger." She gloated over it, nursed it, kissed it.

"I must have it, Nanny."

The Egyptian put her hand lightly on the old woman's shoulder, and Nanny jumped up, pressing the ring to her bosom. Her face had become cunning and ugly; she retreated into a corner.

"Nanny, give me back my ring or I will take it from you."

The cruel light of the diamond was in Nanny's eyes for a moment, and then, shuddering, she said, "Tak your ring awa, tak it out o' my sicht."

In the meantime Gavin was trudging home gloomily composing his second sermon against women. I have already given the entry in my own diary for that day: this is his:— "Notes on Jonah. Exchanged vol. xliii., 'European Magazine,' for Owen's 'Justification' (*per* flying stationer). Began Second Samuel. Visited Nanny Webster." There is no mention of the Egyptian.

Chapter XVI

Continued Misbehaviour Of The Egyptian Woman

BY the following Monday it was known at many looms that something sat heavily on the Auld Licht minister's mind. On the previous day he had preached his second sermon of warning to susceptible young men, and his first mention of the word "woman" had blown even the sleepy heads upright. Now he had salt fish for breakfast, and on clearing the table Jean noticed that his knife and fork were uncrossed. He was observed walking into a gooseberry bush by Susie Linn, who possessed the pioneer spring-bed of Thrums, and always knew when her man jumped into it by suddenly finding herself shot to the ceiling. Lunan, the tinsmith, and two women, who had the luck to be in the street at the time, saw him stopping at Dr. McQueen's door, as if about to knock, and then turning smartly away. His hat blew off in the school wynd, where a wind wanders ever, looking for hats, and he chased it so passionately that Lang Tammas went into Allardyce's smiddy to say—

"I dinna like it. Of course he couldna afford to lose his hat, but he should hae run after it mair reverently."

Gavin, indeed, was troubled. He had avoided speaking of the Egyptian to his mother. He had gone to McQueen's house to ask the doctor to accompany him to the Kaims, but with the knocker in his hand he changed his mind, and now he was at the place of meeting alone. It was a day of thaw, nothing to be heard from a distance but the swish of curling-stones through water on Rashie-bog, where the match for the eldership was going on. Around him, Gavin saw only dejected firs with drops of water falling listlessly from them, clods of snow, and grass that rustled as if animals were crawling through it. All the roads were slack.

I suppose no young man to whom society has not become a cheap thing can be in Gavin's position, awaiting the coming of an attractive girl, without giving thought to what he should say to her. When in the pulpit or visiting the sick, words came in a rush to the little minister, but he had set his teeth to determine what to say to the Egyptian.

This was because he had not yet decided which of two women she was. Hardly had he started on one line of thought when she crossed his vision in a new light, and drew him after her.

Her "Need that make any difference?" sang in his ear like another divit, cast this time at religion itself, and now he spoke aloud, pointing his finger at a fir: "I said at the mud house that I believed you because I knew you. To my shame be it said that I spoke falsely. How dared you bewitch me? In your presence I flung away the precious hours in frivolity; I even forgot the Sabbath. For this I have myself to blame. I am an unworthy preacher of the Word. I sinned far more than you who have been brought up godlessly from your cradle. Nevertheless, whoever you are, I call upon you, before we part never to meet again, to repent of your—"

And then it was no mocker of the Sabbath he was addressing, but a woman with a child's face, and there were tears in her eyes. "Do you care?" she was saying, and again he answered, "Yes, I care." This girl's name was not Woman, but Babbie.

Now Gavin made an heroic attempt to look upon both these women at once." Yes, I believe in you," he said to them, "but henceforth you must send your money to Nanny by another messenger. You are a gypsy and I am a minister; and that must part us. I refuse to see you again. I am not angry with you, but as a minister—"

It was not the disappearance of one of the women that clipped this argument short; it was Babbie singing—

"It fell on a day, on a bonny summer day,
When the corn grew green and yellow,
That there fell out a great dispute
Between Argyle and Airly.
"The Duke of Montrose has written to Argyle
To come in the morning early,
An' lead in his men by the back o' Dunkeld
To plunder the bonny house o' Airly."

"Where are you?" cried Gavin in bewilderment.

"I am watching you from my window so high," answered the Egyptian; and then the minister, looking up, saw her peering at him from a fir.

"How did you get up there?" he asked in amazement.

"On my broomstick," Babbie replied, and sang on—

"The lady looked o'er her window sae high,
And oh! but she looked weary,
And there she espied the great Argyle
Come to plunder the bonny house o' Airly."

"What are you doing there?" Gavin said, wrathfully.

"This is my home," she answered. "I told you I lived in a tree."

"Come down at once," ordered Gavin. To which the singer responded—

" 'Come down, come down, Lady Margaret,' he says;
'Come down and kiss me fairly;
Or before the morning clear day light
I'll no leave a standing stane in Airly.' "

"If you do not come down this instant," Gavin said in a rage, "and give me what I was so foolish as to come for, I—"

The Egyptian broke in—

" 'I wouldna kiss thee, great Argyle,
I wouldna kiss thee fairly;
I wouldna kiss thee, great Argyle,
Gin you shouldna leave a standing stane in Airly.' "

"You have deceived Nanny," Gavin cried, hotly, "and you have brought me here to deride me. I will have no more to do with you."

He walked away quickly, but she called after him, "I am coming down. I have the money," and next moment a snowball hit his hat.

"That is for being cross," she explained, appearing so unexpectedly at his elbow that he was taken aback. "I had to come close up to you before I flung it, or it would have fallen over my shoulder. Why are you so nasty to-day? and, oh, do you know you were speaking to yourself?"

"You are mistaken," said Gavin, severely. "I was speaking to you."

"You didn't see me till I began to sing, did you?"

"Nevertheless I was speaking to you, or rather, I was saying to myself what—"

"What you had decided to say to me?" said the delighted gypsy. "Do you prepare your talk like sermons? I hope you have prepared something nice for me. If it is very nice I may give you this bunch of holly."

She was dressed as he had seen her previously, but for a cluster of holly berries at her breast.

"I don't know that you will think it nice," the minister answered, slowly, "but my duty—"

"If it is about duty," entreated Babbie, "don't say it. Don't, and I will give you the berries."

She took the berries from her dress, smiling triumphantly the while like one who had discovered a cure for duty; and instead of pointing the finger of wrath at her, Gavin stood expectant.

"But no," he said, remembering who he was, and pushing the gift from him, "I will not be bribed. I must tell you—"

"Now," said the Egyptian, sadly, "I see you are angry with me. Is it because I said I lived in a tree? Do forgive me for that dreadful lie."

She had gone on her knees before he could stop her, and was gazing imploringly at him, with her hands clasped.

"You are mocking me again," said Gavin, "but I am not angry with you. Only you must understand—"

She jumped up and put her fingers to her ears.

"You see I can hear nothing," she said.

"Listen while I tell you—"

"I don't hear a word. Why do you scold me when I have kept my promise? If I dared take my fingers from my ears I would give you the money for Nanny. And, Mr. Dishart, I must be gone in five minutes."

"In five minutes!" echoed Gavin, with such a dismal face that Babbie heard the words with her eyes, and dropped her hands.

"Why are you in such haste?' he asked, taking the five pounds mechanically, and forgetting all that he had meant to say.

"Because they require me at home," she answered, with a sly glance at her fir. "And, remember, when I run away you must not follow me."

"I won't," said Gavin, so promptly that she was piqued.

"Why not?" she asked. "But of course you only came here for the money. Well, you have got it. Good-bye."

"You know that was not what I meant," said Gavin, stepping after her. "I have told you already that whatever other people say, I trust you. I believe in you, Babbie."

"Was that what you were saying to the tree?" asked the Egyptian, demurely. Then, perhaps thinking it wisest not to press this point, she continued irrelevantly, "It seems such a pity that you are a minister."

"A pity to be a minister!" exclaimed Gavin, indignantly. "Why, why, you — why, Babbie, how have you been brought up?"

"In a curious way," Babbie answered, shortly, "but I can't tell you about that just now. Would you like to hear all about me?" Suddenly she seemed to have become confidential.

"Do you really think me a gypsy?" she asked.

"I have tried not to ask myself that question."

"Why?"

"Because it seems like doubting your word."

"I don't see how you can think of me at all without wondering who I am."

"No, and so I try not to think of you at all."

"Oh, I don't know that you need do that."

"I have not quite succeeded."

The Egyptian's pique had vanished, but she may have thought that the conversation was becoming dangerous, for she said abruptly—

"Well, I sometimes think about you."

"Do you?" said Gavin, absurdly gratified. "What do you think about me?"

"I wonder," answered the Egyptian, pleasantly, "which of us is the taller."

Gavin's fingers twitched with mortification, and not only his fingers but his toes.

"Let us measure," she said, sweetly, putting her back to his. "You are not stretching your neck, are you?"

But the minister broke away from her. 'There is one subject," he said, with great dignity, "that I allow no one to speak of in my presence, and that is — my height."

His face was as white as his cravat when the surprised Egyptian next looked at him, and he was panting like one who has run a mile. She was ashamed of herself, and said so.

"It is a topic I would rather not speak about," Gavin answered dejectedly, "especially to you."

He meant that he would rather be a tall man in her company than in any other, and possibly she knew this, though all she answered was—

"You wanted to know if I am really a gypsy. Well, I am."

"An ordinary gypsy?"

"Do you think me ordinary?"

"I wish I knew what to think of you."

"Ah, well, that is my forbidden topic. But we have a good many ideas in common after all, have we not, though you are only a minis— I mean, though I am only a gypsy?"

There fell between them a silence that gave Babbie time to remember she must go.

"I have already stayed too long," she said. "Give my love to Nanny, and say that I am coming to see her soon, perhaps on Monday. I don't suppose you will be there on Monday, Mr. Dishart?"

"I — I cannot say."

"No, you will be too busy. Are you to take the holly berries?"

"I had better not," said Gavin, dolefully.

"Oh, if you don't want them—"

"Give them to me," he said, and as he took them his hands shook.

"I know why you are looking so troubled," said the Egyptian, archly. "You think I am to ask you the colour of my eyes, and you have forgotten again."

He would have answered, but she checked him.

"Make no pretence," she said, severely; "I know you think they are blue."

She came close to him until her face almost touched his.

"Look hard at them," she said, solemnly, "and after this you may remember that they are black, black, black!"

At each repetition of the word she shook her head in his face. She was adorable. Gavin's arms — but they met on nothing. She had run away.

When the little minister had gone, a man came from behind a tree and shook his fist in the direction taken by the gypsy. It was Rob Dow, black with passion.

"It's the Egyptian!" he cried. "You limmer, wha are you that hae got haud o' the minister?"

He pursued her, but she vanished as from Gavin in Windyghoul.

"A common Egyptian!" he muttered when he had to give up the search. "But take care, you little devil," he called aloud; "take care; if I catch you playing pranks wi' that man again I'll wring your neck like a hen's!"

Chapter XVII

Intrusion of Haggart Into These Pages Against The Author's Wish

MARGARET having heard the doctor say that one may catch cold in the back, had decided instantly to line Gavin's waistcoat with flannel. She was thus engaged, with pins in her mouth and the scissors hiding from her every time she wanted them, when Jean, red and flurried, abruptly entered the room.

"There! I forgot to knock at the door again," Jean exclaimed, pausing contritely.

"Never mind. Is it Rob Dow wanting the minister?" asked Margaret, who had seen Rob pass the manse dyke.

"Na, he wasna wanting to see the minister."

"Ah, then, he came to see you, Jean," said Margaret, archly.

"A widow man!" cried Jean, tossing her head. "But Rob Dow was in no condition to be friendly wi' onybody the now."

"Jean, you don't mean that he has been drinking again?"

"I canna say he was drunk."

"Then what condition was he in?"

"He was in a — a swearing condition," Jean answered, guardedly. "But what I want to speir at you is, can I gang down to the Tenements for a minute? I'll run there and back."

"Certainly you can go,Jean, but you must not run. You are always running. Did Dow bring you word that you were wanted in the Tenements?"

"No exactly, but I — I want to consult Tammas Haggart about — about something."

"About Dow, I believe, Jean?"

"Na, but about something he has done. Oh, ma'am, you surely dinna think I would take a widow man?"

It was the day after Gavin's meeting with the Egyptian at the Kaims, and here is Jean's real reason for wishing to consult Haggart. Half an hour before she hurried to the parlour she had been at the kitchen door wondering whether she should spread out her washing in the garret, or risk hanging it in the courtyard. She had just decided on the garret when she saw Rob Dow morosely regarding her from the gateway.

"Whaur is he?" growled Rob.

"He's out, but it's no for me to say whaur he is," replied Jean, whose weakness was to be considered a church official. "No that I ken," truthfulness compelled her to add, for she had an ambition to be everything she thought Gavin would like a woman to be.

Rob seized her wrists viciously and glowered into her face.

"You're ane o' them," he said.

"Let me go. Ane o' what?"

"Ane o' thae limmers called women."

"Sal," retorted Jean, with spirit, "you're ane o' thae brutes called men. You're drunk, Rob Dow."

"In the legs, maybe, but no higher. I haud a heap."

"Drunk again, after all your promises to the minister! And you said yoursel' that he had pulled you out o' hell by the root."

"It's himsel' that has flung me back again," Rob said, wildly. "Jean Baxter, what does it mean when a minister carries flowers in his pouch; ay, and takes them out to look at them ilka minute?"

"How do you ken about the holly?" asked Jean, off her guard.

"You limmer," said Dow, "you've been in his pouches."

"It's a lie!" cried the outraged Jean. "I just saw the holly this morning in a jug on his chimley."

"Carefully put by? Is it hod on the chimley? Does he stand looking at it? Do you tell me he's fond like o't?"

"Mercy me!" Jean exclaimed, beginning to shake; "wha is she, Rob Dow?"

"Let me see it first in its jug," Rob answered slyly, "and syne I may tell you."

This was not the only time Jean had been asked to show the minister's belongings. Snecky Hobart, among others, had tried on Gavin's hat in the manse kitchen, and felt queer for some time afterwards. Women had been introduced on tip-toe to examine the handle of his umbrella. But Rob had not come to admire. He snatched the holly from Jean's hands, and casting it on the ground pounded it with his heavy boots, crying, "Greet as you like, Jean.

That's the end o' his flowers, and if I had the tawpie he got them frae I would serve her in the same way."

"I'll tell him what you've done," said terrified Jean, who had tried to save the berries at the expense of her fingers.

"Tell him," Dow roared; "and tell him what I said too. Ay, and tell him I was at the Kaims yestreen. Tell him I'm hunting high and low for an Egyptian woman."

He flung recklessly out of the courtyard, leaving Jean looking blankly at the mud that had been holly lately. Not his act of sacrilege was distressing her, but his news. Were these berries a love token? Had God let Rob Dow say they were a gypsy's love token, and not slain him?

That Rob spoke of the Egyptian of the riots Jean never doubted. It was known that the minister had met this woman in Nanny Webster's house, but was it not also known that he had given her such a talking-to as she could never come above? Many could repeat the words in which he had announced to Nanny that his wealthy friends in Glasgow were to give her all she needed. They could also tell how majestic he looked when he turned the Egyptian out of the house. In short, Nanny having kept her promise of secrecy, the people had been forced to construct the scene in the mud house for themselves, and it was only their story that was known to Jean.

She decided that, so far as the gypsy was concerned, Rob had talked trash. He had seen the holly in the minister's hand, and, being in drink, had mixed it up with the gossip about the Egyptian. But that Gavin had preserved the holly because of the donor was as obvious to Jean as that the vase in her hand was empty. Who could she be? No doubt all the single ladies in Thrums were in love with him, but that, Jean was sure, had not helped them a step forward.

To think was to Jean a waste of time. Discovering that she had been thinking, she was dismayed. There were the wet clothes in the basket looking reproachfully at her. She hastened back to Gavin's room with the vase, but it too had eyes, and they said, "When the minister misses his holly he will question you." Now Gavin had already smiled several times to Jean, and once he had marked passages for her in her "Pilgrim's Progress," with the result that she prized the marks more even than the passages. To lose his good opinion was terrible to her. In her perplexity she decided to consult wise Tammas Haggart, and hence her appeal to Margaret.

To avoid Chirsty, the humourist's wife, Jean sought Haggart at his workshop window, which was so small that an old book sufficed for its shutter. Haggart, whom she could see distinctly at his loom, soon guessed from her knocks and signs (for he was strangely quick in the uptake) that she wanted him to open the window.

"I want to speak to you confidentially," Jean said in a low voice. "If you saw a grand man gey fond o' a flower, what would you think?"

"I would think, Jean," Haggart answered, reflectively, "that he had gien siller for't; ay, I would wonder—"

"What would you wonder?"

"I would wonder how muckle he paid."

"But if he was a — a minister, and keepit the flower — say it was a common rose — fondlike on his chimley, what would you think?"

"I would think it was a black-burning disgrace for a minister to be fond of flowers."

"I dinna haud wi' that."

"Jean," said Haggart, "I allow no one to contradict me."

"It wasna my design. But, Tammas, if a — a minister was fond o' a particular flower — say a rose — and you destroyed it by an accident, when he wasna looking, what would you do?"

"I would gie him another rose for't."

"But if you didna want him to ken you had meddled wi't on his chimley, what would you do?"

"I would put the new rose on the chimley, and he would never ken the differ."

'That's what I'll do," muttered Jean, but she said aloud—

"But it micht be that particular rose he liked?"

"Havers, Jean. To a thinking man one rose is identical wi' another rose. But how are you speiring?"

"Just out o' curiosity, and I maun be stepping now. Thank you kindly, Tammas, for your humour."

"You're welcome," Haggart answered, and closed his window.

That day Rob Dow spent in misery, but so little were his fears selfish that he scarcely gave a thought to his conduct at the manse. For an hour he sat at his loom with his arms folded. Then he slouched out of the house, cursing little Micah, so that a neighbour cried: "You drucken scoundrel!" after him. "He may be a wee drunk," said Micah in his father's defence, "but he's no mortal." Rob wandered to the Kaims in search of the Egyptian, and returned home no happier. He flung himself upon his bed and dared Micah to light the lamp. About gloaming he rose, unable to keep his mouth shut on his thoughts any longer, and staggered to the Tenements to consult Haggart. He found the humourist's door ajar, and Wearyworld listening at it. "Out o' the road!" cried Rob, savagely, and flung the policeman into the gutter.

"That was ill-dune, Rob Dow," Wearyworld said, picking himself up leisurely.

"I'm thinking it was weel-dune," snarled Rob.

"Ay," said Wearyworld, "we needna quarrel about a difference o' opeenion; but, Rob—"

Dow, however, had already entered the house and slammed the door.

"Ay, ay," muttered Wearyworld, departing, "you micht hae stood still, Rob, and argued it out wi' me."

In less than an hour after his conversation with Jean at the window it had suddenly struck Haggart that the minister she spoke of must be Mr. Dishart. In two hours he had confided his suspicions to Chirsty. In ten minutes she had filled the house with gossips. Rob arrived to find them in full cry.

"Ay, Rob," said Chirsty, genially, for gossip levels ranks, "you're just in time to hear a queery about the minister."

"Rob," said the Glen Quharity post, from whom I subsequently got the story, "Mr. Dishart has fallen in — in — what do you call the thing, Chirsty?"

Birse knew well what the thing was called, but the word is a staggerer to say in company.

"In love," answered Chirsty, boldly.

"Now we ken what he was doing in the country yestreen," said Snecky Hobart, "the which has been bothering us sair."

"The manse is fu' o' the flowers she sends him," said Tibbie Craik. "Jean's at her wits'-end to ken whaur to put them a'."

"Wha is she?"

It was Rob Dow who spoke. All saw he had been drinking, or they might have wondered at his vehemence. As it was, everybody looked at every other body, and then everybody sighed.

"Ay, wha is she?" repeated several.

"I see you ken nothing about her," said Rob, much relieved; and he then lapsed into silence.

"We ken a' about her," said Snecky, "except just wha she is. Ay, that's what we canna bottom. Maybe you could guess, Tammas?"

"Maybe I could, Sneck," Haggart replied, cautiously; "but on that point I offer no opinion."

"If she bides on the Kaims road," said Tibbie Craik, "she maun be a farmer's dochter. What say you to Bell Finlay?"

"Na, she's U. P. But it micht be Loups o' Malcolm's sister. She's promised to Muckle Haws; but no doubt she would gie him the go-by at a word frae the minister."

"It's mair likely," said Chirsty, "to be the factor at the Spittal's lassie. The factor has a grand garden, and that would account for such basketfuls o' flowers."

"Whaever she is," said Birse, "I'm thinking he could hae done better."

"I'll be fine pleased wi' ony o' them," said Tibbie, who had a magenta silk, and so was jealous of no one.

"It hasna been proved," Haggart pointed out, "that the flowers came frae thae parts. She may be sending them frae Glasgow."

"I aye understood it was a Glasgow lady," said Snecky. "He'll be like the Tilliedrum minister that got a lady to send him to the college on the promise that he would marry her as soon as he got a kirk. She made him sign a paper."

"The far-seeing limmer," exclaimed Chirsty. "But if that's what Mr. Dishart has done, how has he kept it so secret?"

"He wouldna want the women o' the congregation to ken he was promised till after they had voted for him."

"I winna haud wi' that explanation o't," said Haggart, "but I may tell you that I ken for sure she's a Glasgow leddy. Lads, ministers is near aye bespoke afore they're licensed. There's a michty competition for them in the big toons. Ay, the leddies just stand at the college gates, as you may say, and snap them up as they come out."

"And just as well for the ministers, I'se uphaud," said Tibbie, "for it saves them a heap o' persecution when they come to the like o' Thrums. There was Mr. Meiklejohn, the U. P. minister: he was no sooner placed than every genteel woman in the town was persecuting him. The Miss Dobies was the maist shameless; they fair hunted him."

"Ay," said Snecky; "and in the tail o' the day ane o' them snacked him up. Billies, did you ever hear o' a minister being refused?"

"Never."

"Weel, then, I have; and by a widow woman too. His name was Samson, and if it had been Tamson she would hae ta'en him. Ay, you may look, but it's true. Her name was Turnbull, and she had another gent after her, name o' Tibbetts. She couldna make up her mind atween them, and for a while she just keeped them dangling on. Ay, but in the end she took Tibbets. And what, think you, was her reason? As you ken, thae grand folk has their initials on their spoons and nichtgowns. Ay, weel, she thocht it would be mair handy to take Tibbets, because if she had ta'en the minister the *T*'s would have had to be changed *S*'s. It was thoctfu' o' her."

"Is Tibbets living?" asked Haggart sharply.

"No; he's dead."

"What," asked Haggart, "was the corp to trade?"

"I dinna ken."

"I thocht no'," said Haggart, triumphantly. "Weel, I warrant he was a minister too. Ay, catch a woman giving up a minister, except for another minister."

All were looking on Haggart with admiration, when a voice from the door cried—

"Listen, and I'll tell you a queerer ane than that."

"Dagont," cried Birse, "its Wearywarld, and he has been hearkening. Leave him to me."

When the post returned, the conversation was back at Mr. Dishart.

"Yes, lathies," Haggart was saying, "daftness about women comes to all, gentle and simple, common and colleged, humourists and no humourists. You say Mr. Dishart has preached ower muckle at women to stoop to marriage, but that makes no differ. Mony a humourous thing hae I said about women, and yet Chirsty has me. It's the same wi' ministers. A' at aince they see a lassie no' unlike ither lassies, away goes their learning, and they skirl out, 'You dawtie!' That's what comes to all."

"But it hasna come to Mr. Dishart," cried Rob Dow, jumping to his feet. He had sought Haggart to tell him all, but now he saw the wisdom of telling nothing. "I'm sick o' your blathers. Instead o' the minister's being sweet-hearting yesterday, he was just at the Kaims visiting the gamekeeper. I met him in the Wast town-end, and gaed there and back wi' him."

"That's proof it's a Glasgow leddy," said Snecky.

"I tell you there's no leddy ava!" swore Rob.

"Yea, and wha sends the backets o' flowers, then?"

"There was only one flower," said Rob, turning to his host.

"I aye understood," said Haggart heavily, "that there was only one flower."

"But though there was just ane," persisted Chirsty, "what we want to ken is wha gae him it."

"It was me that gae him it," said Rob; "it was growing on the roadside, and I plucked it and gae it to him."

The company dwindled away shamefacedly, yet unconvinced; but Haggart had courage to say slowly—

"Yes, Rob, I had aye a notion that he got it frae you."

Meanwhile, Gavin, unaware that talk about him and a woman unknown had broken out in Thrums, was gazing, sometimes lovingly and again with scorn, at a little bunch of holly-berries which Jean had gathered from her father's garden. Once she saw him fling them out of his window, and then she rejoiced. But an hour afterwards she saw him pick them up, and then she mourned. Nevertheless, to her great delight, he preached his third sermon against Woman on the following Sabbath. It was universally acknowledged to be the best of the series. It was also the last.

Chapter XVIII

Caddam - Love Leading to a Rupture

Gavin told himself not to go near the mud house on the following Monday; but he went. The distance is half a mile, and the time he took was two hours. This was owing to his setting out due west to reach a point due north; yet with the intention of deceiving none save himself. His reason had warned him to avoid the Egyptian, and his desires had consented to be dragged westward because they knew he had started too soon. When the proper time came they knocked reason on the head and carried him straight to Caddam. Here reason came to, and again began to state its case. Desires permitted him to halt, as if to argue the matter out, but were thus tolerant merely because from where he stood he could see Nanny's doorway. When Babbie emerged from it reason seems to have made one final effort, for Gavin quickly took that side of a tree which is loved of squirrels at the approach of an enemy. He looked round the tree-trunk at her, and then reason discarded him. The gypsy had two empty pans in her hands. For a second she gazed in the minister's direction, then demurely leaped the ditch of leaves that separated Nanny's yard from Caddam, and strolled into the wood. Discovering with indignation that he had been skulking behind the tree, Gavin came into the open. How good of the Egyptian, he reflected, to go to the well for water, and thus save the old woman's arms! Reason shouted from near the manse (he only heard the echo) that he could still make up on it. "Come along," said his desires, and marched him prisoner to the well.

The path which Babbie took that day is lost in blaeberry leaves now, and my little maid and I lately searched for an hour before we found the well. It was dry, choked with broom and stones, and broken rusty pans, but we sat down where Babbie and Gavin had talked, and I stirred up many memories. Probably two of those pans, that could be broken in the hands to-day like shortbread, were Nanny's, and almost certainly the stones are fragments from the great slab that used to cover the well. Children like to peer into wells to see what the world is like on the other side, and so this covering was necessary. Rob Angus was the strong man who bore the stone to Caddam, flinging it a yard before him at a time. The well had also a wooden lid with leather hinges, and over this the stone was dragged.

Gavin arrived at the well in time to offer Babbie the loan of his arms. In her struggle she had taken her lips into her mouth, but in vain did she tug at the stone, which refused to do more than turn round on the wood. But for her presence, the minister's efforts would have been equally futile. Though not strong, however, he had the national horror of being beaten before a spectator, and once at school he had won a fight by telling his big antagonist to come on until the boy was tired of pummelling him. As he fought with the stone now, pains shot through his head, and his arms threatened to come away at the shoulders; but remove it he did.

"How strong you are!" Babbie said with open admiration.

I am sure no words of mine could tell how pleased the minister was; yet he knew he was not strong, and might have known that she had seen him do many things far more worthy of admiration without admiring them. This, indeed, is a sad truth, that we seldom give our love to what is worthiest in its object.

"How curious that we should have met here," Babbie said, in her dangerously friendly way,as they filled the pans. "Do you know I quite started when your shadow fell suddenly on the stone. Did you happen to be passing through the wood?"

"No," answered truthful Gavin, "I was looking for you. I thought you saw me from Nanny's door."

"Did you? I only saw a man hiding behind a tree, and of course I knew it could not be you."

Gavin looked at her sharply, but she was not laughing at him.

"It was I," he admitted; "but I was not exactly hiding behind the tree."

"You had only stepped behind it for a moment," suggested the Egyptian.

Her gravity gave way to laughter under Gavin's suspicious looks, but the laughing ended abruptly. She had heard a noise in the wood, Gavin heard it too, and they both turned round in time to see two ragged boys running from them. When boys are very happy they think they must be doing wrong, and in a wood, of which they are among the natural inhabitants, they always take flight from the enemy, adults, if given time. For my own part, when I see a boy drop from a tree I am as little surprised as if he were an apple or a nut. But Gavin was startled, picturing these spies handing in the new sensation about him at every door, as a district visitor distributes tracts. The gypsy noted his uneasiness and resented it.

"What does it feel like to be afraid?" she asked, eyeing him.

"I am afraid of nothing," Gavin answered, offended in turn.

"Yes, you are. When you saw me come out of Nanny's you crept behind a tree; when these boys showed themselves you shook. You are afraid of being seen with me. Go away, then; I don't want you."

"Fear," said Gavin, "is one thing, and prudence is another."

"Another name for it," Babbie interposed.

"Not at all; but I owe it to my position to be careful. Unhappily, you do not seem to feel — to recognise — to know—"

"To know what?"

"Let us avoid the subject."

"No," the Egyptian said, petulantly. "I hate not to be told things. Why must you be 'prudent'?"

"You should see," Gavin replied, awkwardly, "that there is a — a difference between a minister and a gypsy."

"But if I am willing to overlook it?" asked Babbie, impertinently.

Gavin beat the brushwood mournfully with his staff.

"I cannot allow you," he said, "to talk disrespectfully of my calling. It is the highest a man can follow. I wish—"

He checked himself; but he was wishing she could see him in his pulpit.

"I suppose," said the gypsy, reflectively, "one must be very clever to be a minister."

"As for that—" answered Gavin, waving his hand grandly.

"And it must be nice, too," continued Babbie, "to be able to speak for a whole hour to people who can neither answer nor go away. Is it true that before you begin to preach you lock the door to keep the congregation in?"

"I must leave you if you talk in that way."

"I only wanted to know."

"Oh, Babbie, I am afraid you have little acquaintance with the inside of churches. Do you sit under anybody?"

"Do I sit under anybody?" repeated Babbie, blankly.

Is it any wonder that the minister sighed? "Whom do you sit under?" was his form of salutation to strangers.

"I mean, where do you belong?" he said.

"Wanderers," Babbie answered, still misunderstanding him, "belong to nowhere in particular."

"I am only asking you if you ever go to church?"

"Oh, that is what you mean. Yes, I go often."

"What church?"

"You promised not to ask questions."

"I only mean, what denomination do you belong to?"

"Oh, the — the — Is there an English Church denomination?"

Gavin groaned.

"Well, that is my denomination," said Babbie, cheerfully. "Some day, though, I am coming to hear you preach. I should like to see how you look in your gown."

"We don't wear gowns."

"What a shame! But I am coming, nevertheless. I used to like going to church in Edinburgh."

"You have lived in Edinburgh?"

"We gypsies have lived everywhere," Babbie said, lightly, though she was annoyed at having mentioned Edinburgh.

"But all gypsies don't speak as you do?" said Gavin, puzzled again. "I don't understand you."

"Of course you dinna," replied Babbie, in broad Scotch. "Maybe, if you did, you would think that it's mair imprudent in me to stand here cracking clavers wi' the minister than for the minister to waste his time cracking wi' me."

"Then why do it?"

"Because — Oh, because prudence and I always take different roads."

"Tell me who you are, Babbie," the minister entreated; "at least, tell me where your encampment is."

"You have warned me against imprudence," she said.

"I want," Gavin continued, earnestly, "to know your people, your father and mother."

"Why?"

"Because," he answered, stoutly, "I like their daughter."

At that Babbie's fingers played on one of the pans, and, for the moment, there was no more badinage in her.

"You are a good man," she said, abruptly; "but you will never know my parents."

"Are they dead?"

"They may be; I cannot tell."

"This is all incomprehensible to me."

"I suppose it is. I never asked any one to understand me."

"Perhaps not," said Gavin, excitedly; "but the time has come when I must know everything of you that is to be known."

Babbie receded from him in quick fear.

"You must never speak to me in that way again," she said, in a warning voice.

"In what way?"

Gavin knew what way very well, but he thirsted to hear in her words what his own had implied. She did not choose to oblige him, however.

"You never will understand me," she said. "I daresay I might be more like other people now, if — if I had been brought up differently. Not," she added, passionately, "that I want to be like others. Do you never feel, when you have been living a humdrum life for months, that you must break out of it, or go crazy?"

Her vehemence alarmed Gavin, who hastened to reply—

"My life is not humdrum. It is full of excitement, anxieties, pleasures, and I am too fond of the pleasures. Perhaps it is because I have more of the luxuries of life than you that I am so content with my lot."

"Why, what can you know of luxuries?"

"I have eighty pounds a year."

Babbie laughed. "Are ministers so poor?" she asked, calling back her gravity.

"It is a considerable sum," said Gavin, a little hurt, for it was the first time he had ever heard any one speak disrespectfully of eighty pounds.

The Egyptian looked down at her ring, and smiled.

"I shall always remember your saying that," she told him, "after we have quarrelled."

"We shall not quarrel," said Gavin, decidedly.

"Oh, yes, we shall."

"We might have done so once, but we know each other too well now."

"That is why we are to quarrel."

"About what?" said the minister. "I have not blamed you for deriding my stipend, though how it can seem small in the eyes of a gypsy—"

"Who can afford," broke in Babbie, "to give Nanny seven shillings a week?"

"True," Gavin said, uncomfortably, while the Egyptian again toyed with her ring. She was too impulsive to be reticent except now and then, and suddenly she said, "You have looked at this ring before now. Do you know that if you had it on your finger you would be more worth robbing than with eighty pounds in each of your pockets?"

"Where did you get it?" demanded Gavin, fiercely.

"I am sorry I told you that," the gypsy said, regretfully.

"Tell me how you got it," Gavin insisted, his face now hard.

"Now, you see, we are quarrelling."

"I must know."

"Must know!" You forget yourself," she said, haughtily.

"No, but I have forgotten myself too long. Where did you get that ring?"

"Good afternoon to you," said the Egyptian, lifting her pans.

"It is not good afternoon," he cried, detaining her. "It is good-bye for ever, unless you answer me."

"As you please," she said. "I will not tell you where I got my ring. It is no affair of yours."

"Yes, Babbie, it is."

She was not, perhaps, greatly grieved to hear him say so, for she made no answer.

"You are no gypsy," he continued, suspiciously.

"Perhaps not," she answered, again taking the pans.

"This dress is but a disguise."

"It may be. Why don't you go away and leave me?"

"I am going," he replied, wildly. "I will have no more to do with you. Formerly I pitied you, but—"

He could not have used a word more calculated to rouse the Egyptian's ire, and she walked away with her head erect. Only once did she look back, and it was to say—

"This is prudence — now."

Chapter XIX

Circumstances Leading To The First Sermon In Approval Of Women

A young man thinks he alone of mortals is impervious to love, and so the discovery that he is in it suddenly alters his views of his own mechanism. It is thus not unlike a rap on the funny-bone. Did Gavin make this discovery when the Egyptian left him? Apparently he only came to the brink of it and stood blind. He had driven her from him for ever, and his sense of loss was so acute that his soul cried out for the cure rather than for the name of the malady.

In time he would have realised what had happened, but time was denied him, for just as he was starting for the mud house Babbie saved his dignity by returning to him. It was not her custom to fix her eyes on the ground as she walked, but she was doing so now, and at the same time swinging the empty pans. Doubtless she had come back for more water, in the belief that Gavin had gone. He pronounced her name with a sense of guilt, and she looked up surprised, or seemingly surprised, to find him still there.

"I thought you had gone away long ago," she said stiffly.

"Otherwise," asked Gavin the dejected, "you would not have come back to the well?"

"Certainly not."

"I am very sorry. Had you waited another moment I should have been gone."

This was said in apology, but the wilful Egyptian chose to change its meaning.

"You have no right to blame me for disturbing you," she declared with warmth.

"I did not. I only—"

"You could have been a mile away by this time. Nanny wanted more water."

Babbie scrutinised the minister sharply as she made this statement. Surely her conscience troubled her, for on his not answering her immediately she said, "Do you presume to disbelieve me? What could have made me return except to fill the pans again?"

"Nothing," Gavin admitted eagerly, "and I assure you—"

Babbie should have been grateful to his denseness, but it merely set her mind at rest.

"Say anything against me you choose," she told him. "Say it as brutally as you like, for I won't listen." She stopped to hear his response to that, and she looked so cold that it almost froze on Gavin's lips.

"I had no right," he said, dolefully, "to speak to you as I did."

"You had not," answered the proud Egyptian. She was looking away from him to show that his repentance was not even interesting to her. However, she had forgotten already not to listen.

"What business is it of mine?" asked Gavin, amazed at his late presumption, "whether you are a gypsy or no?"

"None whatever."

"And as for the ring—"

Here he gave her an opportunity of allowing that his curiosity about the ring was warranted. She declined to help him, however, and so he had to go on.

"The ring is yours," he said, "and why should you not wear it?"

"Why, indeed?"

"I am afraid I have a very bad temper."

He paused for a contradiction, but she nodded her head in agreement.

"And it is no wonder," he continued, "that you think me a — a brute."

"I'm sure it is not."

"But Babbie, I want you to know that I despise myself for my base suspicions. No sooner did I see them than I loathed them and myself for harbouring them. Despite this mystery, I look upon you as a noble-hearted girl. I shall always think of you so."

This time Babbie did not reply.

"That was all I had to say," concluded Gavin, "except that I hope you will not punish Nanny for my sins. Good-bye."

"Good-bye," said the Egyptian, who was looking at the well. The minister's legs could not have heard him give the order to march, for they stood waiting.

"I thought," said the Egyptian, after a moment, "that you said you were going."

"I was only — brushing my hat," Gavin answered with dignity. "You want me to go?"

She bowed, and this time he did set off.

"You can go if you like," she remarked now.

He turned at this.

"But you said—" he began, diffidently.

"No, I did not," she answered, with indignation.

He could see her face at last.

"You — you are crying!" he exclaimed, in bewilderment.

"Because you are so unfeeling," sobbed Babbie.

"What have I said, what have I done?" cried Gavin, in an agony of self-contempt. "Oh, that I had gone away at once!"

"That is cruel."

"What is?"

"To say that."

"What did I say?"

"That you wished you had gone away.'

'But surely," the minister faltered, "you asked me to go."

"How can you say so?" asked the gypsy, reproachfully.

Gavin was distracted. "On my word," he said, earnestly, "I thought you did. And now I have made you unhappy. Babbie, I wish I were anybody but myself; I am a hopeless lout."

"Now you are unjust," said Babbie, hiding her face.

"Again? To you?"

"No, you stupid," she said, beaming on him in her most delightful manner, "to yourself!"

She gave him both her hands impetuously, and he did not let them go until she added:

"I am so glad that you are reasonable at last. Men are so much more unreasonable than women, don't you think?"

"Perhaps we are," Gavin said, diplomatically.

"Of course you are. Why, every one knows that. Well, I forgive you; only remember, you have admitted that it was all your fault?"

She was pointing her finger at him like a school mistress, and Gavin hastened to answer—

"You were not to blame at all."

"I like to hear you say that," explained the representative of the more reasonable sex, "because it was really all my fault."

"No, no."

"Yes it was; but of course I could not say so until you had asked my pardon. You must understand that?"

The representative of the less reasonable sex could not understand it, but he agreed recklessly, and it seemed so plain to the woman that she continued confidentially—

"I pretended that I did not want to make it up, but I did."

"Did you?" asked Gavin, elated.

"Yes, but nothing could have induced me to make the first advance. You see why?"

"Because I was so unreasonable?" asked Gavin, doubtfully.

"Yes, and nasty. You admit you were nasty?"

"Undoubtedly, I have an evil temper. It has brought me to shame many times."

"Oh, I don't know," said the Egyptian, charitably. "I like it. I believe I admire bullies."

"Did I bully you?"

"I never knew such a bully. You quite frightened me."

Gavin began to be less displeased with himself.

"You are sure," inquired Babbie, "that you had no right to question me about the ring?"

"Certain," answered Gavin.

"Then I will tell you all about it," said Babbie, "for it is natural that you should want to know."

He looked eagerly at her, and she had become serious and sad.

"I must tell you at the same time," she said, "who I am, and then — then we shall never see each other any more."

"Why should you tell me?" cried Gavin, his hand rising to stop her.

"Because you have a right to know," she replied, now too much in earnest to see that she was yielding a point. "I should prefer not to tell you; yet there is nothing wrong in my secret, and it may make you think of me kindly, when I have gone away."

"Don't speak in that way, Babbie, after you have forgiven me."

"Did I hurt you? It was only because I know that you cannot

trust me while I remain a mystery. I know you would try to trust me, but doubts would cross your mind. Yes, they would; they are the shadows that mysteries cast. Who can believe a gypsy if the odds are against her?"

"I can," said Gavin; but she shook her head, and so would he had he remembered three recent sermons of his own preaching.

"I had better tell you all," she said, with an effort.

"It is my turn now to refuse to listen to you," exclaimed Gavin, who was only a chivalrous boy. "Babbie, I should like to hear your story, but until you want to tell it to me I will not listen to it. I have faith in your honour, and that is sufficient."

It was boyish, but I am glad Gavin said it; and now Babbie admired something in him that deserved admiration. His faith, no doubt, made her a better woman.

"I admit that I would rather tell you nothing just now," she said, gratefully. "You are sure you will never say again that you don't understand me?"

"Quite sure," said Gavin, bravely. "And by-and-by you will offer to tell me of your free will?"

"Oh, don't let us think of the future," answered Babbie. "Let us be happy for the moment."

This had been the Egyptian's philosophy always, but it was ill-suited for Auld Licht ministers, as one of them was presently to discover.

"I want to make one confession, though," Babbie continued, almost reluctantly. "When you were so nasty a little while ago, I didn't go back to Nanny's. I stood watching you from behind a tree, and then, for an excuse to come back, I — I poured out the water. Yes, and I told you another lie. I really came back to admit that it was all my fault, if I could not get you to say that it was yours. I am so glad you gave in first."

She was very near him, and the tears had not yet dried on her eyes. They were laughing eyes, eyes in distress, imploring eyes. Her pale face, smiling, sad, dimpled, yet entreating forgiveness, was the one prominent thing in the world to him just then. He wanted to kiss her. He would have done it as soon as her eyes rested on his, but she continued without regarding him—

"How mean that sounds! Oh, if I were a man I should wish to be everything that I am not, and nothing that I am. I should scorn to be a liar, I should choose to be open in all things, I should try to fight the world honestly. But I am only a woman, and so — well, that is the kind of man I should like to marry."

"A minister may be all these things," said Gavin, breathlessly.

"The man I could love," Babbie went on, not heeding him, almost forgetting that he was there, "must not spend his days in idleness as the men I know do."

"I do not."

"He must be brave, no mere worker among others, but a leader of men."

"All ministers are."

"Who makes his influence felt."

"Assuredly."

"And takes the side of the weak against the strong, even though the strong be in the right."

"Always my tendency."

"A man who has a mind of his own, and having once made it up, stands to it in defiance even of—"

"Of his session."

"Of the world. He must understand me."

"I do."

"And be my master."

"It is his lawful position in the house."

"He must not yield to my coaxing or tempers."

"It would be weakness."

"But compel me to do his bidding; yes, even thrash me if—"

"If you won't listen to reason. Babbie," cried Gavin, "I am that man!"

Here the inventory abruptly ended, and these two people found themselves staring at each other, as if of a sudden they had heard something dreadful. I do not know how long they stood thus, motionless and horrified. I cannot tell even which stirred first. All I know is that almost simultaneously they turned from each other and hurried out of the wood in opposite directions.

Chapter XX

End of the State of Indecision

Long before I had any thought of writing this story, had told it so often to my little maid that she now knows some of it better than I. If you saw me looking up from my paper to ask her, "What was it that Birse said to Jean about the minister's flowers?" or, "Where was Hendry Munn hidden on the night of the riots?" and heard her confident answers, you would conclude that she had been in the thick of these events, instead of born many years after them. I mention this now because I have reached a point where her memory contradicts mine. She maintains that Rob Dow was told of the meeting in the wood by the two boys whom it disturbed, while my own impression is that he was a witness of it. If she is right, Rob must have succeeded in frightening the boys into telling no other person, for certainly the scandal did not spread in Thrums. After all, however, it is only important to know that Rob did learn of the meeting. Its first effect was to send him sullenly to the drink.

Many a time since these events have I pictured what might have been their upshot had Dow confided their discovery to me. Had I suspected why Rob was grown so dour again, Gavin's future might have been very different. I was meeting Rob now and again in the glen, asking, with an affected carelessness he did not bottom, for news of the little minister, but what he told me was only the gossip of the town; and what I should have known, that Thrums might never know it, he kept to himself. I suppose he feared to speak to Gavin, who made several efforts to reclaim him, but without avail.

Yet Rob's heart opened for a moment to one man, or rather was forced open by that man. A few days after the meeting at the well, Rob was bringing the smell of whisky with him down Banker's Close when he ran against a famous staff, with which the doctor pinned him to the wall.

"Ay," said the outspoken doctor, looking contemptuously into Rob's bleary eyes, "so this is what your conversion amounts to? Faugh! Rob Dow, if you were half a man the very thought of what

Mr. Dishart has done for you would make you run past the public-houses."

"It's the thocht o' him that sends me running to them," growled Rob, knocking down the staff. "Let me alane."

"What do you mean by that?" demanded McQueen, hooking him this time.

"Speir at himsel'; speir at the woman."

"What woman?"

"Take your staff out o' my neck."

"Not till you tell me why you, of all people, are speaking against the minister."

Torn by a desire for a confidant and loyalty to Gavin, Rob was already in a fury.

"Say again," he burst forth, "that I was speaking agin the minister and I'll practise on you what I'm awid to do to her."

"Who is she?"

"Wha's wha?"

"The woman whom the minister—"

"I said nothing about a woman," said poor Rob, alarmed for Gavin. "Doctor, I'm ready to swear afore a bailie that I never saw them thegither at the Kaims."

"The Kaims!" exclaimed the doctor, suddenly enlightened. "Pooh! you only mean the Egyptian. Rob, make your mind easy about this. I know why he met her there."

"Do you ken that she has bewitched him; do you ken I saw him trying to put his arms round her; do you ken they have a trysting-place in Caddam wood?"

This came from Rob in a rush, and he would fain have called it all back.

"I'm drunk, doctor, roaring drunk," he said, hastily, "and it wasna the minister I saw ava; it was another man."

Nothing more could the doctor draw from Rob, but he had heard sufficient to smoke some pipes on. Like many who pride themselves on being recluses, McQueen loved the gossip that came to him uninvited; indeed, he opened his mouth to it as greedily as any man in Thrums. He respected Gavin, however, too much to find this new dish palatable, and so his researches to discover whether other Auld Lichts shared Rob's fears were conducted with caution. "Is there no word of your minister's getting a wife yet?" he asked several, but only got for answers, "There's word o' a Glasgow leddy's sending him baskets o' flowers," or "He has his een open, but he's taking his time; ay, he's looking for the blade o' corn in the stack o' chaff."

This convinced McQueen that the congregation knew nothing of the Egyptian, but it did not satisfy him, and he made an opportunity of inviting Gavin into the surgery. It was, to the doctor, the cosiest nook in his house, but to me and many others a room that smelled of hearses. On the top of the pipes and tobacco tins that littered the table there usually lay a death certificate, placed there deliberately by the doctor to scare his sister, who had a passion for putting the surgery to rights.

"By the way," McQueen said, after he and Gavin had talked a little while, "did I ever advise you to smoke?"

"It is your usual form of salutation," Gavin answered, laughing. "But I don't think you ever supplied me with a reason."

"I daresay not. I am too experienced a doctor to cheapen my prescriptions in that way. However, here is one good reason. I have noticed, sir, that at your age a man is either a slave to a pipe or to a woman. Do you want me to lend you a pipe now?"

"Then I am to understand," asked Gavin, slyly, "that your locket came into your possession in your pre-smoking days, and that you merely wear it from habit?"

"Tuts!" answered the doctor, buttoning his coat. "I told you there was nothing in the locket. If there is, I have forgotten what it is."

"You are a hopeless old bachelor, I see," said Gavin, unaware that the doctor was probing him. He was surprised next moment to find McQueen in the ecstasies of one who has won a rubber.

"Now, then," cried the jubilant doctor, "as you have confessed so much, tell me all about her. Name and address, please."

"Confess! What have I confessed?"

"It won't do, Mr. Dishart, for even your face betrays you. No, no, I am an old bird, but I have not forgotten the ways of the fledglings. 'Hopeless bachelor,' sir, is a sweetmeat in every young man's mouth until of a sudden he finds it sour, and that means the banns. When is it to be?"

"We must find the lady first," said the minister, uncomfortably.

"You tell me, in spite of that face, that you have not fixed on her?"

"The difficulty, I suppose, would be to persuade her to fix on me."

"Not a bit of it. But you admit there is some one?"

"Who would have me?"

"You are wriggling out of it. Is it the banker's daughter?"

"No," Gavin cried.

"I hear you have walked up the back wynd with her three times this week. The town is in a ferment about it."

"She is a great deal in the back wynd."

"Fiddle-de-dee! I am oftener in the back wynd than you, and I never meet her there."

"That is curious."

"No, it isn't, but never mind. Perhaps you have fallen to Miss Pennycuick's piano? Did you hear it going as we passed the house?"

"She seems always to be playing on her piano."

"Not she; but you are supposed to be musical, and so when she sees you from her window she begins to thump. If I am in the school wynd and hear the piano going, I know you will turn the corner immediately. However, I am glad to hear it is not Miss Pennycuick. Then it is the factor at the Spittal's lassie? Well done, sir. You should arrange to have the wedding at the same time as the old earl's, which comes off in the summer, I believe."

"One foolish marriage is enough in a day, doctor."

"Eh? You call him a fool for marrying a young wife? Well, no doubt he is, but he would have been a bigger fool to marry an old one. However, it is not Lord Rintoul we are discussing, but Gavin Dishart. I suppose you know that the factor's lassie is an heiress?"

"And, therefore, would scorn me."

"Try her," said the doctor, drily. "Her father and mother, as I know, married on a ten-pound note. But if I am wrong again, I must adopt the popular view in Thrums. It is a Glasgow lady after all? Man, you needn't look indignant at hearing that the people are discussing your intended. You can no more stop it than a doctor's orders could keep Lang Tammas out of church. They have discovered that she sends you flowers twice every week."

"They never reach me," answered Gavin, then remembered the holly and winced.

"Some," persisted the relentless doctor, "even speak of your having been seen together; but of course, if she is a Glasgow lady, that is a mistake."

"Where did they see us?" asked Gavin, with a sudden trouble in his throat.

"You are shaking," said the doctor, keenly, "like a medical student at his first operation. But as for the story that you and the lady have been seen together, I can guess how it arose. Do you remember that gypsy girl?"

The doctor had begun by addressing the fire, but he suddenly wheeled round and fired his question in the minister's face. Gavin, however, did not even blink.

"Why should I have forgotten her?" he replied, coolly.

"Oh, in the stress of other occupations. But it was your getting the money from her at the Kaims for Nanny that I was to speak of. Absurd though it seems, I think some dotard must have seen you and her at the Kaims, and mistaken her for the lady."

McQueen flung himself back in his chair to enjoy this joke.

"Fancy mistaking that woman for a lady!" he said to Gavin, who had not laughed with him.

"I think Nanny has some justification for considering her a lady," the minister said, firmly.

"Well, I grant that. But what made me guffaw was a vision of the harum-scarum, devil-may-care little Egyptian mistress of an Auld Licht manse!"

"She is neither harum-scarum, nor devil-may-care," Gavin answered without heat, for he was no longer a distracted minister. "You don't understand her as I do."

"No, I seem to understand her differently."

"What do you know of her?"

"That is just it," said the doctor, irritated by Gavin's coolness. "I know she saved Nanny from the poorhouse, but I don't know where she got the money. I know she can talk fine English when she chooses, but I don't know where she learned it. I know she heard that the soldiers were coming to Thrums before they knew of their destination themselves, but I don't know who told her. You who understand her can doubtless explain these matters?"

"She offered to explain them to me," Gavin answered, still unmoved, "but I forbade her."

"Why?"

"It is no business of yours, doctor. Forgive me for saying so."

"In Thrums," replied McQueen, "a minister's business is everybody's business. I have often wondered who helped her to escape from the soldiers that night. Did she offer to explain that to you?"

"She did not."

"Perhaps," said the doctor, sharply, "because it was unnecessary?"

"That was the reason."

"You helped her to escape?"

"I did."

"And you are not ashamed of it?" "I am not."

"Why were you so anxious to screen her?"

"She saved some of my people from gaol."

"Which was more than they deserved."

"I have always understood that you concealed two of them in your own stable."

"Maybe I did," the doctor had to allow. "But I took my stick to them next morning. Besides, they were Thrums folk, while you had never set eyes on that imp of mischief before."

"I cannot sit here, doctor, and hear her called names," Gavin said, rising, but McQueen gripped him by the shoulder.

"For pity's sake, sir, don't let us wrangle like a pair of women. I brought you here to speak my mind to you, and speak it I will. I warn you, Mr. Dishart, that you are being watched. You have been seen meeting this lassie in Caddam as well as at the Kaims."

"Let the whole town watch, doctor. I have met her openly."

"And why? Oh, don't make Nanny your excuse.

"I won't. I met her because I love her."

"Are you mad?" cried McQueen. "You speak as if you would marry her."

"Yes," replied Gavin, determinedly, "and I mean to do it."

The doctor flung up his hands.

"I give you up," he said, raging. "I give you up. Think of your congregation, man."

"I have been thinking of them, and as soon as I have a right to do so I shall tell them what I have told you."

"And until you tell them I will keep your madness to myself, for I warn you that, as soon as they do know, there will be a vacancy in the Auld Licht kirk of Thrums."

"She is a woman," said Gavin, hesitating, though preparing to go, "of whom any minister might be proud."

"She is a woman," the doctor roared, "that no congregation would stand. Oh, if you will go, there is your hat."

Perhaps Gavin's face was whiter as he left the house than when he entered it, but there was no other change. Those who were watching him decided that he was looking much as usual, except that his mouth was shut very firm, from which they concluded that he had been taking the doctor to task for smoking. They also noted that he returned to McQueen's house within half an hour after leaving it, but remained no time.

Some explained this second visit by saying that the minister had forgotten his cravat, and had gone back for it. What really sent him back, however, was his conscience. He had said to McQueen that he helped Babbie to escape from the soldiers because of her kindness to his people, and he returned to own that it was a lie.

Gavin knocked at the door of the surgery, but entered without waiting for a response. McQueen was no longer stamping through the room, red and furious. He had even laid aside his pipe. He was sitting back in his chair, looking half-mournfully, half-contemptuously, at something in his palm. His hand closed instinctively when he heard the door open, but Gavin had seen that the object was an open locket.

"It was only your reference to the thing," the detected doctor said, with a grim laugh, "that made me open it. Forty years ago, sir, I — Phew! it is forty-two years, and I have not got over it yet." He closed the locket with a snap. "I hope you have come back, Dishart, to speak more rationally?"

Gavin told him why he had come back, and the doctor said he was a fool for his pains.

"Is it useless, Dishart, to make another appeal to you?"

"Quite useless, doctor," Gavin answered, promptly. "My mind is made up at last."

Chapter XXI

Night — Margaret — Flashing of a Lantern

That evening the little minister sat silently in his parlour. Darkness came, and with it weavers rose heavy-eyed from their looms, sleepy children sought their mothers, and the gate of the field above the manse fell forward to let cows pass to their byre; the great Bible was produced in many homes, and the ten o'clock bell clanged its last word to the night. Margaret had allowed the lamp to burn low. Thinking that her boy slept, she moved softly to his side and spread her shawl over his knees. He had forgotten her. The doctor's warnings scarcely troubled him. He was Babbie's lover. The mystery of her was only a veil hiding her from other men, and he was looking through it upon the face of his beloved.

It was a night of long ago, but can you not see my dear Margaret still as she bends over her son? Not twice in many days dared the minister snatch a moment's sleep from grey morning to midnight, and, when this did happen, he jumped up by-and-by in shame, to revile himself for an idler and ask his mother wrathfully why she had not tumbled him out of his chair? To-night Margaret was divided between a desire to let him sleep and a fear of his self-reproach when he awoke; and so, perhaps, the tear fell that roused him.

"I did not like to waken you," Margaret said apprehensively. "You must have been very tired, Gavin?

"I was not sleeping, mother," he said, slowly. "I was only thinking."

"Ah, Gavin, you never rise from your loom. It is hardly fair that your hands should be so full of other people's troubles."

"They only fill one hand, mother; I carry the people's joys in the other hand, and that keeps me erect, like a woman between her pan and pitcher. I think the joys have outweighed the sorrows since we came here."

"It has been all joy to me, Gavin, for you never tell me of the sorrows. An old woman has no right to be so happy."

"Old woman, mother!" said Gavin. But his indignation was vain. Margaret was an old woman. I made her old before her time.

"As for these terrible troubles," he went on, "I forget them the moment I enter the garden and see you at your window. And, maybe, I keep some of the joys from you as well as the troubles."

Words about Babbie leaped to his mouth, but with an effort he restrained them. He must not tell his mother of her until Babbie of her free will had told him all there was to tell.

"I have been a selfish woman, Gavin."

"You selfish, mother!" Gavin said, smiling. "Tell me when you did not think of others before yourself?"

"Always, Gavin. Has it not been selfishness to hope that you would never want to bring another mistress to the manse? Do you remember how angry you used to be in Glasgow when I said that you would marry some day?"

"I remember," Gavin said, sadly.

"Yes; you used to say, 'Don't speak of such a thing, mother, for the horrid thought of it is enough to drive all the Hebrew out of my head.' Was not that lightning just now?"

"I did not see it. What a memory you have, mother, for all the boyish things I said."

"I can't deny," Margaret admitted with a sigh, "that I liked to hear you speak in that way, though I knew you would go back on your word. You see, you have changed already."

"How, mother?" asked Gavin, surprised.

"You said just now that those were boyish speeches. Gavin, I can't understand the mothers who are glad to see their sons married; though I had a dozen I believe it would be a wrench to lose one of them. It would be different with daughters. You are laughing, Gavin!"

"Yes, at your reference to daughters. Would you not have preferred me to be a girl?"

" 'Deed I would not," answered Margaret, with tremendous conviction. "Gavin, every woman on earth, be she rich or poor, good or bad, offers up one prayer about her firstborn, and that is, 'May he be a boy!'"

"I think you are wrong, mother. The banker's wife told me that there is nothing for which she thanks the Lord so much as that all her children are girls."

"May she be forgiven for that, Gavin!" exclaimed Margaret; "though she maybe did right to put the best face on her humiliation. No, no, there are many kinds of women in the world, but there never was one yet that didn't want to begin with a laddie. You can speculate about a boy so much more than about a girl. Gavin, what is it a woman thinks about the day her son is born? yes, and the day before too? She is picturing him a grown man, and a slip of a lassie taking him from her. Ay, that is where the lassies have their revenge on the mothers. I remember as if it were this morning a Harvie fishwife patting your head and asking who was your sweetheart, and I could never thole the woman again. We were at the door of the cottage, and I mind I gripped you up in my arms. You had on a tartan frock with a sash and diamond socks. When I look back, Gavin, it seems to me that you have shot up from that frock to manhood in a single hour."

"There are not many mothers like you," Gavin said, laying his hand fondly on Margaret's shoulder.

"There are many better mothers, but few such sons. It is easily seen why God could not afford me another. Gavin, I am sure that was lightning."

"I think it was; but don't be alarmed, mother."

"I am never frightened when you are with me."

"And I always will be with you."

"Ah, if you were married—"

"Do you think," asked Gavin, indignantly, "that it would make any difference to you?"

Margaret did not answer. She knew what a difference it would make.

"Except," continued Gavin, with a man's obtuseness, "that you would have a daughter as well as a son to love you and take care of you."

Margaret could have told him that men give themselves away needlessly who marry for the sake of their mother, but all she said was—

"Gavin, I see you can speak more composedly of marrying now than you spoke a year ago. If I did not know better, I should think a Thrums young lady had got hold of you."

It was a moment before Gavin replied; then he said, gaily—

"Really, mother, the way the best of women speak of each other is lamentable. You say I should be better married, and then you take for granted that every marriageable woman in the neighbourhood is trying to kidnap me. I am sure you did not take my father by force in that way."

He did not see that Margaret trembled at the mention of his father. He never knew that she was many times pining to lay her head upon his breast and tell him of me. Yet I cannot but believe that she always shook when Adam Dishart was spoken of between them. I cannot think that the long-cherishing of the secret which was hers and mine kept her face steady when that horror suddenly confronted her as now. Gavin would have suspected much had he ever suspected anything.

"I know," Margaret said, courageously, "that you would be better married; but when it comes to selecting the woman I grow fearful. Oh, Gavin!" she said, earnestly, "it is an awful thing to marry the wrong man!"

Here in a moment had she revealed much, though far from all, and there must have been many such moments between them. But Gavin was thinking of his own affairs.

"You mean the wrong woman, don't you, mother?" he said, and she hastened to agree. But it was the wrong man she meant.

"The difficulty, I suppose, is to hit upon the right one?" Gavin said, blithely.

"To know which is the right one in time," answered Margaret, solemnly. But I am saying nothing against the young ladies of Thrums, Gavin. Though I have scarcely seen them, I know there are good women among them. Jean says—"

"I believe, mother," Gavin interposed, reproachfully, "that you have been questioning Jean about them?"

"Just because I was afraid — I mean because I fancied — you might be taking a liking to one of them."

"And what is Jean's verdict?"

"She says every one of them would jump at you, like a bird at a berry."

"But the berry cannot be divided. How would Miss Pennycuick please you, mother?"

"Gavin!" cried Margaret, in consternation, "you don't mean to — But you are laughing at me again."

"Then there is the banker's daughter?"

"I can't thole her."

"Why, I question if you ever set eyes on her, mother."

"Perhaps not, Gavin; but I have suspected her ever since she offered to become one of your tract distributors."

"The doctor," said Gavin, not ill-pleased, "was saying that either of these ladies would suit me."

"What business has he," asked Margaret, vindictively, "to put such thoughts into your head?"

"But he only did as you are doing. Mother, I see you will never be satisfied without selecting the woman for me yourself."

"Ay, Gavin," said Margaret, earnestly; "and I question if I should be satisfied even then. But I am sure I should be a better guide to you than Dr. McQueen is."

"I am convinced of that. But I wonder what sort of woman would content you?"

"Whoever pleased you, Gavin, would content me," Margaret ventured to maintain. "You would only take to a clever woman."

"She must be nearly as clever as you, mother."

"Hoots, Gavin," said Margaret, smiling, "I'm not to be caught with chaff. I am a stupid, ignorant woman.'

"Then I must look out for a stupid, ignorant woman, for that seems to be the kind I like," answered Gavin, of whom I may confess here something that has to be told sooner or later. It is this: he never realised that Babbie was a great deal cleverer than himself. Forgive him, you who read, if you have any tolerance for the creature, man.

"She will be terribly learned in languages," pursued Margaret, "so that she may follow you in your studies, as I have never been able to do."

"Your face has helped me more than Hebrew, mother," replied Gavin. "I will give her no marks for languages."

"At any rate," Margaret insisted, "she must be a grand housekeeper, and very thrifty."

"As for that," Gavin said, faltering a little, "one can't expect it of a mere girl."

"I should expect it," maintained his mother.

"No,no; but she would have you," said Gavin, happily, "to teach her housekeeping."

"It would be a pleasant occupation to me, that," Margaret admitted. "And she would soon learn; she would be so proud of her position as mistress of a manse."

"Perhaps," Gavin said, doubtfully. He had no doubt on the subject in his college days.

"And we can take for granted," continued his mother, "that she is a lassie of fine character."

"Of course," said Gavin, holding his head high, as if he thought the doctor might be watching him.

"I have thought," Margaret went on, "that there was a great deal of wisdom in what you said at that last marriage in the manse, the one where, you remember, the best man and the bridesmaid joined hands instead of the bride and bridegroom."

"What did I say?" asked the little minister, with misgivings.

"That there was great danger when people married out of their own rank of life."

"Oh — ah — well, of course, that would depend on circumstances."

"They were wise words, Gavin. There was the sermon, too, that you preached a month or two ago against marrying into other denominations. Jean told me that it greatly impressed the congregation. It is a sad sight, as you said, to see an Auld Licht lassie changing her faith because her man belongs to the U. P.'s."

"Did I say that?"

"You did, and it so struck Jean that she told me she would rather be an old maid for life, 'the which,' she said, 'is a dismal prospect,' than marry out of the Auld Licht kirk."

"Perhaps that was a rather narrow view I took, mother. After all, the fitting thing is that the wife should go with her husband; especially if it is he that is the Auld Licht."

"I don't hold with narrowness myself, Gavin," Margaret said, with an effort, "and I admit that there are many respectable persons in the other denominations. But though a weaver might take a wife from another kirk without much scandal, an Auld

Licht minister's madam must be Auld Licht born and bred. The congregation would expect no less. I doubt if they would be sure of her if she came from some other Auld Licht kirk. 'Deed, though she came from our own kirk, I'm thinking the session would want to catechise her. Ay, and if all you tell me of Lang Tammas be true (for, as you know, I never spoke to him), I warrant he would catechise the session."

"I would brook no interference from my session," said Gavin, knitting his brows, "and I do not consider it necessary that a minister's wife should have been brought up in his denomination. Of course she would join it. We must make allowance, mother, for the thousands of young women who live in places where there is no Auld Licht kirk."

"You can pity them, Gavin," said Margaret, "without marrying them. A minister has his congregation to think of."

"So the doctor says," interposed her son.

"Then it was just like his presumption!" cried Margaret. "A minister should marry to please himself."

"Decidedly he should," Gavin agreed, eagerly, "and the bounden duty of the congregation is to respect and honour his choice. If they forget that duty, his is to remind them of it."

"Ah, well, Gavin," said Margaret, confidently, "your congregation are so fond of you that your choice would doubtless be theirs. Jean tells me that even Lang Tammas, though he is so obstinate, has a love for you passing the love of woman. These were her words. Jean is more sentimental than you might think."

"I wish he would show his love," said Gavin, "by contradicting me less frequently."

"You have Rob Dow to weigh against him."

"No; I cannot make out what has come over Rob lately. He is drinking heavily again, and avoiding me. The lightning is becoming very vivid."

"Yes, and I hear no thunder. There is another thing, Gavin. I am one of those that like to sit at home, but if you had a wife she would visit the congregation. A truly religious wife would be a great help to you."

"Religious," Gavin repeated slowly: "Yes, but some people are religious without speaking of it. If a woman is good she is religious. A good woman who has been, let us say, foolishly brought up, only needs to be shown the right way to tread it. Mother, I question if any man, minister or layman, ever yet fell in love because the woman was thrifty, or clever, or went to church twice on Sabbath."

"I believe that is true," Margaret said, "and I would not have it otherwise. But it is an awful thing, Gavin, as you said from the pulpit two weeks ago, to worship only at a beautiful face."

"You think too much about what I say in the pulpit, mother," Gavin said, with a sigh, "though of course a man who fell in love merely with a face would be a contemptible creature. Yet I see that women do not understand how beauty affects a man."

"Yes, yes, my boy — oh, indeed, they do," said Margaret, who on some matters knew far more than her son.

Twelve o'clock struck, and she rose to go to bed, alarmed lest she should not waken early in the morning. "But I am afraid I shan't sleep," she said, "if that lightning continues."

"It is harmless," Gavin answered, going to the window. He started back next moment, and crying, "Don't look out, mother," hastily pulled down the blind.

"Why, Gavin," Margaret said in fear, "you look as if it had struck you."

"Oh, no," Gavin answered, with a forced laugh, and he lit her lamp for her.

But it had struck him, though it was not lightning. It was the flashing of a lantern against the window to attract his attention, and the holder of the lantern was Babbie.

"Good-night, mother."

"Good-night, Gavin. Don't sit up any later."

Chapter XXII

Lovers

ONLY something terrible, Gavin thought, could have brought Babbie to him at such an hour; yet when he left his mother's room it was to stand motionless on the stair, waiting for a silence in the manse that would not come. A house is never still in darkness to those who listen intently; there is a whispering in distant chambers, an unearthly hand presses the snib of the window, the latch rises. Ghosts were created when the first man woke in the night.

Now Margaret slept. Two hours earlier, Jean, sitting on the salt-bucket, had read the chapter with which she always sent herself to bed. In honour of the little minister she had begun her Bible afresh when he came to Thrums, and was progressing through it, a chapter a night, sighing, perhaps, on washing days at a long chapter, such as Exodus twelfth, but never making two of it. The kitchen wag-at-the-wall clock was telling every room in the house that she had neglected to shut her door. As Gavin felt his way down the dark stair, awakening it into protest at every step, he had a glimpse of the pendulum's shadow running back and forward on the hearth; he started back from another shadow on the lobby wall, and then seeing it start too, knew it for his own. He opened the door and passed out unobserved; it was as if the sounds and shadows that filled the manse were too occupied with their game to mind an interloper.

"Is that you?" he said to a bush, for the garden was in semi-darkness. Then the lantern's flash met him, and he saw the Egyptian in the summer-seat.

"At last!" she said, reproachfully. "Evidently a lantern is a poor door-bell."

"What is it?" Gavin asked, in suppressed excitement, for the least he expected to hear was that she was again being pursued for her share in the riot. The tremor in his voice surprised her into silence, and he thought she faltered because what she had to tell him was so woeful. So, in the darkness of the summer-seat, he kissed her, and she might have known that with that kiss the little minister was hers for ever.

Now Babbie had been kissed before, but never thus, and she turned from Gavin, and would have liked to be alone, for she had begun to know what love was, and the flash that revealed it to her laid bare her own shame, so that her impulse was to hide herself from her lover. But of all this Gavin was unconscious, and he repeated his question. The lantern was swaying in her hand, and when she turned fearfully to him its light fell on his face, and she saw how alarmed he was.

"I am going away back to Nanny's," she said suddenly, and rose cowed, but he took her hand and held her.

"Babbie," he said huskily, "tell me what has happened to bring you here at this hour."

She sought to pull her hand from him, but could not.

"How you are trembling!" he whispered. "Babbie," he cried, "something terrible has happened to you, but do not fear. Tell me what it is, and then — then I will take you to my mother: yes, I will take you now."

The Egyptian would have given all she had in the world to be able to fly from him then, that he might never know her as she was, but it could not be, and so she spoke out remorselessly. If her voice had become hard, it was a new-born scorn of herself that made it so.

"You are needlessly alarmed," she said; "I am not at all the kind of person who deserves sympathy or expects it. There is nothing wrong. I am staying with Nanny over-night, and only came to Thrums to amuse myself. I chased your policeman down the Roods with my lantern, and then came here to amuse myself with you. That is all."

"It was nothing but a love of mischief that brought you here?" Gavin asked, sternly, after an unpleasant pause.

"Nothing," the Egyptian answered, recklessly.

"I could not have believed this of you," the minister said; "I am ashamed of you."

"I thought," Babbie retorted, trying to speak lightly until she could get away from him, "that you would be glad to see me. Your last words in Caddam seemed to justify that idea."

"I am very sorry to see you," he answered, reproachfully.

"Then I will go away at once," she said, stepping out of the summer-seat.

"Yes," he replied, "you must go at once."

"Then I won't," she said, turning back defiantly. "I know what you are to say: that the Thrums people would be shocked if they knew I was here; as if I cared what the Thrums people think of me."

"I care what they think of you," Gavin said, as if that were decisive, "and I tell you I will not allow you to repeat this freak."

"You 'will not allow me' echoed Babbie, almost enjoying herself, despite her sudden loss of self-respect.

"I will not," Gavin said resolutely. "Henceforth you must do as I think fit."

"Since when have you taken command of me?" demanded Babbie.

"Since a minute ago," Gavin replied, "when you let me kiss you."

"Let you!" exclaimed Babbie, now justly incensed. "You did it yourself. I was very angry."

"No, you were not."

"I am not allowed to say that even?" asked the Egyptian: 'Tell me something I may say, then, and I will repeat it after you."

"I have something to say to you," Gavin told her, after a moment's reflection; "yes, and there is something I should like to hear you repeat after me, but not to-night."

"I don't want to hear what it is," Babbie said, quickly, but she knew what it was, and even then, despite the new pain at her heart, her bosom swelled with pride because this man still loved her. Now she wanted to run away with his love for her before he could take it from her, and then realising that this parting must be for ever, a great desire filled her to hear him put that kiss into words, and she said, faltering:

"You can tell me what it is if you like."

"Not to-night," said Gavin.

"To-night, if at all," the gypsy almost entreated.

"To-morrow, at Nanny's," answered Gavin, decisively: and this time he remembered without dismay that to-morrow was the Sabbath.

In the fairy tale the beast suddenly drops his skin and is a prince,and I believe it seemed to Babbie that some such change had come over this man, her plaything.

"Your lantern is shining on my mother's window," were the words that woke her from this discovery, and then she found herself yielding the lantern to him. She became conscious vaguely that a corresponding change was taking place in herself.

"You spoke of taking me to your mother," she said, bitterly.

"Yes," he answered at once, "to-morrow;" but she shook her head, knowing that to-morrow he would be wiser.

Give me the lantern," she said, in a low voice, I am going back to Nanny's now."

"Yes," he said, "we must set out now, but I can carry the lantern."

"You are not coming with me!" she exclaimed, shaking herself free of his hand.

"I am coming," he replied, calmly, though he was not calm. "Take my arm, Babbie."

She made a last effort to free herself from bondage, crying passionately, "I will not let you come."

"When I say I am coming," Gavin answered between his teeth, "I mean that I am coming, and so let that be an end of this folly. Take my arm."

"I think I hate you," she said, retreating from him.

"Take my arm," he repeated, and, though her breast was rising rebelliously, she did as he ordered, and so he escorted her from the garden. At the foot of the field she stopped, and thought to frighten him by saying, "What would the people say if they saw you with me now?"

"It does not much matter what they would say," he answered, still keeping his teeth together as if doubtful of their courage. "As for what they would do, that is certain; they would put me out of my church."

"And it is dear to you?"

"Dearer than life."

"You told me long ago that your mother's heart would break if—"

"Yes, I am sure it would."

They had begun to climb the fields, but she stopped him with a jerk.

"Go back, Mr. Dishart," she implored, clutching his arm with both hands. "You make me very unhappy for no purpose. Oh, why should you risk so much for me?"

"I cannot have you wandering here alone at midnight," Gavin answered, gently.

"That is nothing to me," she said, eagerly, but no longer resenting his air of proprietorship.

"You will never do it again if I can prevent it."

"But you cannot," she said, sadly. "Oh, yes, you can, Mr. Dishart. If you will turn back now I shall promise never to do anything again without first asking myself whether it would seem right to you. I know I acted very wrongly to-night."

"Only thoughtlessly," he said.

"Then have pity on me," she besought him, "and go back. If I have only been thoughtless, how can you punish me thus? Mr. Dishart," she entreated, her voice breaking, "if you were to suffer for this folly of mine, do you think I could live?"

"We are in God's hands, dear," he answered, firmly, and he again drew her arm to him. So they climbed the first field, and were almost at the hill before either spoke again.

"Stop," Babbie whispered, crouching as she spoke; "I see some one crossing the hill."

"I have seen him for some time," Gavin answered, quietly; "but I am doing no wrong, and I will not hide."

The Egyptian had to walk on with him, and I suppose she did not think the less of him for that. Yet she said, warningly—

"If he sees you, all Thrums will be in an uproar before morning."

"I cannot help that," Gavin replied. "It is the will of God."

"To ruin you for my sins?"

"If He thinks fit."

The figure drew nearer, and with every step Babbie's distress doubled.

"We are walking straight to him," she whispered. "I implore you to wait here until he passes, if not for your own sake, for your mother's."

At that he wavered, and she heard his teeth sliding against each other, as if he could no longer clench them.

"But, no," he said, moving on again, "I will not be a skulker from any man. If it be God's wish that I should suffer for this, I must suffer."

"Oh, why," cried Babbie, beating her hands together in grief, "should you suffer for me?"

"You are mine," Gavin answered. Babbie gasped. "And if you act foolishly," he continued, "it is right that I should bear the brunt of it. No, I will not let you go on alone; you are not fit to be alone. You need some one to watch over you and care for you and love you, and, if need be, to suffer with you."

"Turn back, dear, before he sees us."

"He has seen us."

Yes, I had seen them, for the figure on the hill was no other than the dominie of Glen Quharity. The park gate clicked as it swung to, and I looked up and saw Gavin and the Egyptian. My eyes should have found them sooner, but it was to gaze upon Margaret's home, while no one saw me, that I had trudged into Thrums so late, and by that time, I suppose, my eyes were of little service for seeing through. Yet, when I knew that of these two people suddenly beside me on the hill one was the little minister and the other a strange woman, I fell back from their side with dread before I could step forward and cry "Gavin!"

"I am Mr. Dishart," he answered, with a composure that would not have served him for another sentence. He was more excited than I, for the "Gavin" fell harmlessly on him, while I had no sooner uttered it than there rushed through me the shame of being false to Margaret. It was the only time in my life that I forgot her in him, though he has ever stood next to her in my regard.

I looked from Gavin to the gypsy woman, and again from her to him, and she began to tell a lie in his interest. But she got no farther than "I met Mr. Dishart accid—" when she stopped, ashamed. It was reverence for Gavin that checked the lie. Not every man has had such a compliment paid him.

"It is natural," Gavin said, slowly, "that you, sir, should wonder why I am here with this woman at such an hour, and you may know me so little as to think ill of me for it."

I did not answer, and he misunderstood my silence.

"No," he continued, in a harder voice, as if I had asked him a question, "I will explain nothing to you. You are not my judge. If you would do me harm, sir, you have it in your power."

It was with these cruel words that Gavin addressed me. He did not know how cruel they were. The Egyptian, I think, must have seen that his suspicions hurt me, for she said, softly, with a look of appeal in her eyes

"You are the schoolmaster in Glen Quharity? Then you will perhaps save Mr. Dishart the trouble of coming farther by showing me the way to old Nanny Webster's house at Windyghoul?"

"I have to pass the house at any rate," I answered eagerly, and she came quickly to my side.

I knew, though in the darkness I could see but vaguely, that Gavin was holding his head high and waiting for me to say my worst. I had not told him that I dared think no evil of him, and he still suspected me. Now I would not trust myself to speak lest I should betray Margaret, and yet I wanted him to know that base doubts about him could never find a shelter in me. I am a timid man who long ago lost the glory of my life by it, and I was again timid when I sought to let Gavin see that my faith in him was unshaken. I lifted my bonnet to the gypsy, and asked her to take my arm. It was done clumsily, I cannot doubt, but he read my meaning and held out his hand to me. I had not touched it since he was three years old, and I trembled too much to give it the grasp I owed it. He and I parted without a word, but to the Egyptian he said, "To-morrow, dear, I will see you at Nanny's," and he was to kiss her, but I pulled her a step farther from him, and she put her hands over her face, crying, "No, no!"

If I asked her some questions between the hill and Windyghoul you must not blame me, for this was my affair as well as theirs. She did not answer me; I know now that she did not hear me. But at the mud house she looked abruptly into my face, and said—

"You love him, too!"

I trudged to the school-house with these words for company, and it was less her discovery than her confession that tortured me. How much I slept that night you may guess.

Chapter XXIII

Contains a Birth, which is Sufficient for One Chapter

"THE kirk bell will soon be ringing," Nanny said on the following morning, as she placed herself carefully on a stool, one hand holding her Bible and the other wandering complacently over her aged merino gown. "Ay, lassie, though you're only an Egyptian I would hae ta'en you wi' me to hear Mr. Duthie, but it's speiring ower muckle o' a woman to expect her to gang to the kirk in her ilka day claethes."

The Babbie of yesterday would have laughed at this, but the new Babbie sighed.

"I wonder you don't go to Mr. Dishart's church now, Nanny," she said, gently. "I am sure you prefer him."

"Babbie, Babbie," exclaimed Nanny, with spirit, "may I never be so far left to mysel' as to change my kirk just because I like another minister better! It's easy seen, lassie, that you ken little o' religious questions."

"Very little," Babbie admitted, sadly.

"But dinna be so waeful about it," the old woman continued, kindly, "for that's no nane like you. Ay, and if you see muckle mair o' Mr. Dishart he'll soon cure your ignorance."

"I shall not see much more of him," Babbie answered, with averted head.

"The like o' you couldna expect it," Nanny said, simply, whereupon Babbie went to the window. "I had better be stepping," Nanny said, rising, "for I am aye late unless I'm on the hill by the time the bell begins. Ay, Babbie, I'm doubting my merino's no sair in the fashion?"

She looked down at her dress half despondently, and yet with some pride.

"It was fowerpence the yard, and no less," she went on, fondling the worn merino, "when we bocht it at Sam'l Curr's. Ay, but it has been turned sax times since syne."

She sighed, and Babbie came to her and put her arms round her, saying, "Nanny, you are a dear."

"I'm a gey auld-farrant-looking dear, I doubt," said Nanny, ruefully.

"Now, Nanny," rejoined Babbie, "you are just wanting me to flatter you. You know the merino looks very nice."

It's a guid merino yet," admitted the old woman, but, oh, Babbie, what does the material matter if the cut isna fashionable? It's fine, isn't it, to be in the fashion?"

She spoke so wistfully that, instead of smiling, Babbie kissed her.

"I am afraid to lay hand on the merino, Nanny, but give me off your bonnet and I'll make it ten years younger in as many minutes."

"Could you?" asked Nanny, eagerly, unloosening her bonnet-strings. "Mercy on me!" she had to add; "to think about altering bonnets on the Sabbath-day! Lassie, how could you propose sic a thing?"

"Forgive me, Nanny," Babbie replied, so meekly that the old woman looked at her curiously.

"I dinna understand what has come ower you," she said: 'There's an unca difference in you since last nicht. I used to think you were mair like a bird than a lassie, but you've lost a' your daft capers o' singing and lauching, and I take ill wi't. Twa or three times I've catched you greeting. Babbie, what has come ower you?"

"Nothing, Nanny. I think I hear the bell."

Down in Thrums two kirk-officers had let their bells loose, waking echoes in Windyghoul as one dog in country parts sets all the others barking, but Nanny did not hurry oft to church. Such a surprising notion had filled her head suddenly that she even forgot to hold her dress off the floor.

"Babbie," she cried, in consternation, "dinna tell me you've gotten ower fond o' Mr. Dishart."

"The like of me, Nanny!" the gypsy answered, with affected raillery, but there was a tear in her eye.

"It would be a wild, presumptious thing," Nanny said, "and him a grand minister, but—"

Babbie tried to look her in the face, but failed, and then all at once there came back to Nanny the days when she and her lover wandered the hill together.

"Ah, my dawtie," she cried, so tenderly, "what does it matter wha he is when you canna help it!"

Two frail arms went round the Egyptian, and Babbie rested her head on the old woman's breast. But do you think it could have happened had not Nanny loved a weaver two-score years before?

And now Nanny has set off for church and Babbie is alone in the mud house. Some will pity her not at all, this girl who was a dozen women in the hour, and all made of impulses that would scarce stand still to be photographed. To attempt to picture her at any time until now would have been like chasing a spirit that changes to something else as your arms clasp it; yet she has always seemed a pathetic little figure to me. If I understand Babbie at all, it is, I think, because I loved Margaret, the only woman I have ever known well, and one whose nature was not, like the Egyptian's, complex, but most simple, as if God had told her only to be good. Throughout my life since she came into it she has been to me a glass in which many things are revealed that I could not have learned save through her, and something of all womankind, even of bewildering Babbie,I seem to know because I knew Margaret.

No woman is so bad but we may rejoice when her heart thrills to love, for then God has her by the hand. There is no love but this. She may dream of what love is, but it is only of a sudden that she knows. Babbie, who was without a guide from her baby days, had dreamed but little of it, hearing its name given to another thing. She had been born wild and known no home; no one had touched her heart except to strike it; she had been educated, but never tamed; her life had been thrown strangely among those who were great in the world's possessions, but she was not of them. Her soul was in such darkness that she had never seen it; she would have danced away cynically from the belief that there is such a thing, and now all at once she had passed from disbelief to knowledge. Is not love God's doing? To Gavin He had given something of Himself, and the moment she saw it the flash lit her own soul.

It was but little of his Master that was in Gavin, but far smaller things have changed the current of human lives; the spider's thread that strikes our brow on a country road may do that. Yet this I will say, though I have no wish to cast the little minister on my pages larger than he was, that he had some heroic hours in Thrums, of which one was when Babbie learned to love him. Until the moment when he kissed her she had only conceived him a quaint fellow whose life was a string of Sundays, but behold what she saw in him now. Evidently to his noble mind her mystery was only some misfortune, not of her making, and his was to be the part of leading her away from it into the happiness of the open life. He did not doubt her, for he loved, and to doubt is to dip love in the mire. She had been given to him by God, and he was so rich in her possession that the responsibility attached to the gift was not grievous. She was his, and no mortal man could part them. Those who looked askance at her were looking askance at him; in so far as she was wayward and wild, he was those things; so long as she remained strange to religion, the blame lay on him.

All this Babbie read in the Gavin of the past night, and to her it was the book of love. What things she had known, said and done in that holy name! How shamefully have we all besmirched it! She had only known it as the most selfish of the passions, a brittle image that men consulted because it could only answer in the words they gave it to say. But here was a man to whom love was something better than his own desires leering on a pedestal. Such love as Babbie had seen hitherto made strong men weak, but this was a love that made a weak man strong. All her life, strength had been her idol, and the weakness that bent to her cajolery her scorn. But only now was it revealed to her that strength, instead of being the lusty child of passions, grows by grappling with and throwing them.

So Babbie loved the little minister for the best that she had ever seen in man. I shall be told that she thought far more of him than he deserved, forgetting the mean in the worthy: but who that has had a glimpse of heaven will care to let his mind dwell henceforth on earth? Love, it is said, is blind, but love is not blind. It is an extra eye, which shows us what is most worthy of regard. To see the best is to see most clearly, and it is the lover's privilege.

Down in the Auld Licht kirk that forenoon Gavin preached a sermon in praise of Woman, and up in the mud house in Windyghoul Babbie sat alone. But it was the Sabbath day to her: the first Sabbath in her life. Her discovery had frozen her mind for a time, so that she could only stare at it with eyes that would not shut; but that had been in the night. Already her love seemed a thing of years, for it was as old as herself, as old as the new Babbie. It was such a dear delight that she clasped it to her, and exulted over it because it was hers, and then she cried over it because she must give it up.

For Babbie must only look at this love and then turn from it. My heart aches for the little Egyptian, but the Promised Land would have remained invisible to her had she not realised that it was only for others. That was the condition of her seeing.

Chapter XXIV

The New World, And The Woman Who May Not Dwell Therein

UP here in the glen school-house after my pupils have straggled home, there comes to me at times, and so sudden that it may be while I am infusing my tea, a hot desire to write great books. Perhaps an hour afterwards I rise, beaten from my desk, flinging all I have written into the fire (yet rescuing some of it on second thoughts), and curse myself as an ingle-nook man, for I see that one can only paint what he himself has felt, and in my passion I wish to have all the vices, even to being an impious man, that I may describe them better. For this may I be pardoned. It comes to nothing in the end, save that my tea is brackish.

Yet though my solitary life in the glen is cheating me of many experiences, more helpful to a writer than to a Christian, it has not been so tame but that I can understand why Babbie cried when she went into Nanny's garden and saw the new world. Let no one who loves be called altogether unhappy. Even love unreturned has its rainbow, and Babbie knew that Gavin loved her. Yet she stood in woe among the stiff berry bushes, as one who stretches forth her hands to Love and sees him looking for her, and knows she must shrink from the arms she would lie in, and only call to him in a voice he cannot hear. This is not a love that is always bitter. It grows sweet with age. But could that dry the tears of the little Egyptian, who had only been a woman for a day?

Much was still dark to her. Of one obstacle that must keep her and Gavin ever apart she knew, and he did not, but had it been removed she would have given herself to him humbly, not in her own longing, but because he wanted her. "Behold what I am," she could have said to him then, and left the rest to him, believing that her unworthiness would not drag him down, it would lose itself so readily in his strength. That Thrums could rise against such a man if he defied it, she did not believe; but she was to learn the truth presently from a child.

To most of us, I suppose, has come some shock that was to make us different men from that hour, and yet, how many days elapsed before something of the man we had been leapt up in us? Babbie thought she had buried her old impulsiveness, and then remembering that from the top of the field she might see Gavin returning from church, she hastened to the hill to look upon him from a distance. Before she reached the gate where I had met her and him, however, she stopped, distressed at her selfishness, and asked bitterly, "Why am I so different from other women; why should what is so easy to them be so hard to me?"

"Gavin, my beloved!" the Egyptian cried in her agony, and the wind caught her words and flung them in the air, making sport of her.

She wandered westward over the bleak hill, and by-and-by came to a great slab called the Standing Stone, on which children often sit and muse until they see gay ladies riding by on palfreys a kind of horse and knights in glittering armour, and goblins, and fiery dragons, and other wonders now extinct, of which bare-legged laddies dream, as well as boys in socks. The Standing Stone is in the dyke that separates the hill from a fir wood, and it is the fairy-book of Thrums. If you would be a knight yourself, you must sit on it and whisper to it your desire.

Babbie came to the Standing Stone, and there was a little boy astride it. His hair stood up through holes in his bonnet, and he was very ragged and miserable.

"Why are you crying, little boy?" Babbie asked him, gently; but he did not look up and the tongue was strange to him.

"How are you greeting so sair?" she asked.

"I'm no greeting very sair," he answered, turning his head from her that a woman might not see his tears. "I am no greeting so sair but what I grat sairer when my mither died."

"When did she die?" Babbie inquired.

"Lang syne," he answered, still with averted face.

"What is your name?"

"Micah is my name. Rob Dow's my father."

"And have you no brothers nor sisters?" asked Babbie, with a fellow-feeling for him.

"No, juist my father," he said.

"You should be the better laddie to him then. Did your mither no tell you to be that afore she died?"

"Ay," he answered, "she telled me ay to hide the bottle frae him when I could get haed o't. She took me into the bed to make me promise that, and syne she died."

"Does your father drink?"

"He hauds mair than ony other man in Thrums," Micah replied, almost proudly.

"And he strikes you?" Babbie asked, compassionately.

"That's a lie," retorted the boy, fiercely. "Leastwise, he doesna strike me except when he's mortal, and syne I can jouk him."

"What are you doing there?"

"I'm wishing. It's a wishing stane."

"You are wishing your father wouldna drink."

"No, I'm no," answered Micah. "There was a lang time he didna drink, but the woman has sent him to it again. It's about her I'm wishing. I'm wishing she was in hell."

"What woman is it?" asked Babbie, shuddering.

"I dinna ken," Micah said, "but she's an ill ane."

"Did you never see her at your father's house?"

"Na; if he could get grip o' her he would break her ower his knee. I hearken to him saying that, when he's wild. He says she should be burned for a witch."

"But if he hates her," asked Babbie, "how can she have sic power ower him?"

"It's no him that she has haud o'," replied Micah, still looking away from her.

"Wha is it then?"

"It's Mr. Dishart."

Babbie was struck as if by an arrow from the wood. It was so unexpected that she gave a cry, and then for the first time Micah looked at her.

"How should that send your father to the drink?" she asked, with an effort.

"Because my father's michty fond o' him," answered Micah, staring strangely at her; "and when the folk ken about the woman, they'll stane the minister out o' Thrums."

The wood faded for a moment from the Egyptian's sight. When it came back, the boy had slid off the Standing Stone and was stealing away.

"Why do you run frae me?" Babbie asked, pathetically.

"I'm fleid at you," he gasped, coming to a standstill at a safe distance: "you're the woman!"

Babbie cowered before her little judge, and he drew nearer her slowly.

"What makes you think that?" she said.

It was a curious time for Babbie's beauty to be paid its most princely compliment.

"Because you're so bonny," Micah whispered across the dyke. Her tears gave him courage. "You micht gang awa," he entreated. "If you kent what a differ Mr. Dishart made in my father till you came, you would maybe gang awa. When he's roaring fou I have to sleep in the wood, and it's awfu' cauld. I'm doubting he'll kill me, woman, if you dinna gang awa."

Poor Babbie put her hand to her heart, but the innocent lad continued mercilessly—

"If ony shame comes to the minister, his auld mither'll die. How have you sic an ill will at the minister?"

Babbie held up her hands like a supplicant.

"I'll gie you my rabbit," Micah said, "if you'll gang awa. I've juist the ane." She shook her head, and, misunderstanding her, he cried, with his knuckles in his eye, "I'll gie you them baith, though I'm michty sweer to part wi' Spotty."

Then at last Babbie found her voice.

"Keep your rabbits, laddie," she said, "and greet no more. I'm gaen awa."

"And you'll never come back no more a' your life?" pleaded Micah.

"Never no more a' my life," repeated Babbie.

"And ye'll leave the minister alane for ever and ever?"

"For ever and ever."

Micah rubbed his face dry, and said, "Will you let me stand on the Standing Stane and watch you gaen awa for ever and ever?"

At that a sob broke from Babbie's heart, and looking at her doubtfully Micah said—

"Maybe you're gey ill for what you've done?"

"Ay," Babbie answered, "I'm gey ill for what I've done."

A minute passed, and in her anguish she did not know that still she was standing at the dyke. Micah's voice roused her:

"You said you would gang awa, and you're no gaen."

Then Babbie went away. The boy watched her across the hill. He climbed the Standing Stone and gazed after her until she was but a coloured ribbon among the broom. When she disappeared into Windyghoul he ran home joyfully, and told his father what a good day's work he had done. Rob struck him for a fool for taking a gypsy's word, and warned him against speaking of the woman in Thrums.

But though Dow believed that Gavin continued to meet the Egyptian secretly, he was wrong. A sum of money for Nanny was sent to the minister, but he could guess only from whom it came. In vain did he search for Babbie. Some months passed and he gave up the search, persuaded that he should see her no more. He went about his duties with a drawn face that made many folk uneasy when it was stern, and pained them when it tried to smile. But to Margaret, though the effort was terrible, he was as he had ever been, and so no thought of a woman crossed her loving breast.

Chapter XXV

Beginning Of The Twenty-Four Hours

I CAN tell still how the whole of the glen was engaged about the hour of noon on the fourth of August month; a day to be among the last forgotten by any of us, though it began as quietly as a roaring March. At the Spittal, between which and Thrums this is a halfway house, were gathered two hundred men in kilts, and many gentry from the neighbouring glens, to celebrate the earl's marriage, which was to take place on the morrow, and thither, too, had gone many of my pupils to gather gossip, at which girls of six are trustier hands than boys of twelve. Those of us, however, who were neither children nor of gentle blood, remained at home, the farmers more taken up with the want of rain, now become a calamity, than with an old man's wedding, and their women-folk wringing their hands for rain also, yet finding time to marvel at the marriage's taking place at the Spittal instead of in England, of which the ignorant spoke vaguely as an estate of the bride's.

For my own part I could talk of the disastrous drouth with Waster Lunny as I walked over his parched fields, but I had not such cause as he to brood upon it by day and night; and the ins and outs of the earl's marriage were for discussing at a tea-table, where there were women to help one to conclusions, rather than for the reflections of a solitary dominie, who had seen neither bride nor bridegroom. So it must be confessed that when I might have been regarding the sky moodily, or at the Spittal, where a free table that day invited all, I was sitting in the school-house, heeling my left boot, on which I have always been a little hard.

I made small speed, not through lack of craft, but because one can no more drive in tackets properly than take cities unless he gives his whole mind to it; and half of mine was at the Auld Licht manse. Since our meeting six months earlier on the hill I had not seen Gavin, but I had heard much of him, and of a kind to trouble me.

"I saw nothing queer about Mr. Dishart," was Waster Lunny's frequent story, "till I hearkened to Elspeth speaking about it to the lasses (for I'm the last Elspeth would tell onything to, though I'm her man), and syne I minded I had been noticing it for months. Elspeth says," he would go on, for he could no more forbear quoting his wife than complaining of her, "that the minister'll listen to you nowadays wi' his een glaring at you as if he had a perfectly passionate interest in what you were telling him (though it may be only about a hen wi' the croup), and then, after all, he hasna heard a sylib. Ay, I listened to Elspeth saying that, when she thoct I was at the byre, and yet would you believe it, when I says to her after lousing time, 'I've been noticing of late that die minister loses what a body tells him,' all she answers is, 'Havers.' Tod, but women's provoking."

"I allow," Birse said, "that on the first Sabbath o' June month, and again on the third Sabbath, he poured out the Word grandly, but I've ta'en note this curran Sabbaths that if he's no michty magnificent he's michty poor. There's something damming up his mind, and when he gets by it he's a roaring water, but when he doesna he's a despisable trickle. The folk thinks it's a woman that's getting in his way, but dinna tell me that about sic a scholar; I tell you he would gang ower a toon o' women like a loaded cart ower new-laid stanes."

Wearyworld hobbled after me up die Roods one day, pelting me with remarks, though I was doing my best to get away from him. "Even Rob Dow sees there's something come ower the minister," he bawled, "for Rob's fou ilka Sabbath now. Ay, but this I will say for Mr. Dishart, that he aye gies me a civil word." I thought I had left the policeman behind with this, but next minute he roared, "and whatever is the matter wi' him it has made him kindlier to me than ever." He must have taken the short cut through Lunan's close, for at the top of the Roods his voice again made up on me. "Dagone you, for a cruel pack to put your fingers to your lugs ilka time I open my mouth."

As for Waster Lunny's daughter Easie, who got her schooling free for redding up the school-house and breaking my furniture, she would never have been off the gossip about the minister, for she was her mother in miniature, with a tongue that ran like a pump after the pans are full, not for use but for the mere pleasure of spilling.

On that awful fourth of August I not only had all this confused talk in my head but reason for jumping my mind between it and the Egyptian (as if to catch them together unawares), and I was like one who, with the mechanism of a watch jumbled in his hand, could set it going if he had the art.

Of the gypsy I knew nothing save what I had seen that night, yet what more was there to learn? I was aware that she loved Gavin and that he loved her. A moment had shown it to me. Now with the Auld Lichts, I have the smith's acquaintance with his irons, and so I could not believe that they would suffer their minister to marry a vagrant. Had it not been for this knowledge, which made me fearful for Margaret, I would have done nothing to keep these two young people apart. Some to whom I have said this maintain that the Egyptian turned my head at our first meeting. Such an argument is not perhaps worth controverting. I admit that even now I straighten under the fire of a bright eye, as a pensioner may salute when he sees a young officer. In the shooting season, should I chance to be leaning over my dyke while English sportsmen pass (as is usually the case if I have seen them approaching), I remember nought of them save that they call me "she," and end their greetings with "whatever" (which Waster Lunny takes to be a southron mode of speech), but their ladies dwell pleasantly in my memory, from their engaging faces to the pretty crumpled thing dangling on their arms, that is a hat or a basket, I am seldom sure which. The Egyptian's beauty, therefore, was a gladsome sight to me, and none the less so that I had come upon it as unexpectedly as some men step into a bog. Had she been alone when I met her I cannot deny that I would have been content to look on her face, without caring what was inside it; but she was with her lover, and that lover was Gavin, and so her face was to me as little for admiring as this glen in a thunderstorm, when I know that some fellow-creature is lost on the hills.

If, however, it was no quick liking for the gypsy that almost tempted me to leave these two lovers to each other, what was it? It was the warning of my own life. Adam Dishart had torn my arm from Margaret's, and I had not recovered the wrench in eighteen years. Rather than act his part between these two I felt tempted to tell them, "Deplorable as the result may be, if you who are a minister marry this vagabond, it will be still more deplorable if you do not."

But there was Margaret to consider, and at thought of her I cursed the Egyptian aloud. What could I do to keep Gavin and the woman apart? I could tell him the secret of his mother's life. Would that be sufficient? It would if he loved Margaret, as I did not doubt. Pity for her would make him undergo any torture rather than she should suffer again. But to divulge our old connection would entail her discovery of me, and I questioned if even the saving of Gavin could destroy the bitterness of that.

I might appeal to the Egyptian. I might tell her even what I shuddered to tell him. She cared for him, I was sure, well enough to have the courage to give him up. But where was I to find her?

Were she and Gavin meeting still? Perhaps the change which had come over the little minister meant that they had parted. Yet what I had heard him say to her on the hill warned me not to trust in any such solution of the trouble.

Boys play at casting a humming-top into the midst of others on the ground, and if well aimed it scatters them prettily. I seemed to be playing such a game with my thoughts, for each new one sent the others here and there, and so what could I do in the end but fling my tops aside, and return to the heeling of my boot?

I was thus engaged when the sudden waking of the glen into life took me to my window. There is seldom silence up here, for if the wind be not sweeping the heather, the Quharity, that I may not have heard for days, seems to have crept nearer to the school-house in the night, and if both wind and water be out of earshot, there is the crack of a gun, or Waster Lunny's shepherd is on a stone near at hand whistling, or a lamb is scrambling through a fence, and kicking foolishly with its hind legs. These sounds I am unaware of until they stop, when I look up. Such a stillness was broken now by music.

From my window I saw a string of people walking rapidly down the glen, and Waster Lunny crossing his potato-field to meet them. Remembering that, though I was in my stocking soles, the ground was dry, I hastened to join the farmer, for I like to miss nothing. I saw a curious sight. In front of the little procession coming down the glen road, and so much more impressive than his satellites that they may be put out of mind as merely ploughmen and the like following a show, was a Highlander that I knew to be Lauchlan Campbell, one of the pipers engaged to lend music to the earl's marriage. He had the name of a thrawn man when sober, but pretty at the pipes at both times, and he came marching down the glen blowing gloriously, as if he had die clan of Campbell at his heels. I know no man who is so capable on occasion of looking like twenty as a Highland piper, and never have I seen a face in such a blaze of passion as was Lauchlan Campbell's that day. His following were keeping out of his reach, jumping back every time he turned round to shake his fist in the direction of the Spittal. While this magnificent man was yet some yards from us, I saw Waster Lunny,who had been in the middle of the road to ask questions, fall back in fear, and not being a fighting man myself, I jumped the dyke. Lauchlan gave me a look that sent me farther into the field, and strutted past, shrieking defiance through his pipes, until I lost him and his followers in a bend of the road.

"That's a terrifying spectacle," I heard Waster Lunny say when the music had become but a distant squeal. "You're bonny at louping dykes, dominie, when there is a wild bull in front o' you. Na, I canna tell what has happened, but at the least Lauchlan maun hae dirked the earl. Thae loons cried out to me as they gaed by that he has been blawing awa' at that tune till he canna halt. What a wind's in the crittur! I'm thinking there's a hell in ilka Highlandman."

"Take care then, Waster Lunny, that you dinna licht it," said an angry voice that made us jump, though it was only Duncan, the farmer's shepherd, who spoke.

"I had forgotten you was a Highlandman yoursel', Duncan," Waster Lunny said nervously, but Elspeth, who had come to us unnoticed, ordered the shepherd to return to the hillside, which he did haughtily.

"How did you no lay haud on that blast o' wind, Lauchlan Campbell," asked Elspeth of her husband, "and speir at him what had happened at the Spittal? A quarrel afore a marriage brings ill luck."

"I'm thinking," said the farmer," that Rintoul's making his ain ill luck by marrying on a young leddy."

"A man s never ower auld to marry," said Elspeth.

"No, nor a woman," rejoined Waster Lunny, "when she gets the chance. But, Elspeth, I believe I can guess what has fired that fearsome piper. Depend upon it, somebody has been speaking disrespectful about the crittur's ancestors."

"His ancestors!" exclaimed Elspeth, scornfully. "I'm thinking mine could hae bocht them at a crown the dozen."

"Hoots," said the farmer, "you're o' a weaving stock, and dinna understand about ancestors. Take a stick to a Highland laddie, and it's no him you hurt, but his ancestors. Likewise it's his ancestors that stanes you for it. When Duncan stalked awa the now, what think you he saw? He saw a farmer's wife dauring to order about his ancestors; and if that's the way wi' a shepherd, what will it be wi' a piper that has the kilts on him a' day to mind him o' his ancestors ilka time he looks down?"

Elspeth retired to discuss the probable disturbance at the Spittal with her family, giving Waster Lunny the opportunity of saying to me impressively—

"Man, man, has it never crossed you that it's a queer thing the like o' you and me having no ancestors? Ay, we had them in a manner o' speaking, no doubt, but they're as completely lost sicht o' as a flagon lid that's fallen ahint the dresser. Hech, sirs, but they would need a gey rubbing to get the rust off them now. I've been thinking that if I was to get my laddies to say their grandfather's name a curran times ilka day, like the Catechism, and they were to do the same wi' their bairns, and it was continued in future generations, we micht raise a fell field o' ancestors in time. Ay, but Elspeth wouldna hear o't. Nothing angers her mair than to hear me speak o' planting trees for the benefit o' them that's to be farmers here after me, and as for ancestors, she would howk them up as quick as I could plant them. Losh, dominie, is that a boot in your hand?"

To my mortification I saw that I had run out of the school-house with the boot on my hand as if it were a glove, and back I went straightway, blaming myself for a man wanting in dignity.

It was but a minor trouble this, however, even at the time; and to recall it later in the day was to look back on happiness, for though I did not know it yet, Lauchlan's playing raised the curtain on the great act of Gavin's life, and the twenty-four hours had begun, to which all I have told as yet is no more than the prologue.

Chapter XXVI

Scene At The Spittal

WITHIN an hour after I had left him Waster Lunny walked into the school-house and handed me his snuff-mull, which I declined politely. It was with this ceremony that we usually opened our conversations.

"I've seen the post," he said, "and he tells me there has been a queer ploy at the Spittal. It's a wonder the marriage hasna been turned into a burial, and all because o' that Highland stirk, Lauchlan Campbell."

Waster Lunny was a man who had to retrace his steps in telling a story if he tried short cuts, and so my custom was to wait patiently while he delved through the ploughed fields that always lay between him and his destination.

"As you ken, Rintoul's so little o' a Scotchman that he's no muckle better than an Englisher. That maun be the reason he hadna mair sense than to tramp on a Highlandman's ancestors, as he tried to tramp on Lauchlan's this day."

"If Lord Rintoul insulted the piper," I suggested, giving the farmer a helping hand cautiously, "it would be through inadvertence. Rintoul only bought the Spittal a year ago, and until then, I daresay,he had seldom been on our side of the Border."

This was a foolish interruption, for it set Waster Lunny off in a new direction.

"That's what Elspeth says. Says she, 'When the earl has grand estates in England, what for does he come to a barren place like the Spittal to be married? It's gey like,' she says, 'as if he wanted the marriage to be got by quietly; a thing,' says she, 'that no woman can stand. Furthermore,' Elspeth says, 'how has the marriage been postponed twice?' We ken what the servants at the Spittal says to that, namely, that the young lady is no keen to take him, but Elspeth winna listen to sic arguments. She says either the earl had grown timid (as mony a man does), when the wedding-day drew near, or else his sister that keeps his house is mad at the thocht o' losing her place; but as for the young lady's being sweer, says

Elspeth, 'an earl's an earl however auld he is, and a lassie's a lassie however young she is, and weel she kens you're never sure o' a man's no changing his mind about you till you're tied to him by law, after which it doesna so muckle matter whether he changes his mind about you or no.' Ay, there's a quirk in it some gait, dominie; but it's a deep water Elspeth canna bottom."

"It is," I agreed; "but you were to tell me what Birse told you of the disturbance at the Spittal."

"Ay, weel," he answered, "the post puts the wite o't on her little leddyship, as they call her, though she winna be a leddyship till the morn. All I can say is that if the earl was saft enough to do sic a thing out o' fondness for her, it's time he was married on her,so that he may come to his senses again. That's what I say; but Elspeth confers me, of course,and says she, 'If the young leddy was so careless o' insulting other folks' ancestors, it proves she has nane o' her ain; for them that has china plates themsels is the maist careful no to break the china plates of others.'"

"But what was the insult? Was Lauchlan dismissed?"

"Na, faags! It was waur than that. Dominie, you're dull in the uptake compared to Elspeth. I hadna tell her half the story afore she jaloused the rest. However, to begin again; there's great feasting and rejoicings gaen on at the Spittal the now, and also a banquet, which the post says is twa dinners in one. Weel, there's a curran Ogilvys among the guests, and it was them that egged on her little leddyship to make the daring proposal to the earl. What was the proposal? It was no less than that the twa pipers should be ordered to play 'The Bonny House o'Airlie.' Dominie, I wonder you can tak it so calm when you ken that's the Ogilvys sang, and that it's aimed at the clan o' Campbell."

"Pooh!" I said. "The Ogilvys and the Campbells used to be mortal enemies, but the feud has been long forgotten."

"Ay, I've heard tell," Waster Lunny said sceptically, "that Airlie and Argyle shakes hands now like Christians; but I'm thinking that's just afore the Queen. Dinna speak now, for I'm in the thick o't. Her little leddyship was all hinging in gold and jewels, the which winna be her ain till the morn; and she leans ower to the earl and whispers to him to get the pipers to play 'The Bonny

House.' He wasna willing, for says he, 'There's Ogilvys at the table, and ane o' the pipers is a Campbell, and we'll better let sleeping dogs lie.' However,the Ogilvys lauched at his caution; and he was so infatuated wi' her little leddyship that he gae in, and he cried out to the pipers to strike up 'The Bonny House.'

Waster Lunny pulled his chair nearer me and rested his hand on my knees.

"Dominie," he said in a voice that fell now and again into a whisper, "them looking on swears that when Lauchlan Campbell heard these monstrous orders his face became ugly and black, so that they kent in a jiffy what he would do. It's said a' body jumped back frae him in a sudden dread, except poor Angus, the other piper, wha was busy tuning up for 'The Bonny House.' Weel, Angus had got no fartherin the tune than the first skirl when Lauchlan louped at him, and ripped up the startled crittur's pipes wi' his dirk. The pipes gae a roar o' agony like a stuck swine, and fell gasping on the floor. What happened next was that Lauchlan wi' his dirk handy for onybody that micht try to stop him, marched once round the table, playing 'The Campbells are coming,' and then straucht out o' the Spittal, his chest far afore him, and his head so weel back that he could see what was going on ahint. Frae the Spittal to here he never stopped that fearsome tune, and I'se warant he's blawing away at it at this moment through the streets o' Thrums."

Waster Lunny was not in his usual spirits, or he would have repeated his story before he left me, for he had usually as much difficulty in coming to an end as in finding a beginning. The drouth was to him as serious a matter as death in the house, and as little to be forgotten for a lengthened period.

"There's to be a prayer-meeting for rain in the Auld Licht kirk the night," he told me as I escorted him as far as my side of the Quharity, now almost a dead stream, pitiable to see, "and I'm gaen; though I'm sweer to leave thae puir cattle o' mine. You should see how they look at me when I gie them mair o' that rotten grass to eat. It's eneuch to mak a man greet, for what richt hae I to keep kye when I canna meat them?"

Waster Lunny has said to me more than once that the great surprise of his life was when Elspeth was willing to take him.

Many a time, however, I have seen that in him which might have made any weaver's daughter proud of such a man, and I saw it again when we came to the river side.

"I'm no ane o' thae farmers," he said truthfully, "that's aye girding at the weather, and Elspeth and me kens that we hae been dealt wi' bountifully since we took this farm wi' gey anxious hearts. That woman, dominie, is eneuch to put a brave face on a coward, and it's no langer syne than yestreen when I was sitting in the dumps, looking at the aurora borealis, which I canna but regard as a messenger o' woe, that she put her hand on my shoulder, and she says, 'Waster Lunny, twenty year syne we began life thegither wi' nothing but the claethes on our back, and an it please God we can begin it again, for I hae you and you hae me, and I'm no cast down if you're no.' Dominie, is there mony sic women in the warld as that?"

"Many a one," I said.

"Ay, man, it shamed me, for I hae a kind o' delight in angering Elspeth, just to see what she'll say. I could hae ta'en her on my knee at that minute, but the bairns was there, and so it wouldna hae dune. But I cheered her up, for, after all, the drouth canna put us so far back as we was twenty years syne, unless it's true what my father said, that the aurora borealis is the devil's rainbow. I saw it sax times in July month, and it made me shut my een. You was out admiring it, dominie, but I can never forget that it was seen in the year twelve just afore the great storm. I was only a laddie then, but I mind how that awful wind stripped a' the standing corn in the glen in less time than we've been here at the water's edge. It was called the deil's besom. My father's hinmost words to me was, 'It's time eneuch to greet, laddie, when you see the aurora borealis.' I mind he was so complete ruined in an hour that he had to apply for relief frae the poor's rates. Think o' that, and him a proud man. He would tak' nothing till one winter day when we was a' starving, and syne I gaed wi' him to speir for't, and he telled me to grip his hand ticht, so that the cauldness o' mine micht gie him courage. They were doling out the charity in the Town's House, and I had never been in't afore. I canna look at it now without thinking of that day when me and my father gaed up the stair thegither. Mr.

Duthie was presiding at the time, and he wasna muckle older than Mr. Dishart is now. I mind he speired for proof that we was needing, and my father couldna speak. He just pointed at me. 'But you have a good coat on your back yoursel',' Mr. Duthie said, for there were mony waiting, sair needing. 'It was lended him to come here,' I cried, and without a word my father opened the coat, and they saw he had nothing on aneath, and his skin blue wi' cauld. Dominie, Mr. Duthie handed him one shilling and saxpence, and my father's fingers closed greedily on't for a minute, and syne it fell to the ground. They put it back in his hand, and it slipped out again, and Mr. Duthie gave it back to him, saying, 'Are you so cauld as that?' But, oh, man, it wasna cauld that did it, but shame o' being on the rates. The blood a' ran to my father's head, and syne left it as quick, and he flung down the siller and walked out o' the Town's House wi' me running after him. We warstled through that winter, God kens how, and it's near a pleasure to me to think o't now, for, rain or no rain, I can never be reduced to sic straits again."

The farmer crossed the water without using the stilts which were no longer necessary, and I little thought, as I returned to the school-house, what terrible things were to happen before he could offer me his snuff-mull again. Serious as his talk had been it was neither of drouth nor of the incident at the Spittal that I sat down to think. My anxiety about Gavin came back to me until I was like a man imprisoned between walls of his own building. It may be that my presentiments of that afternoon look gloomier now than they were, because I cannot return to them save over a night of agony, black enough to darken any time connected with it. Perhaps my spirits only fell as the wind rose, for wind ever takes me back to Harvie, and when I think of Harvie my thoughts are of the saddest. I know that I sat for some hours, now seeing Gavin pay the penalty of marrying the Egyptian, and again drifting back to my days with Margaret, until the wind took to playing tricks with me, so that I heard Adam Dishart enter our home by the sea every time the school-house door shook.

I became used to the illusion after starting several times, and thus when the door did open, about seven o'clock, it was only the wind rushing to my fire like a shivering dog that made me turn my head. Then I saw the Egyptian staring at me, and though her sudden appearance on my threshold was a strange thing, I forgot it in the whiteness of her face. She was looking at me like one who has asked a question of life or death, and stopped her heart for the reply.

"What is it?" I cried, and for a moment I believe I was glad she did not answer. She seemed to have told me already as much as I could bear.

"He has not heard," she said aloud in an expressionless voice, and, turning, would have slipped away without another word.

"Is any one dead?" I asked, seizing her hands and letting them fall, they were so clammy. She nodded, and trying to speak could not.

"He is dead," she said at last in a whisper. "Mr. Dishart is dead," and she sat down quietly.

At that I covered my face, crying, "God help Margaret!" and then she rose, saying fiercely, so that I drew back from her, "There is no Margaret; he only cared for me."

"She is his mother," I said hoarsely, and then she smiled to me, so that I thought her a harmless mad thing. "He was killed by a piper called Lauchlan Campbell," she said, looking up at me suddenly. "It was my fault."

"Poor Margaret!" I wailed.

"And poor Babbie," she entreated pathetically; "will no one say, 'Poor Babbie'?"

Chapter XXVII

First Journey Of The Dominie To Thrums During The Twenty-Four Hours

"How did it happen?" I asked more than once, but the Egyptian was only with me in the body, and she did not hear. I might have been talking to some one a mile away whom a telescope had drawn near my eyes.

When I put on my bonnet, however, she knew that I was going to Thrums, and she rose and walked to the door, looking behind to see that I followed.

"You must not come," I said harshly, but her hand started to her heart as if I had shot her, and I added quickly, "Come." We were already some distance on our way before I repeated my question.

"What matter how it happened?" she answered piteously, and they were words of which I felt the force. But when she said a little later, "I thought you would say it is not true," I took courage, and forced her to tell me all she knew. She sobbed while she spoke, if one may sob without tears.

"I heard of it at the Spittal," she said. 'The news broke out suddenly there that the piper had quarrelled with some one in Thrums, and that in trying to separate them Mr. Dishart was stabbed. There is no doubt of its truth."

"We should have heard of it here," I said hopefully, "before the news reached the Spittal. It cannot be true."

"It was brought to the Spittal," she answered, "by the hill road."

Then my spirits sank again, for I knew that this was possible. There is a path, steep but short, across the hills between Thrums and the top of the glen, which Mr. Glendinning took frequently when he had to preach at both places on the same Sabbath. It is still called the Minister's Road.

"Yet if the earl had believed it he would have sent some one into Thrums for particulars," I said, grasping at such comfort as I could make.

"He does believe it," she answered. "He told me of it himself."

You see the Egyptian was careless of her secret now; but what was that secret to me? An hour ago it would have been much, and already it was not worth listening to. If she had begun to tell me why Lord Rintoul took a gypsy girl into his confidence I should not have heard her.

"I ran quickly," she said. "Even if a messenger was sent he might be behind me."

Was it her words or the tramp of a horse that made us turn our heads at that moment? I know not. But far back in a twist of the road we saw a horseman approaching at such a reckless pace that I thought he was on a runaway. We stopped instinctively, and waited for him, and twice he disappeared in hollows of the road, and then was suddenly tearing down upon us. I recognised in him young Mr. McKenzie, a relative of Rintoul, and I stretched out my arms to compel him to draw up. He misunderstood my motive, and was raising his whip threateningly, when he saw the Egyptian. It is not too much to say that he swayed in the saddle. The horse galloped on, though he had lost hold of the reins. He looked behind until he rounded a corner, and I never saw such amazement mixed with incredulity on a human face. For some minutes I expected to see him coming back, but when he did not I said wonderingly to the Egyptian—

"He knew you."

"Did he?" she answered indifferently, and I think we spoke no more until we were in Windyghoul. Soon we were barely conscious of each other's presence. Never since have I walked between the schoolhouse and Thrums in so short a time, nor seen so little on the way.

In the Egyptian's eyes, I suppose, was a picture of Gavin lying dead; but if her grief had killed her thinking faculties, mine that was only less keen because I had been struck down once before, had set all the wheels of my brain in action. For it seemed to me that the hour had come when I must disclose myself to Margaret.

I had realised always that if such a necessity did arise it could only be caused by Gavin's premature death, or by his proving a bad son to her. Some may wonder that I could have looked calmly thus far into the possible, but I reply that the night of Adam Dishart's home-coming had made of me a man whom the future could not surprise again. Though I saw Gavin and his mother happy in our Auld Licht manse, that did not prevent my considering the contingencies which might leave her without a son. In the schoolhouse I had brooded over them as one may think over moves on a draught-board. It may have been idle, but it was done that I might know how to act best for Margaret if anything untoward occurred. The time for such action had come. Gavin's death had struck me hard, but it did not crush me. I was not unprepared. I was going to Margaret now.

What did I see as I walked quickly along the glen road, with Babbie silent by my side, and I doubt not pods of the broom cracking all around us? I saw myself entering the Auld Licht manse, where Margaret sat weeping over the body of Gavin, and there was none to break my coming to her, for none but she and I knew what had been.

I saw my Margaret again, so fragile now, so thin the wrists, her hair turned grey. No nearer could I go, but stopped at the door, grieving for her, and at last saying her name aloud.

I saw her raise her face, and look upon me for the first time for eighteen years. She did not scream at sight of me, for the body of her son lay between us, and bridged the gulf that Adam Dishart had made.

I saw myself draw near her reverently and say, "Margaret, he is dead, and that is why I have come back," and I saw her put her arms around my neck as she often did long ago.

But it was not to be. Never since that night at Harvie have I spoken to Margaret.

The Egyptian and I were come to Windyghoul before I heard her speak. She was not addressing me. Here Gavin and she had met first, and she was talking of that meeting to herself.

"It was there," I heard her say softly, as she gazed at the bush beneath which she had seen him shaking his fist at her on the night of the riots. A little farther on she stopped where a path from Windyghoul sets off for the well in the wood. She looked up it wistfully, and there I left her behind, and pressed on to the mud house to ask Nanny Webster if the minister was dead. Nanny's gate was swinging in the wind, but her door was shut, and for a moment I stood at it like a coward, afraid to enter and hear the worst.

The house was empty. I turned from it relieved, as if I had got a respite, and while I stood in the garden the Egyptian came to me shuddering, her twitching face asking the question that would not leave her lips.

"There is no one in the house," I said. "Nanny is perhaps at the well."

But the gypsy went inside, and pointing to the fire said, "It has been out for hours. Do you not see? The murder has drawn every one into Thrums."

So I feared. A dreadful night was to pass before I knew that this was the day of the release of Sanders Webster, and that frail Nanny had walked into Tilliedrum to meet him at the prison gate.

Babbie sank upon a stool, so weak that I doubt whether she heard me tell her to wait there until my return. I hurried into Thrums, not by the hill, though it is the shorter way, but by the Roods, for I must hear all before I ventured to approach the manse. From Windyghoul to the top of the Roods it is a climb and then a steep descent. The road has no sooner reached its highest point than it begins to fall in the straight line of houses called the Roods, and thus I came upon a full view of the street at once. A cart was labouring up it. There were women sitting on stones at their doors, and girls playing at palaulays, and out of the house nearest me came a black figure. My eyes failed me; I was asking so much from them. They made him tall and short, and spare and stout, so that I knew it was Gavin, and yet, looking again, feared, but all the time, I think, I knew it was he.

Chapter XXVIII

The Hill Before Darkness Fell — Scene Of The Impending Catastrophe

"YOU are better now?" I heard Gavin ask, presently.

He thought that having been taken ill suddenly I had waved to him for help, because he chanced to be near. With all my wits about me I might have left him in that belief, for rather would I have deceived him than had him wonder why his welfare seemed so vital to me. But I, who thought the capacity for being taken aback had gone from me, clung to his arm and thanked God audibly that he still lived. He did not tell me then how my agitation puzzled him, but led me kindly to the hill, where we could talk without listeners. By the time we reached it I was again wary, and I had told him what had brought me to Thrums, without mentioning how the story of his death reached my ears, or through whom.

"Mr. McKenzie," he said, interrupting me, "galloped all the way from the Spittal on the same errand. However, no one has been hurt much, except the piper himself."

Then he told me how the rumour arose.

"You know of the incident at the Spittal, and that Campbell marched off in high dudgeon? I understand that he spoke to no one between the Spittal and Thrums, but by the time he arrived here he was more communicative; yes, and thirstier. He was treated to drink in several public houses by persons who wanted to hear his story, and by-and-by he began to drop hints of knowing something against the earl's bride. Do you know Rob Dow?"

"Yes," I answered, "and what you have done for him."

"Ah, sir!" he said sighing, "for a long time I thought I was to be God's instrument in making a better man of Rob, but my power over him went long ago. Ten short months of the ministry takes some of the vanity out of a man."

Looking sideways at him I was startled by the unnatural brightness of his eyes. Unconsciously he had acquired the habit of pressing his teeth together in the pauses of his talk, shutting them on some woe that would proclaim itself, as men do who keep their misery to themselves."

"A few hours ago," he went on, "I heard Rob's voice in altercation as I passed the Bull tavern, and I had a feeling that if I failed with him so should I fail always throughout my ministry. I walked into the public-house, and stopped at the door of a room in which Dow and the piper were sitting drinking. I heard Rob saying, fiercely, 'If what you say about her is true, Highlandman, she's the woman I've been looking for this half year and mair; what is she like?' I guessed, from what I had been told of the piper, that they were speaking of the earl's bride, but Rob saw me and came to an abrupt stop, saying to his companion, 'Dinna say another word about her afore the minister.' Rob would have come away at once in answer to my appeal, but the piper was drunk and would not be silenced. 'I'll tell the minister about her, too,' he began. 'You dinna ken what you're doing,' Rob roared, and then, as if to save my ears from scandal at any cost, he struck Campbell a heavy blow on the mouth. I tried to intercept the blow, with the result that I fell, and then some one ran out of the tavern crying, 'He's killed!' The piper had been stunned, but the story went abroad that he had stabbed me for interfering with him. That is really all. Nothing, as you know, can overtake an untruth if it has a minute's start."

"Where is Campbell now?"

"Sleeping off the effect of the blow: but Dow has fled. He was terrified at the shouts of murder, and ran off up the West Town end. The doctor's dogcart was standing at a door there and Rob jumped into it and drove off. They did not chase him far, because he is sure to hear the truth soon, and then, doubtless, he will come back."

Though in a few hours we were to wonder at our denseness, neither Gavin nor I saw why Dow had struck the Highlander down rather than let him tell his story in the minister's presence. One moment's suspicion would have lit our way to the whole truth, but of the spring to all Rob's behaviour in the past eight months we were ignorant, and so to Gavin the Bull had only been the scene of a drunken brawl, while I forgot to think in the joy of finding him alive.

"I have a prayer-meeting for rain presently," Gavin said, breaking a picture that had just appeared unpleasantly before me of Babbie still in agony at Nanny's, "but before I leave you tell me why this rumour caused you such distress."

The question troubled me, and I tried to avoid it. Crossing the hill we had by this time drawn near a hollow called the Toad's-hole, then gay and noisy with a caravan of gypsies. They were those same wild Lindsays, for whom Gavin had searched Caddam one eventful night, and as I saw them crowding round their king, a man well known to me, I guessed what they were at.

"Mr. Dishart," I said abruptly, "would you like to see a gypsy marriage? One is taking place there just now. That big fellow is the king, and he is about to marry two of his people over the tongs. The ceremony will not detain us five minutes, though the rejoicings will go on all night."

I have been present at more than one gypsy wedding in my time, and at the wild, weird orgies that followed them, but what is interesting to such as I may not be for a minister's eyes, and, frowning at my proposal, Gavin turned his back upon the Toad's-hole. Then, as we re-crossed the hill, to get away from the din of the camp, I pointed out to him that the report of his death had brought McKenzie to Thrums, as well as me.

"As soon as McKenzie heard I was not dead," he answered, "he galloped off to the Spittal, without even seeing me. I suppose he posted back to be in time for the night's rejoicings there. So you see,it was not solicitude for me that brought him. He came because a servant at the Spittal was supposed to have done the deed."

"Well, Mr. Dishart," I had to say, "why should I deny that I have a warm regard for you? You have done brave work in our town."

"It has been little," he replied. "With God's help it will be more in future."

He meant that he had given time to his sad love affair that he owed to his people. Of seeing Babbie again I saw that he had given up hope. Instead of repining, he was devoting his whole soul to God's work. I was proud of him, and yet I grieved, for I could not think that God wanted him to bury his youth so soon.

"I had thought," he confessed to me, "that you were one of those who did not like my preaching."

"You were mistaken," I said, gravely. I dared not tell him that, except his mother, none would have sat under him so eagerly as I.

"Nevertheless," he said, "you were a member of the Auld Licht church in Mr. Carfrae's time, and you left it when I came."

"I heard your first sermon," I said.

"Ah," he replied. "I had not been long in Thrums before I discovered that if I took tea with any of my congregation and declined a second cup, they thought it a reflection on their brewing."

"You must not look upon my absence in that light," was all I could say. "There are reasons why I cannot come.'

He did not press me further, thinking I meant that the distance was too great, though frailer folk than I walked twenty miles to hear him. We might have parted thus had we not wandered by chance to the very spot where I had met him and Babbie. There is a seat there now for those who lose their breath on the climb up, and so I have two reasons nowadays for not passing the place by.

We read each other's thoughts, and Gavin said calmly, "I have not seen her since that night. She disappeared as into a grave."

How could I answer when I knew that Babbie was dying for want of him, not half a mile away?

"You seemed to understand everything that night," he went on; "or if you did not, your thoughts were very generous to me."

In my sorrow for him I did not notice that we were moving on again, this time in the direction of Windyghoul.

"She was only a gypsy girl," he said, abruptly, and I nodded. "But I hoped," he continued, "that she would be my wife."

"I understood that," I said.

"There was nothing monstrous to you," he asked, looking me in the face, "in a minister's marrying a gypsy?"

I own that if I had loved a girl, however far below or above me in degree, I would have married her had she been willing to take me. But to Gavin I only answered, "These are matters a man must decide for himself."

"I had decided for myself," he said, emphatically.

"Yet," I said, wanting him to talk to me of Margaret, "in such a case one might have others to consider besides himself."

"A man's marriage," he answered, "is his own affair. I would have brooked no interference from my congregation."

I thought, "There is some obstinacy left in him still"; but aloud I said, "It was of your mother I was thinking."

"She would have taken Babbie to her heart," he said, with the fond conviction of a lover.

I doubted it, but I only asked, "Your mother knows nothing of her?"

"Nothing," he rejoined. "It would be cruelty to tell my mother of her now that she is gone."

Gavin's calmness had left him, and he was striding quickly nearer to Windyghoul. I was in dread lest he should see the Egyptian at Nanny's door, yet to have turned him in another direction might have roused his suspicions. When we were within a hundred yards of the mud house, I knew that there was no Babbie in sight. We halved the distance and then I saw her at the open window. Gavin's eyes were on the ground, but she saw him. I held my breath, fearing that she would run out to him.

"You have never seen her since that night?" Gavin asked me,without hope in his voice.

Had he been less hopeless he would have wondered why I did not reply immediately. I was looking covertly at the mud house, of which we were now within a few yards. Babbie's face had gone from the window, and the door remained shut. That she could hear every word we uttered now, I could not doubt. But she was hiding from the man for whom her soul longed. She was sacrificing herself for him.

"Never," I answered, notwithstanding my pity for the brave girl, and then while I was shaking lest he should go in to visit Nanny, I heard the echo of the Auld Licht bell.

"That calls me to the meeting for rain," Gavin said, bidding me good-night. I had acted for Margaret, and yet I had hardly the effrontery to take his hand. I suppose he saw sympathy in my face, for suddenly the cry broke from him—

"If I could only know that nothing evil had befallen her!"

Babbie heard him and could not restrain a heartbreaking sob.

"What was that?" he said, starting.

A moment I waited, to let her show herself if she chose. But the mud house was silent again.

"It was some boy in the wood," I answered.

"Good-bye," he said, trying to smile.

Had I let him go, here would have been the end of his love story, but that piteous smile unmanned me, and I could not keep the words back.

"She is in Nanny's house," I cried.

In another moment these two were together for weal or woe, and I had set off dizzily for the schoolhouse, feeling now that I had been false to Margaret, and again exulting in what I had done. By-and-by the bell stopped, and Gavin and Babbie regarded it as little as I heeded the burns now crossing the glen road noisily at places that had been dry two hours before.

Chapter XXIX

Story Of The Egyptian

God gives us more than, were we not over-bold, we should dare to ask for, and yet how often (perhaps after saying "Thank God" so curtly that it is only a form of swearing) we are supplicants again within the hour. Gavin was to be satisfied if he were told that no evil had befallen her he loved, and all the way between the school-house and Windyghoul Babbie craved for no more than Gavin's life. Now they had got their desires; but do you think they were content?

The Egyptian had gone on her knees when she heard Gavin speak of her. It was her way of preventing herself from running to him. Then when she thought him gone, he opened the door. She rose and shrank back, but first she had stepped toward him with a glad cry. His disappointed arms met on nothing.

"You, too, heard that I was dead?" he said, thinking her strangeness but grief too sharply turned to joy.

There were tears in the word with which she answered him, and he would have kissed her, but she defended her face with her hand.

"Babbie," he asked, beginning to fear that he had not sounded her deepest woe, "why have you left me all this time? You are not glad to see me now?"

"I was glad," she answered in a low voice, "to see you from the window, but I prayed to God not to let you see me."

She even pulled away her hand when he would have taken it. "No, no, I am to tell you everything now, and then—"

"Say that you love me first," he broke in, when a sob checked her speaking.

"No," she said, "I must tell you first what I have done, and then you will not ask me to say that. I am not a gypsy."

"What of that?" cried Gavin. "It was not because you were a gypsy that I loved you."

"That is the last time you will say you love me," said Babbie. "Mr. Dishart, I am to be married tomorrow.'

She stopped, afraid to say more lest he should fall, but except that his arms twitched he did not move.

"I am to be married to Lord Rintoul," she went on. "Now you know who I am."

She turned from him, for his piercing eyes frightened her. Never again, she knew, would she see the love-light in them. He plucked himself from the spot where he had stood looking at her, and walked to the window. When he wheeled round there was no anger on his face, only a pathetic wonder that he had been deceived so easily. It was at himself that he was smiling grimly rather than at her, and the change pained Babbie as no words could have hurt her. He sat down on a chair, and waited for her to go on.

"Don't look at me," she said, "and I will tell you everything." He dropped his eyes listlessly, and had he not asked her a question from time to time she would have doubted whether he heard her.

"After all," she said, "a gypsy dress is my birthright, and so the Thrums people were scarcely wrong in calling me an Egyptian. It is a pity any one insisted on making me something different. I believe I could have been a good gypsy."

"Who were your parents?" Gavin asked, without looking up.

"You ask that," she said, "because you have a good mother. It is not a question that would occur to me. My mother — If she was bad may not that be some excuse for me? Ah, but I have no wish to excuse myself. Have you seen a gypsy cart with a sort of hammock swung beneath it in which gypsy children are carried about the country? If there are no children, the pots and pans are stored in it. Unless the roads are rough it makes a comfortable cradle, and it was the only one I ever knew. Well, one day I suppose the road was rough, for I was capsized. I remember picking myself up after a little and running after the cart, but they did not hear my cries. I sat down by the roadside and stared after the cart until I lost sight of it. That was in England, and I was not three years old."

"But surely," Gavin said, "they came back to look for you?"

"So far as I know," Babbie answered hardly, "they did not come back. I have never seen them since. I think they were drunk. My only recollection of my mother is that she once took me to see the dead body of some gypsy who had been murdered. She told me to dip my hand in the blood, so that I could say I had done so when I became a woman. It was meant as a treat to me, and is the one kindness I am sure I got from her. Curiously enough, I felt the shame of her deserting me for many years afterwards. As a child I cried hysterically at thought of it; it pained me when I was at school in Edinburgh every time I saw the other girls writing home; I cannot think of it without a shudder, even now. It is what makes me worse than other women."

Her voice had altered, and she was speaking passionately.

"Sometimes," she continued, more gently, "I try to think that my mother did come back for me, and then went away because she heard I was in better hands than hers. It was Lord Rintoul who found me, and I owe everything to him. You will say that he has no need to be proud of me. He took me home on his horse, and paid his gardener's wife to rear me. She was Scotch, and that is why I can speak two languages. It was he, too, who sent me to school in Edinburgh."

"He has been very kind to you," said Gavin, who would have preferred to dislike the earl.

"So kind," answered Babbie, "that now he is to marry me. But do you know why he has done all this?"

Now again she was agitated, and spoke indignantly.

"It is all because I have a pretty face," she said, her bosom rising and falling. "Men think of nothing else. He had no pity for the deserted child. I knew that while I was yet on his horse. When he came to the gardener's afterwards it was not to give me some one to love, it was only to look upon what was called my beauty; I was merely a picture to him, and even the gardener's children knew it and sought to terrify me by saying, 'You are losing your looks; the earl will not care for you any more.' Sometimes he brought his friends to see me, 'because I was such a lovely child, and if they did not agree with him on that point he left without kissing me. Throughout my whole girlhood I was taught nothing but to please him, and the only way to do that was to be pretty. It was the only virtue worth striving for; the others were never thought of when he asked how I was getting on. Once I had fever and nearly died, yet this knowledge that my face was everything was implanted in me so that my fear lest he should think me ugly when I recovered terrified me into hysterics. I dream still that I am in that fever and all my fears return. He did think me ugly when he saw me next. I remember the incident so well still. I had run to him, and he was lifting me up to kiss me when he saw that my face had changed. 'What a cruel disappointment,' he said, and turned his back on me. I had given him a child's love until then, but from that day I was hard and callous."

"And when was it you became beautiful again?" Gavin asked, by no means in the mind to pay compliments.

"A year passed," she continued, "before I saw him again. In that time he had not asked for me once, and the gardener had kept me out of charity. It was by an accident that we met, and at first he did not know me. Then he said, 'Why, Babbie, I believe you are to be a beauty after all!' I hated him for that, and stalked away from him, but he called after me, 'Bravo! she walks like a queen'; and it was because I walked like a queen that he sent me to an Edinburgh school. He used to come to sec me every year, and as I grew up the girls called me Lady Rintoul. He was not fond of me; he is not fond of me now. He would as soon think of looking at the back of a picture as at what I am apart from my face, but he dotes on it, and is to marry it. Is that love? Long before I left school, which was shortly before you came to Thrums, he had told his sister that he was determined to marry me, and she hated me for it, making me as uncomfortable as she could, so that I almost looked forward to the marriage because it would be such a humiliation to her."

In admitting this she looked shamefacedly at Gavin, and then went on—

"It is humiliating him too. I understand him. He would like not to want to marry me, for he is ashamed of my origin, but he cannot help it. It is this feeling that has brought him here, so that the marriage may take place where my history is not known."

"The secret has been well kept," Gavin said, "for they have failed to discover it even in Thrums."

"Some of the Spittal servants suspect it, nevertheless," Babbie answered, "though how much they know I cannot say. He has not a servant now, either here or in England, who knew me as a child.

The gardener who befriended me was sent away long ago. Lord Rintoul looks upon me as a disgrace to him that he cannot live without."

"I dare say he cares for you more than you think," Gavin said gravely.

"He is infatuated about my face, or the pose of my head, or something of that sort," Babbie said bitterly, "or he would not have endured me so long. I have twice had the wedding postponed, chiefly, I believe, to enrage my natural enemy, his sister, who is as much aggravated by my reluctance to marry him as by his desire to marry me. However, I also felt that imprisonment for life was approaching as the day drew near, and I told him that if he did not defer the wedding I should run away. He knows I am capable of it, for twice I ran away from school. If his sister only knew that!"

For a moment it was the old Babbie Gavin saw; but her glee was short-lived, and she resumed sedately—

"They were kind to me at school, but the life was so dull and prim that I ran off in a gypsy dress of my own making. That is what it is to have gypsy blood in one. I was away for a week the first time, wandering the country alone, telling fortunes, dancing and singing in woods and sleeping in barns. I am the only woman in the world well brought up who is not afraid of mice or rats. That is my gypsy blood again. After that wild week I went back to the school of my own will, and no one knows of the escapade but my school-mistress and Lord Rintoul. The second time, however, I was detected singing in the street, and then my future husband was asked to take me away. Yet Miss Feversham cried when I left, and told me that I was the nicest girl she knew, as well as the nastiest. She said she should love me as soon as I was not one of her boarders."

"And then you came to the Spittal?"

"Yes; and Lord Rintoul wanted me to say I was sorry for what I had done, but I told him I need not say that, for I was sure to do it again. As you know, I have done it several times since then; and though I am a different woman since I knew you, I dare say I shall go on doing it at times all my life. You shake your head because you do not understand. It is not that I make up my mind to break out in that way; I may not have had the least desire to do it for weeks, and then suddenly, when I am out riding, or at dinner, or at a dance, the craving to be a gypsy again is so strong that I never think of resisting it; I would risk my life to gratify it. Yes, whatever my life in the future is to be, I know that must be part of it. I used to pretend at the Spittal that I had gone to bed, and then escape by the window. I was mad with glee at those times, but I always returned before morning, except once, the last time I saw you, when I was away for nearly twenty-four hours. Lord Rintoul was so glad to see me come back then, that he almost forgave me for going away. There is nothing more to tell except that on the night of the riot it was not my gypsy nature that brought me to Thrums, but a desire to save the poor weavers. I had heard Lord Rintoul and the sheriff discussing the contemplated raid. I have hidden nothing from you. In time, perhaps, I shall have suffered sufficiently for all my wickedness."

Gavin rose wearily, and walked through the mud house looking at her.

"This is the end of it all," he said harshly, coming to a standstill. "I loved you, Babbie."

"No," she answered, shaking her head: "You never knew me until now, and so it was not me you loved. I know what you thought I was, and I will try to be it now."

"If you had only told me this before," the minister said sadly, "it might not have been too late."

"I only thought you like all the other men I knew," she replied, "until the night I came to the manse. It was only my face you admired at first."

"No, it was never that," Gavin said with such conviction that her mouth opened in alarm to ask him if he did not think her pretty. She did not speak, however, and he continued, "You must have known that I loved you from the first night."

"No; you only amused me," she said, like one determined to stint nothing of the truth. "Even at the well I laughed at your vows."

This wounded Gavin afresh, wretched as her story had made him, and he said tragically, "You have never cared for me at all."

"Oh, always, always," she answered, "since I knew what love was; and it was you who taught me."

Even in his misery he held his head high with pride. At least she did love him.

"And then," Babbie said, hiding her face, "I could not tell you what I was because I knew you would loathe me. I could only go away."

She looked at him forlornly through her tears, and then moved toward the door. He had sunk upon a stool, his face resting on the table, and it was her intention to slip away unnoticed. But he heard the latch rise, and jumping up, said sharply, "Babbie, I cannot give you up."

She stood in tears, swinging the door unconsciously with her hand.

"Don't say that you love me still," she cried; and then, letting her hand fall from the door, added imploringly, "Oh, Gavin, do you?"

Chapter XXX

The Meeting For Rain

Meanwhile the Auld Lichts were in church, waiting for their minister, and it was a full meeting, because nearly every well in Thrums had been scooped dry by anxious palms. Yet not all were there to ask God's rain for themselves. Old Charles Yuill was in his pew, after dreaming thrice that he would break up with the drouth; and Bell Christison had come, though her man lay dead at home, and she thought it could matter no more to her how things went in the world.

You, who do not love that little congregation, would have said that they were waiting placidly. But probably so simple a woman as Meggy Rattray could have deceived you into believing that because her eyes were downcast she did not notice who put the threepenny-bit in the plate. A few men were unaware that the bell was working overtime, most of them farmers with their eyes on the windows, but all the women at least were wondering. They knew better, however, than to bring their thoughts to their faces, and none sought to catch another's eye. The men-folk looked heavily at their hats in the seats in front. Even when Hendry Munn, instead of marching to the pulpit with the big Bible in his hands, came as far as the plate and signed to Peter Tosh, elder, that he was wanted in the vestry, you could not have guessed how every woman there, except Bell Christison, wished she was Peter Tosh. Peter was so taken aback that he merely gaped at Hendry, until suddenly he knew that his five daughters were furious with him, when he dived for his hat and staggered to the vestry with his mouth open. His boots cheeped all the way, but no one looked up.

"I hadna noticed the minister was lang in coming," Waster Lunny told me afterwards, "but Elspeth noticed it, and with a quickness that baffles me she saw I was thinking o' other things. So she let out her foot at me. I gae a low cough to let her ken I wasna sleeping, but in a minute out goes her foot again. Ay, syne I thocht I might hae dropped my hanky into Snecky Hobart's pew, but no, it was in my tails. Yet her hand was on the board, and she was working her fingers in a way that I kent meant she would like to shake me. Next I looked to see if I was sitting on her frock, the which tries a woman sair, but I wasna. 'Does she want to change Bibles wi' me?' I wondered; 'or is she sliding yont a peppermint to me?' It was neither, so I edged as far frae her as I could gang. Weel, would you credit it, I saw her body coming nearer me inch by inch, though she was looking straucht afore her, till she was within kick o' me, and then out again goes her foot. At that, dominie, I lost patience, and I whispered, fierce-like, 'Keep your foot to yoursel', you limmer!' Ay, her intent, you see, was to waken me to what was gaen on, but I couldna be expected to ken that."

In the vestry Hendry Munn was now holding counsel with three elders, of whom the chief was Lang Tammas.

"The laddie I sent to the manse," Hendry said, "canna be back this five minutes, and the question is how we're to fill up that time. I'll ring no langer, for the bell has been in a passion ever since a quarter-past eight. It's as sweer to clang past the quarter as a horse to gallop by its stable."

"You could gang to your box and gie out a psalm, Tammas," suggested John Spens.

"And would a psalm sung wi' sic an object," retorted the precentor, "mount higher, think you, than a bairn's kite? I'll insult the Almighty to screen no minister."

"You're screening him better by standing whaur you are," said the imperturbable Hendry, "for as lang as you dinna show your face they'll think it may be you that's missing instead o' Mr. Dishart."

Indeed, Gavin's appearance in church without the precentor would have been as surprising as Tammas's without the minister. As certainly as the shutting of a money-box is followed by the turning of the key, did the precentor walk stiffly from the vestry to his box a toll of the bell in front of the minister. Tammas's halfpenny rang in the plate as Gavin passed T'nowhead's pew, and Gavin's sixpence with the snapping-to of the precentor's door. The two men might have been connected by a string that tightened at ten yards.

"The congregation ken me ower weel," Tammas said, "to believe I would keep the Lord waiting."

"And they are as sure o' Mr. Dishart," rejoined Spens, with spirit, though he feared the precentor on Sabbaths and at prayer-meetings. "You're a hard man."

"I speak the blunt truth," Whamond answered.

"Ay," said Spens, "and to tak' credit for that may be like blawing that you're ower honest to wear claethes."

Hendry, who had gone to the door, returned now with the information that Mr. Dishart had left the manse two hours ago to pay visits meaning to come to the prayer-meeting before he returned home.

"There's a quirk in this, Hendry," said Tosh. "Was it Mistress Dishart the laddie saw?"

"No," Hendry replied. "It was Jean. She canna get to the meeting because the mistress is nervous in the manse by herself; and Jean didna like to tell her that he's missing, for fear o' alarming her. What are we to do now?"

"He's an unfaithful shepherd," cried the precentor, while Hendry again went out. "I see it written on the walls."

"I dinna," said Spens doggedly.

"Because," retorted Tammas, "having eyes you see not."

'Tammas, I aye thocht you was fond o' Mr. Dishart."

"If my right eye were to offend me," answered the precentor, "I would pluck it out. I suppose you think, and baith o' you farmers too, that there's no necessity for praying for rain the nicht? You'll be content, will ye, if Mr. Dishart just drops in to the kirk some day accidental-like, and offers up a bit prayer?"

"As for the rain," Spens said, triumphantly, "I wouldna wonder though it's here afore the minister. You canna deny, Peter Tosh, that there's been a smell o' rain in the air this twa hours back."

"John," Peter said agitatedly, "dinna speak so confidently. I've kent it," he whispered, "since the day turned; but it wants to tak' us by surprise, lad, and so I'm no letting on."

"See that you dinna make an idol o' the rain," thundered Whamond. "Your thochts is no wi' Him, but wi' the clouds; and whaur your thochts are, there will your prayers stick also."

"If you saw my lambs," Tosh began; and then, ashamed of himself, said, looking upwards, "He holds the rain in the hollow of His hand."

"And He's closing His neive ticht on't again," said the precentor solemnly. "Hearken to the wind rising."

God help me!" cried Tosh, wringing his hands. Is it fair, think you," he said, passionately addressing the sky, "to show your wrath wi' Mr. Dishart by ruining my neeps?"

"You were richt, Tammas Whamond," Spens said, growing hard as he listened to the wind, "the sanctuary o' the Lord has been profaned this nicht by him wha should be the chief pillar o' the building."

They were lowering brows that greeted Hendry when he returned to say that Mr. Dishart had been seen last on the hill with the Glen Quharity dominie.

"Some thinks," said the kirk-officer, "that he's awa hunting for Rob Dow."

"Nothing'll excuse him," replied Spens, "short o' his having fallen over the quarry."

Hendry's was usually a blank face, but it must have looked troubled now, for Tosh was about to say, "Hendry, you're keeping something back," when the precentor said it before him.

"Wi' that story o' Mr. Dishart's murder, no many hours auld yet," the kirk-officer replied evasively, "we should be wary o' trusting gossip."

"What hae you heard?"

"It's through the town," Hendry answered, "that a woman was wi' the dominie."

"A woman!" cried Tosh. "The woman there's been sic talk about in connection wi' the minister? Whaur are they now?"

"It's no kent, but — the dominie was seen goin' hame by himsel'."

"Leaving the minister and her thegither," cried the three men at once.

"Hendry Munn," Tammas said sternly, "there's mair about this; wha is the woman?"

"They are liars," Hendry answered, and shut his mouth tight.

"Gie her a name, I say," the precentor ordered, "or, as chief elder of this kirk, supported by mair than half o' the Session, I command you to lift your hat and go."

Hendry gave an appealing took to Tosh and Spens, but the precentor's solemnity had cowed them.

"They say, then," he answered sullenly, "that it's the Egyptian. Yes, and I believe they ken."

The two farmers drew back from this statement incredulously; but Tammas Whamond jumped at the kirk-officer's throat, and some who were in the church that night say they heard Hendry scream. Then the precentor's fingers relaxed their grip, and he tottered into the middle of the room.

"Hendry," he pleaded, holding out his arms pathetically, "tak' back these words. Oh, man, have pity, and tak' them back."

But Hendry would not, and then Lang Tammas's mouth worked convulsively, and he sobbed, crying, "Nobody kent it, but mair than mortal son, O God, did I love the lad!"

So seldom in a lifetime had any one seen into this man's heart that Spens said, amazed—

"Tammas, Tammas Whamond, it's no like you to break down."

The rusty door of Whamond's heart swung to.

"Who broke down?" he asked fiercely. "Let no member of this Session dare to break down till his work be done."

"What work?" Tosh said uneasily. "We canna interfere."

"I would rather resign," Spens said, but shook when Whamond hurled these words at him—

'And Jesus said unto him, No man, having put his hand to the plow and looking back, is fit for the kingdom of God.'

"It mayna be true," Hendry said eagerly.

"We'll soon see."

"He would gie her up," said Tosh.

"Peter Tosh," answered Whamond sternly, "I call upon you to dismiss the congregation."

"Should we no rather haud the meeting oursel's?"

"We have other work afore us," replied the precentor.

"But what can I say?" Tosh asked nervously. "Should I offer up a prayer?"

"I warn you all," broke in Hendry, "that though the congregation is sitting there quietly, they'll be tigers for the meaning o' this as soon as they're in the street."

"Let no ontruth be telled them," said the precentor. "Peter Tosh, do your duty. John Spens, remain wi' me."

The church emptied silently, but a buzz of excitement arose outside. Many persons tried to enter the vestry, but were ordered away, and when Tosh joined his fellow-elders the people were collecting in animated groups in the square, or scattering through the wynds for news.

"And now," said the precentor, "I call upon the three o' you to come wi' me. Hendry Munn, you gang first."

"I maun bide ahint," Hendry said, with a sudden fear, "to lock up the kirk."

"I'll lock up the kirk," Whamond answered harshly.

"You maun gie me the keys, though," entreated the kirk-officer.

I'll take care o' the keys," said Whamond.

'I maun hae them," Hendry said, "to open the kirk on Sabbath."

The precentor locked the doors, and buttoned up the keys in his trousers pocket.

"Wha kens," he said in a voice of steel, "that the kirk'll be open next Sabbath?"

"Hae some mercy on him, Tammas," Spens implored. "He's no twa-and-twenty."

"Wha kens," continued the precentor, "but that the next time this kirk is opened will be to preach it toom?"

"What road do we tak'?"

"The road to the hill, whaur he was seen last."

Chapter XXXI

Various Bodies Converging On The Hill

It would be coming on for a quarter-past nine, and a misty night, when I reached the schoolhouse, and I was so weary of mind and body that I sat down without taking off my bonnet. I had left the door open, and I remember listlessly watching the wind making a target of my candle, but never taking a sufficiently big breath to do more than frighten it. From this lethargy I was roused by the sound of wheels.

In the daytime our glen road leads to many parts, but in the night only to the doctor's. Then the gallop of a horse makes farmers start up in bed and cry, "Who's ill?" I went to my door and listened to the trap coming swiftly down the lonely glen, but I could not see it, for there was a trailing scarf of mist between the school-house and the road. Presently I heard the swish of the wheels in water, and so learned that they were crossing the ford to come to me. I had been unstrung by the events of the evening, and fear at once pressed thick upon me that this might be a sequel to them, as indeed it was.

While still out of sight the trap stopped, and I heard some one jump from it. Then came this conversation, as distinct as though it had been spoken into my ear:—

"Can you see the school-house now, McKenzie?"

"I am groping for it, Rintoul. The mist seems to have made off with the path."

"Where are you, McKenzie? I have lost sight of you."

It was but a ribbon of mist, and as these words were spoken McKenzie broke through it. I saw him, though to him I was only a stone at my door.

"I have found the house, Rintoul," he shouted, "and there is a light in it, so that the fellow has doubtless returned."

"Then wait a moment for me."

"Stay where you are, Rintoul, I entreat you, and leave him to me. He may recognise you."

"No, no, McKenzie, I am sure he never saw me before. I insist on accompanying you."

"Your excitement, Rintoul, will betray you. Let me go alone. I can question him without rousing his suspicions. Remember, she is only a gypsy to him."

"He will learn nothing from me. I am quite calm now."

"Rintoul, I warn you your manner will betray you, and tomorrow it will be roared through the countryside that your bride ran away from the Spittal in a gypsy dress, and had to be brought back by force."

The altercation may have lasted another minute, but the suddenness with which I learned Babbie's secret had left my ears incapable of learning more. I daresay the two men started when they found me at my door, but they did not remember, as few do remember who have the noisy day to forget it in, how far the voice carries in the night.

They came as suddenly on me as I on them, for though they had given unintentional notice of their approach, I had lost sight of the speakers in their amazing words. Only a moment did young McKenzie's anxiety to be spokesman give me to regard Lord Rintoul. I saw that he was a thin man and tall, straight in the figure, but his head begun to sink into his shoulders and not very steady on them. His teeth had grip of his underlip, as if this was a method of controlling his agitation, and he was opening and shutting his hands restlessly. He had a dog with him which I was to meet again.

"Well met, Mr. Ogilvy," said McKenzie, who knew me slightly, having once acted as judge at a cock-fight in the school-house. "We were afraid we should have to rouse you."

"You will step inside?" I asked awkwardly, and while I spoke I was wondering how long it would be before the earl's excitement broke out.

"It is not necessary," McKenzie answered hurriedly. "My friend and I (this is Mr. McClure) have been caught in the mist without a lamp, and we thought you could perhaps favour us with one."

"Unfortunately I have nothing of the kind," I said, and the state of mind I was in is shown by my answering seriously.

"Then we must wish you a good-night and manage as best we can," he said; and then before he could touch, with affected indifference, on the real object of their visit, the alarmed earl said angrily, "McKenzie, no more of this."

"No more of this delay, do you mean, McClure?" asked McKenzie, and then turning to me said, "By the way, Mr. Ogilvy, I think this is our second meeting to-night. I met you on the road a few hours ago with your wife. Or was it your daughter?"

"It was neither, Mr. McKenzie," I answered, with the calmness of one not yet recovered from a shock. "It was a gypsy girl."

"Where is she now?" cried Rintoul feverishly; but McKenzie, speaking loudly at the same time, tried to drown his interference as one obliterates writing by writing over it.

"A strange companion for a schoolmaster," he said. "What became of her?"

"I left her near Caddam Wood," I replied, "but she is probably not there now."

"Ah, they are strange creatures, these gypsies," he said, casting a warning look at the earl. "Now I wonder where she had been bound for?"

'There is a gypsy encampment on the hill," I answered, though I cannot say why.

"She is there!" exclaimed Rintoul, and was done with me.

"I daresay," McKenzie said, indifferently. "However, it is nothing to us. Good-night, sir."

The earl had started for the trap, but McKenzie's salute reminded him of a forgotten courtesy, and, despite his agitation, he came back to apologise. I admired him for this. Then my thoughtlessness must needs mar all.

"Good-night, Mr. McKenzie," I said. "Goodnight, Lord Rintoul."

I had addressed him by his real name. Never a turnip fell from a bumping, laden cart, and the driver more unconscious of it, than I that I had dropped that word. I re-entered the house, but had not reached my chair when McKenzie's hand fell roughly on me, and I was swung round.

"Mr. Ogilvy," he said, the more savagely I doubt not because his passions had been chained so long, "you know more than you would have us think. Beware, sir, of recognising that gypsy should you ever see her again in different attire. I advise you to have forgotten this night when you waken tomorrow morning."

With a menacing gesture he left me, and I sank into a chair, glad to lose sight of the glowering eyes with which he had pinned me to the wall. I did not hear the trap cross the ford and renew its journey. When I looked out next, the night had fallen very dark, and the glen was so deathly in its drowsiness that I thought not even the cry of murder could tear its eyes open.

The earl and McKenzie would be some distance still from the hill when the office-bearers had scoured it in vain for their minister. The gypsies, now dancing round their fires to music that, on ordinary occasions, Lang Tammas would have stopped by using his fists to the glory of God, had seen no minister, they said, and disbelieved in the existence of the mysterious Egyptian.

"Liars they are to trade," Spens declared to his companions, "but now and again they speak truth, like a standing clock, and I'm beginning to think the minister's lassie was invented in the square."

"Not so," said the precentor, "for we saw her oursel's a short year syne, and Hendry Munn there allows there's townsfolk that hae passed her in the glen mair recently."

"I only allowed," Hendry said cautiously, "that some sic talk had shot up sudden-like in the town. Them that pretends they saw her says that she joukit quick out o' sicht."

"Ay, and there's another quirk in that," responded the suspicious precentor.

"I'se uphaud the minister's sitting in the manse in his slippers by this time," Hendry said.

"I'm willing," replied Whamond, "to gang back and speir, or to search Caddam next; but let the matter drop I winna, though I ken you're a' awid to be hame now."

"And naturally," retorted Tosh, "for the nicht's coming on as black as pick, and by the time we're at Caddam, we'll no even see the trees."

Toward Caddam, nevertheless, they advanced, hearing nothing but a distant wind and the whish of their legs in the broom.

"Whaur's John Spens?" Hendry said suddenly.

They turned back, and found Spens rooted to the ground, as a boy becomes motionless when he thinks he is within arm's reach of a nest, and the bird sitting on the eggs.

"What do you see, man?" Hendry whispered.

"As sure as death," answered Spens, awe-struck, "I felt a drap o' rain."

"It's no rain we're here to look for," said the precentor.

"Peter Tosh," cried Spens, "it was a drap! Oh, Peter! how are you looking at me so queer, Peter, when you should be thanking the Lord for the promise that's in that drap?"

"Come away," Whamond said, impatiently, but Spens answered, "No till I've offered up a prayer for the promise that's in that drap. Peter Tosh, you've forgotten to take off your bonnet."

"Think twice, John Spens," gasped Tosh, "afore you pray for rain this nicht."

The others thought him crazy, but he went on, with a catch in his voice:—

"I felt a drap o' rain mysel', just afore it came on dark so hurried, and my first impulse was to wish that I could carry that drap about wi' me, and look at it. But, John Spens, when I looked up I saw sic a change running ower the sky that I thocht hell had taen the place o' heaven, and that there was waterspouts gathering therein for the drowning o' the world."

"There's no water in hell," the precentor said grimly.

"Genesis ix.," said Spens, "verses 8 to 17. Ay but, Peter, you've startled me, and I'm thinking we should be stepping hame. Is that a licht?"

"It'll be in Nanny Webster's," Hendry said, after they had all regarded the light.

"I never heard that Nanny needed a candle to licht her to her bed," the precentor muttered.

"She was awa to meet Sanders the day as he came out o' the Tilliedrum gaol," Spens remembered, "and I daresay the licht means they're hame again."

"It's well kent—" began Hendry, and would have recalled his words.

"Hendry Munn," cried the precentor, "if you hae minded onything that may help us, out wi't."

"I was just minding," the kirk-officer answered reluctantly, "that Nanny allows it's Mr. Dishart that has been keeping her frae the poorhouse. You canna censure him for that, Tammas."

"Can I no?" retorted Whamond. "What business has he to befriend a woman that belongs to another denomination? I'll see to the bottom o' that this nicht. Lads, follow me to Nanny's, and dinna be surprised if we find baith the minister and the Egyptian there."

They had not advanced many yards when Spens jumped to the side, crying, "Be wary, that's no the wind; it's a machine!"

Immediately the doctor's dog-cart was close to them, with Rob Dow for its only occupant. He was driving slowly, or Whamond could not have escaped the horse's hoofs.

"Is that you, Rob Dow?" said the precentor sourly. "I tell you, you'll be gaoled for stealing the doctor's machine."

"The Hielandman wasna muckle hurt, Rob," Hendry said, more good-naturedly.

"I ken that," replied Rob, scowling at the four of them. "What are you doing here on sic a nicht?"

"Do you see anything strange in the nicht, Rob?" Tosh asked apprehensively.

"It's setting to rain," Dow replied. "I dinna see it, but I feel it."

"Ay," said Tosh, eagerly, "but will it be a saft, cowdie sweet ding-on?"

"Let the heavens open if they will," interposed Spens recklessly. "I would swap the drouth for rain, though it comes down in a sheet as in the year twelve."

"And like a sheet it'll come," replied Dow, "and the deil'll blaw it about wi' his biggest bellowses."

Tosh shivered, but Whamond shook him roughly, saying—

"Keep your oaths to yoursel', Rob Dow, and tell me, hae you seen Mr. Dishart?"

"I hinna," Rob answered curtly, preparing to drive on.

"Nor the lassie they call the Egyptian?"

Rob leaped from the dog-cart, crying, "What does that mean?"

"Hands oft," said the precentor, retreating from him. "It means that Mr. Dishart neglected the prayer-meeting this nicht to philander after that heathen woman."

"We're no sure o't, Tammas," remonstrated the kirk-officer. Dow stood quite still. "I believe Rob kens it's true," Hendry added sadly, "or he would hae flown at your throat, Tammas Whamond, for saying these words."

Even this did not rouse Dow.

"Rob doesna worship the minister as he used to do," said Spens.

"And what for no?" cried the precentor. "Rob Dow, is it because you've found out about this woman?"

"You're a pack o' liars," roared Rob, desperately, "and if you say again that ony wandering hussy has haud o' the minister, I'll let you see whether I can loup at throats."

"You'll swear by the Book," asked Whamond, relentlessly, "that you've seen neither o' them this nicht, nor them thegither at any time?"

"I so swear by the Book," answered poor loyal Rob. "But what makes you look for Mr. Dishart here?" he demanded, with an uneasy look at the light in the mud house.

"Go hame," replied the precentor, "and deliver up the machine you stole, and leave this Session to do its duty. John, we maun fathom the meaning o' that licht."

Dow started, and was probably at that moment within an ace of felling Whamond.

"I'll come wi' you," he said, hunting in his mind for a better way of helping Gavin.

They were at Nanny's garden, but in the darkness Whamond could not find the gate. Rob climbed the paling, and was at once lost sight of. Then they saw his head obscure the window. They did not, however, hear the groan that startled Babbie.

'There's nobody there," he said, coming back, "but Nanny and Sanders. You'll mind Sanders was to be freed the day."

"I'll go in and see Sanders," said Hendry, but the precentor pulled him back, saying, "You'll do nothing o' the kind, Hendry Munn; you'll come awa wi' me now to the manse."

"It's mair than me and Peter'll do, then," said Spens, who had been consulting with the other farmer. 'We're gaun as straucht hame as the darkness'll let us."

With few more words the Session parted, Spens and Tosh setting off for their farms, and Hendry accompanying the precentor. No one will ever know where Dow went. I can fancy him, however, returning to the wood, and there drawing rein. I can fancy his mind made up to watch the mud house until Gavin and the gypsy separated, and then pounce upon her. I daresay his whole plot could be condensed into a sentence, "If she's got rid o' this nicht, we may cheat the Session yet." But this is mere surmise. All I know is, that he waited near Nanny's house, and by-and-by heard another trap coming up Windy ghoul. That was just before the ten o'clock bell began to ring.

Chapter XXXII

Leading Swiftly To The Appalling Marriage

The little minister bowed his head in assent when Babbie's cry, "Oh, Gavin, do you?" leapt in front of her unselfish wish that he should care for her no more.

"But that matters very little now," he said.

She was his to do with as he willed; and, perhaps, the joy of knowing herself loved still, begot a wild hope that he would refuse to give her up. If so, these words laid it low, but even the sentence they passed upon her could not kill the self-respect that would be hers henceforth.

"That matters very little now," the man said, but to the woman it seemed to matter more than anything else in the world.

Throughout the remainder of this interview, until the end came, Gavin never faltered. His duty and hers lay so plainly before him that there could be no straying from it. Did Babbie think him strangely calm? At the Glen Quharity gathering I once saw Rob Angus lift a boulder with such apparent ease that its weight was discredited, until the cry arose that the effort had dislocated his arm. Perhaps Gavin's quietness deceived the Egyptian similarly. Had he stamped, she might have understood better what he suffered, standing there on the hot embers of his passion.

"We must try to make amends now," he said gravely, "for the wrong we have done."

"The wrong I have done," she said, correcting him. "You will make it harder for me if you blame yourself. How vile I was in those days!"

"Those days," she called them; they seemed so far away.

"Do not cry, Babbie," Gavin replied, gently. "He knew what you were, and why, and He pities you. 'For His anger endureth but a moment: in His favour is life: weeping may endure for a night, but joy cometh in the morning.'"

"Not to me."

"Yes, to you," he answered. "Babbie, you will return to the Spittal now, and tell Lord Rintoul everything."

"If you wish it."

"Not because I wish it, but because it is right. He must be told that you do not love him."

"I never pretended to him that I did," Babbie said, looking up. "Oh," she added, with emphasis, "He knows that. He thinks me incapable of caring for any one.

"And that is why he must be told of me," Gavin replied. "You are no longer the woman you were, Babbie, and you know it, and I know it, but he does not know it. He shall know it before he decides whether he is to marry you."

Babbie looked at Gavin, and wondered he did not see that this decision lay with him.

"Nevertheless," she said, "the wedding will take place to-morrow; if it did not, Lord Rintoul would be the scorn of his friends."

"If it does," the minister answered, "he will be the scorn of himself. Babbie, there is a chance."

"There is no chance," she told him. "I shall be back at the Spittal without any one's knowing of my absence, and when I begin to tell him of you, he will tremble, lest it means my refusal to marry him; when he knows it does not, he will wonder only why I told him anything."

"He will ask you to take time—"

"No, he will ask me to put on my wedding-dress. You must not think anything else possible."

"So be it, then," Gavin said firmly.

"Yes, it will be better so," Babbie answered and then, seeing him misunderstand her meaning, exclaimed reproachfully, "I was not thinking of myself. In the time to come, whatever be my lot, I shall have the one consolation, that this is best for you. Think of your mother."

"She will love you," Gavin said, "when I tell her of you."

"Yes," said Babbie, wringing her hands; "she will almost love me, but for what? For not marrying you. That is the only reason any one in Thrums will have for wishing me well."

"No others," Gavin answered, "will ever know why I remained unmarried."

"Will you never marry?" Babbie asked, exultingly. "Ah!" she cried, ashamed, "but you must."

"Never."

Well, many a man and many a woman has made that vow in similar circumstances, and not all have kept it. But shall we who are old smile cynically at the brief and burning passion of the young? "The day," you say, "will come when—" Good sir, hold your peace. Their agony was great, and now is dead, and, maybe, they have forgotten where it lies buried; but dare you answer lightly when I ask you which of these things is saddest?

Babbie believed his "Never," and doubtless, thought no worse of him for it; but she saw no way of comforting him save by disparagement of herself.

"You must think of your congregation," she said. "A minister with a gypsy wife—"

"Would have knocked them about with a flail," Gavin interposed, showing his teeth at the thought of the precentor, "until they did her reverence."

She shook her head, and told him of her meeting with Micah Dow. It silenced him; not, however, on account of its pathos, as she thought, but because it interpreted the riddle of Rob's behaviour.

"Nevertheless," he said ultimately, "my duty is not to do what is right in my people's eyes, but what seems right in my own."

Babbie had not heard him.

"I saw a face at the window just now," she whispered, drawing closer to him.

"There was no face there; the very thought of Rob Dow raises him before you," Gavin answered reassuringly, though Rob was nearer at that moment than either of them thought.

"I must go away at once," she said, still with her eyes on the window. "No, no, you shall not come or stay with me; it is you who are in danger."

"Do not fear for me."

"I must if you will not. Before you came in, did I not hear you speak of a meeting you had to attend to-night?"

"My pray—" His teeth met on the word; so abruptly did it conjure up the forgotten prayer meeting that before the shock could reach his mind he stood motionless, listening for the bell. For one instant all that had taken place since he last heard it might have happened between two of its tinkles; Babbie passed from before him like a figure in a panorama, and he saw, instead, a congregation in their pews.

"What do you see?" Babbie cried in alarm, for he seemed to be gazing at the window.

"Only you," he replied, himself again; "I am coming with you."

"You must let me go alone," she entreated; "if not for your own safety" — but it was only him she considered — "then for the sake of Lord Rintoul. Were you and I to be seen together now, his name and mine might suffer."

It was an argument the minister could not answer, save by putting his hands over his face; his distress made Babbie strong; she moved to the door, trying to smile.

"Go, Babbie!" Gavin said, controlling his voice, though it had been a smile more pitiful than her tears. "God has you in His keeping; it is not His will to give me this to bear for you."

They were now in the garden.

"Do not think of me as unhappy," she said; "it will be happiness to me to try to be all you would have me be."

He ought to have corrected her. "All that God would have me be" is what she should have said. But he only replied, "You will be a good woman, and none such can be altogether unhappy; God sees to that."

He might have kissed her, and perhaps she thought. so.

"I am — I am going now, dear," she said, and came back a step because he did not answer; then she went on, and was out of his sight at three yards' distance. Neither of them heard the approaching dog-cart.

"You see, I am bearing it quite cheerfully," she said. "I shall have everything a woman loves; do not grieve for me so much."

Gavin dared not speak nor move. Never had he found life so hard; but he was fighting with the ignoble in himself, and winning. She opened the gate, and it might have been a signal to the dogcart to stop. They both heard a dog barking, and then the voice of Lord Rintoul—

"That is a light in the window. Jump down, McKenzie, and inquire."

Gavin took one step nearer Babbie, and stopped. He did not see how all her courage went from her, so that her knees yielded, and she held out her arms to him, but he heard a great sob and then his name.

"Gavin, I am afraid."

Gavin understood now, and I say he would have been no man to leave her after that; only a moment was allowed him, and it was their last chance on earth. He took it. His arm went round his beloved, and he drew her away from Nanny's.

McKenzie found both house and garden empty.

"And yet," he said, "I swear some one passed the window as we sighted it."

"Waste no more time," cried the impatient earl. "We must be very near the hill now. You will have to lead the horse, McKenzie, in this darkness; the dog may find the way through the broom for us."

"The dog has run on," McKenzie replied, now in an evil temper. "Who knows, it may be with her now? So we must feel our way cautiously; there is no call for capsizing the trap in our haste." But there was call for haste if they were to reach the gypsy encampment before Gavin and Babbie were made man and wife over the tongs.

The Spittal dog-cart rocked as it dragged its way through the broom. Rob Dow followed. The ten o'clock bell began to ring.

Chapter XXXIII

While The Ten O'Clock Bell Was Ringing

In the square and wynds — weavers in groups:

"No, no, Davit, Mr. Dishart hadna felt the blow the piper gave him till he ascended the pulpit to conduct the prayer-meeting for rain, and then he fainted awa. Tammas Whamond and Peter Tosh carried him to the Session-house. Ay, an awful scene."

"How did the minister no come to the meeting? I wonder how you could expect it, Snecky, and his mother taen so suddenly ill; he's at her bedside, but the doctor has little hope."

"This is what has occurred, Tailor: Mr. Dishart never got the length of the pulpit. He fell in a swound on the vestry floor. What caused it? Oh, nothing but the heat. Thrums is so dry that one spark would set it in a blaze."

"I canna get at the richts o' what keeped him frae the meeting, Femie, but it had something to do wi' an Egyptian on the hill. Very like he had been trying to stop the gypsy marriage there. I gaed to the manse to speir at Jean what was wrang, but I'm thinking I telled her mair than she could tell me."

"Man, man, Andrew, the wite o't lies wi' Peter Tosh. He thocht we was to hae sic a terrible rain that he implored the minister no to pray for it, and so angry was Mr. Dishart that he ordered the whole Session out o' the kirk. I saw them in Couthie's close, and michty dour they looked."

"Yes, as sure as death, Tammas Whamond locked the kirk-door in Mr. Dishart's face."

"I'm, a' shaking? And small wonder, Marget, when I've heard this minute that Mr. Dishart's been struck by lichtning while looking for Rob Dow. He's no killed, but, woe's me! they say he'll never preach again."

"Nothing o' the kind. It was Rob that the lichtning struck dead in the doctor's machine. The horse wasna touched; it came tearing down the Roods wi' the corps sitting in the machine like a living man."

"What are you listening to, woman? Is it to a dog barking? I've heard it this while, but it's far awa."

In the manse kitchen.

"Jean, did you not hear me ring? I want you to — Why are you staring out at the window, Jean?"

"I — I —was just hearkening to the ten o'clock bell, ma'am."

"I never saw you doing nothing before! Put the heater in the fire, Jean. I want to iron the minister's neckcloths. The prayer-meeting is long in coming out, is it not?"

"The — the drouth, ma'am, has been so cruel hard."

"And, to my shame, I am so comfortable that I almost forgot how others are suffering. But my son never forgets, Jean. You are not crying, are you?"

"No, ma'am."

"Bring the iron to the parlour, then. And if the minis— Why did you start, Jean? I only heard a dog barking."

"I thocht, ma'am — at first I thocht it was Mr. Dishart opening the door. Ay, it's just a dog; some gypsy dog on the hill, I'm thinking, for sound would carry far the nicht."

"Even you, Jean, are nervous at nights, I see, if there is no man in the house. We shall hear no more distant dogs barking, I warrant, when the minister comes home."

"When he comes home, ma'am."

On the middle of the hill — a man and a woman:

"Courage, beloved; we are nearly there."

"But, Gavin, I cannot see the encampment."

"The night is too dark."

"But the gypsy fires?"

"They are in the Toad's-hole."

"Listen to that dog barking."

"There are several dogs at the encampment, Babbie."

"There is one behind us. See, there it is!"

"I have driven it away, dear. You are trembling."

"What we are doing frightens me, Gavin. It is at your heels again!"

"It seems to know you."

"Oh, Gavin, it is Lord Rintoul's collie Snap. It will bite you."

"No, I have driven it back again. Probably the earl is following us."

"Gavin, I cannot go on with this."

"Quicker, Babbie."

"Leave me, dear, and save yourself."

"Lean on me, Babbie."

"Oh, Gavin, is there no way but this?"

"No sure way."

"Even though we are married to-night—"

"We shall be married in five minutes, and then, whatever befall, he cannot have you."

"But after?"

"I will take you straight to the manse, to my mother."

"Were it not for that dog, I should think we were alone on the hill."

"But we are not. See, there are the gypsy fires."

On the west side of the hill — two figures:

"Tammas, Tammas Whamond, I've lost you. Should we gang to the manse down the fields?"

"Wheesht, Hendry!"

"What are you listening for?"

"I heard a dog barking."

"Only a gypsy dog, Tammas, barking at the coming storm."

"The gypsy dogs are all tied up, and this one's atween us and the Toad's-hole. What was that?"

"It was nothing but the rubbing of the branches in the cemetery on ane another. It's said, trees mak' that fearsome sound when they're terrified."

"It was a dog barking at somebody that's stoning it. I ken that sound, Hendry Munn."

"May I die the death, Tammas Whamond, if a great drap o' rain didna strike me the now, and I swear it was warm. I'm for running name."

"I'm for seeing who drove awa that dog. Come back wi' me, Hendry."

"I winna. There's no a soul on the hill but you and me and thae daffing and drinking gypsies. How do you no answer me, Tammas? Hie, Tammas Whamond, whaur are you? He's gone! Ay, then I'll mak' tracks hame."

In the broom — a dog cart:

"Do you see nothing yet, McKenzie?"

"Scarce the broom at my knees, Rintoul. There is not a light on the hill."

"McKenzie, can that schoolmaster have deceived us?"

"It is probable."

"Urge on the horse, however. There is a road through the broom, I know. Have we stuck again?"

"Rintoul, she is not here. I promised to help you to bring her back to the Spittal before this escapade became known, but we have failed to find her. If she is to be saved now, it must be by herself. I daresay she has returned already. Let me turn the horse's head. There is a storm brewing."

"I will search this gypsy encampment first, if it is on the hill. Hark! that was a dog's bark. Yes, it is Snap, but he would not bark at nothing. Why do you look behind you so often, McKenzie?"

"For some time, Rintoul, it has seemed to me that we are being followed. Listen!"

"I hear nothing. At last, McKenzie, at last, we are out of the broom."

"And as I live, Rintoul, I see the gypsy lights!"

It might have been a lantern that was flashed across the hill. Then all that part of the world went suddenly on fire. Everything was horribly distinct in that white light. The firs of Caddam were so near that it seemed to have arrested them in a silent march upon the hill. The grass would not hide a pebble. The ground was scored with shadows of men and things. Twice the light flickered and recovered itself. A red serpent shot across it, and then again black night fell.

The hill had been illumined thus for nearly half a minute. During that time not even a dog stirred. The shadows of human beings lay on the ground as motionless as logs. What had been revealed seemed less a gypsy marriage than a picture. Or was it that during the ceremony every person on the hill had been turned into stone? The gypsy king, with his arm upraised, had not had time to let it fall. The men and women behind him had their mouths open, as if struck when on the point of calling out. Lord Rintoul had risen in the dog-cart, and was leaning forward. One of McKenzie's feet was on the shaft. The man crouching in the dog-cart's wake had flung up his hands to protect his face. The precentor, his neck outstretched, had a hand on each knee. All eyes were fixed, as in the death glare, on Gavin and Babbie, who stood before the king, their hands clasped over the tongs. Fear was petrified on the woman's face, determination on the man's.

They were all released by the crack of the thunder, but for another moment none could have swaggered.

"That was Lord Rintoul in the dog-cart," Babbie whispered, drawing in her breath.

"Yes, dear," Gavin answered, resolutely, "and now is the time for me to have my first and last talk with him. Remain here, Babbie. Do not move till I come back."

"But, Gavin, he has seen. I fear him still."

"He cannot touch you now, Babbie. You are my wife."

In the vivid light Gavin had thought the dog-cart much nearer than it was. He called Lord Rintoul's name, but got no answer. There were shouts behind, gypsies running from the coming rain, dogs whining, but silence in front. The minister moved on some paces. Away to the left he heard voices—

"Who was the man, McKenzie?"

"My lord, I have lost sight of you. This is not the way to the camp."

"Tell me, McKenzie, that you did not see what I saw."

"Rintoul, I beseech you to turn back. We are too late."

"We are not too late."

Gavin broke through the darkness between them and him, but they were gone. He called to them, and stopped to listen to their feet.

"Is that you, Gavin?" Babbie asked just then.

For reply, the man who had crept up to her clapped his hand upon her mouth. Only the beginning of a scream escaped from her. A strong arm drove her quickly southward.

Gavin heard her cry, and ran back to the encampment. Babbie was gone. None of the gypsies had seen her since the darkness came back. He rushed hither and thither with a torch that only showed his distracted face to others. He flung up his arms in appeal for another moment of light; then he heard Babbie scream again, and this time it was from a distance. He dashed after her; he heard a trap speeding down the green sward through the broom.

Lord Rintoul had kidnapped Babbie. Gavin had no other thought as he ran after the dog-cart from which the cry had come. The earl's dog followed him, snapping at his heels. The rain began.

Chapter XXXIV

The Great Rain

GAVIN passed on through Windyghoul, thinking in his frenzy that he still heard the trap. In a rain that came down like iron rods every other sound was beaten dead. He slipped, and before he could regain his feet the dog bit him. To protect himself from dykes and trees and other horrors of the darkness he held his arm before him, but soon it was driven to his side. Wet whips cut his brow so, that he had to protect it with his hands, until it had to bear the lash again, for they would not. Now he was forced upon his knees, and would have succumbed, but for a dread of being pinned to the earth. This fight between the man and the rain went on all night, and, long before it ended, the man was past the power of thinking.

In the ringing of the ten o'clock bell Gavin had lived the seventh part of a man's natural life. Only action was required of him. That accomplished, his mind had begun to work again, when suddenly the loss of Babbie stopped it, as we may put out a fire with a great coal. The last thing he had reflected about was a dog-cart in motion, and, consequently, this idea clung to him. His church, his mother, were lost knowledge of, but still he seemed to hear the trap in front.

The rain increased in violence, appalling even those who heard it from under cover. However rain may storm, though it be an army of archers battering roofs and windows, it is only terrifying when the noise swells every instant. In those hours of darkness it again and again grew in force and doubled its fury, and was louder, louder, and louder, until its next attack was to be more than men and women could listen to. They held each other's hands and stood waiting. Then abruptly it abated, and people could speak. I believe a rain that became heavier every second for ten minutes would drive many listeners mad. Gavin was in it on a night that tried us repeatedly for quite half that time.

By-and-by even the vision of Babbie in the dogcart was blotted out. If nothing had taken its place, he would not have gone on probably; and had he turned back objectless, his strength would have succumbed to the rain. Now he saw Babbie and Rintoul being married by a minister who was himself, and there was a fair company looking on, and always when he was on the point of shouting to himself, whom he could see clearly, that this woman was already married, the rain obscured his words and the light went out. Presently the ceremony began again, always to stop at the same point. He saw it in the lightning-flash that had startled the hill. It gave him courage to fight his way onward, because he thought he must be heard if he could draw nearer to the company.

A regiment of cavalry began to trouble him. He heard it advancing from the Spittal, but was not dismayed, for it was, as yet, far distant. The horsemen came thundering on, filling the whole glen of Quharity. Now he knew that they had been sent out to ride him down. He paused in dread, until they had swept past him. They came back to look for him, riding more furiously than ever, and always missed him, yet his fears of the next time were not lessened. They were only the rain.

All through the night the dog followed him. He would forget it for a time, and then it would be so close that he could see it dimly. He never heard it bark, but it snapped at him, and a grin had become the expression of its face. He stoned it, he even flung himself at it, he addressed it in caressing tones, and always with the result that it disappeared, to come back presently.

He found himself walking in a lake, and now even the instinct of self-preservation must have been flickering, for he waded on, rejoicing merely in getting rid of the dog. Something in the water rose and struck him. Instead of stupefying him, the blow brought him to his senses, and he struggled for his life. The ground slipped beneath his feet many times, but at last he was out of the water. That he was out in a flood he did not realize; yet he now acted like one in full possession of his faculties. When his feet sank in water, he drew back; and many times he sought shelter behind banks and rocks, first testing their firmness with his hands. Once a torrent of stones, earth, and heather carried him down a hillside until he struck against a tree. He twined his arms round it, and had just done so when it fell with him. After that, when he touched trees growing in water, he fled from them, thus probably saving himself from death.

What he heard now might have been the roll and crack of the thunder. It sounded in his ear like nothing else. But it was really something that swept down the hill in roaring spouts of water, and it passed on both sides of him so, that at one moment, had he paused, it would have crashed into him, and at another he was only saved by stopping. He felt that the struggle in the dark was to go on till the crack of doom.

Then he cast himself upon the ground. It moved beneath him like some great animal, and he rose and stole away from it. Several times did this happen. The stones against which his feet struck seemed to acquire life from his touch. So strong had he become, or so weak all other things, that whatever clump he laid hands on by which to pull himself out of the water was at once rooted up.

The daylight would not come. He longed passionately for it. He tried to remember what it was like, and could not; he had been blind so long. It was away in front somewhere, and he was struggling to overtake it. He expected to see it from a dark place, when he would rush forward to bathe his arms in it, and then the elements that were searching the world for him would see him and he would perish. But death did not seem too great a penalty to pay for light.

And at last the day did come back, grey and drear. He saw suddenly once more. I think he must have been wandering the glen with his eyes shut, as one does shut them involuntarily against the hidden dangers of black night. How different was daylight from what he had expected! He looked, and then shut his dazed eyes again, for the darkness was less horrible than the day. Had he indeed seen, or only dreamed that he saw? Once more he looked to see what the world was like; and the sight that met his eyes was so mournful that he who had fought through the long night now sank hopeless and helpless among the heather. The dog was not far away, and it, too, lost heart. Gavin held out his hand, and Snap crept timidly toward him. He unloosened his coat, and the dog nestled against him, cowed and shivering, hiding its head from the day. Thus they lay, and the rain beat upon them.

Chapter XXXV

The Glen At Break Of Day

MY first intimation that the burns were in flood came from Waster Lunny, close on the strike of ten o'clock. This was some minutes before they had any rain in Thrums. I was in the schoolhouse, now piecing together the puzzle Lord Rintoul had left with me, and anon starting upright as McKenzie's hand seemed to tighten on my arm. Waster Lunny had been whistling to me (with his fingers in his mouth) for some time before I heard him and hurried out. I was surprised and pleased, knowing no better, to be met on the threshold by a whisk of rain.

The night was not then so dark but that when I reached the Quharity I could see the farmer take shape on the other side of it. He wanted me to exult with him, I thought, in the end of the drought, and I shouted that I would fling him the stilts.

"It's yoursel' that wants them," he answered, excitedly, "if you're fleid to be left alone in the schoolhouse the nicht. Do you hear me, dominie? There has been frichtsome rain among the hills, and the Bog burn is coming down like a sea. It has carried awa the miller's brig, and the steading o' Muckle Pirley is standing three feet in water."

"You're dreaming, man," I roared back, but beside his news he held my doubts of no account.

"The Retery's in flood," he went on, "and running wild through Hazel Wood; T'nowdunnie's tattie field's out o' sicht, and at the Kirkton they're fleid they've lost twa kye."

"There has been no rain here," I stammered, incredulously.

"It's coming now," he replied. "And listen; the story's out that the Backbone has fallen into the loch. You had better cross, dominie, and thole out the nicht wi' us."

The Backbone was a piece of mountain-side overhanging a loch among the hills, and legend said that it would one day fall forward and squirt all the water into the glen. Something of the kind had happened, but I did not believe it then; with little wit I pointed to the shallow Quharity.

"It may come down at any minute," the farmer answered, "and syne, mind you, you'll be five miles frae Waster Lunny, for there'll be no crossing but by the Brig o' March. If you winna come, I maun awa back. I mauna bide langer on the wrang side o' the Moss ditch, though it has been as dry this month back as a rabbit's roady. But if you—" His voice changed. "God's sake, man," he cried, "you're ower late. Look at that! Dinna look — run, run!"

If I had not run before he bade me, I might never have run again on earth. I had seen a great shadowy yellow river come riding down the Quharity. I sprang from it for my life: and when next I looked behind, it was upon a turbulent loch, the further bank lost in darkness. I was about to shout to Waster Lunny, when a monster rose in the torrent between me and the spot where he had stood. It frightened me to silence until it fell, when I knew it was but a tree that had been flung on end by the flood. For a time there was no answer to my cries, and I thought the farmer had been swept away. Then I heard his whistle, and back I ran recklessly through the thickening darkness to the school-house. When I saw the tree rise, I had been on ground hardly wet as yet with the rain; but by the time Waster Lunny sent that reassuring whistle to me I was ankle-deep in water, and the rain was coming down like hail. I saw no lightning.

For the rest of the night I was only out once, when I succeeded in reaching the hen-house, and brought all my fowls safely to the kitchen, except a hen which would not rise off her young. Between us we had the kitchen floor, a pool of water; and the rain had put out my fires already, as effectually as if it had been an overturned broth-pot. That I never took off my clothes that night I need not say, though of what was happening in the glen I could only guess. A flutter against my window now and again, when the rain had abated, told me of another bird that had flown there to die; and with Waster Lunny I kept up communication by waving a light, to which he replied in a similar manner. Before morning, however, he ceased to answer my signals, and I feared some catastrophe had occurred at the farm. As it turned out, the family was fighting with the flood for the year's shearing of wool, half of which eventually went down the waters, with the wool-shed on top of it.

The school-house stands too high to fear any flood, but there were moments when I thought the rain would master it. Not only the windows and the roof were rattling then, but all the walls, and I was like one in a great drum. When the rain was doing its utmost, I heard no other sound; but when the lull came, there was the wash of a heavy river, or a crack as of artillery that told of landslips, or the plaintive cry of the peesweep as it rose in the air, trying to entice the waters away from its nest.

It was a dreary scene that met my gaze at break of day. Already the Quharity had risen six feet, and in many parts of the glen it was two handred yards wide. Waster Lunny's corn-field looked like a bog grown over with rushes, and what had been his turnips had become a lake with small islands in it. No dyke stood whole except one that the farmer, unaided, had built in a straight line from the road to the top of Mount Bare, and my own, the further end of which dipped in water. Of the plot of firs planted fifty years earlier to help on Waster Lunny's crops, only a triangle had withstood the night.

Even with the aid of my field-glass I could not estimate the damage on more distant farms, for the rain, though now thin and soft, as it continued for six days, was still heavy and of a brown colour. After breakfast — which was interrupted by my bantam cock's twice spilling my milk — saw Waster Lunny and his son, Matthew, running towards the shepherd's house with ropes in their hands. The house, I thought, must be in the mist beyond; and then I sickened, knowing all at once that it should be on this side of the mist. When I had nerve to look again, I saw that though the roof had fallen in, the shepherd was astride one of the walls, from which he was dragged presently through the water by the help of the ropes. I remember noticing that he returned to his house with the rope still about him, and concluding that he had gone back to save some of his furniture. I was wrong, however. There was too much to be done at the farm to allow this, but Waster Lunny had consented to Duncan's forcing his way back to the shieling to stop the clock. To both men it seemed horrible to let a clock go on ticking in a deserted house.

Having seen this rescue accomplished, I was letting my glass roam in the opposite direction, when one of its shakes brought into view something on my own side of the river. I looked at it long, and saw it move slightly. Was it a human being? No, it was a dog. No, it was a dog and something else. I hurried out to see more clearly, and after a first glance the glass shook so in my hands that I had to rest it on the dyke. For a full minute, I daresay, did I look through the glass without blinking, and then I needed to look no more. That black patch was, indeed, Gavin.

He lay quite near the school-house, but I had to make a circuit of half a mile to reach him. It was pitiful to see the dog doing its best to come to me, and falling every few steps. The poor brute was discoloured almost beyond recognition; and when at last it reached me, it lay down at my feet and licked them. I stepped over it and ran on recklessly to Gavin. At first I thought he was dead. If tears rolled down my cheeks, they were not for him.

I was no strong man even in those days, but I carried him to the school-house, the dog crawling after us. Gavin I put upon my bed, and I lay down beside him (holding him close to me, that some of the heat of my body might be taken in by his. When he was able to look at me, however, it was not with understanding, and in vain did my anxiety press him with questions. Only now and again would some word in my speech strike upon his brain and produce at least an echo. To "Did you meet Lord Rintoul's dog-cart?" he sat up, saying quickly—

"Listen, the dog-cart!"

"Egyptian" was not that forenoon among the words he knew, and I did not think of mentioning "hill." At "rain" he shivered; but "Spittal" was what told me most.

"He has taken her back," he replied at once, from which I learned that Gavin now knew as much of Babbie as I did.

I made him as comfortable as possible, and despairing of learning anything from him in his present state, I let him sleep. Then I went out into the rain, very anxious and dreading what he might have to tell me when he woke. I waded and jumped my way as near to the farm as I dared go, and Waster Lunny, seeing me, came to the water's edge. At this part the breadth of the flood was not forty yards, yet for a time our voices could no more cross its roar than one may send a snowball through a stone wall. I know not whether the river then quieted for a space, or if it was only that the ears grow used to dins as the eyes distinguish the objects in a room that is at first black to them, but after a little we were able to shout our remarks across, much as boys fling pebbles, many to fall into the water, but one occasionally to reach the other side. Waster Lunny would have talked of the flood, but I had not come here for that.

"How were you home so early from the prayer-meeting last night?" I bawled.

"No meeting . . . . I came straucht hame . . . . but terrible stories . . . . Mr. Dishart," was all I caught after Waster Lunny had flung his words across a dozen times.

I could not decide whether it would be wise to tell him that Gavin was in the school-house and while I hesitated he continued to shout

"Some woman . . . . the Session . . . . Lang Tammas . . . . God forbid . . . . maun back to the farm . . . . byre running like a mill-dam."

He signed to me that he must be off, but my signals delayed him, and after much trouble he got my question, "Any news about Lord Rintoul?" My curiosity about the earl must have surprised him, but he answered—

"Marriage is to be the day . . . . cannon."

I signed that I did not grasp his meaning.

"A cannon is to be fired as soon as they're man and wife," he bellowed. "We'll hear it."

With that we parted. On my way home, I remember, I stepped on a brood of drowned partridge.

I was only out half an hour, but I had to wring my clothes as if they were fresh from the tub.

The day wore on, and I did not disturb the sleeper. A dozen times, I suppose, I had to relight my fire of wet peats and roots; but I had plenty of time to stare out at the window, plenty of time to think. Probably Gavin's life depended on his sleeping, but that was not what kept my hands off him. Knowing so little of what had happened in Thrums since I left it, I was forced to guess, and my conclusion was that the earl had gone off with his own, and that

Gavin in a frenzy had followed them. My wisest course, I thought, was to let him sleep until I heard the cannon, when his struggle for a wife must end. Fifty times at least did I stand regarding him as he slept; and if I did not pity his plight sufficiently, you know the reason. What were Margaret's sufferings at this moment? Was she wringing her hands for her son lost in the flood, her son in disgrace with the congregation? By one o'clock no cannon had sounded, and my suspense had become intolerable. I shook Gavin awake, and even as I shook him demanded a knowledge of all that had happened since we parted at Nanny's gate.

"How long ago is that?" he asked, with bewilderment.

"It was last night," I answered. "This morning I found you senseless on the hillside, and brought you here, to the Glen Quharity school-house. That dog was with you."

He looked at the dog, but I kept my eyes on him, and I saw intelligence creep back, like a blush into his face.

"Now I remember," he said, shuddering. "You have proved yourself my friend, sir, twice in the four-and-twenty hours."

"Only once, I fear," I replied gloomily. "I was no friend when I sent you to the earl's bride last night."

"You know who she is?" he cried, clutching me, and finding it agony to move his limbs.

"I know now," I said, and had to tell him how I knew before he would answer another question. Then I became listener, and you who read know to what alarming story.

"And all that time," I cried reproachfully, when he had done, "you gave your mother not a thought."

"Not a thought," he answered, and I saw that he pronounced a harsher sentence on himself than could have come from me. "All that time!" he repeated, after a moment. "It was only a few minutes, while the ten o'clock bell was ringing."

"Only a few minutes," I said, "but they changed the channel of the Quharity, and perhaps they have done not less to you."

"That may be," he answered gravely, "but it is of the present I must think just now. Mr. Ogilvy, what assurance have I, while lying here helpless, that the marriage at the Spittal is not going on?"

"None, I hope," I said to myself, and listened longingly for the cannon. But to him I only pointed out that no woman need go through a form of marriage against her will.

"Rintoul carried her off with no possible purport," he said, "but to set my marriage at defiance, and she has had a conviction always that to marry me would be to ruin me. It was only in the shiver Lord Rintoul's voice in the darkness sent through her that she yielded to my wishes. If she thought that marriage last night could be annulled by another to-day, she would consent to the second, I believe, to save me from the effects of the first. You are incredulous, sir; but you do not know of what sacrifices love is capable."

Something of that I knew, but I did not tell him. I had seen from his manner rather than his words that he doubted the validity of the gypsy marriage, which the king had only consented to celebrate because Babbie was herself an Egyptian. The ceremony had been interrupted in the middle.

"It was no marriage," I said, with a confidence I was far from feeling.

"In the sight of God," he replied excitedly, "we took each other for man and wife."

I had to hold him down in bed. "You are too weak to stand, man," I said, "and yet you think you could start off this minute for the Spittal."

"I must go," he cried. "She is my wife. That impious marriage may have taken place already."

"Oh that it had!" was my prayer. "It has not," I said to him. "A cannon is to be fired immediately after the ceremony, and all the glen will hear it."

I spoke on the impulse, thinking to allay his desire to be off; but he said, "Then I may yet be in time." Somewhat cruelly I let him rise, that he might realise his weakness. Every bone in him cried out at his first step, and he sank into a chair.

"You will go to the Spittal for me?" he implored.

"I will not," I told him. "You are asking me to fling away my life."

To prove my words I opened the door, and he saw what the flood was doing. Nevertheless, he rose and tottered several times across the room, trying to revive his strength. Though every bit of him was aching, I saw that he would make the attempt.

"Listen to me," I said. "Lord Rintoul can maintain with some reason that it was you rather than he who abducted Babbie. Nevertheless, there will not, I am convinced, be any marriage at the Spittal today. When he carried her off from the Toad's-hole, he acted under impulses not dissimilar to those that took you to it. Then, I doubt not, he thought possession was all the law, but that scene on the hill has staggered him by this morning. Even though she thinks to save you by marrying him, he will defer his wedding until he learns the import of yours."

I did not believe in my own reasoning, but I would have said anything to detain him until that cannon was fired. He seemed to read my purpose, for he pushed my arguments from him with his hands, and continued to walk painfully to and fro.

"To defer the wedding," he said, "would be to tell all his friends of her gypsy origin, and of me. He would risk much to avoid that."

"In any case," I answered, "you must now give some thought to those you have forgotten, your mother and your church."

"That must come afterwards," he said firmly. "My first duty is to my wife."

The door swung-to sharply just then, and he started. He thought it was the cannon.

"I wish to God it had been!" I cried, interpreting his thoughts.

"Why do you wish me ill?" he asked.

"Mr. Dishart," I said solemnly, rising and facing him, and disregarding his question, "if that woman is to be your wife, it will be at a cost you cannot estimate till you return to Thrums. Do you think that if your congregation knew of this gypsy marriage they would have you for their minister for another day? Do you enjoy the prospect of taking one who might be an earl's wife into poverty — ay, and disgraceful poverty? Do you know your mother so little as to think she could survive your shame? Let me warn you, sir, of what I see. I see another minister in the Auld Licht kirk; I see you and your wife stoned through our wynds, stoned from Thrums, as malefactors have been chased out of it ere now; and as certainly as I see these things I see a hearse standing at the manse door, and stern men denying a son's right to help to carry his mother's coffin to it. Go your way, sir, but first count the cost."

His face quivered before these blows, but all he said was, "I must dree my dreed."

"God is merciful," I went on, "and these things need not be. He is more merciful to you, sir, than to some, for the storm that He sent to save you is ruining them. And yet the farmers are to-day thanking Him for every pound of wool, every blade of corn He has left them, while you turn from Him because He would save you, not in your way, but in His. It was His hand that stayed your marriage. He meant Babbie for the earl; and if it is on her part a loveless match, she only suffers for her own sins. Of that scene on the hill no one in Thrums, or in the glen, need ever know. Rintoul will see to it that the gypsies vanish from these parts for ever, and you may be sure the Spittal will soon be shut up. He and McKenzie have as much reason as yourself to be silent. You, sir, must go back to your congregation, who have heard as yet only vague rumours that your presence will dispel. Even your mother will remain ignorant of what has happened. Your absence from the prayer-meeting you can leave to me to explain."

He was so silent that I thought him mine, but his first words undeceived me.

"I thought I had nowhere so keen a friend," he said: "but, Mr. Ogilvy, it is devil's work you are pleading. Am I to return to my people to act a living lie before them to the end of my days? Do you really think that God devastated a glen to give me a chance of becoming a villain? No, sir, I am in His hands, and I will do what I think right."

"You will be dishonoured," I said, "in the sight of God and man."

"Not in God's sight," he replied. "It was a sinless marriage, Mr. Ogilvy, and I do not regret it. God ordained that she and I should love each other, and He put it into my power to save her from that man. I took her as my wife before Him, and in His eyes I am her husband. Knowing that, sir, how could I return to Thrums without her?"

I had no answer ready for him. I knew that in my grief for Margaret I had been advocating an unworthy course; but I would not say so. I went gloomily to the door, and there, presently, his hand fell on my shoulder.

"Your advice came too late, at any rate," he said. "You forget that the precentor was on the hill and saw everything."

It was he who had forgotten to tell me this, and to me it was the most direful news of all.

"My God!" I cried. "He will have gone to your mother and told her." And straightway I began to lace my boots.

"Where are you going?" he asked, staring at me.

"To Thrums," I answered, harshly.

"You said that to venture out into the glen was to court death," he reminded me.

"What of that?" I said, and hastily put on my coat.

"Mr. Ogilvy," he cried, "I will not allow you to do this for me."

"For you?" I said bitterly. "It is not for you."

I would have gone at once, but he got in front of me, asking, "Did you ever know my mother?"

"Long ago," I answered shortly, and he said no more; thinking, I suppose, that he knew all. He limped to the door with me, and I had only advanced a few steps when I understood better than before what were the dangers I was to venture into. Since I spoke to Waster Lunny the river had risen several feet, and even the hillocks in his turnip-field were now submerged. The mist was creeping down the hills. But what warned me most sharply that the flood was not satisfied yet was top of the school-house dyke; it was lined with field-mice. I turned back, and Gavin, mistaking my meaning, said I did wisely.

"I have not changed my mind," I told him, and then had some difficulty in continuing. "I expect," I said, "to reach Thrums safely, even though I should be caught in the mist, but I shall have to go round by the Kelpie brig in order to get across the river, and it is possible that that something may befall me ."

I have all my life been something of a coward, and my voice shook when I said this, so that Gavin again entreated me to remain at the school-house, saying that if I did not he would accompany me.

"And so increase my danger tenfold," I pointed out. "No, no, Mr. Dishart, I go alone; and if I can do nothing with the congregation, I can at least send your mother word that you still live. But if anything should happen to me, I want you—"

But I could not say what I had come back to say. I had meant to ask him, in the event of my death, to take the hundred pounds which were the savings of my life; but now I saw that this might lead to Margaret's hearing of me, and so I stayed my words. It was bitter to me this, and yet, after all, a little thing when put aside the rest.

"Good-bye, Mr. Dishart," I said abruptly. I then looked at my desk, which contained some trifles that were once Margaret's. "Should anything happen to me," I said, "I want that old desk to be destroyed unopened."

"Mr. Ogilvy," he answered gently, "you are venturing this because you loved my mother. If anything does befall you, be assured that I will tell her what you attempted for her sake."

I believe he thought it was to make some such request that I had turned back.

"You must tell her nothing about me," I exclaimed in consternation. "Swear that my name will never cross your lips before her. No, that is not enough. You must forget me utterly, whether I live or die, lest sometime you should think of me and she should read your thoughts. Swear, man."

"Must this be?" he said, gazing at me.

"Yes," I answered more calmly, "it must be. For nearly a score of years I have been blotted out of your mother's life, and since she came to Thrums my one care has been to keep my existence from her. I have changed my burying-ground even from Thrums to the glen, lest I should die before her, and she, seeing the hearse go by the Tenements, might ask, 'Whose funeral is this?"

In my anxiety to warn him, I had said too much. His face grew haggard, and there was fear to speak on it; and I saw, I knew, that some damnable suspicion of Margaret—

"She was my wife!" I cried sharply. "We were married by the minister of Harvie. You are my son.'

Chapter XXXV

Story of The Dominie

WHEN I spoke next, I was back in the schoolhouse, sitting there with my bonnet on my head, Gavin looking at me. We had forgotten the cannon at last.

In that chair I had anticipated this scene more than once of late. I had seen that a time might come when Gavin would have to be told all, and I had even said the words aloud, as if he were indeed opposite me. So now I was only repeating the tale, and I could tell it without emotion, because it was nigh nineteen years old; and I did not look at Gavin, for I knew that his manner of taking it could bring no change to me.

"Did you never ask your mother," I said, addressing the fire rather than him, "why you were called Gavin?"

"Yes," he answered, "it was because she thought Gavin a prettier name than Adam."

"No," I said slowly, "it was because Gavin is my name. You were called after your father. Do you not remember my taking you one day to the shore at Harvie to see the fishermen carried to their boats upon their wives' backs, that they might start dry on their journey?"

"No," he had to reply. "I remember the women carrying the men through the water to the boats, but I thought it was my father who—I mean—"

"I know whom you mean," I said. "That was our last day together, but you were not three years old. Yet you remembered me when you came to Thrums. You shake your head, but it is true. Between the diets of worship that first Sabbath I was introduced to you, and you must have had some shadowy recollection of my face, for you asked, 'Surely I saw you in church in the forenoon, Mr. Ogilvy?' I said 'Yes,' but I had not been in the church in the forenoon. You have forgotten even that, and yet I treasured it."

I could hear that he was growing impatient, though so far he had been more indulgent than I had any right to expect.

"It can all be put into a sentence," I said calmly. "Margaret married Adam Dishart, and afterwards believing herself a widow,she married me. You were born, and then Adam Dishart came back."

That is my whole story, and here was I telling it to my son, and not a tear between us. It ended abruptly, and I fell to mending the fire.

"When I knew your mother first," I went on, after Gavin had said some boyish things that were of no avail to me, "I did not think to end my days as a dominie. I was a student at Aberdeen, with the ministry in my eye, and sometimes on Saturdays I walked forty miles to Harvie to go to church with her. She had another lover, Adam Dishart, a sailor turned fisherman; and while I lingered at corners, wondering if I could dare to meet her and her mother on their way to church, he would walk past with them. He was accompanied always by a lanky black dog, which he had brought from a foreign country. He never signed for any ship without first getting permission to take it with him, and in Harvie they said it did not know the language of the native dogs. I have never known a man and dog so attached to each other."

"I remember that black dog," Gavin said. "I have spoken of it to my mother, and she shuddered, as if it had once bitten her."

"While Adam strutted by with them," I continued, "I would hang back, raging at his assurance or my own timidity; but I lost my next chance in the same way. In Margaret's presence something came over me, a kind of dryness in the throat, that made me dumb. I have known divinity students stricken in the same way, just as they were giving out their first text. It is no aid in getting a kirk or wooing a woman.

"If anyone in Harvie recalls me now, it is as a hobbledehoy who strode along the cliffs, shouting Homer at the sea-mews. With all my learning, I, who gave Margaret the name of Lalage, understood women less than any fishermen who bandied words with them across a boat. I remember a Yule night when both Adam and I were at her mother's cottage, and, as we were leaving, he had the audacity to kiss Margaret. She ran out of the room, and Adam swaggered off, and, when I recovered from my horror, I apologised for what he had done. I shall never forget how her mother looked at me, and said, 'Ay, Gavin, I see they dinna teach everything at

Aberdeen.' You will not believe it, but I walked away doubting her meaning. I thought more of scholarship then than I do now. Adam Dishart taught me its proper place.

"Well, that is the dull man I was; and yet, though Adam was always saying and doing the things I was making up my mind to say and do, I think Margaret cared more for me. Nevertheless, there was something about him that all women seemed to find lovable, a dash that made them send him away and then well-nigh run after him. At any rate, I could have got her after her mother's death if I had been half a man. But I went back to Aberdeen to write a poem about her, and while I was at it Adam married her."

I opened my desk and took from it a yellow manuscript.

"Here," I said, "is the poem. You see, I never finished it."

I was fingering the thing grimly when Gavin's eye fell on something else in the desk. It was an ungainly clasp knife, as rusty as if it had spent a winter beneath a hedge.

"I seem to remember that knife," he said.

"Yes," I answered, "you should remember it. Well, after three months Adam tired of his wife."

I stopped again. This was a story in which only the pauses were eloquent.

"Perhaps I have no right to say he tired of her. One day, however, he sauntered away from Harvie whistling, his dog at his heels as ever, and was not seen again for nearly six years. When I heard of his disappearance I packed my books in that kist and went to Harvie, where I opened a school. You see, everyone but Margaret believed that Adam had fallen over the cliffs and been drowned."

"But the dog?" said Gavin.

"We were all sure that, if he had fallen over it had jumped after him. The fisher-folk said that he could have left his shadow behind as easily as it. Yet Margaret thought for long that he had tired of Harvie merely and gone back to sea, and not until two years had passed would she marry me. We lived in Adam's house. It was so near the little school that when I opened the window in summer-time she could hear the drone of our voices. During the weeks before you were born I kept that window open all day long, and often I went to it and waved my hand to her.

"Sometimes, when she was washing or baking, I brought you to the school. The only quarrel she and I ever had was about my teaching you the Lord's Prayer in Greek as soon as you could say father and mother. It was to be a surprise for her on your second birthday. On that day, while she was ironing, you took hold of her gown to steady yourself, and began 'Πάτερ ημώγ ο εύ τοις υραυοις and to me, behind the door, it was music. But at 'άγιασθήτω' of which you made two syllables, you cried, and Margaret snatched you up, thinking this was some new ailment. After I had explained to her that it was the Lord's Prayer in Greek, she would let me take you to the schoolhouse no more.

"Not much longer could I have taken you in any case, for already we are at the day when Adam Dishart came back. It was the 7th of September, and all the week most of the women in Harvie had been setting off at dawn to the harvest-fields and straggling home at nights, merry and with yellow corn in their hair. I had sat on in the school-house that day after my pupils were gone. I still meant to be a minister, and I was studying Hebrew, and so absorbed in my book that as the daylight went, I followed it step by step as far as my window, and there I read, without knowing, until I chanced to look up, that I had left my desk. I have not opened that book since.

"From the window I saw you on the waste ground that separated the school from our home. You were coming to me on your hands and feet, and stopping now and again to look back at your mother, who was at the door, laughing and shaking her fist at you. I beckoned to you, and took the book back to my desk to lock it up. While my head was inside the desk I heard the school-house door pushed open, and thinking it was you I smiled, without looking up. Then something touched my hand, and I still thought it was you; but I looked down, and I saw Adam Dishart's black dog.

"I did not move. It looked up at me and wagged its tail. Then it drew back; I suppose, because I had no words for it. I watched it run half round the room, and stop and look at me again. Then it slunk out.

"All that time one of my hands had been holding the desk open. Now the lid fell. I put on my bonnet and went to the door. You were only a few yards away, with flowers in your fist. Margaret was laughing still. I walked round the school, and there was no dog visible. Margaret nodded to me, meaning that I should bring you home. You thrust the flowers into my hand, but they fell. I stood there, dazed.

"I think I walked with you some way across the waste ground. Then I dropped your hand, and strode back to the school. I went down on my knees, looking for marks of a dog's paws, and I found them.

"When I came out again, your mother was no longer at our door, and you were crying because I had left you. I passed you and walked straight to the house. Margaret was skinning rushes for wicks. There must have been fear in my face, for as soon as she saw it she ran to the door to see if you were still alive. She brought you in with her, and so had strength to cry, 'What is it? Speak!'

" 'Come away,' I said, 'come away,' and I was for drawing her to the door, but she pressed me into a chair. I was up again at once.

" 'Margaret,' I said, 'ask no questions. Put on your bonnet, give me the boy, and let us away.'

"I could not take my eyes off the door, and she was walking to it to look out when I barred the way with my arm.

" 'What have you seen?' she cried; and then, as I only pointed to her bonnet, she turned to you, and you said, 'Was it the black dog, father?'

"Gavin, then she knew; and I stood helpless and watched my wife grow old. In that moment she lost the sprightliness I loved the more, because I had none of it myself, and the bloom went from her face, never to return.

" 'He has come back,' she said.

"I told her what I had seen, and while I spoke she put on her bonnet, and I exulted, thinking and then she took off her bonnet, and I knew she would not go away with me.

" 'Margaret,' I cried, 'I am that bairn's father.'

" 'Adam's my man,' she said, and at that I gave her a look for which God might have struck me dead. But instead of blaming me she put her arms round my neck.

"After that we said very little. We sat at opposite sides of the fire, waiting for him, and you played on the floor. The harvesters trooped by, and there was a fiddle; and when it stopped, long stillness, and then a step. It was not Adam. You fell asleep, and we could hear nothing but the sea. There was a harvest moon.

"Once a dog ran past the door, and we both rose. Margaret pressed her hands on her breast. Sometimes she looked furtively at me, and I knew her thoughts. To me it was only misery that had come, but to her it was shame, so that when you woke and climbed into her lap she shivered at your touch. I could not look at her after that, for there was a horror of me growing in her face.

"Ten o'clock struck, and then again there was no sound but the sea pouring itself out on the beach. It was long after this, when to me there was still no other sound, that Margaret screamed, and you hid behind her. Then I heard it.

" 'Gavin,' Margaret said to me, 'be a good man all your life.'

"It was louder now, and then it stopped. Above the wash of the sea we heard another sound — a sharp tap, tap. You said, 'I know what sound that is; it's a man knocking the ashes out of his pipe against his boot.'

"Then the dog pushed the door off the latch, and Adam lurched in. He was not drunk, but he brought the smell of drink into the room with him. He was grinning like one bringing rare news, and before she could shrink back or I could strike him he had Margaret in his arms.

" 'Lord, lass,' he said, with many jovial oaths, 'to think I'm back again! There, she's swounded. What folks be women, to be sure!"

" 'We thought you were dead, Adam,' she said, coming to.

" 'Bless your blue eyes,' he answered gleefully; 'often I says to myself, "Meggy will be thinking I'm with the fishes," and then I chuckles.'

" 'Where have you been all this time?' I demanded sternly.

" 'Gavin,' he said effusively, 'your hand. And don't look so feared, man; I bear no malice for what you've done. I heard all about it at the Cross Anchors.'

" 'Where have you been these five years and a half?' I repeated.

" 'Where have I no been, lad?' he replied.

" 'At Harvie,' I said.

" 'Right you are,' said he good-naturedly. 'Meggy, I had no

intention of leaving you that day, though I was yawning myself to death in Harvie, but I sees a whaler, and I thinks, "That's a tidy boat and I'm a tidy man, and if they'll take me and the dog, off we go.'"

" 'You never wrote to me,' Margaret said.

" 'I meant to send you some scrapes,' he answered, 'but it wasna till I changed ships that I had the chance, and then I minds, "Meggy kens I'm no hand with the pen." But I swear I often thought of you, lass; and look you here, that's better than letters, and so is that, and every penny of it is yours.'

"He flung two bags of gold upon the table, and their chink brought you out from behind your mother.

" 'Hallo!' Adam cried.

" 'He is mine,' I said. 'Gavin, come here.' But Margaret held you back.

" 'Here's a go,' Adam muttered, and scratched his head. Then he slapped his thigh. 'Gavin,' he said, in his friendliest way, 'we'll toss for him.'

"He pulled the knife that is now in my desk from his pocket, spat on it, and flung it up. 'Dry, the kid's ours, Meggy,' he explained; wet, he goes to Gavin.' I clenched my fist to— But what was the use? He caught the knife, and showed it to me.

" 'Dry,' he said triumphantly; 'so he is ours, Meggy. Kiddy, catch the knife. It is yours; and, mind, you have changed dads. And now that we have settled that, Gavin, there's my hand again.'

"I went away and left them, and I never saw Margaret again until the day you brought her to Thrums. But I saw you once, a few days after Adam came back. I was in the school-house, packing my books, and you were playing on the waste ground. I asked you how your mother was, and you said, 'She's fleid to come to the door till you gang awa, and my father's buying a boat.'

" 'I'm your father,' I said; but you answered confidently—

" 'You're no a living man. You're just a man I dreamed about; and I promised my mother no to dream about you again.'

" 'I am your father,' I repeated.

" 'My father's awa buying a fishing-boat,' you insisted; 'and when I speir at my mother whaur my first father is, she says I'm havering.'

" 'Gavin Ogilvy is your name,' I said. 'No,' you answered, 'I have a new name. My mother telled me my name is aye to be Gavin Dishart now. She telled me, too, to fling awa this knife my father gave me, and I've flung it awa a lot o' times, but I aye pick it up again.'

" 'Give it to me,' I said, with the wicked thoughts of a fool in my head.

"That is how your knife came into my possession. I left Harvie that night in the carrier's cart, but I had not the heart to return to college. Accident brought me here, and I thought it a fitting place in which to bury myself from Margaret."

Chapter XXXVII

Second Journey Of The Dominie To Thrums During The Twenty-Four Hours

Here was a nauseous draught for me. Having finished my tale, I turned to Gavin for sympathy; and, behold, he had been listening for the cannon instead of to my final words. So, like an old woman at her hearth, we warm our hands at our sorrows and drop in faggots, and each thinks his own fire a sun, in presence of which all other fires should go out. I was soured to see Gavin prove this, and then I could have laughed without mirth, for had not my bitterness proved it too?

"And now," I said, rising, "whether Margaret is to hold up her head henceforth lies no longer with me, but with you."

It was not to that he replied.

"You have suffered long, Mr. Ogilvy," he said. "Father," he added, wringing my hand. I called him son; but it was only an exchange of musty words that we had found too late. A father is a poor estate to come into at two-and-twenty.

"I should have been told of this," he said.

"Your mother did right, sir," I answered slowly, but he shook his head.

"I think you have misjudged her," he said. "Doubtless while my fa—, while Adam Dishart lived, she could only think of you with pain, but after his death—"

"After his death," I said quietly, "I was still so horrible to her that she left Harvie without letting a soul know whither she was bound. She dreaded my following her."

"Stranger to me," he said, after a pause, "than even your story is her being able to keep it from me. I believed no thought ever crossed her mind that she did not let me share."

"And none, I am sure, ever did," I answered, "save that, and such thoughts as a woman has with God only. It was my lot to bring disgrace on her. She thought it nothing less, and she has hidden it all these years for your sake, until now it is not burdensome. I suppose she feels that God had taken the weight off her. Now you are to put a heavier burden in its place."

He faced me boldly, and I admire him for it now.

"I cannot admit," he said, "that I did wrong in forgetting my mother for that fateful quarter of an hour. Babbie and I loved each other, and I was given the opportunity of making her mine or losing her for ever. Have you forgotten that all this tragedy you have told me of only grew out of your own indecision? I took the chance that you let slip by."

"I had not forgotten it," I replied. "What else made me tell you last night that Babbie was in Nanny's house?"

"But now you are afraid — now when the deed is done, when for me there can be no turning back. Whatever be the issue, I should be a cur to return to Thrums without my wife. Every minute I feel my strength returning, and before you reach Thrums I will have set out to the Spittal."

There was nothing to say after that. He came with me in the rain as far as the dyke, warning me against telling his people what was not true.

"My first part," I answered, "will be to send word to your mother that you are in safety. After that I must see Whamond. Much depends on him."

"You will not go to my mother?"

"Not so long as she has a roof over her head," I said, "but that may not be for long."

So, I think, we parted — each soon to forget the other in a woman.

But I had not gone far when I heard something that stopped me as sharply as if it had been McKenzie's hand once more on my shoulder. For a second the noise appalled me, and then, before the echo began, I knew it must be the Spittal cannon. My only thought was one of thankfulness. Now Gavin must see the wisdom of my reasoning. I would wait for him until he was able to come with me to Thrums. I turned back, and in my haste I ran through water I had gone round before.

I was too late. He was gone, and into the rain. I shouted his name in vain; that he had started for the Spittal there could be no doubt, that he would ever reach it was less certain. The earl's collie was still crouching by the fire, and, thinking it might be a guide to him, I drove the brute to the door, and chased it in the direction he probably had taken. Not until it had run from me did I resume my own journey. I do not need to be told that you who read would follow Gavin now rather than me; but you must bear with the dominie for a little while yet, as I see no other way of making things clear.

In some ways I was not ill-equipped for my attempt. I do not know any one of our hillsides as it is known to the shepherd, to whom every rabbit-hole and glimmer of mica is a landmark; but he, like his flock, has only to cross a dyke to find himself in a strange land, while I have been everywhere in the glen.

In the foreground the rain slanted, transparent till it reached the ground, where a mist seemed to blow it along as wind ruffles grass. In the distance all was a driving mist. I have been out for perhaps an hour in rains as wetting, and I have watched floods from my window, but never since have I known the fifth part of a season's rainfall in eighteen hours; and if there should be the like here again, we shall be found better prepared for it. Men have been lost in the glen in mists so thick that they could plunge their fingers out of sight in it as into a meal girnel; but this mist never came within twenty yards of me. I was surrounded by it, however, as if I was in a round tent; and out of this tent I could not walk, for it advanced with me. On the other side of this screen were horrible noises, at whose cause I could only guess, save now and again when a tongue of water was shot at my feet, or great stones came crashing through the canvas of mist. Then I ran whereever safety prompted, and thus tangled my bearings, until I was like that one in the child's game who is blindfolded and turned round three times that he may not know east from west.

Once I stumbled over a dead sheep and a living lamb; and in a clump of trees which puzzled me for they were where I thought no trees should be a wood-pigeon flew to me, but struck my breast with such force that I picked it up dead. I saw no other living thing, though half a dozen times I must have passed within cry of farmhouses. At one time I was in a corn-field, where I had to lift my hands to keep them out of water, and a dread filled me that I had wandered in a circle, and was still on Waster Lunny's land. I plucked some corn and held it to my eyes to see if it was green; but it was yellow, and so I knew that at last I was out of the glen.

People up here will complain if I do not tell how I found the farmer of Green Brae's fifty pounds. It is one of the best-remembered incidents of the flood, and happened shortly after I got out of the cornfield. A house rose suddenly before me, and I was hastening to it when as suddenly three of its walls fell. Before my mind could give a meaning to what my eyes told it, the water that had brought down the house had lifted me off my feet and flung me among waves. That would have been the last of the dominie had I not struck against a chest, then halfway on its voyage to the sea. I think the lid gave way under me; but that is surmise, for from the time the house fell till I was on the river in a kist that was like to be my coffin, is almost a blank. After what may have been but a short journey, though I had time in it to say my prayers twice, we stopped, jammed among fallen trees; and seeing a bank within reach, I tried to creep up it. In this there would have been little difficulty had not the contents of the kist caught in my feet and held on to them, like living things afraid of being left behind. I let down my hands to disentangle my feet, but failed; and then, grown desperate, I succeeded in reaching firm ground, dragging I knew not what after me. It proved to be a pillow-slip. Green Brae still shudders when I tell him that my first impulse was to leave the pillowslip unopened. However, I ripped it up, for to undo the wet strings that had ravelled round my feet would have wearied even a man with a needle to pick open the knots; and among broken gimlets, the head of a grape, and other things no beggar would have stolen, I found a tin canister containing fifty pounds. Waster Lunny says that this should have made a religious man of Green Brae, and it did to this extent, that he called the fall of the cottar's house providential. Otherwise the cottar, at whose expense it may be said the money was found, remains the more religious man of the two.

At last I came to the Kelpie's Brig, and I could have wept in joy (and might have been better employed), when, like everything I saw on that journey, it broke suddenly through the mist, and seemed to run at me like a living monster. Next moment I ran back, for as I stepped upon the bridge I saw that I had been about to walk into the air. What was left of the Kelpie's Brig ended in mid-stream. Instead of thanking God for the light without which I should have gone abruptly to my death, I sat down, miserable and hopeless.

Presently I was up, and trudging to the Loups of Malcolm. At the Loups the river runs narrow and deep between cliffs, and the spot is so called because one Malcolm jumped across it when pursued by wolves. Next day he returned boastfully to look at his jump, and gazing at it turned dizzy and fell into the river. Since that time chains have been hung across the Loups, to reduce the distance between the farms of Carwhimple and Keep-What-You-Can from a mile to a hundred yards. You must cross the chains on your breast. They were suspended there by Rob Angus, who was also the first to breast them.

But I never was a Rob Angus. When my pupils practise what they call the high jump, two small boys hold a string aloft, and the bigger ones run at it gallantly until they reach it, when they stop meekly and creep beneath. They will repeat this twenty times, and yet never, when they start for the string, seem to know where their courage will fail. Nay, they will even order the small boys to hold the string higher. I have smiled at this, but it was the same courage while the difficulty is far off that took me to the Loups. At sight of them I turned away.

I prayed to God for a little of the mettle of other men, and He heard me, for with my eyes shut I seemed to see Margaret beckoning from across the abyss as if she had need of me. Then I rose calmly and tested the chains, and crossed them on my breast. Many have done it with the same danger, at which they laugh, but without that vision I should have held back.

I was now across the river, and so had left the chance of drowning behind, but I was farther from Thrums than when I left the schoolhouse, and this countryside was almost unknown to me. The mist had begun to clear, so that I no longer wandered into fields; but though I kept to the roads, I could not tell that they led toward Thrums, and in my exhaustion I had often to stand still.

Then to make a new start in the mud was like pulling stakes out of the ground. So long as the rain faced me I thought I could not be straying far; but after an hour I lost this guide, for a wind rose that blew it in all directions.

In another hour, when I should have been drawing near Thrums, I found myself in a wood, and here I think my distress was greatest; nor is this to be marvelled at, for instead of being near Thrums, I was listening to the monotonous roar of the sea. I was too spent to reason, but I knew that I must have travelled direct east, and must be close to the German Ocean. I remember putting my back against a tree and shutting my eyes, and listening to the lash of the waves against the beach, and hearing the faint toll of a bell, and wondering listlessly on what lighthouse it was ringing. Doubtless I would have lain down to sleep for ever had I not heard another sound near at hand. It was the knock of a hammer on wood, and might have been a fisherman mending his boat. The instinct of self-preservation carried me to it, and presently I was at a little house. A man was standing in the rain, hammering new hinges to the door; and though I did not recognise him, I saw with bewilderment that the woman at his side was Nanny.

"It's the dominie," she cried, and her brother added—

"Losh, sir, you hinna the look o' a living man."

"Nanny," I said, in perplexity, "what are you doing here?"

"Whaur else should I be?" she asked.

I pressed my hands over my eyes, crying, "Where am I?"

Nanny shrank from me, but Sanders said, "Has the rain driven you gyte man? You're in Thrums."

"But the sea," I said, distrusting him. "I hear it. Listen!"

"That's the wind in Windyghoul," Sanders answered, looking at me queerly. "Come awa into the house."

Chapter XXXVIII

Thrums During The Twenty-Four Hours — Defence Of The Manse

Hardly had I crossed the threshold of the mud house when such a sickness came over me that I could not have looked up, though Nanny's voice had suddenly changed to Margaret's. Vaguely I knew that Nanny had put the kettle on the fire — a woman's first thought when there is illness in the house — and as I sat with my hands over my face I heard the water dripping from my clothes to the floor.

"Why is that bell ringing?" I asked at last, ignoring all questions and speaking through my fingers. An artist, I suppose, could paint all expression out of a human face. The sickness was having that effect on my voice.

"It's the Auld Licht bell," Sanders said; "and it's almost as fearsome to listen to as last nicht's rain. I wish I kent what they're ringing it for."

"Wish no sic things," said Nanny nervously. "There's things it's best to put off kenning as lang as we can."

"It's that ill-cleakit witch, Effie McBean, that makes Nanny speak so doleful," Sanders told me. "There was to be a prayer-meeting last nicht, but Mr. Dishart never came to 't, though they rang till they wraxed their arms; and now Effie says it'll ring on by itsel' till he's brocht hame a corp. The hellicat says the rain's a dispensation to drown him in for neglect o' duty. Sal, I would think little o' the Lord if He needed to create a new sea to drown one man in. Nanny, you cuttie, that's no swearing; I defy you to find a single lonely oath in what I've said."

"Never mind Effie McBean," I interposed. "What are the congregation saying about the minister's absence?"

"We ken little except what Effie telled us," Nanny answered. "I was at Tilliedrum yestreen, meeting Sanders as he got out o' the gaol, and that awfu on-ding began when we was on the Bellies Braes. We focht our way through it, but not a soul did we meet;

and wha would gang out the day that can bide at hame? Ay, but Effie says it's kent in Thrums that Mr. Dishart has run off wi'— wi' an Egyptian."

"You're waur than her, Nanny," Sanders said roughly, "for you hae twa reasons for kenning better. In the first place, has Mr. Dishart no keeped you in siller a' the time I was awa? and for another, have I no been at the manse?"

My head rose now.

"He gaed to the manse," Nanny explained, "to thank Mr. Dishart for being so good to me. Ay, but Jean wouldna let him in. I'm thinking that looks gey grey."

"Whatever was her reason," Sanders admitted, "Jean wouldna open the door; but I keeked in at the parlour window, and saw Mrs. Dishart in't looking very cosy-like and lauching; and do you think I would hae seen that if ill had come ower the minister?"

"Not if Margaret knew of it," I said to myself, and wondered at Whamond's forbearance.

"She had a skein o' worsted stretched out on her hands," Sanders continued, "and a young leddy was winding it. I didna see her richt, but she wasna a Thrums leddy."

"Effie McBean says she's his intended, come to call him to account," Nanny said; but I hardly listened, for I saw that I must hurry to Tammas Whamond's. Nanny followed me to the gate with her gown pulled over her head, and said excitedly—

"Oh, dominie, I warrant it's true. It'll be Babbie. Sanders doesna suspect, because I've telled him nothing about her. Oh, what's to be done? They were baith so good to me."

I could only tell her to keep what she knew to herself.

"Has Rob Dow come back?" I called out after I had started.

"Whaur frae?" she replied; and then I remembered that all these things had happened while Nanny was at Tilliedrum. In this life some of the seven ages are spread over two decades, and others pass as quickly as a stage play. Though a fifth of a season's rain had fallen in a night and a day, it had scarcely kept pace with Gavin.

I hurried to the town by the Roods. That brae was as deserted as the country roads, except where children had escaped from their mothers to wade in it. Here and there dams were keeping the water away from one door to send it with greater volume to another, and at points the ground had fallen in. But this I noticed without interest. I did not even realise that I was holding my head painfully to the side where it had been blown by the wind and glued by the rain. I have never held my head straight since that journey.

Only a few looms were going, their peddles in water. I was addressed from several doors and windows; once by Charles Yuill.

"Dinna pretend," he said, "that you've walked in frae the school-house alane. The rain chased me into this house yestreen, and here it has keeped me, though I bide no further awa than Tillyloss."

"Charles," I said in a low voice, "why is the Auld Licht bell ringing?"

"Hae you no heard about Mr. Dishart?" he asked.

"Oh, man! that's Lang Tammas in the kirk by himsel', tearing at the bell to bring the folk thegither to depose the minister."

Instead of going to Whamond's house in the school wynd I hastened down the Banker's close to the kirk, and had almost to turn back, so choked was the close with floating refuse. I could see the bell swaying, but the kirk was locked, and I battered on the door to no purpose. Then, remembering that Hendry Munn lived in Coutt's trance, I set off for his house. He saw me crossing the square, but would not open his door until I was close to it.

"When I open," he cried, "squeeze through quick;" but though I did his bidding, a rush of water darted in before me. Hendry re-closed the door by flinging himself against it.

"When I saw you crossing the square," he said, "it was surprise enough to cure the hiccup."

"Hendry," I replied instantly, "why is the Auld Licht bell ringing?"

He put his finger to his lip. "I see," he said imperturbably, "you've met our folk in the glen and heard frae them about the minister."

"What folk?"

"Mair than half the congregation," he replied, "started for Glen Quharity twa hours syne to help the farmers. You didna see them?"

"No; they must have been on the other side of the river." Again that question forced my lips. "Why is the bell ringing?"

"Canny, dominie," he said, "till we're up the stair. Mysy Moncur's lug's at her key-hole listening to you."

"You lie, Hendry Munn," cried an invisible woman. The voice became more plaintive: "I ken a heap, Hendry, so you may as well tell me a'."

"Lick away at the bone you hae," the shoemaker replied heartlessly, and conducted me to his room up one of the few inside stairs then in Thrums, Hendry's oldest furniture was five boxes, fixed to the wall at such a height that children could climb into them from a high stool. In these his bairns slept, and so space was economised. 1 could never laugh at the arrangement, as I knew that Betty had planned it on her death-bed for her man's sake. Five little heads bobbed up in their beds as I entered, but more vexing to me was Wearyworld on a stool.

"In by, dominie," he said sociably. "Sal, you needna fear burning wi' a' that water on you. You're in mair danger o' coming a-boil."

"I want to speak to you alone, Hendry," I said bluntly.

"You winna put me out, Hendry?" the alarmed policeman entreated. "Mind, you said in sic weather you would be friendly to a brute beast. Ay, ay, dominie, what's your news? It's welcome, be it good or bad. You would meet the townsfolk in the glen, and they would tell you about Mr. Dishart. What, you hinna heard? Oh, sirs, he's a lost man. There would hae been a meeting the day to depose him if so many hadna gaen to the glen. But the morn'll do as weel. The very women is cursing him, and the laddies has begun to gather stanes. He's married on an Egyp—"

"Hendry!" I cried, like one giving an order.

"Wearyworld, step!" said Hendry sternly, and then added soft-heartedly, "Here's a bit news that'll open Mysy Moncur's door to you. You can tell her frae me that the bell's ringing just because I forgot to tie it up last nicht, and the wind's shaking it, and I winna gang out in the rain to stop it."

"Ay," the policeman said, looking at me sulkily, "she may open her door for that, but it'll no let me in. Tell me mair. Tell me wha the leddy at manse is."

"Out you go," answered Hendry. "Once she opens the door, you can shove your foot in, and syne she's in your power." He pushed

Wearyworld out, and came back to me, saying, "It was best to tell him the truth, to keep him frae making up lies."

"But is it the truth? I was told Lang Tammas—" "Ay, I ken that story; but Tammas has other work on hand."

"Then tie up the bell at once, Hendry," I urged.

"I canna," he answered gravely. "Tammas took the keys o' the kirk frae me yestreen, and winna gie them up. He says the bell's being rung by the hand o' God."

"Has he been at the manse? Does Mrs. Dishart know—?"

"He's been at the manse twa or three times, but Jean barred him out. She'll let nobody in till the minister comes back, and so the mistress kens nothing. But what's the use o' keeping it frae her ony langer?"

"Every use," I said.

"None," answered Hendry sadly. "Dominie, the minister was married to the Egyptian on the hill last nicht, and Tammas was witness. Not only were they married, but they've ran aff thegither."

"You are wrong, Hendry," I assured him, telling as much as I dared. "I left Mr. Dishart in my house."

"What! But if that is so, how did he no come back wi' you?"

"Because he was nearly drowned in the flood."

"She'll be wi' him?"

"He was alone."

Hendry's face lit up dimly with joy, and then he shook his head. "Tammas was witness," he said. "Can you deny the marriage?"

"All I ask of you," I answered guardedly, "is to suspend judgment until the minister returns."

"There can be nothing done, at ony rate," he said, "till the folk themsel's come back frae the glen; and I needna tell you how glad we would a' be to be as fond o' him as ever. But Tammas was witness."

"Have pity on his mother, man."

"We've done the best for her we could," he replied. "We prigged wi' Tammas no to gang to the manse till he was sure the minister was living. 'For if he has been drowned,' we said, 'his mother need never ken what we were thinking o' doing.' Ay, and we are sorry for the young leddy, too."

"What young lady is this you all talk of?" I asked.

"She's his intended. Ay, you needna start. She has come a' the road frae Glasgow to challenge him about the gypsy. The pitiful thing is that Mrs. Dishart lauched awa her fears, and now they're baith waiting for his return, as happy as ignorance can make them."

"There is no such lady," I said.

"But there is," he answered, doggedly, "for she came in a machine late last nicht, and I was ane o' a dozen that baith heard and saw it through my window. It stopped at the manse near half an hour. What's mair, the lady hersel' was at Sam'l Farquharson's in the Tenements the day for twa hours."

I listened in bewilderment and fear.

"Sam'l's bairn's down wi' scarlet fever and like to die, and him being a widow-man he has gone useless. You mauna blame the wives in the Tenements for hauding back. They're fleid to smit their ain litlins; and as it happens, Sam'l's friends is a' aff to the glen. Weel, he ran greeting to the manse for Mr. Dishart, and the lady heard him crying to Jean through the door, and what does she do but gang straucht to the Tenements wi' Sam'l. Her goodness has naturally put the folk on her side against the minister."

"This does not prove her his intended," I broke in.

"She was heard saying to Sam'l," answered the kirk-officer, "that the minister being awa, it was her duty to take his place. Yes, and though she little kent it, he was already married."

"Hendry," I said, rising, "I must see this lady at once. Is she still at Farquharson's house?"

"She may be back again by this time. Tammas set off for Sam'l's as soon as he heard she was there, but he just missed her. I left him there an hour syne. He was waiting for her, determined to tell her all."

I set off for the Tenements at once, declining Hendry's company. The wind had fallen, so that the bell no longer rang, but the rain was falling doggedly. The streets were still deserted. I pushed open the precentor's door in the school wynd, but there was no one in the house. Tibbie Birse saw me, and shouted from her door—

"Hae you heard o' Mr. Dishart? He'll never daur show face in Thrums again."

Without giving her a word I hastened to the Tenements.

"The leddy's no here," Sam'l Farquharson told me, "and Tammas is back at the manse again, trying to force his way in."

From Sam'l, too, I turned, with no more than a groan; but he cried after me, "Perdition on the man that has played that leddy false."

Had Margaret been at her window she must have seen me, so recklessly did I hurry up the minister's road, with nothing in me but a passion to take Whamond by the throat. He was not in the garden. The kitchen door was open. Jean was standing at it with her apron to her eyes.

"Tammas Whamond?" I demanded, and my face completed the question.

"You're ower late," she wailed. "He's wi' her. Oh, dominie, whaur's the minister?"

"You base woman!" I cried, "why did you unbar the door?"

"It was the mistress," she answered. "She heard him shaking it, and I had to tell her wha it was. Dominie, it's a' my wite! He tried to get in last nicht, and roared threats through the door, and after he had gone awa she speired wha I had been speaking to. I had to tell her, but I said he had come to let her ken that the minister was taking shelter frae the rain in a farmhouse. Ay, I said he was to bide there till the flood gaed down, and that's how she has been easy a' day. I acted for the best, but I'm sair punished now; for when she heard Tammas at the door twa or three minutes syne, she ordered me to let him in, so that she could thank him for bringing the news last nicht, despite the rain. They're in the parlour. Oh, dominie, gang in and stop his mouth."

This was hard. I dared not go to the parlour, Margaret might have died at sight of me. I turned my face from Jean.

"Jean," said someone, opening the inner kitchen door, "why did you—?"

She stopped, and that was what turned me round. As she spoke I thought it was the young lady; when I looked I saw it was Babbie, though no longer in a gypsy's dress. Then I knew that the young lady and Babbie were one.

Chapter XXXIX

How Babbie Spent The Night Of August Fourth

How had the Egyptian been spirited here from the Spittal? I did not ask the question. To interest myself in Babbie at that dire hour of Margaret's life would have been as impossible to me as to sit down to a book. To others, however, it is only an old woman on whom the parlour door of the manse has closed, only a garrulous dominie that is in pain outside it. Your eyes are on the young wife. When Babbie was plucked off the hill, she thought as little as Gavin that her captor was Rob Dow. Close as he was to her, he was but a shadow until she screamed the second time, when he pressed her to the ground and tied his neckerchief over her mouth. Then, in the moment that power of utterance was taken from her, she saw the face that had startled her at Nanny's window. Half-carried, she was borne forward rapidly, until someone seemed to rise out of the broom and strike them both. They had only run against the doctor's trap; and huddling her into it, Dow jumped up beside her. He tied her hands together with a cord. For a time the horse feared the darkness in front more than the lash behind; but when the rains became terrific, it rushed ahead wildly — probably with its eyes shut.

In three minutes Babbie went through all the degrees of fear. In the first she thought Lord Rintoul had kidnapped her; but no sooner had her captor resolved himself into Dow, drunk with the events of the day and night, than in the earl's hands would have lain safety. Next, Dow was forgotten in the dread of a sudden death which he must share. And lastly, the rain seemed to be driving all other horrors back, that it might have her for its own. Her perils increased to the unbearable as quickly as an iron in the fire passes through the various stages between warmth and white heat. Then she had to do something; and as she could not cry out, she flung herself from the dog-cart. She fell heavily in Caddam Wood, but the rain would not let her lie there stunned. It beat her back to consciousness, and she sat up on her knees and listened breathlessly, staring in the direction the trap had taken, as if her eyes could help her ears.

All night, I have said, the rain poured, but those charges only rode down the deluge at intervals, as now and again one wave greater than the others stalks over the sea. In the first lull it appeared to Babbie that the storm had swept by, leaving her to Dow. Now she heard the rubbing of the branches, and felt the torn leaves falling on her gown. She rose to feel her way out of the wood with her bound hands, then sank in terror, for someone had called her name. Next moment she was up again, for the voice was Gavin's, who was hurrying after her, as he thought, down Windyghoul. He was no farther away than a whisper might have carried on a still night, but she dared not pursue him, for already Dow was coming back. She could not see him, but she heard the horse whinny and the rocking of the dog-cart. Dow was now at the brute's head, and probably it tried to bite him, for he struck it, crying—

"Would you? Stand still till I find her. I heard her move this minute."

Babbie crouched upon a big stone, and sat motionless while he groped for her. Her breathing might have been tied now, as well as her mouth. She heard him feeling for her, first with his feet and then with his hands, and swearing when his head struck against a tree.

"I ken you're within hearing," he muttered, "and I'll hae you yet. I have a gully-knife in my hand. Listen!"

He severed a whin stalk with the knife, and Babbie seemed to see the gleam of the blade.

"What do I mean by wanting to kill you?" he said, as if she had asked the question. "Do you no ken wha said to me, 'Kill this woman'? It was the Lord. 'I winna kill her,' I said, 'but I'll cart her out o' the country.' 'Kill her,' says He; 'why encumbereth she the ground?'

He resumed his search, but with new tactics. "I see you now," he would cry, and rush forward, perhaps within a yard of her. Then she must have screamed had she the power. When he tied that neckerchief round her mouth he prolonged her life.

Then came the second hurricane of rain, so appalling that had Babbie's hands been free she would have pressed them to her ears. For a full minute she forgot Dow's presence. A living thing touched her face. The horse had found her. She recoiled from it, but its frightened head pressed heavily on her shoulder. She rose and tried to steal away, but the brute followed, and as the rain suddenly exhausted itself she heard the dragging of the dog-cart. She had to halt.

Again she heard Dow's voice. Perhaps he had been speaking throughout the roar of the rain. If so, it must have made him deaf to his own words. He groped for the horse's head, and presently his hand touched Babbie's dress, then jumped from it, so suddenly had he found her. No sound escaped him, and she was beginning to think it possible that he had mistaken her for a bush, when his hand went over her face. He was making sure of his discovery.

"The Lord has delivered you into my hands," he said in a low voice, with some awe in it. Then he pulled her to the ground, and, sitting down beside her, rocked himself backwards and forwards, his hands round his knees. She would have bartered the world for power to speak to him.

"He wouldna hear o' my just carting you to some other countryside," he said confidentially. " 'The devil would just blaw her back again, says He, 'therefore kill her.' 'And if I kill her,' I says, 'they'll hang me.' 'You can hang yoursel',' says He. 'What wi'?' I speirs. 'Wi' the reins o' the dog-cart,' says He. 'They would break,' says I. 'Weel, weel,' says He, 'though they do hang you, nobody'll miss you.' 'That's true,' says I, 'and You are a just God.' "

He stood up and confronted her.

"Prisoner at the bar," he said, "hae ye onything to say why sentence of death shouldna be pronounced against you? She doesna answer. She kens death is her deserts."

By this time he had forgotten probably why his victim was dumb.

"Prisoner at the bar, hand back to me the soul o' Gavin Dishart. You winna? Did the devil, your master, summon you to him and say, 'Either that noble man or me maun leave Thrums?' He did. And did you, or did you no, drag that minister, when under your spell, to the hill, and there marry him ower the tongs? You did. Witnesses, Rob Dow and Tammas Whamond."

She was moving from him on her knees, meaning when out of arm's reach to make a dash for life.

"Sit down," he grumbled, "or how can you expect a fair trial? Prisoner at the bar, you have been found guilty of witchcraft."

For the first time his voice faltered.

"That's the difficulty, for witches canna die, except by burning or drowning. There's no blood in you for my knife, and your neck wouldna twist. Your master has brocht the rain to put out a' the fires, and we'll hae to wait till it runs into a pool deep enough to drown you.

"I wonder at You, God. Do You believe her master'll mak' the pool for her? He'll rather stop his rain. Mr. Dishart said You was mair powerful than the devil, but it doesna look like it. If You had the power, how did you no stop this woman working her will on the minister? You kent what she was doing, for You ken a' things. Mr. Dishart says You ken a' things. If You do, the mair shame to You. Would a shepherd, that could help it, let dogs worry his sheep? Kill her! It's fine to cry 'Kill her,' but whaur's the bonfire, whaur's the pool? You that made the heaven and the earth and all that in them is, can You no set fire to some wet whins, or change this stane into a mill-dam?"

He struck the stone with his fist, and then gave a cry of exultation. He raised the great slab in his arms and flung it from him. In that moment Babbie might have run away, but she fainted. Almost simultaneously with Dow she knew this was the stone which covered the Caddam well. When she came to, Dow was speaking, and his voice had become solemn.

"You said your master was mair powerful than mine, and I said it too, and all the time you was sitting here wi' the very pool aneath you that I have been praying for. Listen!"

He dropped a stone into the well, and she heard it strike the water.

"What are you shaking at?" he said in reproof. "Was it no yoursel' that chose the spot? Lassie, say your prayers. Are you saying them?"

He put his hand over her face, to feel if her lips were moving, and tore off the neckerchief.

And then again the rain came between them. In that rain one could not think. Babbie did not know that she had bitten through the string that tied her hands. She planned no escape. But she flung herself at the place where Dow had been standing. He was no longer there, and she fell heavily, and was on her feet again in an instant and running recklessly. Trees intercepted her, and she thought they were Dow, and wrestled with them. By-and-by she fell into Windyghoul, and there she crouched until all her senses were restored to her, when she remembered that she had been married lately.

How long Dow was in discovering that she had escaped, and whether he searched for her, no one knows. After a time he jumped into the dog-cart again, and drove aimlessly through the rain. That wild journey probably lasted two hours, and came to an abrupt end only when a tree fell upon the trap. The horse galloped off, but one of Dow's legs was beneath the tree, and there he had to lie helpless; for though the leg was little injured, he could not extricate himself. A night and day passed, and he believed that he must die; but even in this plight he did not forget the man he loved. He found a piece of slate, and in the darkness cut these words on it with his knife:

"Me being about to die, I solemnly swear I didna see the minister marrying an Egyptian on the hill this nicht. May I burn in Hell if this is no true.

(Signed) "Rob Dow."

This document he put in his pocket, and so preserved proof of what he was perjuring himself to deny.

Chapter XL

Babbie and Margaret - Defence Of The Manse Continued

The Egyptian was mournful in Windyghoul, up which she had once danced and sung; but you must not think that she still feared Dow. I felt McKenzie's clutch on my arm for hours after he left me, but she was far braver than I; indeed, dangers at which I should have shut my eyes only made hers gleam, and I suppose it was sheer love of them that first made her play the coquette with Gavin. If she cried now, it was not for herself; it was because she thought she had destroyed him. Could I have gone to her then, and said that Gavin wanted to blot out the gypsy wedding, that throbbing little breast would have frozen at once, and the drooping head would have been proud again, and she would have gone away for ever without another tear.

What do I say? I am doing a wrong to the love these two bore each other. Babbie would not have taken so base a message from my lips. He would have had to say the words to her himself before she believed them his. What would he want her to do now? was the only question she asked herself. To follow him was useless, for in that rain and darkness two people might have searched for each other all night in a single field. That he would go to the Spittal, thinking her in Rintoul's dog-cart, she did not doubt; and his distress was painful to her to think of. But not knowing that the burns were in flood, she under-estimated his danger.

Remembering that the mud house was near, she groped her way to it, meaning to pass the night there; but at the gate she turned away hastily, hearing from the door the voice of a man she did not know to be Nanny's brother. She wandered recklessly a short distance, until the rain began to threaten again, and then, falling on her knees in the broom, she prayed to God for guidance. When she rose, she set off for the manse.

The rain that followed the flash of lightning had brought Margaret to the kitchen.

"Jean, did you ever hear such a rain? It is trying to break into the manse."

"I canna hear you, ma'am; is it the rain you're feared at?"

"What else could it be?"

Jean did not answer.

"I hope the minister won't leave the church, Jean, till this is over?"

"Nobody would daur, ma'am. The rain'll turn the key on them all."

Jean forced out these words with difficulty, for she knew that the church had been empty, and the door locked for over an hour.

"This rain has come as if in answer to the minister's prayer, Jean."

"It wasna rain like this they wanted."

"Jean, you would not attempt to guide the Lord's hand. The minister will have to reprove the people for thinking too much of him again, for they will say that he induced God to send the rain. To-night's meeting will be remembered long in Thrums."

Jean shuddered, and said, "It's mair like an ordinary rain now, ma'am."

"But it has put out your fire, and I wanted another heater. Perhaps the one I have is hot enough, though."

Margaret returned to the parlour, and from the kitchen Jean could hear the heater tilted backward and forward in the box-iron — a pleasant, homely sound when there is happiness in the house. Soon she heard a step outside, however, and it was followed by a rough shaking of the barred door.

"Is it you, Mr. Dishart?" Jean asked nervously.

"It's me, Tammas Whamond," the precentor answered. "Unbar the door."

"What do you want? Speak low."

"I winna speak low. Let me in. I have news for the minister's mother."

"What news?" demanded Jean.

"Jean Proctor, as chief elder of the kirk I order you to let me do my duty."

"Whaur's the minister?"

"He's a minister no longer. He's married a gypsy woman and run awa wi' her."

"You lie, Tammas Whamond. I believe—"

"Your belief's of no consequence. Open the door, and let me in to tell your mistress what I hae seen."

"She'll hear it first frae his ain lips if she hears it ava. I winna open the door."

"Then I'll burst it open."

Whamond flung himself at the door, and Jean, her fingers rigid with fear, stood waiting for its fall. But the rain came to her rescue by lashing the precentor until even he was forced to run from it.

"I'll be back again," he cried. "Woe to you, Jean Proctor, that hae denied your God this nicht."

"Who was that speaking to you, Jean?" asked Margaret, re-entering the kitchen. Until the rain abated, Jean did not attempt to answer.

"I thought it was the precentor's voice," Margaret said.

Jean was a poor hand at lying, and she stuttered in her answer.

"There is nothing wrong, is there?" cried Margaret, in sudden fright. "My son—"

"Nothing, nothing."

The words jumped from Jean to save Margaret from falling. Now she could not take them back. "I winna believe it o' him," said Jean to herself. "Let them say what they will, I'll be true to him; and when he comes back he'll find her as he left her."

"It was Lang Tammas," she answered his mistress; "but he just came to say that—"

"Quick, Jean! what?"

"—Mr. Dishart has been called to a sick-bed in the country, ma'am to the farm o' Look-About-You; and as it's sic a rain, he's to bide there a' nicht."

"And Whamond came through that rain to tell me this? How good of him. Was there any other message?"

"Just that the minister hoped you would go straight to your bed, ma'am," said Jean, thinking to herself, "There can be no great sin in giving her one mair happy nicht; it may be her last."

The two women talked for a short time, and then read verse about in the parlour from the third chapter of Mark.

"This is the first night we have been left alone in the manse," Margaret said, as she was retiring to her bedroom, "and we must not grudge the minister to those who have sore need of him. I notice that you have barred the doors."

"Ay, they're barred. Nobody can win in the nicht."

"Nobody will want in, Jean," Margaret said, smiling.

"I dinna ken about that," answered Jean below her breath. "Ay, ma'am, may you sleep for baith o' us this nicht, for I daurna gang to my bed."

Jean was both right and wrong, for two persons wanted in within the next half-hour, and she opened the door to both of them. The first to come was Babbie.

So long as women sit up of nights listening for a footstep, will they flatten their faces at the window, though all without be black. Jean had not been back in the kitchen for two minutes before she raised the blind. Her eyes were close to the glass, when she saw another face almost meet hers, as you may touch your reflection in a mirror. But this face was not her own. It was white and sad. Jean suppressed a cry, and let the blind fall, as if shutting the lid on some uncanny thing.

"Won't you let me in?" said a voice that might have been only the sob of a rain-beaten wind; "I am nearly drowned."

Jean stood like death; but her suppliant would not pass on.

"You are not afraid?" the voice continued; "raise the blind again, and you will see that no one need fear me."

At this request Jean's hands sought each other's company behind her back.

"Wha are you?" she asked, without stirring. "Are you — the woman?"

"Yes."

"Whaur's the minister?"

The rain again became wild, but this time it only tore by the manse as if to a conflict beyond.

"Are you aye there? I daurna let you in till I'm sure the mistress is bedded. Gang round to the front, and see if there's ony licht burning in the high west window."

"There was a light," the voice said presently, "but it was turned out as I looked."

"Then I'll let you in, and God kens I mean no wrang by it."

Babbie entered shivering, and Jean re-barred the door. Then she looked long at the woman whom her master loved. Babbie was on her knees at the hearth, holding out her hands to the dead fire.

"What a pity it's a fause face."

"Do I look so false?"

"Is it true? You're no married to him?"

"Yes, it is true."

"And yet you look as if you was fond o' him. If you cared for him, how could you do it?"

"That was why I did it."

"And him could hae had wha he liked."

"I gave up Lord Rintoul for him."

"What? Na, na, you're the Egyptian."

"You judge me by my dress."

"And soaking it is. How you're shivering — what neat fingers — what bonny little feet. I could near believe what you tell me. Aff wi' these rags, and I'll gie you on my black frock, if — if you promise me no to gang awa wi't."

So Babbie put on some clothes of Jean's, including the black frock, and stockings and shoes.

"Mr. Dishart cannot be back, Jean," she said, "before morning, and I don't want his mother to see me till he comes."

"I wouldna let you near her the nicht, though you gaed on your knees to me. But whaur is he?"

Babbie explained why Gavin had set off for the Spittal; but Jean shook her head incredulously, saying, "I canna believe you're that grand leddy, and yet ilka time I look at you I could near believe it."

In another minute Jean had something else to think of, for there came a loud rap upon the front door.

"It's Tammas Whamond back again," she moaned; "and if the mistress hears, she'll tell me to let him in."

"You shall open to me," cried a hoarse voice.

"That's no Tammas's word," Jean said in bewilderment.

"It is Lord Rintoul," Babbie whispered.

"What? Then it's truth you telled me."

The knocking continued; a door upstairs opened, and Margaret spoke over the banisters.

"Have you gone to bed, Jean? Someone is knocking at the door, and a minute ago I thought I heard a carriage stop close by. Perhaps the farmer has driven Mr. Dishart home."

"I'm putting on my things, ma'am," Jean answered; then whispered to Babbie, "What's to be done?"

"He won't go away," Babbie answered: "You will have to let him into the parlour, Jean. Can she see the door from up there?"

"No; but though he was in the parlour?"

"I shall go to him there."

"Make haste, Jean," Margaret called. 'If it is any persons wanting shelter, we must give it them on such a night."

"A minute, ma'am," Jean answered. To Babbie she whispered, "What shall I say to her?"

"I — I don't know," answered Babbie ruefully. "Think of something, Jean. But open the door now. Stop, let me into the parlour first."

The two women stole into the parlour.

"Tell me what will be the result o' his coming here," entreated Jean.

"The result," Babbie said firmly, "will be that he shall go away and leave me here."

Margaret heard Jean open the front door and speak to some person or persons whom she showed into the parlour.

Chapter XLI

Rintoul and Babbie — Break-down Of The Defence Of The Manse

"You dare to look me in the face!"

They were Rintoul's words. Yet Babbie had only ventured to look up because he was so long in speaking. His voice was low, but harsh, like a wheel on which the brake is pressed sharply.

"It seems to be more than the man is capable of," he added sourly.

"Do you think," Babbie exclaimed, taking fire, "that he is afraid of you?"

"So it seems; but I will drag him into the light, wherever he is skulking."

Lord Rintoul strode to the door, and the brake was off his tongue already.

"Go," said Babbie coldly, "and shout and stamp through the house; you may succeed in frightening the women, who are the only persons in it."

"Where is he?"

"He has gone to the Spittal to see you."

"He knew I was on the hill."

"He lost me in the darkness, and thought you had run away with me in your trap."

"Ha! So he is off to the Spittal to ask me to give you back to him."

"To compel you," corrected Babbie.

"Pooh!" said the earl nervously, "that was but mummery on the hill."

"It was a marriage."

"With gypsies for witnesses. Their word would count for less than nothing. Babbie, I am still in time to save you."

"I don't want to be saved. The marriage had witnesses no court could discredit."

"What witnesses?"

"Mr. McKenzie and yourself."

She heard his teeth meet. When next she looked at him, there were tears in his eyes as well as in her own. It was perhaps the first time these two had ever been in close sympathy. Both were grieving for Rintoul.

"I am so sorry," Babbie began in a broken voice; then stopped, because they seemed such feeble words.

"If you are sorry," the earl answered eagerly, "it is not yet too late. McKenzie and I saw nothing. Come away with me, Babbie, if only in pity for yourself."

"Ah, but I don't pity myself."

"Because this man has blinded you."

"No, he has made me see."

"This mummery on the hill—"

"Why do you call it so? I believe God approved of that marriage, as He could never have countenanced yours and mine."

"God! I never heard the word on your lips before."

"I know that."

"It is his teaching, doubtless?"

"Yes."

"And he told you that to do to me as you have done was to be pleasing in God's sight?"

"No; he knows that it was so evil in God's sight that I shall suffer for it always."

"But he has done no wrong, so there is no punishment for him?"

"It is true that he has done no wrong, but his punishment will be worse, probably, than mine."

"That," said the earl, scoffing, "is not just."

"It is just. He has accepted responsibility for my sins by marrying me."

"And what form is his punishment to take?"

"For marrying me he will be driven from his church and dishonoured in all men's eyes, unless — unless God is more merciful to us than we can expect."

Her sincerity was so obvious that the earl could no longer meet it with sarcasm.

"It is you I pity now," he said, looking wonderingly at her. "Do you not see that this man has deceived you? Where was his boasted purity in meeting you by stealth, as he must have been doing, and plotting to take you from me?"

"If you knew him," Babbie answered, "you would not need to be told that he is incapable of that. He thought me an ordinary gypsy until an hour ago."

"And you had so little regard for me that you waited until the eve of what was to be our marriage, and then, laughing at my shame, ran off to marry him."

"I am not so bad as that," Babbie answered, and told him what had brought her to Thrums. "I had no thought but of returning to you, nor he of keeping me from you. We had said good-bye at the mud house door — and then we heard your voice."

"And my voice was so horrible to you that it drove you to this!"

"I — I love him so much."

What more could Babbie answer? These words told him that, if love commands, home, the friendships of a life-time, kindnesses incalculable, are at once as nought. Nothing is so cruel as love if a rival challenges it to combat.

"Why could you not love me, Babbie?" said the earl sadly. "I have done so much for you."

It was little he had done for her that was not selfish. Men are deceived curiously in such matters. When they add a new wing to their house, they do not call the action virtue; but if they give to a fellow creature for their own gratification, they demand of God a good mark for it. Babbie, however, was in no mood to make light of the earl's gifts, and at his question she shook her head sorrowfully.

"Is it because I am too — old?"

This was the only time he ever spoke of his age to her.

"Oh no, it is not that," she replied hastily, "I love Mr. Dishart — because he loves me, I think."

"Have I not loved you always?"

"Never," Babbie answered simply. "If you had, perhaps then I should have loved you."

"Babbie," he exclaimed, "if ever man loved woman, and showed it by the sacrifices he made for her, I—"

"No," Babbie said, "you don't understand what it is. Ah! I did not mean to hurt you."

"If I don't know what it is, what is it?" he asked, almost humbly. "I scarcely know you now."

"That is it," said Babbie.

She gave him back his ring, and then he broke down pitifully. Doubtless there was good in him, but I saw him only once, and with nothing to contrast against it I may not now attempt to breathe life into the dust of his senile passion. These were the last words that passed between him and Babbie:—

"There was nothing," he said wistfully, "in this wide world that you could not have had by asking me for it. Was not that love?"

"No," she answered. "What right have I to everything I cry for?"

"You should never have had a care had you married me. That is love."

"It is not. I want to share my husband's cares, as I expect him to share mine."

"I would have humoured you in everything."

"You always did: as if a woman's mind were for laughing at, like a baby's passions."

"You had your passions, too, Babbie. Yet did I ever chide you for them? That was love."

"No, it was contempt. Oh," she cried passionately, "what have not you men to answer for who talk of love to a woman when her face is all you know of her; and her passions, her aspirations, are for kissing to sleep, her very soul a plaything? I tell you, Lord Rintoul, and it is all the message I send back to the gentleman at the Spittal who made love to me behind your back, that this is a poor folly, and well calculated to rouse the wrath of God."

Now Jean's ear had been to the parlour keyhole for a time, but some message she had to take to Margaret, and what she risked saying was this—

"It's Lord Rintoul and a party that has been catched in the rain, and he would be obliged to you if you could gie his bride shelter for the nicht."

Thus the distracted servant thought to keep Margaret's mind at rest until Gavin came back.

"Lord Rintoul!" exclaimed Margaret. "What a pity Gavin has missed him. Of course she can stay here. Did you say I had gone to bed? I should not know what to say to a lord. But ask her to come up to me after he has gone — and, Jean, is the parlour looking tidy?"

Lord Rintoul having departed, Jean told Babbie how she had accounted to Margaret for his visit. "And she telled me to gie you dry claethes and her compliments, and would you gang up to the bedroom and see her?"

Very slowly Babbie climbed the stairs. I suppose she is the only person who was ever afraid of Margaret. Her first knock on the bedroom door was so soft that Margaret, who was sitting up in bed, did not hear it. When Babbie entered the room, Margaret's first thought was that there could be no other so beautiful as this, and her second was that the stranger seemed even more timid than herself. After a few minutes' talk she laid aside her primness, a weapon she had drawn in self-defence lest this fine lady should not understand the grandeur of a manse, and at a "Call me Babbie, won't you?" she smiled.

"That is what some other person calls you!" said Margaret archly. "Do you know that he took twenty minutes to say good-night? My dear," she added hastily, misinterpreting Babbie's silence, "I should have been sorry had he taken one second less. Every tick of the clock was a gossip, telling me how he loves you."

In the dim light a face that begged for pity was turned to Margaret.

"He does love you, Babbie?" she asked, suddenly doubtful.

Babbie turned away her face, then shook her head.

"But you love him?"

Again Babbie shook her head.

"Oh, my dear," cried Margaret, in distress, "if this is so, are you not afraid to marry him?"

She knew now that Babbie was crying, but she did not knew why Babbie could not look her in the face.

"There may be times," Babbie said, most woeful that she had not married Rintoul, "when it is best to marry a man though we do not love him."

"You are wrong, Babbie," Margaret answered gravely; "if I know anything at all, it is that."

"It may be best for others."

"Do you mean for one other?" Margaret asked, and the girl bowed her head. "Ah, Babbie, you speak like a child."

"You do not understand."

"I do not need to be told the circumstances to know this — that if two people love each other, neither has any right to give the other up."

Babbie turned impulsively to cast herself on the mercy of Gavin's mother, but no word could she say; a hot tear fell from her eyes upon the coverlet, and then she looked at the door, as if to run away.

"But I have been too inquisitive," Margaret began; whereupon Babbie cried, "Oh no, no, no: you are very good. I have no one who cares whether I do right or wrong."

"Your parents—"

"I have had none since I was a child."

"It is the more reason why I should be your friend," Margaret said, taking the girl's hand.

"You do not know what you are saying. You cannot be my friend."

"Yes, dear, I love you already. You have a good face, Babbie, as well as a beautiful one."

Babbie could remain in the room no longer. She bade Margaret good-night and bent forward to kiss her; then drew back, like a Judas ashamed.

"Why did you not kiss me?" Margaret asked in surprise, but poor Babbie walked out of the room without answering.

Of what occurred at the manse on the following day until I reached it, I need tell little more. When Babbie was tending Sam'l Farquharson's child in the Tenements, she learned of the flood in Glen Quharity, and that the greater part of the congregation had set off to the assistance of the farmers; but fearful as this made her for Gavin's safety, she kept the new anxiety from his mother. Deceived by another story of Jean's, Margaret was the one happy person in the house.

"I believe you had only a lover's quarrel with Lord Rintoul last night," she said to Babbie in the afternoon. "Ah, you see I can guess what is taking you to the window so often. You must not think him long in coming for you. I can assure you that the rain which keeps my son from me must be sufficiently severe to separate even true lovers. Take an old woman's example, Babbie. If I thought the minister's absence alarming, I should be in anguish; but as it is, my mind is so much at ease that, see, I can thread my needle."

It was in less than an hour after Margaret spoke thus tranquilly to Babbie that the precentor got into the manse.

Chapter XLII

Margaret, The Precentor, And God Between

Unless Andrew Luke, who went to Canada, be still above ground, I am now the only survivor of the few to whom Lang Tammas told what passed in the manse parlour after the door closed on him and Margaret. With the years the others lost the details, but before I forget them the man who has been struck by lightning will look at his arm without remembering what shrivelled it. There even came a time when the scene seemed more vivid to me than to the precentor, though that was only after he began to break up.

"She was never the kind o' woman," Whamond said, "that a body need be nane feared at. You can see she is o' the timid sort. I couldna hae selected a woman easier to speak bold out to, though I had ha'en my pick o' them."

He was a gaunt man, sour and hard, and he often paused in his story with a puzzled look on his forbidding face.

"But, man, she was so michty windy o' him. If he had wanted to put a knife into her, I believe that woman would just hae telled him to take care not to cut his hands. Ay, and what innocent-like she was. If she had heard enough, afore I saw her, to make her uneasy, I could hae begun at once; but here she was, shaking my hand and smiling to me, so that aye when I tried to speak I gaed through ither. Nobody can despise me for it, I tell you, mair than I despise mysel'.

"I thocht to mysel', 'Let her hae her smile out, Tammas Whamond; it's her hinmost.' Syne wi' shame at my cowardiness I tried to yoke to my duty as chief elder o' the kirk, and I said to her, as thrawn as I could speak, 'Dinna thank me; I've done nothing for you.'

" 'I ken it wasna for me you did it,' she said, 'but for him; but oh, Mr. Whamond, will that make me think the less o' you? He's my all,' she says, wi' that smile back in her face, and a look mixed up wi't that said as plain, 'and I need no more.' I thocht o' saying that some builds their house upon the sand, but — dagont, dominie, it's a solemn thing the pride mithers has in their laddies. I mind aince my ain mither — what the devil are you glowering at, Andrew Luke? Do you think I'm greeting?

" 'You'll sit down, Mr. Whamond,' she says, next.

" 'No, I winna,' I said, angry-like. 'I didna come here to sit.'

"I could see she thocht I was shy at being in the manse-parlour; ay, and I thocht she was pleased at me looking shy. Weel, she took my hat out o' my hand, and she put it on the chair at the door, whaur there's aye an auld chair in grand houses for the servant to sit on at family exercise.

" 'You're a man, Mr. Whamond,' says she, 'that the minister delights to honour, and so you'll oblige me by sitting in his own arm-chair.'

Gavin never quite delighted to honour the precentor, of whom he was always a little afraid, and perhaps Margaret knew it. But you must not think less of her for wanting to gratify her son's chief elder. She thought, too, that he had just done her a service. I never yet knew a good woman who did not enjoy flattering men she liked.

"I saw my chance at that," Whamond went on, "and I says to her sternly, 'In worldy position,' I says, 'I'm a common man, and it's no for the like o' sic to sit in a minister's chair; but it has been God's will,' I says, 'to wrap around me the mantle o' chief elder o' the kirk, and if the minister falls awa frae grace, it becomes my duty to take his place.'

"If she had been looking at me, she maun hae grown feared at that, and syne I could hae gone on though my ilka word was a knock-down blow. But she was picking some things aft the chair to let me down on't.

" 'It's a pair o' mittens I'm working for the minister,' she says, and she handed them to me. Ay, I tried no to take them, but — Oh, lads, it's queer to think how saft I was.

" 'He's no to ken about them till they're finished,' she says, terrible fond-like.

"The words came to my mouth, 'They'll never be finished,' and I could hae cursed myself for no saying them. I dinna ken how it was, but there was something pitiful in seeing her take up the mittens and begin working cheerily at one, and me kenning all the time that they would never be finished. I watched her fingers, and I said to mysel', 'Another stitch, and that maun be your last.' I said that to mysel' till I thocht it was the needle that said it, and I wondered at her no hearing.

"In the tail of the day I says, 'You needna bother; he'll never wear them,' and they sounded sic words o' doom that I rose up off the chair. Ay, but she took me up wrang, and she said, 'I see you have noticed how careless o' his ain comforts he is, and that in his zeal he forgets to put on his mittens, though they may be in his pocket a' the time. Ay,' says she, confident-like, 'but he winna forget these mittens, Mr. Whamond, and I'll tell you the reason; it's because they're his mother's work.'

"I stamped my foot, and she gae me an apologetic look, and she says, 'I canna help boasting about his being so fond o' me.'

"Ay, but here was me saying to mysel', 'Do your duty, Tammas Whamond; you sluggard, do your duty,' and without lifting my een frae her fingers I said sternly, 'The chances are,' I said, 'that these mittens will never be worn by the hands they are worked for.'

" 'You mean,' says she, 'that he'll gie them awa to some ill-off body, as he gies near a' thing he has? Ay, but there's one thing he never parts wi', and that's my work. There's a young lady in the manse the now,' says she, 'that offered to finish the mittens for me, but he would value them less if I let ony other body put a stitch into them.'

"I thocht to mysel', 'Tammas Whamond, the Lord has opened a door to you, and you'll be disgraced for ever if you dinna walk straucht in.' So I rose again, and I says, boldly this time, 'Whaur's that young leddy? I hae something to say to her that canna be kept waiting.'

" 'She's up the stair,' she says, surprised, 'but you canna ken her, Mr. Whamond, for she just came last nicht.'

" 'I ken mair o' her than you think,' says I; 'I ken what brocht her here, and I ken wha she thinks she is to be married to, and I've come to tell her that she'll never get him.'

" 'How no?' she said, amazed-like.

" 'Because,' said I, wi' my teeth thegither, 'he is already married.'

"Lads, I stood waiting to see her fall, and when she didna fall I just waited langer, thinking she was slow in taking it a' in.

" 'I see you ken wha she is,' she said, looking at me, 'and yet I canna credit your news.'

" 'They're true,' I cries.

" 'Even if they are,' says she, considering, 'it may be the best thing that could happen to baith o' them.'

"I sank back in the chair in fair bewilderment, for I didna ken at that time, as we a' ken now, that she was thinking o' the earl when I was thinking o' her son. Dominie, it looked to me as if the Lord had opened a door to me, and syne shut it in my face.

"Syne wi' me sitting there in a kind o' awe o' the woman's simpleness, she began to tell me what the minister was like when he was a bairn, and I was saying a' the time to mysel', 'You're chief elder o' the kirk, Tammas Whamond, and you maun speak out the next time she stops to draw breath.' They were terrible sma', common things she telled me, sic as near a' mithers minds about their bairns, but the kind o' holy way she said them drove my words down my throat, like as if I was some infidel man trying to break out wi' blasphemy in a kirk.

" 'I'll let you see something,' says she, 'that I ken will interest you.' She brocht it out o' a drawer, and what do you think it was? As sure as death it was no more than some o' his hair when he was a litlin, and it was tied up sic carefully in paper that you would hae thocht it was some valuable thing.

" 'Mr. Whamond,' she says solemnly, 'you've come thrice to the manse to keep me frae being uneasy about my son's absence, and you was the chief instrument under God in bringing him to Thrums, and I'll gie you a little o' that hair.'

"Dagont, what did I care about his hair? and yet to see her fondling it! I says to mysel', 'Mrs. Dishart,' I says to mysel', I was the chief instrument under God in bringing him to Thrums, and I've come here to tell you that I'm to be the chief instrument under God in driving him out o't.' Ay,but when I focht to bring out these words, my mouth snecked like a box.

" 'Dinna gie me his hair,' was a' I could say, and I wouldna take it frae her; but she laid it in my hand, and and syne what could I do? Ay, it's easy to speak about thae things now, and to wonder how I could hae so disgraced the position o' chief elder o' the kirk, but I tell you I was near greeting for the woman. Call me names, dominie; I deserve them all."

I did not call Whamond names for being reluctant to break Margaret's heart. Here is a confession I may make. Sometimes I say my prayers at night in a hurry, going on my knees indeed, but with as little reverence as I take a drink of water before jumping into bed, and for the same reason, because it is my nightly habit. I am only patterning words I have by heart to a chair then, and should be as well employed writing a comic Bible. At such times I pray for the earthly well-being of the precentor, though he has been dead for many years. He crept into my prayers the day he told me this story, and was part of them for so long that when they are only a recitation he is part of them still.

"She said to me," Whamond continued, "that the women o' the congregation would be fond to handle the hair. Could I tell her that the women was waur agin him than the men? I shivered to hear her.

" 'Syne when they're a' sitting breathless listening to his preaching,' she says, 'they'll be able to picture him as a bairn, just as I often do in the kirk mysel'.'

"Andrew Luke, you're sneering at me, but I tell you if you had been there and had begun to say, 'He'll preach in our kirk no more,' I would hae struck you. And I'm chief elder o' the kirk.

"She says, 'Oh, Mr. Whamond, there's times in the kirk when he is praying and the glow on his face is hardly mortal, so that I fall a shaking, wi' a mixture o' fear and pride, me being his mother; and sinful though I am to say it, I canna help thinking at sic times that I ken what the mother o' Jesus had in her heart when she found Him in the temple.'

"Dominie, it's sax-and-twenty years since I was made an elder o' the kirk. I mind the day as if it was yestreen. Mr. Carfrae made me walk hame wi' him, and he took me into the manse parlour,and he set me in that very chair. It was the first time I was ever in the manse. Ay, he little thocht that day in his earnestness, and I little thocht mysel' in the pride o' my lusty youth, that the time was coming when I would swear in that reverenced parlour. I say swear, dominie, for when she had finished I jumped to my feet, and I cried, 'Hell!' and I lifted up my hat. And I was chief elder.

"She fell back frae my oath," he said, "and syne she took my sleeve and speired, 'What has come ower you, Mr. Whamond? Hae you ony thing on your mind?'

" 'I've sin on it,' I roared at her. 'I have neglect o' duty on it. I am one o' them that cries "Lord, Lord," and yet do not the things which He commands. He has pointed out the way to me, and I hinna followed it.'

" 'What is it you hinna done that you should hae done?' she said. 'Oh, Mr. Whamond, if you want my help, it's yours.'

" 'Your son's a' the earth to you,' I cried, 'but my eldership's as muckle to me. Sax-and-twenty years hae I been an elder, and now I maun gie it up.'

" 'Wha says that?' she speirs.

" 'I say it,' I cried. 'I've shirked my duty. I gie up my eldership now. Tammas Whamond is na langer an elder o' the kirk'; ay, and I was chief elder.

"Dominie, I think she began to say that when the minister came hame he wouldna accept my resignation, but I paid no heed to her. You ken what was the sound that keeped my ears frae her words; it was the sound o' a machine coming yont the Tenements. You ken what was the sicht that made me glare through the window instead o' looking at her; it was the sight o' Mr. Dishart in the machine. I couldna speak, but I got my body atween her and the window, for I heard shouting, and I couldna doubt that it was the folk cursing him.

"But she heard too, she heard too, and she squeezed by me to the window. I couldna look out; I just walked saft-like to the parlour door, but afore I reached it she cried joyously —

" 'It's my son come back, and see how fond o' him they are. They are running at the side o' the machine, and the laddies are tossing their bonnets in the air.

" 'God help you, woman!' I said to mysel', 'it canna be bonnets — it's stanes and divits mair likely that they're flinging at him.' Syne I creeped out o' the manse. Dominie, you mind I passed you in the kitchen, and didna say a word?"

Yes, I saw the precentor pass through the kitchen, with such a face on him as no man ever saw him wear again. Since Tammas Whamond died we have had to enlarge the Thrums cemetery twice; so it can matter not at all to him, and but little to me, what you who read think of him. All his life children ran from him. He was the dourest, the most unlovable man in Thrums. But may my right hand wither, and may my tongue be cancer-bitten, and may my mind be gone into a dry rot, before I forget what he did for me and mine that day.

Chapter XLIII

Rain – Mist – The Jaws

To this day we argue in the glen about the sound mistaken by many of us for the firing of the Spittal cannon, some calling it thunder and others the tearing of trees in the torrent. I think it must have been the roll of stones into the Quharity from Silver Hill, of which a corner has been missing since that day. Silver Hill is all stones, as if creation had been riddled there, and in the sun the mica on them shines like many pools of water.

At the roar, as they thought, of the cannon, the farmers looked up from their struggles with the flood to say, 'That's Rintoul married," as clocks pause simultaneously to strike the hour. Then every one in the glen save Gavin and myself was done with Rintoul. Before the hills had answered the noise, Gavin was on his way to the Spittal. The dog must have been ten minutes in overtaking him, yet he maintained afterwards that it was with him from the start. From this we see that the shock he had got carried him some distance before he knew that he had left the school-house. It also gave him a new strength, that happily lasted longer than his daze of mind.

Gavin moved northward quicker than I came south, climbing over or wading through his obstacles, while I went round mine. After a time, too, the dog proved useful, for on discovering that it was going homeward it took the lead, and several times drew him to the right road to the Spittal by refusing to accompany him on the wrong road. Yet in two hours he had walked perhaps nine miles without being four miles nearer the Spittal. In that flood the glen milestones were three miles apart.

For some time he had been following the dog doubtfully, for it seemed to be going too near the river. When they struck a cart-track, however, he concluded rightly that they were nearing a bridge. His faith in his guide was again tested before they had been many minutes on this sloppy road. The dog stopped, whined, looked irresolute, and then ran to the right, disappearing into the mist in an instant. He shouted to it to come back, and was surprised to hear a whistle in reply. This was sufficient to make him dash after the dog, and in less than a minute he stopped abruptly by the side of a shepherd.

"Have you brocht it?" the man cried, almost into Gavin's ear; yet the roar of the water was so tremendous that the words came faintly, as if from a distance. "Wae is me; is it only you, Mr. Dishart?"

"Is it only you!" No one in the glen would have addressed a minister thus except in a matter of life or death, and Gavin knew it.

"He'll be ower late," the shepherd exclaimed, rubbing his hands together in distress. "I'm speaking o' Whinbusses' grieve. He has run for ropes, but he'll be ower late."

"Is there someone in danger?" asked Gavin, who stood, he knew not where, with this man, enveloped in mist.

"Is there no? Look!"

"There is nothing to be seen but mist; where are we?"

"We're on the high bank o' the Quharity. Take care, man; you was stepping ower into the roaring water. Lie down and tell me if he's there yet. Maybe I just think that I see him, for the sicht is painted on my een."

Gavin lay prone and peered at the river, but the mist came up to his eyes. He only knew that the river was below, from the sound.

"Is there a man down there?" he asked, shuddering.

"There was a minute syne; on a bit island."

"Why does he not speak?"

"He's senseless. Dinna move; the mist's clearing, and you'll see if he's there syne. The mist has been lifting and falling that way ilka minute since me and the grieve saw him."

The mist did not rise. It only shook like a blanket, and then again remained stationary. But in that movement Gavin had seen twice, first incredulously, and then with conviction.

"Shepherd," he said, rising, "it is Lord Rintoul."

"Ay, it's him; and you saw his feet was in the water. They were dry when the grieve left me. Mr. Dishart, the ground he is on is being washed awa bit by bit. I tell you, the flood's greddy for him and it'll hae him — Look, did you see him again?"

"Is he living?"

"We saw him move. Hst! Was that a cry?"

It was only the howling of the dog, which had recognised its master and was peering over the bank, the body quivering to jump, but the legs restless with indecision.

"If we were down there," Gavin said, "we could hold him secure till rescue comes. It is no great jump."

"How far would you make it? I saw him again!"

"It looked further that time."

'That's it! Sometimes the ground he is on looks so near that you think you could almost drop on it, and the next time it's yards and yards awa. I've stood ready for the spring, Mr. Dishart, a dozen times, but I aye sickened. I daurna do it. Look at the dog; just when it's starting to jump, it pulls itsel' back."

As it had heard the shepherd, the dog jumped at that instant.

"It sprang too far," Gavin said.

"It didna spring far enough."

They waited, and presently the mist thinned for a moment, as if it was being drawn out. They saw the earl, but there was no dog.

"Poor brute," said the shepherd, and looked with awe at Gavin.

"Rintoul is slipping into the water," Gavin answered. "You won't jump?"

"No, I'm wae for him, and—"

"Then I will," Gavin was about to say, but the shepherd continued, "And him only married twa hours syne."

That kept the words in Gavin's mouth for half a minute, and then he spoke them.

"Dinna think o't," cried the shepherd, taking him by the coat. "The ground he is on is slippery. I've flung a dozen stanes at it, and them that hit it slithered off. Though you landed in the middle o't, you would slide into the water."

"He shook himsel' free o' me," the shepherd told afterwards, "and I saw him bending down and measuring the distance wi' his een as cool as if he was calculating a drill o' tatties. Syne I saw his lips moving in prayer. It wasna spunk he needed to pray for, though. Next minute there was me, my very arms prigging wi' him to think better o't, and him standing ready to loup, his knees bent, and not a tremble in them. The mist lifted, and I — Lads, I couldna gie a look to the earl. Mr. Dishart jumped; I hardly saw him, but I kent,

I kent, for I was on the bank alane. What did I do? I flung mysel' down in a sweat, and if een could bore mist mine would hae done it. I thocht I heard the minister's death-cry, and may I be struck if I dinna believe now that it was a skirl o' my ain. After that there was no sound but the jaw o' the water; and I prayed, but no to God, to the mist to rise, and after an awful time it rose, and I saw the minister was safe; he had pulled the earl into the middle o' the bit island, and was rubbing him back to consciousness. I sweat when I think o't yet."

The Little Minister's jump is always spoken of as a brave act in the glen, but at such times I am silent. This is not because, being timid myself, I am without admiration for courage. My little maid says that three in every four of my poems are to the praise of prowess, and she has not forgotten how I carried her on my shoulder once to Tilliedrum to see a soldier who had won the Victoria Cross, and made her shake hands with him, though he was very drunk. Only last year one of my scholars declared to me that Nelson never said "England expects every man this day to do his duty," for which I thrashed the boy and sent him to the cooling stone. But was it brave of Gavin to jump? I have heard some maintain that only misery made him so bold, and others that he jumped because it seemed a fine thing to risk his life for an enemy. But these are really charges of cowardice, and my boy was never a coward. Of the two kinds of courage, however, he did not then show the nobler. I am glad that he was ready for such an act, but he should have remembered Margaret and Babbie. As it was, he may be said to have forced them to jump with him. Not to attempt a gallant deed for which one has the impulse may be braver than the doing of it.

"Though it seemed as lang time," the shepherd says, "as I could hae run up a hill in, I dinna suppose it was many minutes afore I saw Rintoul opening and shutting his een. The next glint I had o' them they were speaking to ane another; ay, and mair than speaking. They were quarrelling. I couldna hear their words, but there was a moment when I thocht they were to grapple. Lads, the memory o' that'll hing about my death-bed. There was twa men, edicated to the highest pitch, ane a lord and the other minister, and the flood was taking awa a mouthful o' their footing ilka minute, and the jaws o' destruction was gaping for them, and yet they were near fechting. We ken now it was about a woman. Ay, but does that make it less awful?"

No, that did not make it less awful. It was even awful that Gavin's first words when Rintoul opened his eyes and closed them hastily were "Where is she?" The earl did not answer; indeed for the moment the words had no meaning to him.

"How did I come here?" he asked feebly.

"You should know better than I. Where is my wife?"

"I remember now," Rintoul repeated several times. "Yes, I had left the Spittal to look for you — you were so long in coming. How did I find you?"

"It was I who found you," Gavin answered. "You must have been swept away by the flood."

"And you too?"

In a few words Gavin told how he came to be beside the earl.

"I suppose they will say you have saved my life," was Rintoul's commentary.

"It is not saved yet. If help does not come, we shall be dead men in an hour. What have you done with my wife?"

Rintoul ceased to listen to him, and shouted sums of money to the shepherd, who shook his head and bawled an answer that neither Gavin nor the earl heard. Across that thundering water only Gavin's voice could carry, the most powerful ever heard in a Thrums pulpit, the one voice that could be heard all over the Commonty during the time of the tent preaching. Yet he never roared, as some preachers do of whom we say, "Ah, if they could hear the Little Minister's word!"

Gavin caught the gesticulating earl by the sleeve, and said, "Another man has gone for ropes. Now, listen to me; how dared you go through a marriage ceremony with her, knowing her already to be my wife?"

Rintoul did listen this time.

"How do you know I married her?" he asked sharply.

"I heard the cannon."

Now the earl understood, and the shadow on his face shook

and lifted, and his teeth gleamed. His triumph might be short-lived, but he would enjoy it while he could.

"Well," he answered, picking the pebbles for his sling with care, "you must know that I could not have married her against her will. The frolic on the hill amused her, but she feared you might think it serious, and so pressed me to proceed with her marriage to-day, despite the flood."

This was the point at which the shepherd saw the minister raise his fist. It fell, however, without striking.

"Do you really think that I could doubt her?" Gavin said compassionately, and for the second time in twenty-four hours the earl learned that he did not know what love is.

For a full minute they had forgotten where they were. Now, again, the water seemed to break loose, so that both remembered their danger simultaneously, and looked up. The mist parted for long enough to show them that where had only been the shepherd, was now a crowd of men, with here and there a woman. Before the mist again came between, the minister had recognized many members of his congregation.

In his unsuccessful attempt to reach Whinbusses, the grieve had met the relief party from Thrums. Already the weavers had helped Waster Lunny to stave off ruin, and they were now on their way to Whinbusses, keeping together through fear of mist and water. Every few minutes Snecky Hobart rang his bell to bring in stragglers.

"Follow me," was all the panting grieve could say at first, but his agitation told half his story. They went with him patiently, only stopping once, and then excitedly, for they had come suddenly on Rob Dow. Rob was still lying a prisoner beneath the tree, and the grieve now remembered that he had fallen over this tree, and neither noticed the man under it, nor been noticed by the man. Fifty hands released poor Dow, and two men were commissioned to bring him along slowly while the others hurried to the rescue of the earl. They were amazed to learn from the shepherd that Mr. Dishart also was in danger, and after "Is there a woman wi' him?" some cried, "He'll get off cheap wi' drowning," and "It's the judgment o' God."

The island on which the two men stood was now little bigger than the round tables common in Thrums, and its centre was some feet farther from the bank than when Gavin jumped. A woman, looking down at it, sickened, and would have toppled into the water, had not John Spens clutched her. Others were so stricken with awe that they forgot they had hands.

Peter Tosh, the elder, cast a rope many times, but it would not carry. The one end was then weighted with a heavy stone, and the other tied round the waists of two men. But the force of the river had been under-estimated. The stone fell short into the torrent, which rushed off with it so furiously that the men were flung upon their faces and trailed to the verge of the precipice. A score of persons sprang to their rescue, and the rope snapped. There was only one other rope, and its fate was not dissimilar. This time the stone fell into the water beyond the island, and immediately rushed down stream. Gavin seized the rope, but it pressed against his body, and would have pushed him off his feet, had not Tosh cut it. The trunk of the tree that had fallen on Rob Dow was next dragged to the bank and an endeavour made to form a sloping bridge of it. The island, however, was now soft and unstable, and, though the trunk was successfully lowered it only knocked lumps off the island, and finally it had to be let go, as the weavers could not pull it back. It splashed into the water, and was at once whirled out of sight. Some of the party on the bank began hastily to improvise a rope of cravats and the tags of the ropes still left, but the mass stood helpless and hopeless.

"You may wonder that we could have stood still, waiting to see the last o' them," Birse, the post, has said to me in the school-house, "but, dominie, I couldna hae moved, magre my neck. I'm a hale man, but if this minute we was to hear the voice o' the Almighty saying solemnly, 'Afore the clock strikes again, Birse, the post, will fall down dead of heart disease,' what do you think you would do? I'll tell you. You would stand whaur you are, and stare, tongue-tied, at me till I dropped. How do I ken? By the teaching o' that nicht. Ay, but there's a mair important thing I dinna ken, and that is whether I would be palsied wi' fear like the earl, or face death with the calmness o' the minister."

Indeed, the contrast between Rintoul and Gavin was now impressive. When Tosh signed that the weavers had done their all and failed, the two men looked in each other's faces, and Gavin's face was firm and the earl's working convulsively. The people had given up attempting to communicate with Gavin save by signs, for though they heard his sonorous voice, when he pitched it at them, they saw that he caught few words of theirs. "He heard our skirls," Birse said, "but couldna grip the word ony mair than we could hear the earl. And yet we screamed, and the minister didna. I've heard o' Highlandmen wi' the same gift, so that they could be heard across a glen."

"We must prepare for death," Gavin said solemnly to the earl, "and it is for your own sake that I again ask you to tell me the truth. Worldly matters are nothing to either of us now, but I implore you not to carry a lie into your Maker's presence."

"I will not give up hope," was all Rintoul's answer, and he again tried to pierce the mist with offers of reward. After that he became doggedly silent, fixing his eyes on the ground at his feet. I have a notion that he had made up his mind to confess the truth about Babbie when the water had eaten the island as far as the point at which he was now looking.

Chapter XLIV

End Of The Twenty-Four Hours

Out of the mist came the voice of Gavin, clear and strong—

"If you hear me, hold up your hands as a sign."

They heard, and none wondered at his voice crossing the chasm while theirs could not. When the mist cleared, they were seen to have done as he bade them. Many hands remained up for a time because the people did not remember to bring them down, so great was the awe that had fallen on all, as if the Lord was near.

Gavin took his watch from his pocket, and he said—

"I am to fling this to you. You will give it to Mr. Ogilvy, the schoolmaster, as a token of the love I bear him."

The watch was caught by James Langlands, and handed to Peter Tosh, the chief elder present.

"To Mr. Ogilvy," Gavin continued, "you will also give the chain. You will take it off my neck when you find the body.

"To each of my elders, and to Hendry Munn, kirk-officer, and to my servant Jean, I leave a book, and they will go to my study and choose it for themselves.

"I also leave a book for Nanny Webster, and I charge you, Peter Tosh, to take it to her, though she be not a member of my church.

"The pictorial Bible with 'To my son on his sixth birthday' on it, I bequeath to Rob Dow. No, my mother will want to keep that. I give to Rob Dow my Bible with the brass clasp.

"It is my wish that every family in the congregation should have some little thing to remember me by. This you will tell my mother.

"To my successor I leave whatsoever of my papers he may think of any value to him, including all my notes on Revelation, of which I meant to make a book. I hope he will never sing the paraphrases.

"If Mr. Carfrae's health permits, you will ask him to preach the funeral sermon; but if he be too frail, then you will ask Mr. Trail, under whom I sat in Glasgow. The illustrated 'Pilgrim's Progress' on the drawers in my bedroom belongs to Mr. Trail, and you will return it to him with my affection and compliments.

"I owe five shillings to Hendry Munn for mending my boots, and a smaller sum to Baxter, the mason. I have two pounds belonging to Rob Dow, who asked me to take charge of them for him. I owe no other man anything, and this you will bear in mind if Matthew Cargill, the flying stationer, again brings forward a claim for the price of Whiston's 'Josephus,' which I did not buy from him.

"Mr. Moncur, of Aberbrothock, had agreed to assist me at the Sacrament, and will doubtless still lend his services. Mr. Carfrae or Mr. Trail will take my place if my successor is not elected by that time. The Sacrament cups are in the vestry press, of which you will find the key beneath the clock in my parlour. The tokens are in the topmost drawer in my bedroom.

"The weekly prayer-meeting will be held as usual on Thursday at eight o'clock, and the elders will officiate.

"It is my wish that the news of my death be broken to my mother by Mr. Ogilvy, the schoolmaster, and by no other. You will say to him that this is my solemn request, and that I bid him discharge it without faltering and be of good cheer.

"But if Mr. Ogilvy be not now alive, the news of my death will be broken to my mother by my beloved wife. Last night I was married on the hill, over the tongs, but with the sanction of God, to her whom you call the Egyptian, and despite what has happened since then, of which you will soon have knowledge, I here solemnly declare that she is my wife, and you will seek for her at the Spittal or elsewhere till you find her, and you will tell her to go to my mother and remain with her always, for these are the commands of her husband."

It was then that Gavin paused, for Lord Rintoul had that to say to him which no longer could be kept back. All the women were crying sore, and also some men whose eyes had been dry at the coffining of their children.

"Now I ken," said Cruickshanks, who had been an atheist, "that it's only the fool wha' says in his heart, 'There is no God.'

Another said, "That's a man."

Another said, "That man has a religion to last him all through."

A fourth said, "Behold, the Kingdom of Heaven is at hand."

A fifth said, "That's our minister. He's the minister o' the Auld Licht Kirk o'Thrums. Woe is me, we're to lose him."

Many cried, "Our hearts was set hard against him. Lord, are You angry wi' Your servants that You're taking him frae us just when we ken what he is?"

Gavin did not hear them, and again he spoke:—

"My brethren, God is good. I have just learned that my wife is with my dear mother at the manse. I leave them in your care and in His."

No more he said of Babbie, for the island was become very small.

"The Lord calls me hence. It is only for a little time I have been with you, and now I am going away, and you will know me no more. Too great has been my pride because I was your minister, but He who sent me to labour among you is slow to wrath; and He ever bore in mind that you were my first charge. My people, I must say to you, 'Farewell.'"

Then, for the first time, his voice faltered, and wanting to go on he could not. "Let us read," he said, quickly, "in the Word of God in the fourteenth of Matthew, from the twenty-eighth verse." He repeated these four verses:

"'And Peter answered Him and said, Lord, if it be Thou, bid me come unto Thee on the water.

"'And He said, Come. And when Peter was come down out of the ship, he walked on the water, to go to Jesus.

"'But when he saw the wind boisterous, he was afraid; and beginning to sink, he cried, saying, Lord, save me.

"'And immediately Jesus stretched forth His hand, and caught him, and said unto him, O thou of little faith, wherefore didst thou doubt?'"

After this Gavin's voice was again steady, and he said, "The sand-glass is almost run out. Dearly beloved, with what words shall I bid you good-bye?"

Many thought that these were to be the words, for the mist parted, and they saw the island tremble and half of it sink.

"My people," said the voice behind the mist, "this is the text I leave with you: 'Lay not up for yourselves treasures upon earth, where moth and rust doth corrupt, and where thieves break through and steal; but lay up for yourselves treasures in heaven, where neither moth nor rust doth corrupt, and where thieves do not break through nor steal.' That text I read in the flood, where the hand of God has written it. All the pound-notes in the world would not dam this torrent for a moment, so that we might pass over to you safely. Yet it is but a trickle of water, soon to be dried up. Verily, I say unto you, only a few hours ago the treasures of earth stood between you and this earl, and what are they now compared to this trickle of water? God only can turn rivers into a wilderness, and the water-springs into dry ground. Let His Word be a lamp unto your feet and a light unto your path; may He be your refuge and your strength. Amen."

This amen he said quickly, thinking death was now come. He was seen to raise his hands, but whether to Heaven, or involuntarily to protect his face as he fell, none was sure, for the mist again filled the chasm. Then came a clap of stillness. No one breathed.

But the two men were not yet gone, and Gavin spoke once more.

"Let us sing in the twenty-third Psalm."

He himself raised the tune, and so long as they heard his voice they sang—

"The Lord's my shepherd, I'll not want;
He makes me down to lie In pastures green;
He leadeth me The quiet water by.

"My soul He doth restore again;
And me to walk doth make
Within the paths of righteousness
Ev'n for His own name's sake.

"Yea, though I walk in Death's dark vale,
Yet will I fear none ill;
For Thou art with me; and Thy rod
And staff—

But some had lost the power to sing in the first verse, and others at "Death's dark vale," and when one man found himself singing alone he stopped abruptly. This was because they no longer heard the minister.

"O Lord!" Peter Tosh cried, "lift the mist, for it's mair than we can bear."

The mist rose slowly, and those who had courage to look saw Gavin praying with the earl. Many could not look, and some of them did not even see Rob Dow jump.

For it was Dow, the man with the crushed leg, who saved Gavin's life, and flung away his own for it.

Suddenly he was seen on the edge of the bank, holding one end of the improvised rope in his hand. As Tosh says—

"It all happened in the opening and shutting o' an eye. It's a queer thing to say, but though I prayed to God to take awa the mist, when He did raise it I couldna look. I shut my een tight, and held my arm afore my face, like ane feared o' being struck. Even when I daured to look, my arm was shaking so that I could see Rob both above it and below it. He was on the edge, crouching to leap. I didna see wha had haud o' the other end o' the rope. I heard the minister cry, 'No, Dow, no!' and it gaed through me as quick as a stab that if Rob jumped he would knock them both into the water. But he did jump, and you ken how it was that he didna knock them off."

It was because he had no thought of saving his own life. He jumped, not at the island now little bigger than the seat of a chair, but at the edge of it, into the foam, and with his arm outstretched. For a second the hand holding the rope was on the dot of land. Gavin tried to seize the hand; Rintoul clutched the rope. The earl and the minister were dragged together in safety, and both left the water senseless. Gavin was never again able to lift his left hand higher than his head. Dow's body was found next day near the school-house.

Chapter XLV

Talk Of A Little Maid Since Grown Tall

My scholars have a game they call "The Little Minister," in which the boys allow the girls as a treat to join. Some of the characters in the real drama are omitted as of no importance — the dominie, for instance — and the two best fighters insist on being Dow and Gavin. I notice that the game is finished when Dow dives from a haystack, and Gavin and the earl are dragged to the top of it by a rope. Though there should be another scene, it is only a marriage, which the girls have, therefore, to go through without the help of the boys. This warns me that I have come to an end of my story for all except my little maid. In the days when she sat on my knee and listened, it had no end, for after I told her how her father and mother were married a second time, she would say, "And then I came, didn't I? Oh, tell me about me!" So it happened that when she was no higher than my staff she knew more than I could write in another book, and many a time she solemnly told me what I had told her, as—

"Would you like me to tell you a story? Well, it's about a minister, and the people wanted to be bad to him, and then there was a flood, and a flood is lochs falling instead of rain, and so of course he was nearly drownded, and he preached to them till they liked him again, and so they let him marry her, and they like her awful too, and, just think! it was my father; and that's all. Now tell me about grandmother when father came home."

I told her once again that Margaret never knew how nearly Gavin was driven from his kirk. For Margaret was as one who goes to bed in the daytime and wakes in it, and is not told that there has been a black night while she slept. She had seen her son leave the manse the idol of his people, and she saw them rejoicing as they brought him back. Of what occurred at the Jaws, as the spot where Dow had saved two lives is now called, she learned, but not that these Jaws snatched him, and her, from an ignominy more terrible than death; for she never knew that the people had meditated driving him from his kirk. This Thrums is bleak and perhaps forbidding, but there is a moment of the day when a setting sun dyes it pink, and the people are like their town. Thrums was never colder in times of snow than were his congregation to their minister when the Great Rain began, but his fortitude rekindled their hearts. He was an obstinate minister, and love had led him a dance, but in the hour of trial he had proved himself a man.

When Gavin reached the manse, and saw not only his mother but Babbie, he would have kissed them both; but Babbie could only say, "She does not know," and then run away crying. Gavin put his arm round his mother, and drew her into the parlour, where he told her who Babbie was. Now Margaret had begun to love Babbie already, and had prayed to see Gavin happily married; but it was a long time before she went upstairs to look for his wife, and kiss her and bring her down. "Why was it a long time?" my little maid would ask, and I had to tell her to wait until she was old and had a son, when she would find out for herself.

While Gavin and the earl were among the waters, two men were on their way to Mr. Carfrae's home, to ask him to return with them and preach the Auld Licht kirk of Thrums vacant; and he came, though now so done that he had to be wheeled about in a little coach. He came in sorrow, yet resolved to perform what was asked of him if it seemed God's will; but, instead of banishing Gavin, all he had to do was to re-marry him and kirk him, both of which things he did, sitting in his coach, as many can tell. Lang Tammas spoke no more against Gavin, but he would not go to the marriage, and he insisted on resigning his eldership for a year and a day. I think he only once again spoke to Margaret. She was in the manse garden when he was passing, and she asked him if he would tell her now why he had been so agitated when he visited her on the day of the flood. He answered gruffly, "It's no business o' yours." Dr. McQueen was Gavin's best man. He died long ago of scarlet fever. So severe was the epidemic that for a week he was never in bed. He attended fifty cases without suffering, but as soon as he had bent over Hendry Munn's youngest boys, who both had it, he said, "I'm smitted," and went home to die. You may be sure that Gavin proved a good friend to Micah Dow. I have the piece of slate on which Rob proved himself a good friend to

Gavin; it was in his pocket when we found the body. Lord Rintoul returned to his English estates, and never re-visited the Spittal. The last thing I heard of him was that he had been offered the Lord-Lieutenantship of a county, and had accepted it in a long letter, in which he began by pointing out his unworthiness. This undid him, for the Queen, or her councillors, thinking from his first page that he had declined the honour, read no further, and appointed another man. Waster Lunny is still alive, but has gone to another farm. Sanders Webster, in his gratitude, wanted Nanny to become an Auld Licht, but she refused, saying, "Mr. Dishart is worth a dozen o' Mr. Duthie, and I'm terrible fond o' Mrs. Dishart, but Established I was born, and Established I'll remain till I'm carried out o' this house feet foremost."

"But Nanny went to Heaven for all that," my little maid told me. "Jean says people can go to Heaven though they are not Auld Lichts, but she says it takes them all their time. Would you like me to tell you a story about my mother putting glass on the manse dyke? Well, my mother and my father is very fond of each other, and once they was in the garden, and my father kissed my mother, and there was a woman watching them over the dyke, and she cried out — something naughty."

"It was Tibbie Birse," I said, and what she cried was, 'Mercy on us, that's the third time in half an hour!' So your mother, who heard her, was annoyed, and put glass on the wall."

"But it's me that is telling you the story. You are sure you don't know it? Well, they asked father to take the glass away, and he wouldn't, but he once preached at mother for having a white feather in her bonnet, and at another time he preached at her for being too fond of him. Jean told me. That's all."

No one seeing Babbie going to church demurely on Gavin's arm could guess her history. Sometimes I wonder whether the desire to be a gypsy again ever comes over her for a mad hour, and whether, if so, Gavin takes such measures to cure her as he threatened in Caddam Wood. I suppose not; but here is another story:—

"When I ask mother to tell me about her once being a gypsy she says I am a bad 'quisitive little girl, and to put on my hat and come with her to the prayer-meeting; and when I asked father to let me see mother's gypsy frock he made me learn Psalm forty-eight by heart. But once I see'd it, and it was a long time ago, as long as a week ago. Micah Dow gave me rowans to put in my hair, and I like Micah, because he calls me Miss, and so I woke in my bed because there was noises, and I ran down to the parlour, and there was my mother in her gypsy frock, and my rowans was in her hair, and my father was kissing her, and when they saw me they jumped; and that's all."

"Would you like me to tell you another story? It is about a little girl. Well, there was once a minister and his wife, and they hadn't no little girls, but just little boys, and God was sorry for them, so He put a little girl in a cabbage in the garden, and when they found her they were glad. Would you like me to tell you who the little girl was? Well, it was me, and uhh! I was awful cold in the cabbage. Do you like that story?"

"Yes; I like it best of all the stories I know."

"So do I like it, too. Couldn't nobody help loving me, 'cause I'm so nice? Why am I so fearful nice?"

"Because you are like your grandmother."

"It was clever of my father to know when he found me in the cabbage that my name was Margaret. Are you sorry grandmother is dead?"

"I am glad your mother and father were so good to her and made her so happy."

"Are you happy?"

"Yes."

"But when I am happy I laugh."

"I am old, you see, and you are young."

"I am nearly six. Did you love grandmother? Then why did you never come to see her? Did grandmother know you was here? Why not? Why didn't I know about you till after grandmother died?"

"I'll tell you when you are big."

"Shall I be big enough when I am six?"

"No, not till your eighteenth birthday."

"But birthdays comes so slow. Will they come quicker when I am big?"

"Much quicker."

On her sixth birthday Micah Dow drove my little maid to the school-house in the doctor's gig, and she crept beneath the table and whispered—

"Grandfather!"

"Father told me to call you that if I liked, and I like," she said when I had taken her upon my knee. "I know why you kissed me just now. It was because I looked like grandmother. Why do you kiss me when I look like her?'

"Who told you I did that?"

"Nobody didn't tell me. I just found out. I loved grandmother too. She told me all the stories she knew."

"Did she ever tell you a story about a black dog?"

"No. Did she know one?"

"Yes, she knew it."

"Perhaps she had forgotten it?"

"No, she remembered it."

"Tell it to me."

"Not till you are eighteen."

"But will you not be dead when I am eighteen? When you go to Heaven, will you see grandmother?"

"Yes."

"Will she be glad to see you?"

My little maid's eighteenth birthday has come, and I am still in Thrums, which I love, though it is beautiful to none, perhaps, save to the very done, who lean on their staves and look long at it, having nothing else to do till they die. I have lived to rejoice in the happiness of Gavin and Babbie; and if at times I have suddenly had to turn away my head after looking upon them in their home surrounded by their children, it was but a moment's envy that I could not help. Margaret never knew of the dominie in the glen. They wanted to tell her of me, but I would not have it. She has been long gone from this world; but sweet memories of her still grow, like honeysuckle, up the white walls of the manse, smiling in at the parlour window and beckoning from the door, and for some filling all the air with fragrance. It was not she who raised the barrier between her and me, but God Himself; and to those who maintain otherwise, I say they do not understand the purity of a woman's soul. During the years she was lost to me her face ever came between me and ungenerous thoughts, and now I can say, all that is carnal in me is my own, and all that is good I got from her. Only one bitterness remains. When I found Gavin in the rain, when I was fighting my way through the flood, when I saw how the hearts of the people were turned against him — above all, when I found Whamond in the manse — I cried to God, making promises to Him, if He would spare the lad for Margaret's sake, and He spared him; but these promises I have not kept.

Lightning Source UK Ltd.
Milton Keynes UK
UKOW05f0753191113

221393UK00001B/25/P